BLOOD SUMMIT

A NOVEL BY

ROBERT PIMM

ABOUT THE AUTHOR

Born in England, raised in Africa, Robert Pimm is a graduate of Cambridge University and a former writer for the Financial Times. He lives in Vienna. You can read more about him at http://robertpimm.com/ and follow him on Twitter @RobertPimm.

Robert Pimm's other writing includes *Biotime,* a science fiction black comedy, and *The Hotel Stories*, featuring the world's most brilliant, unpredictable and occasionally homicidal hotel manager, known as Ms N to guard her anonymity.

Matthew Parris says of Robert Pimm: "Funny, pacy, sexy... Pimm has the sharpness of observation and amused cynicism of a political insider... raunchy, clever and melancholy."

ACKNOWLEDGEMENTS

My thanks go to the member of a western intelligence agency who made time between engagements in Kabul to proof-read my references to bombs and ballistics. To Rainer Lingenthal, formerly of the German Interior Ministry, and officials in the German Chancellor's Office (Kanzleramt) who provided advice on security procedures. To Thomas Volkmann and Elke Kleinwächter-Jarnot for showing me the Reichstag. To the members of the MOD who showed me around their training facilities and let me fire weapons. To a government legal specialist who helped me on state immunity. To Michael Trott of the Forensic Science Service for advice on blood, DNA and the destructive effects of fire. To Albert Borowitz, whose book "Terrorism for Self-Glorification – The Herostratus Syndrome" provides valuable insights on a little-discussed aspect of terrorist motivation.   To the authors of the 9/11 Commission Report, whose pages show how governments really work in a crisis.

All the mistakes are mine.

THE GERMAN PHONETIC ALPHABET

A - Anton; **Ä** - Ärger; **B** - Berta; **C** - Cäsar; **CH** - Charlotte; **D** - Dora; **E** - Emil; **F** - Friedrich; **G** - Gustav; **H** - Heinrich; **I** - Ida; **J** - Julius; **K** - Kaufmann; **L** - Ludwig; **M** - Martha; **N** - Nordpol; **O** - Otto; **Ö** - Ökonom; **P** - Paula; **Q** - Quelle; **R** - Richard; **S** - Samuel; **Sch** - Schule; **T** - Theodor; **U** - Ulrich; **Ü** - Übermut; **V** - Viktor; **W** - Wilhelm; **X** - Xanthippe; **Y** - Ypsilon; **Z** – Zacharias

"One of the commonest forms of madness is the desire to be noticed."

- MARK TWAIN

"I was an acute nobody... I was 'Mr Nobody' until I killed the biggest Somebody on earth."

- MARK CHAPMAN
Murderer of John Lennon

To Pamela

BLOOD SUMMIT

PROLOGUE

Two years earlier

THERE WERE CHILDREN PLAYING IN THE STREET OUTSIDE HER door. Turkish, Uli Wenger guessed from their dark skin and bright clothes. He walked around them. The first insect Uli ever killed had been a child. Today, he had more important business.

The surface of the door was rough with dirt and spray paint. Sixteen buzzers studded the wall. The target lived on the third floor. Uli pressed the button by her name.

There was a crackle. 'Yes?'

'Post,' Uli said. 'A package.'

'OK.' The door popped open.

The hallway was cool and dark and smelled of damp stone. Two bicycles stood against a wall. Uli climbed the stairs. At the second floor, he took from his shoulder-bag a cardboard carton and a blue and yellow postman's jacket. Then he trudged up the final flight and rang the bell.

This was the moment. If another door on the landing should open, Uli would walk slowly back down the stairs. He counted the seconds. Patience was everything. She was behind the door. She was looking at him through the spy-hole.

The door opened.

'Hello, is that – '

Uli Wenger barged into the apartment and wrapped his arm around the target's face, crushing her nose and mouth. He reached for the knife at his belt. He had used it twice today already.

But unlike the men whose throats Uli had cut that morning, the woman did not struggle. She was a head shorter than him, wiry and angular. He never relaxed his grip. Suddenly she was dropping to the floor, a dead weight. He staggered. In that instant, she hooked one leg behind his and threw herself backwards.

Self-defence classes, Uli thought as he fell. It would make no difference. His head smashed into the bare floorboards. The woman landed on top of him. He lashed out instinctively with his free hand. His fist connected with her head, a solid, satisfying blow.

Uli jumped up. Already, the woman was scrambling to her feet, backing away. He edged towards her, fully alert. She would be dead in sixty seconds. Behind her on the wall he saw a poster of a man in a tunic brandishing a sword at an army of skeletons. The image meant nothing to Uli. He held his knife forward, ready to slash her throat. She must not scream. His fall had made too much noise already. The neighbours might be calling the police.

But the woman did not cry out. She lifted her hand to a drop of blood at the corner of her mouth. When she spoke, her voice was filled not with fear, but with anger.

'What is this? Are you crazy?'

Uli felt a pulse of panic. It was as if she knew his history. His weakness. But that was impossible. Only Mouse had known, and she was dead. He hesitated, gripping the knife more tightly in his hand.

'Leave me alone!' An order. But then she made a mistake. 'Please.'

The spell was broken. Uli stepped forward. She tried to trip him again, but this time he was ready: when she reached out her foot, he grabbed her and threw her down. She gasped as she hit the floor. For a moment, she lay still. It was enough. He fell on her, pressing his left hand over her mouth and slamming the knife into the carotid triangle at the base of her neck. When he jerked the blade free he was rewarded with a torrent of blood. For twenty seconds, he held her. Then he knelt, and cleaned the knife on her shirt.

The woman's eyes were open.

'Why?' she whispered. 'Why kill me?'

Uli did not know the answer. His employer had named today's targets without giving a reason. The objective might be to test the efficiency with which Uli could kill. Or it could be something else entirely.

He shrugged. 'Do you not know?'

Her eyes widened, but she could not speak.

'I do not know either,' Uli said. 'And I do not care.' He waited a few seconds longer, with his hand on her pulse. Then he rose and left the apartment.

CHAPTER 1

HELEN GALE WAS BRIEFING THE AMBASSADOR ON THE Children's Summit when the first rock hit the window. 'The Prime Minister flies in at 1500 tomorrow,' she said. 'The trouble is, Air Force One is due at 1450. Obviously, the German Federal Chancellor won't have time to greet the President of the United States at the airport.'

'Who wants to meet a child in a sandpit?' the ambassador said.

'The President's been called worse things.'

'Not by the Chancellor. After a speech on US foreign policy. When someone's left the microphone on.'

'So now the big story is when they're going to kiss and make up.' Helen shook her head. 'Not literally, more's the pity.'

'Any idea who the Germans will send to greet the PM?'

'No,' Helen said. 'The No.10 press office are insisting on a cabinet minister at least.'

'They insist? Bully for them.' Sir Leonard Lennox ran his fingers through the white thicket of his hair, making it wilder than ever. 'And won't you say three p.m.? We're not soldiers. Though sometimes I wish we – '

CRACK.

'What the hell is that?' The ambassador was on his feet.

'Stay away from the window.'

CRACK.

Now there were two stars in the wall of bandit glass which fronted the street. Helen fought the urge to run and look out.

Remember Paris. She didn't want to be diced alive by flying shards if a bomb went off outside. But the ambassador was already standing there.

'If they had a bomb they'd not be throwing stones, would they, now?' The lowland burr was calm. 'The police are moving in already.'

'What about the intelligence warnings?' Helen said. 'We know G8 targets are under threat.'

'We can't bolt for cover each time GCHQ eavesdrops on a seditionist.' The ambassador shook his head. 'Come and have a look-see. It's not every day we're attacked by a mob.'

Salvos of stones were rattling against the toughened glass. Because the panes were larger at one end of the ambassador's office than the other, each impact had a different tone, like a monstrous xylophone.

Helen covered the distance to the window in three strides. 'When the ambassador instructs a lowly first secretary to break the rules, she must obey.'

'Don't give me that nonsense, Helen. You don't know what rules are.'

Thousands of faces stared up at them through the summer rain. *JOBS NOT BOMBS*, a banner read. *GLOBALISATION WITHOUT US.* Most of the protesters seemed peaceful. A child on someone's shoulders carried a placard reading *CHILDREN'S SUMMIT: JUST SAY NO.* Helen smiled. If you took politics seriously, you'd go mad. Like the people across the street. A dozen masked figures were tearing up the cobblestones and flinging them at the embassy building. At her, Helen Gale. A phalanx of police officers was pushing towards them through the crowd.

How could the stone-throwers be so sure they were right? Helen's own life held no such certainties. Eight months earlier, she had been unsure whether to move to Berlin. Only Nigel's refusal to leave London had convinced her she must go to Germany. He had told her to quit her job, stay with him, and start a family.

Helen had longed to throw herself into the arms of the only man she had ever loved. She had also felt an urge to slam the door on the only man who sometimes roused her to hatred. At last, she had come to Berlin, despising Nigel for not understanding her, and despairing at herself for not making him understand. She watched the crowd. Did she belong inside the building looking down? Or out in the street, looking up?

'How much longer will the glass hold?' The ambassador might have been asking when the rain would stop.

'In theory, it's fine. But I'd hate any demonstrators to be injured by one of their own rocks falling on their heads. I'll call Dieter Kremp.'

'The most arrogant man in Berlin? Good luck.'

'I like confidence in a man, up to a point. But you – ' Helen wagged her finger at the ambassador as she gave the mock order ' – must get away from the window. I'm telling you in my official capacity as Post Security Officer.'

'Yes, miss.' The ambassador raised his considerable eyebrows but did not move. Helen reached for her phone. Before she could dial, the door burst open.

Jason Short, Head of Political Section and Deputy Head of Mission, was Helen's boss. He was, indeed, limited in stature: in an embassy where first names were standard, he was widely referred to as Mr Short. He was the proud owner of a colossal collection of fitted suits and silk ties and had long, thinning hair, like an ageing rock star. Short was always keen to impress Sir Leonard Lennox, and the Summit would coincide with a decision in London on the appointment of the next British ambassador to Bangkok. This was a job to which Short aspired. Unfortunately for Helen, Jason saw office politics as a zero-sum game in which the best way to look good was to make everyone else look as bad as possible.

He stared at her.

'What are you doing here? Don't you know there's a riot on?'

'I am aware, yes,' Helen said.

'You're Post Security Officer. You should be talking to the staff, reassuring them.'

'I'm trying to call Dieter Kremp at the Summit Security Unit.' Helen held up the phone. 'If you'll give me a moment.'

'Phoning your boyfriend?'

Short was avoiding eye contact, focusing on a point around Helen's neck. Was he looking at the cornflowers on her cotton dress? Or was he staring at her breasts? She turned to Leonard Lennox.

'Ambassador, we're in your way here. Shall I make this call from my office?'

The ambassador shrugged. 'You're not in my way. Speed is of the essence.'

At that moment, something happened. Helen's first impression was of a colossal thunderclap directly above her head. As she winced and started to bring her hands up to her ears, the lights dimmed. There was a click as the computer on the ambassador's desk flickered and began to re-boot.

The ambassador. Helen whirled round. The toughened windows were intact except for a single tiny hole in the glass. Sir Leonard Lennox turned towards her. There was something wrong with the top of his head. Blood was streaming down so fast she could see it dripping from his chin onto his shirt. He lifted a hand to his forehead. Then, slowly, he fell to his knees.

'A bomb,' he said. 'I think I'm hurt.'

CHAPTER 2

IT WAS NOT ACCIDENT BUT DESIGN WHICH MADE ULI WENGER so hard to see. His disguise was brilliant. Only one person in the crowd could recognise him. She would never tell a soul.

More marchers were appearing. The merciless punctuality made planning easy. Uli was in control. In thirty-six hours, he would hold a knife to the throat of the world. A few hours after that, the world would embrace him as its saviour.

Two minutes to go. Uli turned in his pocket the old D-mark coin Gustav had given him. The big man believed the euro currency had debased the fatherland. Uli was indifferent to Germany and the D-mark, but he'd taken the coin. Gustav and Martha were the most reliable killers in his Chaos Team.

He heard a crack of thunder and rain began to fall. Uli stood at the corner of Unter den Linden and waited. He must have line of sight. The demonstrators filled the road, trudging like a column of ants through the indifferent city. Flanking the procession, a handful of policemen sweltered in rain capes. The protesters carried banners: Uli saw something about un-employment. The US President in a sandpit with a missile in each hand. People hated the Americans because they seemed powerful. But sometimes power bred weakness. It only took one man to change history.

Suddenly a squad of trouble-makers in combat boots, their faces masked, started prising up the fist-sized cobblestones which made Berlin a rioter's dream. Uli's eyes narrowed. This was not part of the plan. If the police stepped in, the demonstration might be disrupted. Where was she? He scanned the crowd as the first stones flew towards the British embassy.

There. The trim figure looked out of place in the sullen mob. Her back was straight, her gaze fierce. And she was meant to be invisible. Uli cursed silently. He had thought she could work with him. He had been wrong. If any more proof were needed, this botched surveillance was it. Now to turn a problem into a solution.

The day-bag on the woman's shoulder was fitted with a pinhole-lens video surveillance camera and two spare batteries weighing six hundred and fifty grams in total. It also contained, Uli knew, a half-litre bottle of Evian water which, when full, had weighed a further five hundred grams. By contrast, the military-grade C4 plastic explosive and radio-controlled detonator sewn into the lining of the bag weighed less than one hundred grams in total. It was a tiny bomb, but more than adequate to do the job. It lay directly against the target's upper body.

At that moment, the woman saw him. She looked puzzled. Now was the time. It would be better if she were closer to the embassy. But that was a secondary objective. Uli put his other hand in his pocket, closed the contact, and stepped around the corner into Pariser Platz.

The sound of the explosion in the narrow street was immense. A long moment of silence followed. Then the screaming started.

Uli Wenger had just killed two birds with one stone.

CHAPTER 3

Jason Short ran across the ambassador's office and stood over Leonard Lennox.

'Are you all right, sir?'

'Of course he's not all right,' Helen said. 'We must stop the bleeding.' She grabbed a cloth from under a vase of flowers on a side-table, folded it, and pressed it against the wound.

'Can you hold that in place?'

The ambassador nodded. 'Yes.'

Helen dialled a number. 'Ram? The ambo's injured. Come quickly.'

'It wasn't a big bomb.' Sir Leonard Lennox spoke slowly. 'The bandit glass is intact. Maybe a bit of shrapnel hit me.'

A small bomb. She saw at once the ambassador was right. They wouldn't be standing here if a car bomb had exploded. Yet who would attack a building using a hand-carried bomb in the street outside? It made no sense. And what about the protest?

'My God,' she said. 'The demonstrators!'

'At least they've stopped throwing stones.' Short smirked.

'We must evacuate the building,' Helen said. 'And call London. Can you phone them?'

Short nodded. 'Of course.'

Ram Kuresh bustled into the room, a red plastic medical kit in his hand. He looked at the ambassador, then at Short hovering over him.

'Out of the way, Mr Short,' he said. 'This is a job for trained hands.' The first-aider radiated calm. He turned to the ambassador. 'You poor thing. Let me look at that.'

The Tannoy crackled into life. 'This is Eric Taylor, chief security officer. A bomb has exploded outside the embassy. Please leave the building and assemble in the courtyard.'

'Probably a bomb there too, primed to go off in five minutes.' The colour had returned to Short's cheeks. He straightened his silk tie. 'What does Helen think? Our Post Security Officer? Should we go out?'

Helen breathed deeply. She'd always been fond of Balfour's dictum that nothing mattered very much and few things mattered at all. But this was different.

'The courtyard is secure,' she said. 'Eric knows best.' She turned to Ram. 'What's happening in the annex?'

'Our rooms are clear.' Ram continued to fuss over bandages. 'A few people stopped to put their papers away, I'm afraid.' The SIS office, of which he was the only avowedly gay member, was in a self-contained suite of rooms behind an old-fashioned Cambridge door. To ask the spooks to leave their papers out would be like telling the Pope to skip mass.

'Will the ambassador make it down the stairs?'

'He will. With luck, it is only a flesh wound, but we must get it checked. And heads bleed like crazy.'

Helen looked at Short, who had not moved. 'Are you calling London?'

'Helen. Try to stay calm.' Short took out a phone and peered at it as though trying to recall its purpose. 'I'm taking care of it.'

Leaving Short to report the bomb made Helen uneasy. But she could not take the job back. She left the room and descended the grand staircase to the exit.

The courtyard of the embassy was a grey granite chasm used as a turning circle for visiting vehicles. Now it was filled with bedraggled embassy staff, clustered around floor wardens in the rain. Helen moved among them, checking everyone was accounted for.

Her phone rang.

'Helen. Blore here. Are you all OK?'

'Yes, all good thanks. But wide awake. Did you hear it?'

'Loud and clear.' The US embassy, where Blore Harl worked, was around the corner. 'I guess this confirms the warnings.' He meant the secret intelligence they had both seen.

'But a crowded street is a soft target,' Helen said. 'No-one's allowed within half a mile of the Reichstag.'

'Washington won't like it.'

'Let's hope they cancel the bloody Children's Summit.' Helen wiped rain off her face. 'Do you think it's even possible to invest more effort for less results?'

'Said a British embassy spokeswoman.'

'Don't get me started.'

'I guess the Secret Service will decide,' the American said. 'Hey, I'll get out your hair. See you on the security tour tomorrow.'

Helen rang off and moved towards the street. Something was nagging her. What had she been about to do when the bomb went off? Phone Dieter. The thought filled her with foreboding. But she had to call him.

The deputy head of the Summit Security Unit was expecting her.

'I suppose this means you want even more security for the Reichstag?' When Dieter Kremp was angry, his German sounded more clipped, more official.

'I'm fine, Dieter, thanks for asking. No-one seriously injured.'

He ignored her. 'For months, you and your American friends have been trying to frighten us with warnings about terrorists. Now there is a bomb. You must be happy.'

'Can you send someone over? The Wilhelmstrasse's a mess.'

'Police, medics and a forensic team should all be there. And someone from the SSU. Are they not?'

'I don't know. I'm in the embassy.'

'Who is the embassy contact point?'

Helen thought for a moment. 'Better be me. Jason likes everything to go through him. But this is important.'

'Is he still driving you insane?'

'If he would lay off me, I could ignore him. But he's obsessed with Bangkok.'

'I, too am obsessed. Are you free tonight?'

The change of tack caught Helen off guard. 'No idea. It's the first time we've had a bomb the day before a summit.' She grinned in the darkness. 'But I have wine in the fridge.'

'When will you be home?'

'Ten. Maybe eleven.'

'Sweet dreams.' Dieter rang off.

Helen saw Eric Taylor looming out of the rain. The locally-engaged ex-squaddie was elderly, with a refreshing indifference to hierarchies. He held up a hand.

'Hold it, Helen. Where are you going?'

'The street. People may be injured.'

'There's a few down, aye.' Eric inclined his close-cropped head towards her. 'All on the other side of the road. Bloody odd way to blow up an embassy.'

'Any ambulances?'

Eric bent his head closer still. 'They can't get past the security bollards.'

'I've done a first-aid course.' Helen moved towards the entrance. 'Maybe I could help.'

'Do you think it's safe to go out?'

'We can't just watch. Will you open the gate?'

'What if I won't?'

'I'll climb over the top. It'll look weird on the evening news.'

'OK.' The security officer nodded. 'But I'm shutting it behind you.'

The front guard desk, with its reinforced concrete pedestal and 35-millimetre bullet-resistant glass, was undamaged. Helen waited as Eric opened the ram-resistant steel gates enough for her to step through, then heard them slam shut behind her.

Outside was bedlam. Officers of the Bundespolizei, the Federal Police, were sealing off the street, submachine guns slung over their shoulders. A host of ambulances, police cars and fire engines had congregated beyond the traffic control bollards. Teams of orange-jacketed paramedics were clustered around the epicentre of the blast. A film crew from Wild TV had penetrated the cordon and was pointing a camera at a victim on a stretcher. A man in the charcoal-grey uniform of the Summit Security Unit stood talking on the phone.

Helen crossed the road towards the TV crew. They were filming a boy no more than five or six years old. She flashed on Nigel's plea to start a family. The boy's face was white with shock. A medic was bandaging his leg. Helen crouched down alongside him.

'My knee hurts,' the boy said.

'The doctor will help you.' She hoped it was true.

'I am thirsty.' His voice cracked. 'Something to drink.'

The film crew seemed oblivious to what the boy was saying. The medic had his hands full of dressings. Helen rose.

'I'll fetch water,' she said. 'Hold on.'

She ran back to the embassy. Inside, Eric Taylor saw her and opened the gate.

'Water,' Helen said. 'Quickly.'

'In the back, love.' The security officer jerked his thumb over his shoulder. 'Glasses in the top cupboard.'

She had never before seen the kitchenette which led off the security booth. It seemed to take ages to find a glass, fill it with water at the sink, and carry it outside. By the time she stepped back onto the street, two paramedics were lifting the child's stretcher. Helen moved closer, conscious of the water slopping onto the ground. As they carried the boy away, she heard someone say something about the bollards blocking access to the wounded.

A team of policemen was setting up a plastic awning to keep

the rain off the site of the explosion. One of them approached Helen.

'I saw you come out of the embassy. Please go back inside.'

'Of course.' Helen replied in German with an exaggerated English accent. She did not move, but looked up at the ambassador's office, a pale-blue shard of steel and glass protruding from the sandstone cladding of the embassy. 'Why do you think they set the bomb off on this side of the street?'

'No idea,' the policeman said.

'But look. The walls of the embassy are solid concrete. What could they hope to achieve?'

'Maybe they weren't attacking the embassy,' the policeman said. 'Are you going now?'

'Yes,' Helen said. 'I'm going. And thanks for your help. I think you just said something important.'

She turned and crossed the road to the embassy gates.

CHAPTER 4

AS HE RAN TOWARDS THE SUMMIT SECURITY UNIT COMMAND bunker, Dieter Kremp was reminded with a jolt how much he hated the logo for the Children's Summit. A Berlin bear on its back, for Christ's sake, balancing a cute kid on each of its sharp-clawed paws. The bear was grinning playfully – hungrily, more like – as it performed this unnatural act.

Dieter scowled. The politicians claimed that the package of economic reforms the Summit would agree was so revolutionary it would transform the lives not only of today's children but of their children, too. That was why a hundred kids from across the world had been invited to attend the opening ceremony. Dieter didn't care about that. But he hated the fact that one of the two-metre-high bears-with-children had been stuck to the steel plates which formed the perimeter of the Safety Zone. It made him curse each time he entered the Bunker: a mess on the metal, like bird-shit on a Porsche.

Dieter placed his eye to the retina scanner and the door slid open, releasing a chill blast of air. He could tolerate the stupid logo. Helen Gale was harder. Half the time he wanted to kill the blonde Englishwoman. The rest of the time he wanted to screw her. Either way, she drove him crazy.

The Bunker was nearly empty. That was part of Johann Frost's security concept: SSU staff should be on the ground, not at desks. Inside was just one officer.

Katia Vonhof was monitoring the main security console.

With her unkempt mane of black, shoulder-length hair and gaunt features, Katia barely registered with Dieter as a woman. But her mastery of computers and video surveillance technology was awesome. Where did Johann find these people?

Yet again, Dieter was filled with admiration for the charismatic boss of the Summit Security Unit. The name of Johann Frost was little known outside the counter-terrorism community. When he had first been appointed, senior figures in the police and military had questioned whether someone raised in what had been East Germany would have the qualities and connections for such a vital mission. Johann had confounded them all by filling the SSU with the best counter-terrorism specialists the country had to offer.

It had been Johann's idea to extend the trawl for the twenty-four members of the new Summit Security Unit beyond GSG 9, the elite anti-terrorist squad in which both he and Dieter had been trained. The SSU chief had spent months travelling around Germany, selecting recruits from regional police forces, army formations, and even the Ministry of the Interior. Then, bringing to bear extraordinary leadership, he had melded the disparate elements of the unit into a team the equal of anything in Europe or beyond. In exchange training, members of the SSU nominated by Johann had held their own with the best the US Delta Force and the British SAS had to offer. Two of them, the brothers Lukas and Philipp Klein from Mainz, had finished top in the sniping competition at Fort Bragg. Dieter looked at Katia Vonhof. If there had been a surveillance technology event in North Carolina she would have won it blindfold.

'Who is at the British Embassy?' he asked her.

'Johann has gone there.' The young SSU officer did not look round, but continued to scan the images on her bank of monitors.

'He went himself?'

'Yes.'

Dieter sat down at one of the desks which ringed the room and keyed in his code. No-one had a dedicated terminal in the Bunker, any more than they had a single script to follow in the event of an emergency. Flexibility was the key. Flexibility, and vision. It had been Johann Frost's vision to train a cadre so small, and so expert, that they could deliver security which was omnipresent yet invisible. Once the delegations entered the Safety Zone, the only armed forces on the ground would be the SSU team.

Almost. That was where the trouble had started. Within hours of the German government circulating the security concept for the Children's Summit, the US Secret Service had stated that if they could not assign their own armed agents to protect the President inside the Reichstag, the President would not attend. End of discussion.

Dieter called it an insult to Germany; to the Summit Security Unit; to Johann Frost. But the Federal Chancellor had rolled right over. It was more important that the President attended the Summit than that Johann, the man responsible for security, could run his own show. Both Johann and Dieter had tendered their resignations. But when Interior Minister Tilo Pollex had called personally to ask them to stay on, the leader and deputy leader of the SSU had swallowed their pride.

Once they had got their way with the Secret Service agents, the Americans had started pushing everyone around. The next battleground had been the Threat Assessment Committee. That was where Dieter had first met Helen Gale.

Threat assessment was part of the planning for all international gatherings. The idea was to pool intelligence of possible dangers from terrorism and civil disturbance and assess the implications for security. It was meant to be a routine round of meetings and paperwork. Johann had delegated the job to Dieter without hesitating. But the Committee had become a nightmare.

The British alone had sent two representatives each from the Secret Intelligence Service and the Security Service, plus a bluff policeman with rolled-up sleeves from Scotland Yard's counter-terrorist unit who'd looked as if he would happily kill with his bare hands any terrorists he might come across. This herd of experts had been corralled by the sixth member of the delegation: a freckled blonde in a short skirt from the British embassy in Berlin. Dieter had assumed Helen Gale to be someone's secretary. Only later had he realised the magnitude of his mistake.

The French, Russian, Italian, Canadian and Japanese delegations were as bloated as the British team. But the Americans had sent three times as many: CIA, FBI, NSA, Department of Homeland Security, Secret Service – the list seemed endless. Sometimes Dieter wondered if terror groups measured their success not in how many people they killed, but in how many experts were siphoned off onto the futile treadmill that was counter-terrorism. By that measure, the terrorists had already won.

The telephone rang.

'Johann here. Anything new on the embassy bombing? I am there now.'

Dieter glanced at his monitor. 'No-one has claimed it.'

'Call me if they do. I am talking to the forensic people: if we can ID the bomb, we can ID the bomb-maker. Can you send back-up? '

'Only Katia is here.'

'What about Petra? She should be finished at the US embassy by now.'

'I haven't seen her.' Dieter checked the duty log. Johann was right, as usual. SSU officer Petra Bleibtreu had been running through sniper positions with the Secret Service. But her meeting had been due to finish an hour ago.

'Maybe the Americans wanted more information,' Johann said.

'They do not ask for much, the *Amis*.'

Johann grunted. 'Especially not the Secret Service. A pleasure to work with.'

'How does it look in the Wilhelmstrasse?' Dieter said. 'The British say they have casualties.'

'I cannot move for ambulances.'

'Good. Will you update the Interior Ministry?'

'Sounds bureaucratic. You do it.' Johann rang off.

Dieter returned to his computer screen. Reuters were reporting that the police had rounded up a selection of prominent Islamists. As if the bombers would be sitting around at home. At least the Berlin cops could act without consulting the Threat Assessment Committee first.

If the size of the Committee seemed cumbersome, the meetings were unmanageable. The first few sessions had adopted a table-round format, each delegation vying to show that it knew more about the threats facing the Summit than anyone else. But it soon became clear that when it came to compiling blood-curdling intelligence, the Anglo-Saxons were in a league of their own.

Everyone knew that Washington and London devoted a grotesque proportion of their gross national product to amassing secrets. Some information came from actual human beings. But most came from electronic eavesdropping: by the National Security Agency on the part of the US, and by the Government Communications Headquarters, or GCHQ, on behalf of the British. Dieter had never heard anything like it. By the time he had sat through the first recitation of the threats which the CIA and SIS believed hung over the Summit, he found it hard to imagine that a single aggrieved individual, much less any terrorist group, could have been left off the list.

The result was that Dieter Kremp and the German staff of the Summit Security Unit found themselves engulfed in a tidal wave of advice on how to do their job. If one security airlock controlled access to the Reichstag, it should be two; if two, four. If SSU officers planned to wear body armour, had they considered the latest Kevlar products? And had the German authorities thought of adding a second ring of barriers around the Reichstag to deter suicide bombers? At the third meeting of the committee, Dieter announced straight-faced that Berlin had decided to retrofit the city's entire fleet of police BMW saloons with Chobham composite armour at a cost of one million euro per vehicle. Only one person had smiled at his joke. Helen Gale.

It was the British diplomat's intellect and unpredictability which made her so formidable. At some meetings she barely spoke, but doodled on a pad or gazed at her laptop as if she didn't give a damn what the meeting decided. Other times, she would suddenly raise some intercepted phone call by terrorist group X, and ask how Dieter proposed to respond. That was always it. *How he proposed to respond.*

Whatever the threat might be, you could be sure this was the first Dieter had heard of it. And you could be certain that the entire 20-strong CIA contingent would speak right out in support of Helen Gale. Then the British and Americans would refuse to accept any response which didn't increase security for the Summit. It became a joke in Berlin: if any more fortifications were added, the entire Reichstag would sink into the sandy subsoil.

Until three months ago, Dieter Kremp had viewed Helen Gale as more of a threat to the Summit's success than any possible combination of terrorists.

Then Paris had happened. Helen Gale's spook pals had let their distinguished Foreign Secretary step into a car outside their Paris embassy; allowed the ambassador, a security man and a driver to get in with him; surrounded the vehicle with diplomats; then covered their ears as four kilograms of what the French called *le plastique* ripped seven people to pieces. Thirty more had been hospitalised, many of them hit by flying debris. These were the experts telling the SSU how to run the Summit.

It would be too much to say that when the Threat Assessment Committee met the day after Paris, Helen Gale had been transformed. But for the first time, Dieter had seen her self-possession slip to reveal a hint of – what? Loneliness? Loss? Whatever it was, that glimpse of vulnerability had triggered in him a rush of desire. Was it possible that a dazzling, Cambridge-educated diplomat might be within reach of the son of a metal-worker from the Ruhr?

Dieter Kremp always made decisions quickly. After the meeting, he had taken Helen Gale to one side and asked her out for a drink. He had been surprised when she had accepted; and astonished when, after a meal, a club and more cocktails than he could count, she invited him back to her flat in the Voxstrasse. That night she had seemed desperate to have him. Maybe the bomb in Paris had shaken her; she had been willing to do anything that first night. Almost anything. She was passionate yet controlled; serious, but with flashes of deadpan humour; wild, yet determined to set the rules. That was a challenge: Dieter had never met a woman he could not dominate. Well, there was always time. The British embassy in Berlin had just been blown up, the day before the Summit

That was a tragedy. But for Dieter Kremp, it might be an opportunity. Would Helen Gale feel vulnerable tonight? It would be wrong to let a chance like this go by.

CHAPTER 5

HELEN WATCHED SIR LEONARD LENNOX GROW ANGRY. IT WAS a rare, but frightening sight. Even when the ambassador was calm, his rugged features tended to darken in response to obstacles or unreason. Now, the combination of brilliant white bandages and a choleric outburst made his face look black with rage.

'They say *what?*'

Basil Nutter grimaced, glanced around the conference table and said nothing. Decades of experience in the back rooms of embassies from Abidjan to Yerevan had left the wizened but career-challenged diplomat equipped with two convictions. The first was that the key to a contented life was to avoid drawing attention to yourself. The second was that efforts by governments to influence the media were at best pointless and in most cases counter-productive. Basil was arguably, therefore, ill-fitted to the job of embassy press officer. He seemed physically to have shrunk as the Summit loomed. This morning's blast had left his brow, and his suit, more deeply creased than ever.

Helen had been thinking of the injured child in the street. She saw Basil's plight and intervened.

'Ambassador,' she said. 'You need a cigarette. Possibly two.'

'First sensible idea I've heard all day.' A lighter and a packet of Benson and Hedges were in the ambassador's big hands in an instant. 'And before you say anything, Jason, this is an emergency. Since the windows have been blown out by a terrorist bomb, we're technically outside anyway.'

Jason Short said nothing, but looked at the overwhelmingly intact windows and pursed his lips.

The ambassador lit a cigarette, blew a stream of smoke towards the ceiling, and turned to Basil.

'Tell me about this story.'

'It's on Wild TV,' Basil said. 'The demonstrators are blaming us for the blast.'

'Bollocks.' The ambassador was calmer already. 'Do they think we blew up our own embassy?'

'Uktam Zholobov has issued a statement supporting them.'

'We can ignore Zholobov,' Leonard Lennox said. 'If he wants to influence the Summit, he should come and join in. God knows, the Russian government have invited him enough times.'

'He won't sit at the same table.' Helen shook her head. 'He says they want to destroy his dodgy energy empire.'

'He's probably right.' The ambassador turned to Basil Nutter. 'What are the demonstrators saying?'

'They claim the embassy had an intelligence warning that a terrorist attack was imminent. But that we didn't warn the organisers of the march.'

'How the hell did they know about the intelligence?' Short glared at Helen. 'I suppose you told your pal Dieter Kremp.'

Helen sighed, and typed on her laptop the words *KILL JASON*.

'It is my job to exchange intelligence with the Germans and other partners in the Threat Assessment Committee,' she said. 'There have been dozens of reports about attacks on the Summit. But no references to British targets.'

'Did anyone tell the protesters about these warnings?' Short said.

'Well,' Helen blinked. 'It would look a bit odd if this embassy started putting out terror warnings to the German public. I'm not sure the German government would thank us.'

'British embassy says, "Not our problem",' Short said. 'That should calm things down.'

'Hold it.' The ambassador held up his hand. 'Wild TV are always desperate for scoops. But are they talking out of their arses here? Or could someone really make a case against this embassy for not giving intelligence to the general public?' He looked round the table. 'Helen. You were in the Cabinet Office assessments staff, weren't you? You must have seen a bit of secret intelligence.'

'More than I ever want to see again.' On Helen's laptop, a fractal pattern was engulfing the screen. 'That's the trouble. Every day, intelligence services sift through millions of pieces of data. For every incident, there are a thousand false alarms. It's hard to know when to publicise a threat.'

Short shook his head. 'I don't see how it's our fault if someone blows themselves up outside our embassy.'

Helen ignored him. 'The famous case was in 1988, when someone called the American embassy in Helsinki to say a Pan Am flight from Frankfurt to the US would be blown up in the next two weeks by the Abu Nidhal terrorist organisation. It was an unusually specific threat, so the US aviation authorities issued a warning. But not everyone heard about it. Two weeks later, Pan Am Flight 103 blew up over Lockerbie.'

'I thought the Libyans blew up Pan Am 103,' the ambassador said.

'That was what the courts decided. They said the phone call was probably a hoax. There are always cranks posting bogus warnings that London or New York is about to be attacked with anthrax or bubonic plague. The families of Pan Am 103 couldn't sue the bombers, because they didn't know who they were. Instead, they sued Pan Am. Some people argued the US government was responsible for not publishing the Helsinki warning, or that the CIA were negligent for letting terrorists put a bomb on the plane.'

'But you said there hadn't been any warnings about attacks on the embassy,' the ambassador said.

'No. But there have been threats to the Summit, and we're

a member of the G8.' Helen shrugged. 'If someone wanted to play the blame game, they could point at us.'

No-one spoke.

'Um, there is another problem,' Basil said.

'Let's hear it.' The ambassador lit a second cigarette.

'Wild TV say the embassy's security bollards prevented ambulance crews reaching the injured, and may have caused the death of the demonstrator.' The press officer's anxiety had transformed his expression into a fixed grin. 'What with this and the intelligence story, the press may decide to bury us in ordure.'

'What are the casualty figures?' the ambassador said.

'Twelve injured and one dead,' Helen said. 'But no way the delay caused the death. The dead woman was literally blown to pieces.'

'Don't we know who she is?' Short said.

'It's a mystery. None of the demonstrators has identified the body. The police think it may have been a suicide bomber.'

'A suicide bomber with a very tiny bomb,' Short said. All the men laughed.

Helen took a deep breath. It was true she had spent two years in the Cabinet Office assessments staff in London. Her job there had been to spot connections where others saw confusion. What had the policeman in the street said? She pressed her lips together and felt blood course through them.

'How do we know the bomb was aimed at us?' she said.

Short shook his head. 'London agree that this was an attack on the embassy.'

'You told London we'd been attacked,' Helen said. 'That's how assumptions become facts. But how did you know we were the target?'

The ambassador said nothing, but put one hand up to the bandages on his head. Jason Short laughed again.

Helen forged on. 'In Paris, the bomb targeted the Foreign Secretary. He died, with six other people, four of them ours. Today, not one of the dead or seriously injured – without wanting to belittle your wounds, ambassador – was in the embassy. Doesn't that strike you as odd?'

'So, to summarise,' Short said, 'the ambassador has been injured by a terrorist bomb. The demonstrators blame us for not warning them, and for stopping help from reaching them afterwards. And Helen has a theory that the explosion outside the building had no connection to the embassy.' He paused for effect. 'What we need to decide is what to do next.'

Helen closed her laptop. No-one was listening. Time for Plan B.

'We should go on the offensive,' she said. 'Show we care about the people who have been injured, rather than skulk indoors looking furtive. We do care about the protesters, don't we?'

'We do,' Leonard Lennox said.

'Then let's show it.'

'That could be the second sensible idea I've heard today.' The ambassador lit another cigarette. 'Tell me more.'

The flag car was a Mercedes. Helen was used to seeing the British diplomatic pennant fluttering alongside the three-pointed star. But Sir Leonard Lennox was from a different generation.

'I know the Indians have Jaguar, and BMW's making Rolls Royces,' he muttered as the fat tyres bulged under the weight of the armour-plating. 'But a black Merc. Where's the fun in that?'

'The Rolls was black, the Merc is black. What's the difference?' Helen said.

Leonard Lennox shook his head. 'Sometimes, Helen, I don't know whether you're joking or not.'

Helen gazed out of the window. The guard outside the embassy had been augmented by heavily armed officers of the Bundespolizei, the Federal Police, in their dark-blue uniforms. A crowd of protesters had gathered by the bollards. A news crew from Wild TV stood recording it all. She shivered. The air-conditioning in the car was fierce after the damp heat outside.

She hoped there would be cameras at the hospital, for Basil's sake. The press officer had been tearing around shouting into his phone as Ram Kuresh wrapped fresh bandages around the head of Leonard Lennox.

'You've got to make people feel sorry for him without making him look pathetic,' the shambolically-suited press man had urged between calls. 'Think ambassadorial.'

'Do not worry,' Ram had said. 'I am thinking maharajah.'

Basil was still calling press contacts when they reached the hospital. The main entrance was a futuristic modern portico tacked onto the front of a 1960s East German prefabricated block. The walls on either side were plastered with posters protesting against health-care reform, American military adventurism, and the costs of the Children's Summit. The rain had stopped and the pavements were steaming in the sunshine.

'I can't see any news crews.' The ambassador's face was darkening again.

'Perhaps they're inside,' Basil said.

'Let us hope so.'

But when they entered the building, they saw only a clutter of hospital trolleys, outpatients and listless visitors. There was not a TV camera in sight.

The ambassador seemed inclined to make the best of things. 'Sod it,' he said. 'We can still talk to some poor injured buggers.' And like an auto-homing missile he was off, eyes bright with empathy, looking for a bed to stand by. Helen watched Basil tail him, tape recorder at the ready.

They had been walking for several minutes when she saw through a doorway a huddle of camera crews. *Yes!* They were all there: RBB, ARD, Wild TV again. At last. The audience the ambassador needed. She turned off to check it out.

The ward was quiet. Several beds were occupied by sedated bomb victims. Helen looked round for the injured boy. The hush lent the place a chill air. Then she saw him. Clad in a grey surgical gown on a bed surrounded by TV crews, the child looked more pitiful than ever. A tent of raised sheets covered the lower part of his body. A woman in a green pullover with a bandage on her forehead sat holding his hand.

Helen felt a surge of emotion. Her own concerns seemed irrelevant next to the grief of a mother for her child. She stepped closer. The boy seemed to be asleep.

Someone was talking. Helen saw a woman being interviewed among the TV cameras. It took her a moment to tune in to what she was saying.

'…because his life has become a tragedy. Because it could have been prevented. And because responsibility is clear. Thank you.'

The knot of people loosened. Now to recruit some media interest for the ambassador. Helen tapped one of the cameramen on the shoulder.

'Hi, I'm from the British embassy. Do you think your people would – '

The man reacted unexpectedly. Ignoring Helen, he turned towards the clump of journalists. 'Guess what? She's from the embassy.'

There was a stir. 'The *British* embassy?' A man's voice. 'Unbelievable.' He sounded delighted.

'Believe it.' Helen smiled. A TV camera turned towards her, the recording light on. She sensed danger. A second lens turned her way, then a third, the cameras closing in.

The woman who had been interviewed turned to Helen. She was short, with big breasts and hips and straight dark hair down to her shoulders. She was dressed entirely in black: dense trousers, a long-sleeved army-surplus shirt tucked into a belt, and glasses with thick rectangular frames. At first sight, she projected an impression of immense severity. But behind the lenses her eyes were constantly moving.

'You bastards have a nerve.' The woman in black spat the words out.

Helen stood up straight. 'What did you say?'

29

'You are from the British embassy, is that right? You work for the British government?'

'Yes, we – '

'How does it feel?' The woman's voice rose a tone. 'To have caused so much suffering?'

Helen licked her lips and nodded, to show she was listening. Was this being transmitted live? 'Sorry. I don't quite understand.'

'Look at this child. Does that make you feel good?'

'I feel pity for him.'

'Do not play games. You are not sorry. Do you even know who he is? Have you taken the trouble to find out?'

'I only just arrived at the hospital.' Helen looked at the bed. Perhaps the boy would wake up and explain how Helen had tried to help him. But his eyes stayed closed.

'Of course. An exercise in *public relations*.' The woman used the English words. 'Well, his mother says he just learned to ride a bicycle. He won't be riding it anytime soon.'

'I hope he recovers quickly.'

'I bet you do. Because we are suing the British embassy for damages of fifty million euro, on behalf of the victims of today's crime. Perhaps paying that will make you sorry.'

The TV cameras were still on. The woman in the rectangular glasses was breathing quickly and seemed unsteady on her feet. Was she nervous? Her arms were close to her sides.

'I hope you're not suggesting that the embassy is responsible for the bomb which exploded today,' Helen said. 'That would be crazy.'

'Let us talk about what is and is not crazy. Do you deny that security barriers to protect British diplomats delayed ambulances from reaching victims of the bomb? Do you deny that the officer responsible for security in the embassy, Helen Gale, received intelligence warnings of a terrorist attack on a G8 target in Berlin? Do you deny that the embassy did nothing to warn the peaceful protesters outside?'

How did she know so much? 'We don't comment on intelligence matters.'

'Perhaps you will have more to say when this comes to court.' The woman paused, as if about to continue, then stopped. She took off her glasses and wiped her eyes with the back of her hand. 'OK, that is enough.' She turned away.

Helen saw the lights on the cameras go out. She reached for the woman's shoulder.

'What's this about suing the embassy?'

The woman spun round, shrinking from Helen's touch. *'Hands off.'* Without her glasses, she looked vulnerable and exposed.

Helen stepped back. 'I'm sorry, I just – '

'What do you want?'

'Who are you?'

'None of your business.' The woman turned to go.

Helen lowered her voice. 'I'm not your enemy, you know. I hate all this as much as you do.'

The woman turned back. She looked at Helen as if seeing her for the first time. 'My name is Sabine Wolf. I work as a trauma counsellor for the Victims' Legal Support Group. I try to repair the harm which the powerful do to the powerless. And you are wrong. You are my enemy.'

'We should be fighting whoever did this, not each other.'

'Your government did this. You did this.'

'No.' Helen glanced at the sleeping boy, and held out her card. 'We're on the same side.'

The woman studied the card. 'You are Helen Gale. Strange. Well, I don't need this.' She took the crisp white rectangle and tore it in two. 'And I don't need any fake sympathy. All I want is your money.' Sabine Wolf replaced her glasses and with them a brisker, business persona. 'You understand you are the respondent in the case. The person we are saying is responsible for these injuries. The Victims' Legal Support Group is suing you, Helen Gale, personally for fifty million euro. You had better start saving.'

CHAPTER 6

ONE DAY, ULI WENGER THOUGHT, HE WOULD BE TAGGED. If he lived that long. The technology existed: the state would inject a chip into each citizen and track them by satellite. If Uli were in charge, he would have people tagged tomorrow. He would want to know where everyone was, so he could torment them as they had tormented him.

But for now, there were no tags. That was good. Otherwise, what he planned for tomorrow would be impossible. The insects had saved him. The insects hated change. They liked their old-fashioned ID cards, which could be forged and bought and fixed. They did not want the government to know where they were. So Uli could stay what he wanted to be. Someone who officially did not exist.

On the path through the Grunewald forest he stopped in the shade of a tree and waited ten minutes. The man he was seeing today troubled him. Last time they had met, in an old Prussian fort in the west of the city, Ivan had tracked Uli all the way to the rendezvous point. Uli had seen nothing. That would not happen again.

He felt sweat prickle on his back. The afternoon was close and still. Every cop in Berlin was at the Reichstag, or the British embassy. The woods were quiet. Not even a snake could move silently amongst the twigs and leaves. Not even Ivan, surely. Uli listened, then resumed the gentle climb.

It was a shame he could not meet the man who was paying

for all this. Herr Kraft, Uli called him, Mr Power. Uli thought he knew who it was. But for such a man to meet Uli Wenger was impossible. A personality, meeting an un-person. And so, today, Uli would meet another un-person. His name could not really be Ivan. That was too Russian, too generic. Somewhere nearby, he would be waiting, checking for the all-clear, like Uli. Ivan didn't trust anyone either.

At a clearing, Uli stepped off the path, settled on a fallen log, and sat so still that after a few seconds a sparrow was within a metre of him, fussing among the leaves. He needed no book or newspaper to pass the time: he was content to stare ahead, eyes blank, mind roaming. Now he was watching them hurt Mouse and planning how he would strike back. Then, after he had rescued her, she had lain there in the bath-tub with her pale, perfect skin, eyes closed, so beautiful. Still, and silent. The water so red.

'*Guten Tag.*'

It took all his self-control not to move. Someone had spoken right in front of him. Yet he had seen nothing. Heard nothing.

'Hello there.' He glanced at the bushes by the path. No-one.

Ivan peered round the trunk of the tree behind which he was sitting, hidden from sight. 'Hi. Good to see you again.' His smile was so regular, his hair so blond, his back so straight, it gave Uli the creeps. He looked like a cop, or one of those perfect workers from the old socialist realism murals in East Berlin. Today it was the off-duty look: trainers, sweatshirt and jeans, dull colours for the June forest. No need to get excited. There were no Russian cops in Berlin these days. And not many cops gave you money to kill people.

The Russian walked towards him. Uli kept his hand in his coat pocket, as if he might have a weapon. The pocket was empty, of course. The cops would never search Uli. But if they did, they would always find him clean.

Ivan sat down next to Uli. Like a walker stopping to consult a map. He paused, listening perhaps, then pulled from his inside pocket a newspaper, the Süddeutsche Zeitung, folded to a certain page. Ivan was a professional too. Nothing to attract attention if he were stopped. The Russian spread the page out on his knee and pointed to eight faces among a panel of photographs, a group of men and women.

'One. Two. Three. Four. Five. Six. Seven. Eight.'

Uli looked at the faces. He recognised them all. He cared about none of them. He turned to Ivan. 'Is that it?'

'A personal request. No Russians.'

'I cannot promise anything. We are not talking about a surgical strike.'

The Russian folded his newspaper. 'Do what I say. I know who you are.'

You cannot conceive of who I am. 'Some of my people hate Russians.'

'You will answer for them.' Ivan nodded. 'Do you have something for me?'

'Yes. Usual place.' Uli did not need to say out loud *the latest security reports for the Children's Summit, sanitised as usual.*

'Your sources are good.'

'Yes.' Uli did not bother to smile.

'Enjoy your walk.' The Russian rose to go. 'You remember? One to eight?'

'No problem.' Uli stood too. Nothing had changed hands: anything they needed physically to transfer passed through a series of left-luggage lockers at the Berlin Central Station. Not an incriminating word had been spoken: like Uli, the Russian was passionate about the threat of technical surveillance. Ivan did not say goodbye, but simply walked away. It was tempting to follow and find out where he went. But Ivan was crafty. And Uli had no time. If he did not return to town soon, others would be wondering where he was. That was a risk he could not take. Not when he stood on the brink of an achievement which would pay back everything. Even Mouse.

CHAPTER 7

IT WAS TEN MINUTES PAST ELEVEN AT NIGHT WHEN HELEN logged off her computer in the embassy. She sat for a moment in her swivel chair and stared out at the street. What was she doing here?

Helen had applied to the Foreign Office direct from Cambridge, even before she knew she had been awarded a starred First in her French and Russian finals. Diplomacy was an obvious career path for a linguist, and the idea of maybe one day becoming an ambassador had seemed impossibly exotic.

The Office, as it was known to insiders, had proved a stimulating employer. After twelve months in London on the Russia desk, she had been packed off to spend two years learning Mandarin Chinese, followed by a posting to Beijing. She had been due to return to London when a spy scandal in Moscow and a mass expulsion of British diplomats led to an all-posts trawl for Russian speakers. What was not to like about working at the British embassy in Moscow? Instead of returning to her studio flat in Fulham, she had next unpacked her suitcases in the Moscow Kempinski Hotel, at the start of three years in the Russian capital. Then had come a slot in the Cabinet Office analysing intelligence on terrorist threats, during which time she had met Nigel, fallen in love, and married. Now, she was in Berlin, alone again.

None of these jobs had been dull.

Yet Helen had always found herself curiously indifferent to

the policy-making process which seemed to fascinate her Foreign Office peers. Seeing a minimum of two sides to every argument, most policy wonks seemed to delight in making a watertight case for one of them. Helen, by contrast, found it hard to persuade herself either that any single point of view was correct, or that it mattered very much one way or the other.

This sense of detachment had served her well. For all its innate conservatism, the Foreign Office was conscious that iconoclasts were a precious commodity, and tended to encourage dissent from those capable of expressing it in lucid prose. But Helen found herself drawn to issues where the rights and wrongs were clear. That was why she enjoyed counter-terrorism work. Stopping terrorists from killing people was definitely worth the bother.

Helen tried to remember what time she had told Dieter she would finish. Not that it mattered. She grinned and watched her computer screen fade to black. She was not responsible for him, any more than he was for her. And that was how it would stay.

All around her, the embassy was silent. Jason Short had left hours ago. Yet she had felt the need to work late. Was she trying to prove to herself that her decision to come to Germany had been right? She began packing away her things. The telephone rang.

It was Nigel.

'Helen. I heard about the bomb. Are you OK darling?'

'Yes. Thanks for asking.' *Half a day after the event.*

'I've been running around like mad.' It was as if he'd heard her thoughts. 'I'm in Berlin tomorrow for the Summit. I'll get lots of face time on TV.'

She felt thrilled he was coming and his career was thriving, then angry with herself for caring. 'I thought you hated summits.'

'Correct. There's never any news. If anything juicy happens, the journalists are the last to know. But this one's different. I'm being embedded.'

'Like a tick? Or an arrow?'

'I'll be like one of those war reporters. Except that instead of the marines, I'll be watching the Prime Minister cut swathes through our enemies at the conference table.'

'If you can make a G8 Summit sound exciting you'll deserve a Pulitzer.'

'Thank you. I'll do my best. The good news is – ' Nigel stopped, as if to draw breath. 'The good news is, there's a heads-only dinner on the evening of the first day which journalists can't attend. So, I wondered if my wife and I might get together for a chat.'

'A chat? Why?'

Again, Nigel hesitated. 'I thought it would be nice to see how you are. Talk about us.'

'Sounds delightful. Let's do it. I'm fine, by the way.'

'I'm not suggesting you aren't. But we haven't talked for months.'

'Whose fault is that?'

'Helen. I have two teenage daughters.'

'I know, and a bitter ex-wife. You've already used up a life-time's worth of bile. So now you stay in a Zen state of maddening calmness whenever your present wife tries to have an argument with you. You know nothing makes me lose my temper more than you being so bloody serene all the time.'

Nigel chuckled. 'Remind me to bang the table and rant a little when we meet. Look, I know I was old-fashioned about not quitting my job to swan off to Berlin with you. I'm sorry I said you were crazy to go there alone, when you could have stayed in London and – '

'Become a brood mare.'

'The point is, I don't want to give up what we have, Helen. I still want children with you. Can you imagine that?'

Helen pictured the injured boy. She remembered arguments with Nigel in London. She imagined him holding a child. Her child. She bit her lip and said nothing.

'Could we talk about it?'

'Nigel.' She tried to keep her voice level. 'I am not giving up my job.'

'As you've told me about a million times. Shall I call you tomorrow night?'

'Yes. Please. Call me. Is there anything else?'

'There is a bit of business, yes. Will anyone from the embassy be at the Summit?'

'A bit of business. Why am I not surprised?' Helen refocused her thoughts. 'The ambo should be there, if he's well enough. He was hurt by the bomb.'

'Yes, I heard. The consensus seems to be that the terrorists were lucky, injuring the ambassador with such a small bomb.'

'Yes. I'm not sure it was even aimed at us.'

'What? You think it went off outside the embassy by accident?'

'Don't you think it's strange, injuring so many demonstrators?'

'That reminds me,' Nigel said. 'Someone's saying it's all the embassy's fault. No, your fault. Our terrorism people have a piece in the online edition. Don't get too famous, will you? I'm not sure I could stand the competition.'

'Nigel. Don't even think about competing with me.'

'Very well. See you tomorrow.'

'See you.'

He rang off.

Helen made her way down the deserted corridor. After the embassy was locked up each night, the only way to leave the building from her floor was to descend the emergency stairs to the garage. For reasons no-one had been able to establish, the motion sensors which operated the staircase lights worked only fitfully, with the result that Helen had to feel her way along the banisters down to the ground floor in darkness.

She reached the foot of the stairs, fumbled for the door to the garage, and pulled it open. There was a blaze of light. As her eyes adjusted, the first thing she saw was the chief security officer, Eric Taylor, standing with his back to her. The door clicked shut.

Eric whirled round, a cloth in his hand. Behind him, the cowl of a motorcycle gleamed.

'Helen! You gave me a fright. You're in late.'

'No choice. Did you know the Prime Minister is coming tomorrow for the G8 Summit? And we had a bomb outside the embassy today?'

'No-one tells me anything.' Eric grinned and walked round his motorcycle so he was facing her. He resumed his polishing. 'What's this about someone suing you? That's daft.'

'Of course it's daft. But in theory they could have a case.'

'You're having me on.'

'Something about the embassy's duty of care. Apparently they could argue that if we knew a bomb might go off, we should have warned people.'

'Sounds shite to me.' Eric's hand continued to move on the cowl.

'Right. If they can sue me for that, I can sue Jason for uselessness.'

Helen was smiling. But the case bothered her. Throughout the afternoon, no-one in the Foreign Office in London had shown any interest in the possibility that she might be sued by the victims of the Berlin bomb blast. The only people to call her had been the Press Office, in search of a line to take with journalists.

In desperation, Helen had contacted Julia Strang, a young lawyer in the FCO Legal Adviser's department with whom she had shared a flat when she first moved to London. Julia's advice had not been encouraging.

'It's more political than legal,' she had said. 'If the plaintiffs lodge a case in the German courts, we could claim state immunity. But claiming immunity these days reeks of gunboats and starched collars. Ministers hate doing it unless they're sure the case is bogus. The view of the embassy will carry weight. Who's your boss?'

'A guy called Jason Short. All he cares about is becoming ambassador in Bangkok. Actually, he hates me.'

'Not good. What about the ambassador?'

'He's OK. But he's in hospital.'

'Not good either. What you want is for the Office to stand up for you. But it might be a while before anyone focuses.'

'What happens until then?'

'If these guys want publicity, they might organise an affiliate to sue you in the UK to by-pass immunity. That would increase British media interest.'

'But I haven't done anything.'

'Helen, I know you're innocent. You know you're innocent.' Julia had clicked her tongue. 'But proving something in a court of law is never straightforward. Meanwhile, unfortunately, you're in the firing line.'

Now, standing under the strip-lights of the Embassy garage, Helen realised that Eric's sympathy had brought her to the verge of tears. That was, to quote Julia Strang, not good. British diplomats did not normally weep in front of their colleagues. 'That's a beautiful bike,' she said.

'Man at peace with his motorcycle, that's me.' Eric glanced at her, then resumed his polishing. 'It's time you went home. Don't let the bastards get you down.'

'Good night, Eric.'

'Good night.'

Outside the embassy, the police and Bundespolizei officers guarding the building peered at her, as if suspicious that she might have committed a crime. Even in the dim glow of Berlin's curiously under-powered streetlights, Helen could see smudges on the road surface left by the explosion. According to the police, the dead woman's head and upper body had been destroyed by the blast. Who was she? The intelligence suggested the threat to the Summit came from organised terrorist groups. So why had the bomber not been skilled enough to move close to the building she was attacking? And why had the bomb been so small?

She walked past East German blocks of flats and turned alongside the Holocaust Memorial. In the night, the ranks of concrete blocks looked like giant, densely packed tombstones. She had been shocked when Leonard Lennox collapsed halfway through his tour of the hospital. It had happened after she had briefed him on her disastrous interview with the trauma counsellor, Sabine Wolf; when he fell, Helen's first thought had been that she had killed him with her ineptitude. But the hospital staff said he was suffering from blood loss and shock. Now he lay recuperating at the Charité Hospital. It was uncertain whether he would recover in time to accompany the Prime Minister to the Summit. If not, that dubious privilege would fall to his deputy, Jason Short.

Helen found the thought of the ambassador lying in hospital more distressing than she could explain. Maybe it was something to do with her father. After walking out of the house when she was fourteen to throw himself into a relationship with a girl of twenty-six, he had cut himself off from Helen and her mother. Since then, Helen had often found herself attracted to men who held out the promise of stability. It was hard to see what else a leader-writer for the Times twenty years her senior and a German counter-terrorist cop had in common.

She passed the Canadian embassy. Everyone said the discovery phase was the most thrilling part of a relationship. The trouble was, the more she discovered about a man, the less she found thrilling. When she'd first met Nigel at a press conference in No. 11 Downing Street, she'd been entranced by the respect with which the distinguished journalist treated her. She was used to men lusting after her. In that, Nigel was no different from all the rest. But he also seemed to admire her for who she was, and what she had achieved. Combined with his maturity and intellect, it was a winning combination.

Only after they were married had she realised that however sincerely Nigel wanted her as his wife, he could not grasp the importance she attached to control of her own body and her own life. They had been arguing about it ever since. Dieter, with his edge of danger and exquisite, toned musculature, was no substitute. He was outstanding at what the management manuals called task – getting the job done. But when it came to maintenance of a relationship – empathy, sensitivity and listening – he scored zero across the board.

Nearly home now. Her flat was in the Potsdamer Platz, a nondescript muddle of modernist architecture thrown up when the Wall came down. Its anonymity and convenience suited her. Every morning before breakfast she ran five kilometres along the tracks which criss-crossed the nearby Tiergarten. After work, it took her fifteen minutes to walk home.

Even the fact that her block was half-empty was a blessing: there were none of the noise problems which plagued more popular developments. Many flats belonged to investors like Oleg Sukanashvili, the entrepreneur whom Helen had met on her posting in Moscow. It was Oleg who had alerted Helen to the vacancy. She smiled at the thought of the shambling, bear-like Georgian.

One of Helen's predecessors in the Moscow embassy, a first secretary named Stephen Million, had once done Oleg Sukanashvili a favour. No-one seemed to know what it had been. Million had left Russia under a cloud and no longer worked for the Foreign Office. Sukanashvili and his commercial enterprises had subsequently been treated with circumspection by embassy staff in Moscow. Helen had been warned on her arrival in the Russian capital to avoid the big Georgian if ever their paths crossed.

She had taken the first opportunity to seek Sukanashvili out.

He had not been difficult to find. The Georgian was a consummate networker, and regularly appeared at commercial events in the Russian capital, accompanied by two spectacularly menacing bodyguards. When Helen approached him, his first, ironic, response had been that he could have nothing to do with her since the embassy had warned staff to keep clear of him. Once she had explained that she wanted to meet him for exactly that reason, however, his fat face had creased into a smile.

'The cult of the eccentric,' he had said. 'It is this resistance to conformity that I love about the British. It is because of this that I owe the embassy a debt. But they will not let me repay it.'

The Georgian, too, refused to tell Helen what Stephen Million had done to earn his gratitude. 'You must ask Stephen,' he would say. But over the three years of her posting in Moscow he had showered her with what she wanted most: insights into political and economic life in the Russian capital. He never asked for anything in return: her friendship seemed to satisfy him. But they had lost contact when she returned to London.

It was not until she moved to Berlin that Helen learned Sukanashvili had left Russia two years after her and taken up residence in Germany, 'for reasons of taxation and health', as he described it. She had been delighted to see him again. The Georgian was not the contact he had been in Moscow: he took no interest in German politics. But Helen valued the old rogue's friendship.

Oleg Sukanashvili made it seem as if the concepts of guile and wisdom had been patented, if not actually invented, in the small republic in the south Caucasus. Since she could not speak Georgian and he had no English, their meetings gave Helen a chance to practise her Russian. His contempt for political correctness was exceeded only by his loathing of political authority: his views on the Children's Summit were as unprintable as his tirades against the Summit's opponents. Perhaps she'd call him when she got home, and talk about the bomb. Sukanashvili was never short of an opinion.

She approached her building with keys at the ready. The entrance lay at one end of a deserted alley. The multitude of nearby bars and restaurants meant that the tall glass door always smelt slightly of piss or vomit. That was the down side of living in a half-empty apartment block. You could feel all alone.

In the empty lobby, order was restored. She checked her post – nothing – summoned the lift, and waited. There was a noise behind her. She spun round. The door to the basement garage always clicked when anyone entered or left the building. But no-one was there. The lift doors opened and she rode up to the sixth floor. The corridor was grey and bare. Tastefully minimalist decor, the brochure had said. Right. She glanced at her watch. Eleven thirty-five.

She still hadn't called her mother. Perhaps her mother would have called her. A lonely woman in North Wales reaching out to a lonely woman in Berlin. Her mother rarely missed a chance to explain why Helen should go back to Nigel. She sighed. Telephone parenting was the last thing she needed right now.

Her door was the third on the right. Since entering the building, she had not seen a soul. She jangled the keys, then yawned as she opened the door. Some nights, she dreaded returning to her deserted flat. Tonight, she found herself praying she would find no-one there.

CHAPTER 8

KREUZBERG WAS ONE OF THE FEW DISTRICTS OF WHAT HAD been West Berlin where Sabine Wolf felt at home. Before 1989, the Turkish quarter on the banks of the Spree had been defined by the Wall, hemmed in on three sides by the East. The low rents had attracted outsiders: cut off by culture and concrete, immigrants and the liberal intellectuals who identified with them had created their own city, peopling the streets and squares with cafés and bazaars. Now the Wall had vanished. But Kreuzberg's shabby charm continued to attract alternative thinkers who had discovered, rather shame-facedly, that Berlin's revived status as Germany's capital offered a wealth of profitable new employment opportunities. One such person was Maria von Bock.

Sabine had been preparing for bed when Maria called and asked her out for a drink "and some good news". Most nights, a call from her girlfriend would have triggered a pulse of excitement in Sabine. But today was different.

It was the fault of the English girl. The two halves of the visiting card still nestled in Sabine's pocket: white, with the printing embossed. An anachronistic symbol of power which did not seem to fit its owner. With her blonde hair, cotton print dress and string sandals, Helen Gale looked more like a PhD student than a diplomat. Although fine-featured and alert, she had none of the brash confidence of the beautiful. To confront her, Sabine had overcome a fear of authority which went to her core. Yet the more worked-up Sabine had become, the calmer

Helen Gale had been. It was as if her slender frame was supported by a skeleton of stainless steel.

The contradictions did not end there. Helen Gale seemed to have all the confidence Sabine lacked: she had grabbed her shoulder at the hospital like one of the wardens in the *Spezialkinderheim,* the special children's home where Sabine had grown up. Yet when the diplomat had seen the injured boy, she had seemed close to tears. Sabine took off her heavy glasses and rubbed her eyelids as she put on her shoes to go out. It would be easier if they were suing a man in a suit.

Maria was waiting in the garden at the rear of the cafe. On the table in front of her stood an iced coffee, a shot of whisky and a stack of legal papers. When she saw Sabine, she rose slowly to her feet. She had broad shoulders and a stern, intelligent face, half-hidden by a mass of wiry hair. Only the expensive cut of her summer clothes betrayed the fact that Maria von Bock was one of Berlin's most highly-paid lawyers. They kissed lightly on the lips.

Sabine sat down. Then she saw Maria was still standing.

'You're flustered.' The lawyer looked down at her. 'What is it?'

'Nothing.' The words came out more emphatically than Sabine had intended. Her throat felt dry. 'I didn't want to be late.'

'You're lying.' Maria's eyes glittered as she sensed Sabine's discomfort. 'I call you to give you some fabulous news, and this is how you repay me.'

'Honestly. Please. Just sit down.'

'I don't believe you,' Maria said. 'I'll let it go this time, because I'm in a good mood. But remember, I'm watching.' She sat and sipped her whisky. When she put the glass down she was smiling. 'You look lovely tonight, by the way. I think you've lost weight.'

'You know I don't want to lose weight.' Sabine tried to smile back. 'I've tried being thin, and I didn't like it.'

'Poor little East German girl.' Maria reached her hand across the table. 'You do need me to look after you, don't you?'

'Yes,' Sabine said. The warmth of Maria's hand calmed her. 'You're good to me.'

'Want to hear my news, now?'

'Yes. Please.'

'Well, get this. You know we're preparing to take legal action against the Gale woman in London and Berlin? We found out two hours ago that the British embassy here doesn't even have a lawyer. They have some kind of honorary legal adviser. And guess what? He's dead.'

'Are you sure? Maybe his identity is secret.' For some reason the news made Sabine anxious.

'Of course I'm sure.' Maria scowled, then smiled again. 'My people double-checked. It's a gift! Embassies do nothing, right, they're post-boxes, modems, for passing messages between governments.' Tiny beads of sweat glistened on Maria's shoulders. 'Anyhow, it seems they don't need much legal advice. So they pay someone a retainer, and expect to get advice when they need it. Well, it seems the British embassy haven't contacted their firm here, Golletz and Golletz, for nearly a year. During that time their main man, old Golletz himself, has croaked. No-one else in the firm even knew they worked for the Brits, they're running around looking for an accounting sub-head.' Maria's eyes sparkled. 'Meanwhile, no legal advice for the embassy.'

Sabine thought of Helen Gale. 'Could they claim diplomatic immunity?'

'Well, technically, they could. But in practice, that immunity crap is finished in Europe. If a doctor or a parasite businessman makes a mistake which harms people, they get sued for every cent they have. Why should a diplomat be different?'

'I don't know.' Sabine rubbed her eyes.

A waiter brought a glass of chilled white wine. Maria ordered another whisky. 'The point is, the British government had information that could have saved lives. By not publishing it, they acted *unreasonably or irrationally*.' She said the words in English. 'That makes them culpable. Plus, we'll launch judicial review proceedings and seek discovery of the intelligence here and in England. It'll drive them insane.' Maria sipped her iced coffee. 'Maybe they'll cut their losses and give us something. Like this Helen Gale woman. Perhaps she deserves to rot in jail. Do you know any of the people hurt today?'

'I met some in the hospital. They have horrible injuries.'

'Has anyone identified the dead woman yet?'

'No.' Sabine frowned. 'It makes no sense. None of the organisations which fixed up the demo has claimed her. Even the stone-throwers are all accounted for.'

'Maybe she was a foreign protester,' Maria said. 'Here for the Summit.'

Something was troubling Sabine. 'How do we know about these intelligence warnings? Aren't they secret?'

'Sure they are. We don't know what the warnings said. But everyone knows they exist, it's on the Internet. One of the lads in the office turned it up this morning, when we started researching the bomb.'

'And why is Uktam Zholobov helping us?'

'He hates the Summit even more than we do. He'll do anything to stop it.'

'He's an oligarch. He pumps oil and gas in Siberia. He hates everything we stand for.'

'He does.' Maria ran a manicured finger round her empty whisky glass and licked it. 'But we need all the help we can get to fight the G8. Those big countries still want to rule the world. We have to stop them.'

'They are so strong.' Sabine felt herself breathing too quickly.

'Yeah. Thank God for the Internet. It helps us fight back.'

'But they control the Internet, too.'

'You're such a wimp.' Maria squeezed Sabine's hand. 'My own little scaredy-puss. Remember, we are many. They are few. If we stick a knife in enough times, they'll bleed to death.' She mimed a stabbing motion.

Sabine nodded. 'Do you think they're really worried about

attacks on the Reichstag? An army of terrorists couldn't get inside.'

'All the more reason why the Brits should have warned us of the danger outside. Now they know what it feels like to be under attack.' The wiry-haired lawyer held up a sheaf of papers. 'And when the American President and the other *very important persons* arrive in Berlin tomorrow, we'll show them how it feels to be under attack, too.'

CHAPTER 9

DIETER KREMP WENT OFF DUTY AT 10 P.M.
'You plan to sleep? Tonight?' The head of the Summit
Security Unit, Johann Frost, was gazing at monitors showing
the great empty hallways of the Reichstag.

'Sure. Tomorrow, I must be at the top of my game. Tonight,
I know the summit venue is in good hands.' Dieter slapped
his boss on the back. It was like hitting a boulder. 'What's the
latest on Petra?'

'I told you. I am taking care of it.' Johann Frost's jaw
tightened.

'I'm sorry, I – '

'Do you think I am unaware how great a problem Petra's
absence poses?'

Dieter flinched. 'No.'

'In the first place, she is vital to our operations when the G8
heads of state and government arrive tomorrow. Second, if the
media find out that one of the twenty-four members of the SSU
has vanished the day before the Summit, they will crucify us.
Third, we must face the possibility that Petra's disappearance
is linked to the terrorist threat we face.' Johann Frost tapped
his finger on the desk. 'We do not know if this increases the
danger to the Summit. But we must assume the worst. So, I am
moving two more SSU members from the perimeter to inside
the summit venue.'

'Who?'

'You and Lukas Klein. There will be hundreds of Secret Service agents and GSG 9 operatives at the perimeter. You and Lukas will be more effective within the building.'

'What's your guess on Petra?'

Johann Frost's face darkened. 'I have alerted a few trusted contacts in the Berlin police,' he said. 'There is no sign of her. I hope for her sake that she has suffered a heart attack or an accident and her body has not yet been found. If she reappears in the next few hours with an excuse, I shall punish her more than she can imagine.'

Dieter took a step back. 'Has it leaked that she's missing?'

'No. Wild Media are sniffing around as usual. They have been obsessed by the SSU ever since their documentary collapsed.'

'They were stupid to think we'd tell them how we planned to protect the Summit.'

'Yes.' Johann waved a hand. 'See you tomorrow morning at six.'

Dieter hurried to the locker room. Not much time. He stripped off his uniform and changed into black leather trousers, a dark blue fisherman's sweater, and a matt-black leather jacket. Burglar's gear. Then he placed his eye to the retina scanner, waited for the door to click open, and slipped out into the night.

He knew his plan was absurd. The Children's Summit would make or break his career. He had eight hours to ensure his mental and physical fitness were at an all-time peak ahead of whatever challenges tomorrow might bring. Instead of steering his BMW S1000RR motorcycle south he should head north, towards his flat in Moabit.

But this was a chance too good to miss.

The journey lasted three minutes. He secured the BMW in a dark corner near his destination and kept his helmet on. You never knew where a closed-circuit TV camera might be lurking. Then he dug from his pocket the unmarked keys he'd had cut, and entered the lobby.

The door to the apartment was heavy-duty steel. Only the

best was good enough to protect the prize within. Confronted by the sheer metal, any normal intruder would have tried his luck elsewhere. But if you had a key, the thickness of the armour made no difference. Dieter stepped inside and locked the door behind him.

There was no alarm. Nothing to show that security had been penetrated. That was what the spies liked to talk about, penetrating security. Well, Dieter knew a thing or two about that.

The whole flat smelt of her. Sporty – too fresh, almost, too purposeful. Dieter preferred heavier perfumes, like the sultry scents of the tarts on the Savignyplatz and Oranienburgerstrasse. Some cops made a habit of hassling the Berlin whores, most of whom were from Eastern Europe. The uniforms would brag how they'd forced some miserable immigrant to perform sexual favours in the back seat of a police cruiser. The whole sordid scene disgusted Dieter. But the smell of the women was intoxicating.

Deep down, Dieter knew it was not the perfumes which excited him. It was what came with the smell. Helplessness. Desperation. Nothing excited him more than the power to dominate. That was what made tonight so special. To the outside world, this was a woman of consequence. Yet soon he, Dieter Kremp, would have her in his control.

In the bedroom, the smell of her was stronger. The room was bare – less a home than a temporary lodging. On the dressing table a telephone was flashing a message signal. There was a drying rack with knickers hanging in rows. He picked up a pair, ran the soft fabric against his cheek, then replaced it, smoothing the cloth over the white, plastic-sheathed metal. Light from the street-lamps slanted up through the shutters, painting bars on the ceiling.

Standing in the centre of the bedroom, he undressed. Everything, even the black thong underpants he had ordered from the back pages of the *St Pauli Nachrichten*. For a moment, he admired himself in the full-length mirror: the dim light could not conceal the fact that his body was in peak condition. A fighter in the prime of life.

He gathered his clothes and knelt to slide them underneath the bed. Rising to his feet he felt gloriously unconstrained by clothing, a man in his natural state. Except for the knife in his hand, with its tempered steel blade and serrated edge.

The bedside clock said ten twenty-five. Any minute now. The built-in wardrobes were ideal. He chose one filled with blouses and summer clothes. The hangers slid easily across, the cupboards were half-empty. He stepped inside, placing the helmet, then the knife, by his feet. The louvred doors gave him a perfect view of the bed and the area by the dressing table. Already he was feeling stimulated, his upper body caressed by her clothes. He pictured Johann Frost, flicking from camera to camera in the Reichstag through the night. What a waste of an evening. Dieter looked through the louvres at the bedroom and smiled.

Thirty minutes later he was still waiting. His excitement was history. He was beginning to feel cold, standing naked in the cupboard. The apartment must be air-conditioned. What kind of woman worked so late? In seven hours, he had to be back on duty at the Reichstag.

The minutes ticked by. Dieter retrieved his leather jacket from under the bed and put it over his shoulders for warmth. He could slip it off when the time came. In the darkness, he imagined taking the G8 security experts on their final tour of the summit venue tomorrow morning. They would be impressed: no other reaction was possible. The monumental stone structure was secure against a bomb of up to a thousand kilograms, in the unlikely event that a vehicle could get near the building. All the entrance doors had been welded shut and the windows sealed: the only ingress was through two access tunnels which the police, backed up by the SSU, could control with absolute confidence. Most of the Summit Security Unit would be inside the building, ensuring –

Dieter heard a key in the door.

She did not enter the bedroom at once. There was a scuffling noise from the hall as she kicked off her shoes, then a pause. Perhaps she was hanging up her coat, or doing something with her briefcase. Silence. Then running water. Kitchen sounds – the clink of a glass, the quiet whoosh of a fridge door closing. The padding of feet on the carpet. Yes! Dieter felt his breathing quicken as the light clicked on, his excitement rose again. There she was, a glass of white wine in her hand, wearing a cotton dress with blue flowers on it. She seemed more feminine in her bare feet. But her face was set, as if preparing for a challenge. Dieter frowned. He had hoped she might feel fragile after today's bombing. For a moment, his excitement dissipated. That full, tight feeling of engorgement was gone.

Then things clicked back into gear.

The English girl stretched. She reached both arms towards the ceiling, stood up on the tips of her toes, then ran her hands down her body and gripped the hem of her dress as if preparing to peel it off over her head. Dieter nearly gasped out loud. Then he relaxed as she turned and pulled open a drawer. She took out some matches, lit two slender white candles which stood on the dresser by the telephone, and turned off the bedroom light. She was looking at herself in the full-length mirror, sideways on to Dieter in his cupboard. Her blonde hair gleamed in the candlelight. She cupped her breasts in her hands as if trying to gauge how they looked under the dress. The intimate gesture had him trembling with excitement.

The telephone rang. He saw her pick it up.

'Hello, mum. Yes, I'm fine. Of course, I would have phoned you if I'd been hurt. No, not if I'd been dead, I suppose.'

Inside his cupboard, Dieter stared at her back.

How long would her mother want to talk? The clock by the bed showed eleven forty-five. Six hours before he was back on duty. What was he doing here, naked in a cupboard?

'I can't talk, mum. It's nearly midnight. Big day tomorrow. Yes, I know Nigel's been writing articles about the Summit. That's his job. And I know he's coming to Berlin. Yes. I don't know if I'll see him. We'll both be quite busy, I expect. You don't have to tell me that. The fact is, mum, he's irresistible to you, but not to me. No, I don't mean it literally. I can't talk now. Bye.'

Helen Gale turned back to the mirror. Then, with a sigh, she began to take off her clothes.

To Dieter the sigh was all wrong. But the spectacle of her undressing drove him from frustration to arousal in an instant. The dress came off in a single motion. He could hardly breathe. She reached to undo her bra, some kind of clip at the front. Her breasts fell free, round and pale. She was touching them, picking at some bit of fluff, a speck of something, he couldn't see, he was trembling, he had to bend his legs to release the tension.

To his horror his knee brushed the cupboard door. A tiny noise. Had she heard? She turned, as if puzzled, and walked towards the cupboard. Closer. She was right in front of him, he could see the marks the bra had made on her skin, he stopped breathing, mouth open. Then, with a shake of her head, she turned back, sat on the edge of the bed. As he watched, she slid her thumbs inside her knickers and pulled them down. Then she rolled over onto her back on the bed, eyes closed. One hand was stretched out towards the bedside table. Reaching for something. A thin black cylinder. There was a humming sound.

Dieter longed to see her move the black cylinder around her breasts, between her legs. That would be something. But instead, she raised it to her mouth, sweeping its smooth head around her lips. They moved under the pressure, pulled this way and that. She sighed again, moving her legs on the bed. No. This wasn't right. Again, his instant of arousal had been lost. He felt panic. That made him shrink even faster. He must stop her.

Dieter Kremp pulled open the door of the cupboard, stepped out, and threw himself on top of Helen Gale. He tore the cylinder from her hands and threw it against the wall. Then he kissed her hard on the lips, crushing her head into the pillows, and pulled back. He could hear the device still buzzing on the other side of the room.

She opened her eyes.

'God, Dieter.' Her smile was weary but mischievous. 'I thought I would never tempt you out. What were you doing in there, wanking?' She put her hand down and grasped him, soft now, ruined. How did she know a word like that in German? 'Oh, I'm sorry.' She looked up at him. 'Poor you.'

Didn't she understand? First, she brought her damned sex toy up to her mouth. Then she pitied him. Furious, he rolled off her and stamped across the room to kill the buzzing. If he told her the real reason he'd lost it, she'd laugh her head off. Jealous of a vibrator.

'It can happen.' He sat down next to her. 'Not your fault.'

He meant to imply the opposite. But if Helen Gale noticed his attempt to blame her for his flaccidity, she gave no sign of it. Instead she reached for him again, and squeezed him firmly. He felt himself respond.

'Don't worry, Mr magnificent SSU man. You're my powerful, raging lion. And you look great. Come and give me a cuddle.'

This was better. As their lips met, his fingers moved across her skin, exploring her. She liked that, he knew. They embraced, bodies together, legs entangled. Now she was trying to roll onto her side next to him, pulling him towards her, but he didn't want that, it wouldn't work. He pushed her down and held her arms. For a moment, he saw a shadow cross her face. She liked him to take his time. He lowered his head to her shoulders, a gentle nuzzling. Now he was moving on her, nice and slow, the strokes growing gradually longer. More sighs. Was she building up to something? Yes. Breathing faster now. Still he held her arms pinned down. She was fit, strong for a woman, but he was far heavier. Faster. Any moment now. She was ready.

Smoothly, in one motion, he pulled himself out of her and, pinioning her arms with his knees, knelt up, one hand under her head, lifting her up towards him. Her mouth was opening. *At last...*

'What are you doing?' Her head was straining, pushing against the hand cradling it. Dumbly, he went on trying to push, he could feel her lips moving on him as she shouted, she could hardly move her head. 'Get *off* me! I'll bite the fucking thing in two.' She was moving powerfully beneath him now, but was still held by his weight. Helpless. He thought of the knife in the cupboard. But that was just a fantasy. Wasn't it?

'Dieter!'

Below him, her face was a wild mask. Not fear, but rage. Dieter felt his muscles go slack. What was he doing? How could he, a police officer, even think of forcing Helen Gale to perform a sexual act? This wasn't some game. This was non-consensual sex. Rape. He rolled over onto the bed next to her, laying his arm loosely, resistibly, across her body. 'Sorry. I got carried away.'

'You're sorry?' Her voice was rising. 'I had a bomb at work today. I get home and have to talk to my mother about why I should never have left Nigel. Even then I didn't want to let you down, Dieter. I actually like sex with you. On a good day. But just when we're having a half-way good time, you hold me down and try and do something you know I don't want. What the hell were you thinking of?'

'Sorry. It was stupid.'

'It was. Unbelievable.'

'Can we just lie together?' Perhaps something could still be salvaged.

'Does the idea that I'm not in the mood make any sense to you? You may as well push off.' She stood and moved towards the phone. 'I wasn't going to make this call tonight but I will, now.'

'Please don't.'

She did not reply. Dieter watched as she picked up her mobile. Then she began to talk, in Russian.

That was it. Dieter sat on the opposite side of the bed and began to dress. He had never met Helen's Georgian friend. All he knew was that he was old – so Helen said – and called himself a businessman. A Georgian businessman. Everyone knew what that meant.

What did a British diplomat have in common with a mafia boss? The fact Dieter could not understand a word Helen was saying did not help. She could be discussing his sexual performance, for all he knew. He reached into the cupboard for his jacket, helmet and knife. And what was her problem with what he had been trying to do? Or to put it another way, why was he so keen to force her? He knew the answer, of course. It was an act of control. That was what made Helen Gale so maddening. He wanted to dominate her, as he would any woman. Yet it was her confidence and power which attracted him to her. He pulled on his jacket.

'I'm going,' he said.

Helen Gale put a hand over the receiver. 'See you tomorrow.'

Dieter nodded and closed the front door behind him. She didn't mean tomorrow, of course. She meant today.

CHAPTER 10

HELEN AWOKE DRENCHED IN SWEAT. SOMETHING WAS HAPpening... no. Something had happened. Dieter. *Stupid bastard.* His hand under her head. His knees. The telephone was ringing.

She clicked on the light. Four a.m. Dieter. Disgust rose in her. Then she smiled. How long had he been standing naked in that cupboard?

The phone.

'Is that Helen Gale?' She did not recognise the voice. But she knew the tones of a Whitehall official.

'Speaking.'

'This is the No.10 duty officer. My name's Danny McGregor. There's been a development in Berlin. We need the embassy's take on it.'

'Go ahead.' Helen scrabbled in the drawer for the A4 pad and pen which lived there. 'You'll have to tell me what's happened. I've been asleep.'

'Of course. There's a report on Wild TV that the person killed by yesterday's bomb attack on the embassy was a member of the Summit Security Unit.'

'Sounds like a garble. The woman killed yesterday was a demonstrator.'

'Yes. That's what your embassy told us.' The voice in London was calm. 'But as soon as the DNA results came through, they found a match. Her name is Petra Bleibtreu. She was in the SSU.'

'That's weird.' Helen felt the sleep fall away from her. This was when she loved her job. 'When do you need something? Apart from instantly.'

'Can you get back to me in fifteen minutes? If you have ideas for a line to take, we'll have them too.' There was a rustling of papers. 'I think we have today's lead story. Sky are still talking about a suicide bomber. But Wild TV say she was assassinated. They reckon it shows security for the summit is a joke.'

'They always say that. Give me a few minutes.'

'Thanks. Sorry to ruin your night.'

Danny McGregor had not ruined her night. He had ruined her day. Or perhaps it had been ruined already, after Dieter's performance. Helen didn't mind playing along with Dieter's voyeuristic games. If you were in the mood, it could be exciting to imagine your lover watching you undress. But why did men obsess about women being helpless? That was one thing she would never pretend.

Helen pulled on a T-shirt, marched into her study and clicked on the computer. There it was: a Wild News breaking story. The name Petra Bleibtreu meant nothing to Helen. But Dieter would know her. The SSU would be working like crazy to find out how one of their people could have been killed at a demonstration outside the British embassy. Helen shook her head. No way was she calling Dieter Kremp.

Ten minutes left. Normally she would discuss with the ambassador any advice she was giving No.10. But tonight, he was in hospital. That left Jason Short. Calling him would be worse than useless. In the unlikely event that he had a useful insight, he would never share it with Helen.

Who could you call at 4 a.m.? She tried the Interior Ministry 24-hour number, but gave up after sixty seconds of instructions about which button to press for a range of inappropriate services. The German Foreign Ministry duty centre answered immediately, but could only suggest she telephone the police or the Summit Security Unit. A helpful-sounding officer at the Berlin Police headquarters promised to put her through to the team investigating the case, but after she had held for two minutes, the line went dead.

She looked at her watch. Ten minutes gone. So far, she had found out nothing. She could not report back empty-handed. Who else was there? She clicked on a couple of German web-sites. None of them added anything to the Wild News story. By her monitor was an A4 list of phone numbers headed HELEN'S EMERGENCY: fire, police, embassy duty officer, consular services, FCO Emergency Centre, No.10, Cabinet Office Briefing Room, her mum, Nigel. At the bottom, she had added in manuscript Dieter's number, and contact details for the new Washington Post correspondent in Berlin, Karen Daniels. That was it. Helen dialled again.

She had only met Karen Daniels twice, at drinks parties. Both times, they had had long discussions. The tiny American journalist seemed always to find the most comfortable armchair in the room, curl her legs up under herself and stay put for hours at a time, letting people come to her. Often, she would be on the phone, her huge voice booming out as if she were alone in the room. No-one thought her behaviour eccentric or antisocial because Karen was blind.

Karen never spoke about her disability. But Blore Harl from the US embassy had told Helen it had happened in Russia years earlier, when Karen was researching a story on the privatisation of state assets. She had not gone blind, Blore had said. She had been blinded, and left for dead in a skip outside the Lenin Museum in Moscow, by someone who wanted to stop her digging deeper. They had achieved their goal. Karen had been medevaced back to the US and spent months in hospital. But after she had recovered, she had returned to journalism. Indeed, she now had the best network of contacts in Berlin. It was as if people would tell a blind person things they would never tell someone else. Helen had taken Karen into her confidence about Nigel and Dieter the first time they met.

'Karen Daniels, Washington Post.' The voice was wide awake.

'Ms Karen Daniels, this is your 4 a.m. wake-up call. Hi. It's Helen.'

'Helen! You're calling about Petra Bleibtreu, right? Do you know anything? Or perhaps you have an exclusive for me about the legal case against you? That sucks, by the way.'

'No comment?'

'OK. But I still think it sucks.'

'And I am calling about Petra Bleibtreu. But I know nothing.'

'No-one does. But that's never got in the way of a good story. How can I help?'

'I'm after ideas on why a member of the SSU was blown up outside the British embassy in the middle of a crowd of demonstrators.'

'You want ideas? Sounds subversive.' Karen's laugh was deep and husky. 'But you're right. It makes no sense.'

'There is one strange thing.' Helen wondered how much she should tell the journalist. 'Why was the bomb detonated so far from our concrete perimeter wall? Do you think maybe the embassy wasn't the target?'

'Ha! The logic being that the bomb was too small to damage anything except the crowd. What is this? Original thinking week? What do you think they were trying to blow up?'

'It can't be a coincidence that the one person killed is a member of the Summit Security Unit. Maybe Petra Bleibtreu was the target.'

'Was she carrying the bomb herself, or what?'

'Maybe she didn't know she had it.' Helen thought of Karen, in Moscow. 'Maybe she was attacked because she found something out. About the Summit.'

'Helen, this is great. Can I quote you?'

'Yeah. British diplomat floats wacko theory. No way.' Helen looked at her watch. 'I'm out of time. What have you got?'

'Zilch. Only the SSU seem to know anything. They're not

talking to journalists.' The American paused. 'I have to ask you this, Helen. What does Dieter Kremp say?'

'I haven't asked him.'

'You're kidding. Why not?' Karen's surprise was so loud that Helen had to hold the receiver away from her ear. 'I thought you had special access?' She guffawed.

'I tried. He's not answering.' The lie made Helen realise she'd been stupid. She should have called Dieter straight away. 'I'll try again now.'

'Good. Are you coming on the tour tomorrow?'

'Yes. I didn't know journalists were invited.'

'They're not. I'm being embedded in the US delegation. Where do you think your man Nigel got the idea?'

'At least he learns fast.'

'Helen. He's a smart, lovely guy.'

'My mother thinks so, too. See you tomorrow.' Helen bit her lip. What a stupid choice of words.

But the blind woman seemed not to notice. 'I'll be there. Ring me if Kremp tells you anything.'

Helen ended the call. Was there time to call Dieter? But her phone went at once.

'Helen? This is Danny McGregor. What have you got?'

'OK. You know the ambassador's in hospital after the bomb. This is just me, plus a couple of people I've talked to off the record.'

'Go ahead.'

'The Petra Bleibtreu story stinks. The fact she was killed outside the embassy could mean there's something about that attack we don't understand.'

'Hold it. Someone told us yesterday the embassy was the target.' For the first time, the No.10 duty officer was beginning to sound officious. 'Has that advice changed?'

We can't be certain we were the target, no. It wasn't me who – '

'The Embassy's... advice... has changed.' Helen could hear

the clatter of Danny McGregor's keyboard. 'What do you think this means for the Summit? Is it still safe for the PM to attend?'

'Well. We don't know for sure - '

'Wrong answer. Give me your evaluation. Now.'

'OK.' Helen tried to marshal her thoughts. 'The fact someone has killed a member of the Summit Security Unit seems to confirm reports we've seen – ' she paused so McGregor would know she was talking about intelligence ' – of a terrorist threat to the Summit. Set against that, we've already factored that threat into our security concept. This was a tiny bomb. And the Reichstag is protected against vehicle-borne or hand-carried explosives by defensive measures which our own Security Service has pronounced fit for purpose.' Helen licked her lips. 'So as seen from here, the identification of Petra Bleibtreu doesn't increase the threat to the PM.'

'Doesn't... increase... the danger.' More clattering. 'Thank you, Helen.' Danny McGregor sounded more cheerful now. 'At least that's unambiguous.' He was silent for a moment as he read what he'd just written. 'Can we say we have full confidence in security arrangements for the Summit?'

'Have we said it before?'

'We've been saying it for months.'

'Well, let's say it again. Nothing's changed.'

'Wrong,' Danny McGregor said. 'One thing has changed big-time.'

'What's that, then?'

'The Summit starts today. This time, we'd better be right.'

CHAPTER 11

'THE TOUR OF DIPLOMATS AND SECURITY OFFICIALS FROM THE G8 countries is here,' Katia Vonhof said. 'What shall I do with them?'

'Pack out the Heckler & Kochs.' Dieter's eyes were black with fatigue. 'I shall have to kill them all.'

'Do you want me to lead the tour?' The SSU computer specialist looked embarrassed rather than amused. 'You look like you had a rough night.'

'I am fine. Where is Johann?'

'Talking to the police. He says it is vital to find out where Petra was yesterday between leaving the US embassy and the explosion.'

'I cannot see why she was at the demonstration. Or why anyone would kill her.'

'Johann will find out. Nothing can stop him. He is very angry.' Katia looked at her screen. 'The *Amis* are saying Petra's death shows the terrorist threat is higher than ever. They want to seal one of the tunnels into the Reichstag. What shall I tell them?'

'Say no. The tunnels to the summit venue are as secure as...' Dieter found himself thinking about Helen Gale again. 'They are secure. The emergency drills showed it would take five times as long to evacuate through one tunnel as through two.'

'True,' Katia Vonhof said. 'But the Americans do not care how quickly people can get out of the Reichstag. They are trying to stop anyone from getting in.'

Ten minutes later, Dieter entered the room where the visitors had gathered. Its official designation was Room 6.556, Jakob-Kaiser House South. At once he felt tension in the air. *They smell blood.*

Smolenski, the Russian, was standing by the door with Mura from the French embassy. Mura stepped forward at once to shake Dieter's hand. The no-nukes – Japan, Canada and Italy – were sitting round a table by the coffee machine, enjoying their first cappuccino of the day. In the opposite corner, as far away from Dieter as the room allowed, the usual crowd of Anglo-Saxons had gathered. He recognised Blore Harl from the US embassy, accompanied by two tough-looking men and a tough-looking woman in dark suits – yet another team of Secret Service agents, presumably. Two of the three had mobile phones to their heads. Next to Blore was Helen, looking cool in a beige business suit. She was talking to a short, fat woman with curly black hair and dark glasses, who sat on a chair by the floor-to-ceiling windows with her hand on the head of a German shepherd dog. That must be the journalist, Karen Daniels. Dieter shook his head. Only the Americans would send a blind journalist and her dog on a security tour of the Reichstag.

'So. Be welcome.' Dieter hated speaking English. Here they were in the heart of the biggest German-speaking city on the planet, and he had no more chance of using his native language than of speaking Swahili. 'This tour is lasting ninety minutes. We start now.'

Helen went on talking to Karen Daniels.

'Thanks, Dieter.' Blore Harl's eyes betrayed nothing of his mood. 'Before we start, can I ask one question? Who killed Petra Bleibtreu, and why?'

'This is not a press conference.' Smolenski spoke English with the precision of a trained intelligence operative. 'I suggest we do the tour first. Mr Kremp can field questions later, if there is time.'

'I can answer this.' Dieter didn't want charity from the Russian. 'The police think Ms Bleibtreu was killed by a bomb no larger than a packet of cigarettes. It may be that she had taken the bomb from a terrorist and was trying to make it safe. Or someone might have placed the bomb in Ms Bleibtreu's bag without her knowledge, and detonated it when she approached the embassy. The police will let us know when they have more information. There are now eighty-five minutes remaining for our tour.'

'Nothing on the perps?' Blore Harl said.

'I beg your pardon?'

'I can translate.' Helen had turned her pale face towards Dieter. 'He means the perpetrators. Who did it.'

'No,' Dieter said. 'But members of the Threat Assessment Committee are aware of evidence that certain known terrorist groups may try to disrupt the Summit. There are now eighty minutes remaining for our tour.'

'May we begin, please?' The French security official, Mura, put his hand on Dieter's arm. 'The Elysée has asked for a security update at 10 o'clock, in the light of developments overnight.' He squeezed Dieter's arm as he said this. Perhaps this gesture was intended to show sympathy for the death of Petra Bleibtreu. Perhaps it was to emphasise the closeness of the Franco-German relationship. Whatever the reason, Dieter had to suppress an urge to smash the Frenchman in the face.

'The tour is starting now,' he said. 'First, look at the view from this window.' Everyone except Karen Daniels moved towards the sloping wall of glass which faced the Reichstag.

'The summit venue,' Dieter said, ' is an easy building to secure. It is not connected to any other structures above ground level, and is separated from neighbouring buildings by a free-fire zone of between fifty and eighty metres. We face here the south-east corner of the building. To the west and south, the summit venue faces open ground. On the other two sides are parliamentary accommodation: to the north, the Paul-Löbe House, to the east, the Jakob-Kaiser House North. Both these buildings have been evacuated for the duration of the Summit and will be patrolled by German and US security personnel. All windows have been sealed. German and US snipers are positioned on the four corner towers of the Reichstag and on neighbouring buildings.'

'What if a sniper takes a shot at a delegate?' It was Blore Harl again.

'You have alerted us before to the so-called rogue sniper danger,' Dieter said. 'In this case, it is no danger. The only access to the summit venue will be through two underground tunnels. The main tunnel leads from Jakob-Kaiser House North. All delegates and security personnel will enter and leave the building by this route. The second tunnel, into the Paul-Löbe House, will be opened only if we need to evacuate the building. Both tunnels are controlled by strong units of armed officers.

'The use of tunnels to access the summit venue has a special benefit. The areas which surround the building at ground level will be empty. Between now and the end of the Summit, any vehicle or pedestrian entering the Safety Zone will be subject to fire without warning from snipers armed with high-powered precision weapons.'

There was a silence. Then Karen Daniels spoke. Her voice was so loud Dieter almost stepped back.

'What about a suicide assault? Say, a dozen guys with explosive belts and hand grenades go straight through the empty office blocks and down the tunnels?'

'Over one thousand armed police, special forces and US Secret Service agents are protecting the perimeter of the Safety Zone,' Dieter said. 'In the event of an incident during the Summit, personnel inside the venue could seal the tunnels by operating the security doors installed at the request of our American partners.'

'They're beauties,' one of the Secret Service agents said.

Dieter ignored him. 'We will now inspect the summit venue,' he said.

They started by descending seven storeys to the basement.

They were confronted immediately by one of the late security additions. The passage which led under the Dorotheenstrasse from the Jakob-Kaiser House South to the evacuated Jakob-Kaiser House North had been sealed by a floor-to-ceiling wall of pre-fabricated concrete sections, punctured at one end by a security gate. Katia Vonhof and Peter Sturm from the SSU were visible through an armoured glass panel. Dieter smiled to himself. Johann Frost had found Peter Sturm in a police martial arts training unit in Kiel, together with another recruit, Sara Lutz. Peter stood nearly two metres tall. His size and Katia's gaunt efficiency would intimidate anyone.

'Welcome.' Katia Vonhof's voice came from a loudspeaker. 'You are all pre-registered for access to the Safety Zone. The security chamber is equipped with air analysis equipment. If you have guns or explosives, please do not enter the chamber, or the mechanism will be sealed until the police arrive.'

Several people smiled. Katia Vonhof did not.

'Once you are inside the airlock, please place your eyes to the retina scanners,' she went on.

Everyone looked at Karen Daniels, who stood holding the harness of her guide dog.

'In the case of any person for whom retina records are not available, there is a manual override. This operates only when a member of the Summit Security Unit keys in the appropriate codes.'

Dieter stood proudly by the airlock as the visitors passed through. Who could fail to be impressed by such efficiency? Such discipline? Such sheer physical strength?

Helen kept half a dozen people between herself and Dieter as the tour group moved closer to the Reichstag. He looked absurd, strutting around in his grey SSU uniform, like Charlie Chaplin on steroids.

'Hi, Helen.' Blore Harl had fallen back alongside her. 'How's it going?'

'Terrific.' It was a relief to talk to the phlegmatic American. 'Dieter's impossible. Jason's a bastard. It's too hot. And some NGO is suing me for not warning them we were going to be blown up yesterday. Thank God it'll be over soon.'

The American nodded. 'Have you seen what's above our heads?'

Helen looked up and saw four full-sized rowing eights suspended in the atrium. Three were painted in the red, gold and black of the German flag. The fourth, and highest, was blue.

'In Germany, three per cent of the cost of new public buildings is invested in art.' Blore ran his fingers through his hair as if perplexed at such generosity.

'I like it.' Helen gazed up at the smooth curves of the boats. 'It's as if we're under water.'

'In that case, we're in deep.' Blore watched her with his dark, intense eyes. 'At least the Reichstag is secure. The Secret Service rate it one of the safest conference venues in the world.'

'Do they have a Top 10?'

'More or less, sure. It's perfect. Free-fire Safety Zone. Massive stone walls. Two secure sub-ground entrances. And there's an independent communications centre on the third floor. If someone bombs the local power station or takes out the SSU command bunker, the world's leaders will still have sound and light and can communicate with the outside world.'

'So, Johann and Dieter did a good job.'

'Hell, yes. Of course, the Secret Service insist on doing everything that matters themselves.'

'Sounds paranoid.'

'It's their job to be paranoid. But even Presidents need a life: you can't have twenty agents fussing around them every time they go to the john. The Secret Service create a security bubble: a safe environment whose perimeter can be guarded. Inside the bubble, the President can move around freely.'

Helen nodded. 'I thought you wanted a Secret Service team inside the Reichstag?'

'Sure, we'll have a team inside. But the focus is on the integrity of the bubble. There'll be half a dozen agents in the Reichstag, and a couple of hundred on the perimeter.'

'No wonder Dieter's so bloody grumpy.'

'It's the same wherever the President goes. Even London. There are always agents within arm's length. But Berlin is scary right now. Demonstrators. Crazies. That bomb at your embassy.'

'I thought the President was against the goals of the Summit?'

'Middle America hates the free-trade package the G8 will agree. But the President wants to go down in history as someone who made a difference. Wall Street wants a deal. So does the press – Wild Media have been campaigning like crazy.'

Helen placed her hand against the wall. The concrete was cool and smooth. 'Do you think the Summit will make a difference?'

'It depends whether you think people getting richer is a good thing. All the big economic success stories have been the result of getting rid of trade barriers. Look at China and India.'

'And busting monopolies?'

'Sure. Like Uktam Zholobov's Russian oil and gas empire. Or Wild Media, here in Europe.' Blore scanned the basement, as if half-expecting to find a TV crew. 'It's no use liberalising trade if monopolies can keep competitors out of key markets.'

'Why is Wild supporting the Summit? He likes free trade as much as colon surgery. The liberalisation package will pain him just as much.' Helen pressed her lips together. 'At least Zholobov is consistent. You know Wild is visiting the US embassy this morning? Probably explaining why black is now white.'

Blore shrugged. 'All these media tycoons like to get their names in the papers. Wild pushed hard to be Germany's business guy at the Reichstag. He says he'll do whatever it takes to get a deal signed.'

'Yeah. Like it matters.'

'Helen. What do you think does matter?'

They had fallen behind the main tour party. Blore was standing next to a large canvas on the wall showing what looked like white and black bedsprings tacked to a pink background.

'Crap art matters,' Helen said. 'Stopping people killing people. Champagne and a good man for breakfast.'

'That sounds like Helen.' Karen Daniels had appeared. For once, she spoke quietly. 'Can I take your arm? I've been holding onto David, but his muscles are giving me bad thoughts.'

'Sure.' Helen saw the journalist had her hand on the arm of a powerfully-built Secret Service agent, who grinned self-consciously. 'Won't your dog mind?'

'Otto? He's used to it. Just don't make any sudden movements, or he'll rip your throat out.'

'I should introduce him to Jason.'

'Actually, Otto thinks all people are as gentle as he is. I can't bear to disillusion him.'

Helen moved alongside the journalist. The blind woman took her arm.

'We are now ready to enter the summit venue.' Dieter Kremp was standing at the tunnel entrance with his chest thrust out. 'I believe you will agree, security is adequate.'

'Helen,' Karen Daniels said, 'would you mind telling me what you see?'

'Sure.' Helen placed her hand over Karen's. 'We're at the main tunnel leading into the Reichstag. There's a long, brightly-lit passage, with a moving walkway rising slightly from where we're standing.'

'I don't like moving walkways.'

'No problem. You can walk along a space alongside it with a pedestal and a section of old, brick-built tunnel. You know the Reichstag was burned down in 1933? They say whoever did it came through there.'

'You ever notice that, about places with lots of history? Nearly all of it's bad. What about the famous steel doors?'

'They are beauties, all right. Two at each end of the passage.

Maybe three metres high and four wide, gleaming steel. They're made to seal the opening completely. I wouldn't fancy getting my finger caught in one.'

'And the people? You don't mind, do you?'

'Get real. Do you think I want to listen to Dieter droning on?' Helen looked around, imagining she was doing a radio broadcast. 'OK. At this end of the passage, two Bundespolizei people – Federal Police – are stationed at a dinky concrete security booth. They're armed, dressed in blue. One man, one woman, both perfect specimens. They're standing next to the booth while an SSU guy fiddles around inside.'

The man inside the booth stood up. It was Peter Sturm, the giant SSU officer who had checked them through the Safety Zone perimeter. He looked at them impassively.

'What are you doing in there?' Karen spoke with authority.

'I am checking for explosives.' Sturm held out a piece of equipment like a chunky hand-held vacuum cleaner.

'Find anything?'

'No.' The SSU man sounded bored. But Helen saw a flicker of disdain in his eye as he looked at the blind journalist.

Karen seemed to hear it. 'That's enough of him,' she said. 'What else do you see?'

'At the far end of the tunnel, inside the Reichstag, there are more SSU people and a Secret Service agent, just hanging out.'

'Like a welcome committee.'

'More like bouncers outside a dodgy nightclub.'

'These doors will remain open unless there is evidence of a direct threat,' Dieter Kremp was saying. 'This is because they are heavy, and take several minutes to open and close. Follow me, please.'

Karen and Helen walked past the section of brick tunnel.

'What do you think?' The journalist spoke in a whisper. 'Still *alles in Ordnung?*'

'I agree with Blore,' Helen said. 'The security arrangements look terrific. The way they have a whole empty office building as a security airlock outside each tunnel entrance is sublime.'

'Your man Dieter seems edgy.'

'Edgy? Arrogant and pushy, you mean.' Helen shrugged. 'That's how he is.'

'I thought you were fond of him.'

'He's definitely male.'

'And muscular, I'm told.'

'In parts. His ears lack muscles of any kind. They've atrophied from lack of use.'

'He must be good at something.'

'Yes,' Helen patted Karen's hand on her arm. 'He is.'

Up ahead, one of the Secret Service agents was talking to Blore Harl. The American nodded and squared up to Dieter.

'I am told you haven't sealed the second tunnel. Why is that?'

The German stared at the diplomat. 'We have not sealed the second tunnel, because this would be dangerous for the delegates.'

'But with respect, doesn't the death of one of your officers mean we need extra vigilance?' Blore Harl's face showed no emotion.

'If you can suggest a way in which the death of Petra Bleibtreu increases the threat to the Summit, I will call a meeting of the Threat Assessment Committee,' Dieter said. 'But this will not be possible until tomorrow.'

'Are you refusing to meet our request?' Blore Harl scratched his chin. 'I think we may have to insist.'

Smolenski cleared his throat and spoke in a level tone. 'The Russian government wishes to ensure that the second tunnel remains available in case the Reichstag needs to be evacuated. To seal it would be short-sighted and, frankly, absurd.'

Dieter turned to Smolenski. 'There is no question of refusing the request of the US government,' he said. 'Or that of the Russian government. But we cannot start building walls without input from the Threat Assessment Committee.'

Two of the Secret Service agents huddled around Blore Harl. The third was on the phone.

Helen heard her own ring-tone.

'Helen? It's Jason. I understand you altered the embassy's threat assessment last night without consulting me.'

She held the telephone at arm's length and took a breath before answering. 'We're in the Reichstag. Can I call you back?'

'In the ambassador's absence, I am responsible for the output of this embassy.'

'The threat assessment hasn't changed. We thought it was safe for the Prime Minister to come yesterday. We think it's safe today. Even if the Secret Service are still arguing about everything in sight.'

'Why? What are they saying?'

'They're trying to seal up both the underground tunnels into the Reichstag. So that no-one can get in or out.'

'What?'

'Only one of them, actually. It's daft. The place is like a bunker already.'

'Helen. Imagine if something went wrong, and it turned out we had missed a chance to improve security. We should support the Americans.'

'But this – '

'That's an instruction. Do it. I'll hold.'

Dieter and Blore Harl were still arguing. When Helen spoke, they fell silent.

'I am instructed to tell you,' she said, 'that the British government supports the American proposal to seal the second tunnel.'

Dieter scowled. 'The usual suspects,' he said. 'I take note of your request.'

Helen returned to her phone. 'Mission accomplished.'

'At least we can say we weighed in,' Short said. Have you seen the newspapers, by the way?'

'No. I was up early for this tour.'

'Ah. Well, you should know that Uktam Zholobov is

supporting the legal case against you by the bomb victims. He has contributed one hundred thousand euro to the fighting fund.'

'Why?' Helen placed a hand over her other ear to block out the exchanges between Dieter and the Americans. 'What has a Russian oil tycoon got against me?'

'He has an opinion piece in today's Wild Zeitung. He says the embassy's failure to release intelligence which could have saved lives…' Short paused then went on, translating as he read '… reflects the indifference of the G8 governments to the real interests of ordinary people. He calls for the Summit to be cancelled.'

'That's not true. We gave the intelligence to the Germans.'

'But did we think about the demonstrators? I don't recall we ever discussed it.'

'Jason. You're supposed to be on my side.'

'I am aware of my responsibilities, Helen. Sorry, I must go. Some of us have work to do.'

Short rang off.

'Bad news?' Karen was still holding Helen's arm.

'Unbelievable. Now Uktam Zholobov is on my case.'

'The oligarch who's trying to stop the summit?'

'Why should he fund a legal case against me?'

'He wants attention, I guess. The only thing men are worse at than listening, Helen, is being ignored.' Karen grinned. Helen smiled back, then found herself wondering if there was any point. But her smile lingered as they caught up with the rest of the group.

The stairs from the tunnel led up to the East Lobby of the Reichstag: a high, bright space. Dieter gestured towards a metal structure which towered above them like a titanic propeller blade. Helen found it rather beautiful.

'This flak shield is a further security improvement made at the suggestion of one delegation, supported by a second delegation.' Dieter did not look at Blore or Helen. 'The restoration of the Reichstag as the seat of government of a re-united Germany had as its basis the transparency principle. This means, the people can see the politicians. Therefore, the plenary chamber has glass walls, and a glass ceiling which opens into the dome above.'

Several people looked up.

'Of course, even German politicians have enemies.' Dieter's face stretched into a humourless grin. 'The plenary chamber is protected by bullet-proof glass. But one delegation, supported by a second delegation, suggested a theoretical danger that a terrorist armed with an armour-piercing weapon who had succeeded in penetrating the Safety Zone could fire a projectile into the summit venue through the walls of armoured glass from the roof of a building nearby. Even though these areas are controlled by sniper teams. We have therefore installed flak shields to protect the delegates. We have also covered the glass walls of the plenary chamber with white plastic, so that no terrorist can see inside. This is, of course, the opposite of transparency. The cost was four million euro.'

'Money well spent,' Blore Harl said.

Dieter opened his mouth, but never answered. Helen felt an instant of shock, as if something had just rushed past her, then heard a deep, rumbling roar.

'What was that?' Karen gripped Helen's arm. 'Can you see anything?'

'No.' Helen stared around. So far as she could tell, the building was undamaged.

'That was a bomb. A large bomb.' Dieter Kremp had his phone in his hand. There was a moment of frenetic silence as everyone dialled, or tried to go on-line, then a burst of telephone conversation.

Dieter was the first to end his call. He walked towards Blore Harl, who had not yet managed to ring out, and reached for him with both arms.

'I am sorry,' he said. 'I think we must abandon this tour. A car bomb has exploded at the American embassy.'

CHAPTER 12

ON 7 AUGUST 1998, TERRORISTS DETONATED MASSIVE TRUCK
bombs outside the United States embassies in Dar Es Salaam
and Nairobi. Over 200 Kenyans, Tanzanians and Americans
were killed and over 5,000 wounded.

The following year, a review board headed by retired admiral
William J Crowe recommended that the US government spend
$1.4 billion a year over the next ten years to improve security at
United States diplomatic facilities overseas. Measures proposed
included blast perimeter walls three metres high with anti-ram
protection; toughened windows, with secure frames to prevent
panes of safety glass from flying inwards in the event of an explosion; safe havens for embassy staff; blast-channelling corridors;
and the elimination of internal glass fixtures and fittings. The
most important measure was setback: the establishment of as
wide an area as possible around potential targets, into which no
vehicle could pass. The best way to protect a building, it turned
out, was to make it difficult to bring a bomb anywhere near it.

Uli Wenger knew all there was to know about the Crowe
review. He understood the conflict between making an embassy
secure against terrorist attack, and making it look welcoming to
visitors. And he knew that despite the money spent on security
since 1999, only a fraction of US embassies worldwide met the
counter-terrorism standards whose importance the East Africa
bombings had made clear.

The US embassy in Berlin, however, was one of the exceptions.

Ground had been broken in 2004, seven years after the East Africa bombings and three years after the terrorist attacks of 11 September 2001. Security had been paramount in every aspect of the embassy's design, from the installation of anti-ram bollards to the diversion of several Berlin streets to increase the setback distance. One side-effect had been to shrink the building: so much of the plot was taken up by security works and the setback zone that there was less space left to build the embassy. To Uli, the structure eventually erected seemed ill-suited to represent the mightiest nation on earth. But it was exceptionally bomb-proof. In fact, if you wanted to blow it up, you would somehow have to smuggle a bomb into the heart of the building. Uli and members of his Chaos Team had been inside the US embassy several times. But he had no intention of sacrificing himself or anyone else for a secondary target.

As a result, the thirty-kilo bomb which had just exploded at the rear of the embassy in the Behrenstrasse had done the building remarkably little damage. There would be shattered nerves inside: thirty kilos of high explosive made a hell of a bang. A few insects had been exterminated: the families and dependents of the locally-engaged security guards whose job it was to check deliveries would be needing to read the small print of their insurance policies. The Behrenstrasse was littered with burned-out vehicles. Dozens of the hollow concrete steles in the Holocaust Memorial across the road had been toppled. But tomorrow's newspapers, if they found space to report on the US embassy bombing in the light of the drama which would by then have unfolded elsewhere, would probably take the view that the attack had failed.

Uli knew better. The attack had been simple and successful. The devastation of the Holocaust Memorial might cheer Gustav and Martha. Dora enjoyed anything which made the German government look foolish. But that was a bonus, like the panic generated by the execution at the British embassy the day before.

The plan for killing Petra Bleibtreu had come to Uli when

he was preparing today's bombing. He had thought he could use her. She had proved unreliable. So, she had died, thirty-six hours earlier than she would have died anyway. The bomb which had killed her had helped magnify the impact of today's blast.

Ambulances and fire engines were already at the scene, their blue and red lights bright against the sombre sky. Soon the first demonstrators would show up, no doubt blaming the Americans for building their embassy in a spot where an attack on it would cause so many casualties. It was time for Uli to leave.

He walked towards the Brandenburg Gate. The only risk now was that the Summit would be cancelled. The size of the bomb had been calibrated to minimise that danger. A smaller explosion might have had little impact. A bomb which left the embassy in ruins, even if it had been possible to achieve, would have made cancellation inevitable. Even this explosion seemed risky to Uli. But Herr Kraft had insisted that the Summit would go ahead. Uli did not know how he could be so certain. But Herr Kraft was a man who knew about politics. And, as his plans for the Children's Summit showed, he was a man who liked taking risks.

Uli was passing the Pariser Platz when a woman came running towards him. To avoid her would look suspicious. He let her block his path.

'Excuse me? Hello?' She was a German, well-dressed, authoritative.

'What is it?' Uli clenched his fists. He had to escape.

'I work in the US embassy. What has happened?'

'No idea. Ask a policeman. Look, there's one over there.'

'But – '

'Over there.' Uli turned and walked away.

'That is unacceptable.' The woman's voice was rising. 'I will be reporting you to your superiors.'

He kept walking through the gathering crowds, and felt his pulse slow. Sometimes his disguise posed its own dangers. But it was essential to the enterprise he had planned. And it only had to serve for a few hours more.

CHAPTER 13

HELEN SAW THE BLOOD DRAIN FROM BLORE HARL'S FACE. THE American stood motionless in the East Lobby of the Reichstag, surrounded by Secret Service agents shouting into their phones. At last he spoke.

'Dieter. I must go.' He turned to Helen and Karen. 'Do you mind if I leave you two together?'

'Sure.' The journalist hesitated, her hand still warm on Helen's arm. 'Do you think they will nix the Summit now?'

'They must.' Blore shook his head. 'We can't send the President of the United States into a war zone.'

'But Air Force One is half-way here.'

'I suspect they have the technology on board to turn the plane around.' Blore smiled thinly.

'I hope your embassy is OK,' Helen said. 'Sorry, that sounds feeble.'

'They say there's no-one dead inside. It would take a nuke to damage that place.' Blore turned to go. 'Let's hope these bastards don't have one.' He made for the stairs, followed by the Secret Service agents.

'Stop.' It was Dieter Kremp. 'You cannot leave alone. Everyone must exit the building together.'

'You have to be kidding.' Blore kept on walking. 'This is a crisis.'

'You will make it a crisis if you try to move around the Safety

Zone alone.' Dieter had his phone in his hand. 'If you can wait thirty seconds, I am summoning one of my colleagues.'

'I'm not waiting,' Blore said.

'You will not be able to depart out of the building. I am in charge here.' Dieter began talking on the phone.

'I need to go, too,' Helen said.

'What's your rush?' Karen said.

'The embassy will be reporting to London. The ambo's still in hospital and God knows what Jason will do if he's left in charge.'

'Who gets your reports?'

'No.10. The Foreign Office. The security agencies. Everyone involved in the Summit.'

'And Jason would be…?'

'My brilliant boss. Jason Short'

Karen patted the thick fur on Otto's flank. 'Jason Short. I remember. I never call him, because he never says anything. Maybe he doesn't know anything.'

Again, Helen couldn't help smiling at the blind journalist. 'I'll call him now. Ten euro for you if he thanks me for ringing.'

If Short was grateful, he hid it well. 'I need you here,' he said, 'not holding hands with your boyfriend at the Reichstag. Ten minutes.' He hung up.

Helen re-dialled. This time she reached Short's secretary, Elaine Hunter.

'He can't be disturbed, Helen. I'm awfully sorry.'

'Is he in the office?'

'Yes.'

'OK. Could you tell our would-be ambassador to Bangkok that if he hangs up on me again, I'll report him for harassment? Not that I ever would, between you and me, but then I can't report him for being a jerk. Thanks.'

'Harassment, got it.' Elaine did not sound displeased by this development. 'Hold on.'

Helen heard Elaine repeat her words to Short, who must have been nearby. There was a click.

'What the hell has got into you? If you want harassment, I'll give you harassment.'

Helen found it easy to keep her temper with Karen by her side. 'I will be there as fast as I can. The American embassy think the Summit should be called off. Any read-out from No.10?'

There was a pause, as though Short was trying to stop himself from slamming the phone down. 'If you think threatening your reporting officer will improve your chances of a good appraisal, Helen, you're off your head.'

'Jason. I don't give a monkey's about my annual appraisal.'

There was another silence before Short spoke. 'Ten minutes. Goodbye.'

'Was he more polite this time?' Karen asked. The tour party was moving towards the exit. Blore and the Secret Service agents had gone on ahead, escorted by the hulking figure of Peter Sturm from the Security Summit Unit.

'Yes. He said goodbye. But I don't think he meant it.'

'There's a Leonard Cohen song about that.'

'The pathetic thing is, I'm desperate to get back to the embassy. Even if it means a fight with Jason. I don't care whether the Summit goes ahead. But the Prime Minister deciding whether to stay away because of a terrorist bomb is a big deal. We have to make the right decision.'

'Do you think they should come?'

'No. Blore's right.'

'You think the whole Summit is off?'

'Well, logically it should be. But this isn't logic. It's politics. No world leader wants to look like a surrender monkey.'

'I wonder what Wild News will say? Wait!' Karen's hand tightened on Helen's arm. 'Maxim Wild was at the US embassy this morning. Suppose he's been hurt? What a story. I must go there.'

'How will you report it?'

'What do you mean?'

'Well…' *When you're blind*, Helen was thinking.

84

'I know. Same way I report anything. First of all, I'll ask Otto to take me there. Then I'll ask people what they see. They're always happy to talk. Sometimes I feel I can see more now than I could when I had eyes.'

'Good luck.'

'Give Jason a kiss from me.'

As soon as she left the Jakob-Kaiser House, Helen plugged in her earphones and switched on the FM radio.   Deutsche Welle, too, had focused on the presence of Maxim Wild at the US embassy.

There is still no news on casualties inside the building,' the dry-as-dust commentator was saying. *'But parallels are already being drawn with the tragic murder of Maxim Wild's father, legendary tycoon Mr Rudolph Wild, by the Red Army Faction in 1982.'*

Helen hopped channels as she pushed her way through crowds of people streaming towards the site of the explosion. The BBC reported several deaths in the blast. But no G8 government had yet made a statement about the Summit. The road was jammed with stationary traffic. When she reached Unter den Linden, the reason was clear: the boulevard had been sealed off with red-and-white-striped metal barriers.

She forced her way through a crowd of building workers and held out her diplomatic pass to the policeman at the barrier.

'Could I come through, please? I need to reach the British embassy.'

'No-one is allowed through. Bomb danger.'

'Of course. I understand. But I'm happy to take the risk. I can cross the street in thirty seconds. Please. It's urgent. I work at the embassy.'

'I do not care if you are the Queen of England.' The policeman glanced towards the grinning audience of bare-chested construction workers. 'No-one is crossing this road until we have cleared twelve suspect vehicles from the Pariser Platz.'

Helen glanced around. It would be impossible to cross Unter den Linden any nearer than the Friedrichstrasse – a half-hour walk. She thought of Short, giving advice to No.10. She had to get back. But how?

There was one possibility. She retraced her steps northwards, stopped at a security booth and again held out her pass.

'Helen Gale, British embassy. I am here to see Monsieur Mura,' she said in French.

'You are in luck. He has just come back in.' The uniformed guard dialled a number. 'A young lady is here to see you. Helen Gale, British embassy.' He nodded at Helen. 'He will send someone to collect you.'

'I am so sorry,' Helen said. 'But could you ask him to come down personally, please? Tell him it will only take a moment.'

The guard did so. Mura seemed to take some persuading. At last the guard replaced the phone. 'He is coming.'

Helen stood in the lofty lobby of the French embassy and flicked back through the stations on her radio.

'…*latest figures are of six dead, and thirty injured.*' It was a Wild Radio reporter. 'Mr Maxim Wild is leaving the building now to make a statement. With him is the American ambassador.'

There were the sounds of other reporters hastily concluding their presentations as the ambassador and Wild approached. Then she heard the ambassador's sombre voice. He expressed sympathy for the victims of the blast and their families and his thanks to the emergency services. There was a shift of tone as he moved to his prepared text.

'Today's tragedy inevitably casts doubt on the security for the Children's Summit, which is due to open at 4 o'clock this afternoon,' he said. 'This embassy, whose vital functions have not been affected by the efforts of terrorists to attack the United States today, is reporting fully to the authorities in Washington. It is too early to anticipate their response to that advice. Mr Wild will now make a statement.'

There was a burst of questions before Maxim Wild's voice

asserted itself. Helen had often seen Wild on television. He was a small man, slightly balding, with an avuncular smile which seemed disconcertingly sincere. She could picture him blinking at the crowd, more like your favourite dotty uncle than a powerful media tycoon.

'I have one message today, and one message only.' Wild's English was perfect, his accent plummy with barely a hint of German. 'This message is that the Summit must go on. Yes, John, I am sorry if that is not the advice you are giving your government.' There was a pause, presumably as Wild beamed an apologetic smile at the ambassador. 'But to abandon now a project set to do so much good, a project which will benefit not only our children, but our children's children, would be to give the terrorists what they want. It would be cowardly.' Helen heard clapping and whistling in the background.

'The importance which the Wild Media Group attaches to the success of the Summit,' Wild went on, 'is shown by our determination to ensure that security measures are in place to defeat the terrorists. This is a task in which the German government has failed. Today's tragedy and the cowardly attack yesterday on the British embassy prove that you cannot appease terrorists. In that, nothing has changed since the murder of my beloved father by the Red Army Faction in 1982. To defeat terrorism, we must show strength. And courage.' The little tycoon's voice barely rose. 'The Summit must succeed. I, for one, will be there.'

There was a further burst of applause.

'Hello, Helen. To what do I owe the honour?'

Helen removed her earphones. Mura was standing beside her.

'Pierre. The honour is mine. I need your help.'

'At your service.'

'I have to get back to the Wilhelmstrasse. But they've closed off Unter den Linden. Can you let me out through the front door of your embassy?'

'Into Pariser Platz?' Mura's eyebrows went up. 'That is where they think the car bombs may be. We have evacuated that side of the building.'

'It's the only way through,' Helen said. 'Once I'm outside, I'll be across the street in no time.'

'You do not think the threat of bombs is real?'

Mura's question was a good one. It was a classic terrorist tactic to detonate a bomb in one place in order to drive people towards the site of a second bomb.

'I have to get back. The ambassador is away, and Jason Short is in charge of the embassy.'

'I understand. Very well. Follow me.' Mura led the way into the interior of the building. Groups of people evacuated from their offices were chatting and drinking coffee. The décor felt functional after the postmodernist extravaganza of the British embassy. But as they neared the public areas around the main entrance, the colours became brighter and the materials more sumptuous.

In the foyer stood two French security officials. Both wore loose-fitting uniforms and had their heads shaven brutally short. They stood on either side of the door, their backs to a wall of massive concrete. One stepped forward as Mura approached.

'Go back. Immediately.'

'This is an English diplomat,' Mura said. 'She wishes to cross Pariser Platz to reach her embassy.'

'I cannot let her go out,' the guard said. 'It is my responsibility.'

'No. It is my responsibility,' Helen said in French. 'Look. You have three – ' she racked her brain for the word – 'witnesses.'

'You do not mind being blown up?' Helen's questioner watched her with piercing blue eyes. 'Are you sure?'

What were the chances of a bomb in the Pariser Platz? So far, the terrorists had not done anything predictable. Even if there were a bomb, how likely was it to explode in the next minute? And who was she exposing to danger, apart from herself?

'It is my decision,' Helen said. 'Do you want me to write it down? Sign in blood?'

'That will not be necessary.' The guard looked at Mura. 'I suppose she can go out if she wants.'

'She is tough. She will be fine.' Mura held out his hand to Helen. 'Walk quickly.'

'Nice knowing you,' the security guard said. He pulled open the entrance door.

Helen's first impression was of a peaceful scene. The deserted expanse of the Pariser Platz shimmered in the midday heat. The architecture was monumental. The flower-beds were manicured. Then she saw a group of bomb disposal experts, clad in bulky helmets and blast-resistant suits, gathered around a car. One of them looked up.

'Hey! You! Get inside!' The voice was muffled.

Helen took no notice. She set off at a brisk walk across the cobblestones.

'Stop!'

Already, the voices were behind her. The bomb squad had more important things to worry about than a suicidal pedestrian. The emptiness of the square was exhilarating. The barrier at the mouth of the Wilhelmstrasse was straight ahead. A policeman stood against it with his back to her.

Helen cleared her throat, and the policeman turned.

'What are you doing there? Quick. Get in.' He pushed open a section of barrier.

'Thanks. I was trapped on the wrong side.' Helen set off towards the embassy.

'How did that happen?'

'My own stupidity.' She was shouting over her shoulder. 'Thank you.'

'No problem.'

Twenty-four hours after the bomb blast which had taken the life of Petra Bleibtreu, the British embassy was a sorry spectacle. It wasn't just the stone-crazed windows, or the steel street-gates shut tight. With the future of the Summit uncertain, the whole building seemed marooned in torpor. The police and Bundespolizei officers on guard looked crumpled by the heat.

It was a relief to see Eric Taylor in the security kiosk. He raised an arm in greeting as the gates trundled open for Helen to slip inside. Then he popped his head round the door.

'Hello, Helen. Hear the bomb?'

'Yes. Even at the Reichstag. Are you OK here? It must have been terrifying.'

'Aye. We've got the whole Hotel Adlon between us and the US Embassy,' Eric said. 'But people are a bit shook up. I'll be glad when the ambassador's back.'

'What's the latest?'

'He's out of hospital. Due here any minute, thank God. But don't tell his nibs upstairs. Might ruin his day.'

'Jason is enjoying being in charge, is he?'

'Just a bit. Moved into the ambassador's office, hasn't he?'

'Can it be that no-one has told him the ambo is out of hospital and heading his way?'

'How could they have?' Eric Taylor grinned. 'He hasn't asked.'

Helen crossed the courtyard, climbed the stairs to the Wintergarden, and walked into the ambassador's office. Short was sitting at the desk staring at a computer screen. In a corner the television was chattering away. The picture showed the Holocaust Memorial. The German text read: *BOMB AT US EMBASSY DESTROYS JEWISH MONUMENT.*

'So. Decided to put in an appearance, have we?' Short continued to stare at his terminal. His fingers hovered over the keys, but he typed nothing.

'What have we told London about the US embassy bomb?'

'It was big. Twenty to thirty kilos. No serious injuries inside the building, but a good deal of trauma. Completely different scenario from our situation yesterday. I've recommended that the Prime Minister cry off the Summit.'

Helen blinked at her boss. People who spent their time

fighting to promote themselves were easy to underestimate. Short had seen a chance to put his name to a key piece of work, and had seized it with both hands.

'Any reply?'

'Everyone's waiting on the Yanks. It's their embassy. Big glazing job, I imagine.' Short waved at the panes broken the day before. 'Now we'll never get these windows fixed.'

'The US ambassador was on the radio just now. He wanted to call the whole thing off, too.' Helen made to leave. 'I'll call Blore.'

'Don't go yet, Helen.' Short reached out and tapped a single key on his keyboard. 'You should know that there has been some debate in London about whether you should be suspended from duty. Pending the outcome of this legal case.'

'What?' Helen found herself gripping the back of a chair. 'Where did that come from?'

'It was my idea.' Short was still staring at the computer; he had not looked at Helen once. 'I can see that you are having trouble coping: not following clearance procedures, resisting instructions, threatening colleagues. I do not think you belong at the embassy in that state. If you take some time off, you can commit your energy to clearing your name.'

'But if the Office suspends me, it will look as if I'm guilty.'

'No need to get worked up. London haven't decided anything yet. Got other things on their minds, I expect. But I suggest you take the rest of the day off.'

'Day off? Who's taking a day off?' The deep tones of Sir Leonard Lennox came from the doorway. 'All hands to the pumps, more like. Jason, what are you doing in my chair? Clear off.'

'Of course.' Short sprang up as if the seat had been electrified. 'We were just discussing next steps.'

'First thing is, we must tell the PM to come straight to Berlin. I know you've already advised the opposite, and well done for that. Good piece of work.' The ambassador nodded at Short. 'But we'll have to say I've risen from my death-bed and overruled you.'

He smiled at Helen as though meeting her for the first time. 'The head's fine, by the way. Nothing a lobotomy couldn't sort out.'

'Maybe we should all have one.' Helen looked at Short. 'But why do you think the Summit should go ahead?'

'Same reasons as Maxim Wild. Personally, I think the chap is an attention-seeking second-rater, but his political instincts are spot-on. If the terrorists want us to cancel the Summit, we should disappoint them.'

'But how do we know what the terrorists want?'

'Good point.' Leonard Lennox sat down in his chair and began whirling round in his seat. 'We don't. But which is likelier: that terrorists let off bombs in Berlin to encourage world leaders to attend the Summit, or that the aim is to scare them off?'

'Scare them off.' Short said. 'You are right, ambassador. The Summit should go ahead.'

'What is the problem, Helen?' The ambassador leant forward over his desk. 'Are we missing something? Come on, spit it out.'

'It makes no sense. It is as if the bombers are trying to cause a panic, but in a half-baked kind of way.'

'And why do you think they might do that? Do you have a theory?'

Helen walked to the window and looked down at the street to where Petra Bleibtreu had been killed. 'Could it be a trick? They make us raise our defences at the Reichstag, while all the time they're planning to attack us somewhere else?'

The ambassador nodded. 'OK. Let's suppose. Where else might they attack?'

There was a silence. Jason Short was shaking his head. At last, Helen turned away from the window. 'I don't know.'

'Hm.' The ambassador frowned. 'What about this SSU officer killed outside the embassy?'

'I don't know,' Helen said again.

At last Short spoke. 'The only thing we know for certain, ambassador, is that the terrorists are trying to stop the Summit,' he said. 'I think your reasoning stands. We should advise the PM to go ahead.'

The ambassador was still looking at Helen. She couldn't think of anything to say. Where else could the terrorists attack? At the airport? In mid-air? Every possibility had been provided for.

At last the ambassador nodded and tidied some papers on his desk. 'Well, history shows it is a bold man who disagrees with you, Helen, but in this case, I shall make an exception. Now, Jason. What's this cock and bull story about Helen taking time off in the middle of a Summit?'

Short's face took on an expression of concern. 'It's this legal case, sir. London are worried the pressure might be too much for her.'

'Who in London is worried?'

'Medical and Welfare Unit, I think it is.'

'I've never heard such tripe. Helen lives for pressure. Don't you, Helen?'

'Well, I – '

'I shall call the HR Director as soon as we have sorted out No.10.'

The ambassador reached for the telephone. But as he did so, it rang.

'Leonard Lennox? Yes?' He stood up, then sat down again. 'Good. Very good. I see. Excellent. I agree. Everything is ready. Goodbye.'

He replaced the receiver, a smile on his lips. 'Too late. No.10 received our advice that the PM should stay at home. Then the President called for a quick word from the mid-Atlantic. Guess what they decided?'

'They're both coming?' Helen wasn't sure whether to be delighted or dismayed.

'Correct. The President and the Prime Minister have announced that they won't let terrorists stop them meeting wherever they please. The Summit goes ahead this afternoon. Unless, of course, the terrorists come up with something we haven't thought of.'

CHAPTER 14

'WHY DOES AIR FORCE ONE NEVER CRASH?' SABINE WOLF said.

'Black magic.' Maria von Bock was peering through a pair of expensive binoculars. 'The US President is protected by the powers of evil.'

'All US Presidents? Or just this one?'

'Every evil one of them, of course.'

'But some US presidents have been assassinated,' Sabine said. 'Does that mean they weren't evil?'

'Stop splitting hairs, for God's sake. What's got into you?' Suddenly Maria von Bock smiled. 'Suppose someone hijacked Air Force One and flew it into the Reichstag? That would be cool.'

'That's sick. Too many innocent victims.'

She knew at once this was a contradiction too many. Slowly, Maria lowered the binoculars. She looked at Sabine, her face set.

'Who do you think you are, judging who is innocent and who isn't? Do you want to stop the Summit, or not?'

'How about taking bribes from Uktam Zholobov?' Sabine pictured Helen Gale and felt curiously emboldened. 'That can't be right.'

'It's not a bribe, scaredy-puss. You have to use the tools of capitalism to fight capitalism.'

'Isn't that like fighting for peace?' Sabine risked a smile. 'And fucking for virginity?'

Maria did not smile. Her eyes glittered. 'They didn't teach

you much in those poxy East German schools, did they? Don't you know the President is Commander-in-Chief of the US armed forces? Think about it: how many people have they killed in the last few decades? It's like Hitler. If someone had murdered him in 1933 it would have saved millions of lives.'

Sabine couldn't help herself. 'You know the rule. As soon as you use Hitler to justify an argument, you've lost.'

'Don't get smart with me, orphan-girl. Sometimes a few people have to suffer to prevent greater suffering somewhere else.'

'Suffering? What do you know about suffering?'

'Oh! Poor little Sabine.' Maria's mouth curled into a sneer. 'When you start moaning about your childhood in the work-houses of East Germany to justify an argument, I know you've lost.' She turned away. 'Behold: the enemy.'

Beyond the end of the runway, the looming bulk of the presidential Boeing hung in the sky. The throb of its engines was muffled by the shrill howls of the accompanying jet fighters as they turned back towards the US Air Force base at Ramstein. A speck in the distance marked a second aircraft carrying the rest of the Presidential team: hundreds of security staff, journalists, drivers, secretaries, diplomats, medical staff and, famously, a hairdresser. The President, too, might be in the second aircraft: it was impossible to be sure.

Sabine lifted her hand to her mouth. 'Look! Someone's shooting at the plane!'

Maria did not move. 'Those are flares. They're to confuse heat-seeking missiles. In case someone does take a shot at them.'

'Oh.' Sabine felt foolish. 'Did you bring any missiles?'

'No. Well, yes.' Maria indicated the straw basket at her feet. 'But there's no way I can throw them far enough.'

Maria and Sabine, along with thousands of other protesters, had gathered at the airport to demonstrate against the arrival of the G8 leaders. The atmosphere was festive: sausage stands and beer stalls had been set up as soon as a crowd began to form. Colourful banners demanded an end to international arms sales and the introduction of a shorter working week. A band of drummers, dressed as mutant farm animals to highlight the dangers of genetic engineering, was keeping up an infectious rhythm. Some students had stripped naked and painted "*AMIS GO HOME*" on their bodies, one letter to each protester, to the delight of nearby photographers. But the protest had been dampened by a police decision to corral the demonstrators in a loop of the airport perimeter fence nearly two kilometres from the terminal.

'My office is checking whether cooping us up out here violates our right to self-expression,' Maria said. 'To think, I brought eggs. Even one of your East German shot-put champions couldn't reach the President from here.'

'No.' Usually by this stage in an argument with Maria, Sabine would have capitulated. But today, something kept her battling on. 'I can still recognise a bribe, though. Even if I did grow up in a worker's paradise.'

'Money has no ideology.'

'That's not true.'

'Calm down, orphan-girl. You don't know what you're talking about.'

'But surely Uktam Zholobov doesn't want the same things we do?'

'Sabine.' Maria's voice was terse. 'Why are you so in such a state? Don't you want to fight back against the military industrial complex?'

'It makes no sense. We are trying to bury capitalism, and a capitalist gives us money.'

'Zholobov hates globalisation. Don't forget he is boycotting the Summit.'

'Zholobov is as big a bastard as anyone who's attending.'

Maria von Bock was silent. Her eyes hardened. 'It's that girl, isn't it? At the British embassy. Ever since you met her, you've been all mixed up.'

'What girl?' Suddenly the sun felt intolerably hot.

'Helen Gale. The pen-pusher we're putting in the debtors' prison.'

'I don't care about her.' Sabine wondered if it was true.

'Fancy her, do you? Plenty of other girls will, too, once she's in jail.'

'Do you think it's right, Uktam Zholobov paying for us to sue her? It's like the powerful picking on the defenceless.'

'Defenceless? She has a whole government behind her. See that plane? They can buy one any time they want. You needn't worry about Helen Gale, scaredy-puss.'

'No. I guess not.' Sabine clutched the fence to steady herself. Then she pointed across the airfield and forced a smile. 'Look how they've parked the aircraft. We can't even see the president come down the steps.'

'Maybe it's like Stalin.' Maria patted Sabine's head. 'They have six identical presidents, to confuse assassins.'

Again, Sabine thought of Helen Gale. 'I wonder who organises the Presidential look-alikes?'

'Let's hope the assassins kill all of them.' Maria took an egg from the basket at her feet and threw it over the fence. It landed silently amidst the tussocks of grass. 'Let's hope they butcher every single person at the Summit.'

'You would not say that if you had seen someone killed.'

Maria shook her head. 'Who have you seen killed, then?'

'I have seen worse.'

'Worse than dying? Don't be absurd.'

'There are plenty of things worse than dying.'

Maria von Bock looked at Sabine. 'OK, suffering girl. Let me rephrase that. I hope everyone at the Summit suffers a fate worse than death. Are you happy now?

CHAPTER 15

'THE AMBASSADOR MAY HAVE A CRUSH ON YOU, HELEN. BUT I'm not happy with your performance.'

Helen looked up to find Jason Short in the doorway to her office. His long, thinning hair gleamed under the fluorescent lights. He looked tired and irritable. But she did not have time to fight him now.

'I'm trying to make the Summit safe. So are you. Let's get on with it.'

Short shook his head. 'The first rule of policy is consistency. If I tell No.10 the bomb was aimed at the embassy and you tell them it wasn't, we both look like idiots.'

'This is about Bangkok, isn't it?'

'Then you tell London the killing of a member of the SSU leaves the threat to the Summit unchanged, hours before a bomb blows up the US embassy. We must have set some kind of world record for bad advice.'

'A bomb at the US embassy doesn't necessarily make the Reichstag more dangerous.'

'It makes it safer, does it? Why don't you tell London that? We might win a special award for daftness.'

'I suppose if there is one you would know.'

'It's you who's making the embassy a laughing-stock, Helen.'

Her phone rang. She picked it up at once.

'This is Oleg Sukanashvili. I am rescuing you.'

'How do you know I need rescuing?' It felt good to speak Russian, knowing Short could not understand.

'Your Prime Minister is coming. The Summit is starting. It is the eye of the storm,' the Georgian said. 'A good time to rescue people. Let me invite you to lunch.'

'Impossible. No time.'

'For food, there is always time. You must be strong for the Summit. I invite you for a doner kebab at the Cafe Motiv. Five minutes' walk for you, fifteen minutes to eat.'

Helen looked at Short, whose mouth had puckered into a tight ring of rage, and made her mind up.

'OK,' she said to Sukanashvili. 'See you there.' She stood. 'I have to go,' she said to Short. 'Something important has come up.'

'Going to see a Russian on the day of the Summit? You are out of your tree.' Short turned to go. 'Oh, and if you have any new security revelations, do tell me before you ring London. There's a good girl.'

Before she left, Helen popped in to see Ram Kuresh.

'I'm escaping for a few minutes,' she said. 'Can you ring me if anything comes in?'

'You know someone has claimed responsibility?' the SIS man said. 'For the US embassy bomb?'

'What's the source?'

'Someone phoned Al Jazeera. The Action Group for Peace and Justice. No-one has heard of them.'

'But you must have some idea who they are.'

'No. We do not have the foggiest idea.'

'Anything else?'

'There is one other thing, coming in on secret channels. But it is so far being tightly held, while they assess it. There is so much noise on the airwaves, it is hard to know what to take seriously.'

'Call me.'

'Certainly. But you may have to come to my office to look at it.'

Helen felt her mood lighten as she stepped out into the Wilhelmstrasse. Sukanashvili was right: the Children's Summit had as good as started. The great summit train would now grind inexorably forward to its conclusion, along rails laid and greased in hundreds of meetings and contacts over the past year. The ambassador was at the airport. Transport and security arrangements were in place. Tonight, she would hear what Nigel had to say about life, love, happiness and no doubt children. Now, it was time to eat a kebab.

The streets around the US embassy were crammed with sightseers. What if the bombers wanted more victims? With terrorism, anyone could be a target. You could never protect a whole country against random acts of violence. But it was possible to defend a single building. The Reichstag was the best fortress paranoia could construct.

Her phone rang.

'Ram?'

'It's your husband, darling. The name is Nigel. Who is Ram?'

'Ram is someone who understands women. What do you want?'

'I am crushed. And here I was, hoping you might help me.'

Helen imagined Nigel hunched over a laptop, a telephone headset in his ear as he hammered out another heavyweight commentary. 'Try me. This is about work, I suppose?'

'I am afraid so.' His voice dropped. 'But I am looking forward to seeing you for dinner this evening.'

'Good.' Helen skirted a clump of protesters. 'Me too.'

Nigel was silent. The effort of expressing emotion had probably exhausted him. 'What is it you want?' Helen said.

'Well. It's these rumours about a fresh threat to the Summit. New intelligence. Hush-hush. Do you know anything?'

'I thought you were part of our delegation?'

'Ah. Yes. Well, it seems some people are more part of the delegation than others. When it comes to secret intelligence, I'm very much at the rear of the aircraft.'

'I know nothing.' Helen thought of Ram Kuresh. 'Even if I did, I can't dish out secret intelligence on the phone.'

'You would tell me whatever you wanted, if you were in the mood.' Nigel's voice became more insistent. 'Let me offer you something in exchange. I happen to know that the home pages of my esteemed organ are doing an opinion piece on the legal action against you in the UK. Perhaps I could ask them to give it a favourable spin.'

'Who is taking action against me in the UK?'

'Something called the British Victims' Legal Support Group. It seems suing you in the UK is a way to by-pass diplomatic immunity.'

'Great.'

'So, how about a nugget, darling? What's the latest threat?'

'You know about the responsibility claim from the Action Group for Peace and Justice?'

'Obviously.'

'That is the latest thing I've heard. Nigel. Please. If you care about me at all, get your people to cut me some slack.'

Silence. 'I do care, Helen. I will see what I can do.'

'Thanks.'

'Wish me luck in the Reichstag.' The phone went dead.

Helen stood at the kerb and stared at the little red traffic light man, his arms outstretched as if determined to bar her way. Should she cross on red? She looked around, anxious not to set a bad example if children were nearby. Her own children, of course, would only cross on green. If she ever had any. How could she, if her career took her all around the globe and no man she could respect would ever follow her? Maybe she would find out when she saw Nigel.

The red man had disappeared, to be replaced by a jaunty green figure in a hat, stepping out with enthusiasm. Helen crossed to the Café Motiv.

From the outside, the Motiv looked like any other Berlin doner shop. A glistening cylinder of processed lamb gyrated slowly next to the grill in the front window. Garish red and yellow signs advertised roast chicken, pizzas, and a host of other life-shortening forms of food intake. A seedy beer garden occupied a stretch of pavement, overshadowed by the hulk of the Czech embassy across the street.

But beneath its greasy veneer, the Motiv was distinguished by doners which were always sliced steaming from the spit; by its location in the heart of the government quarter; and by the ability of its owner to spot a government minister or a celebrity before they opened the front door. Signed photos of customers decorated the walls, from the parsimonious former finance minister who was said to have eaten there daily to a one-time US president whose signature Helen felt deserved a closer inspection. Oleg Sukanashvili was sitting in a dark corner beneath the President's portrait, hemmed in between a plastic-topped table and a wood-panelled wall.

'Helen. Welcome.' The Georgian manoeuvred his bulk out from behind the table and kissed Helen on both cheeks. He smelt of expensive cologne. 'Sit down.' He nodded at the owner behind the counter, and squeezed himself back into his chair. 'Let me guess. You have just finished an argument. Business? Or personal?'

'Good so far.'

'This is something you care about. So, it is personal. A relationship.' Sukanashvili's deep-set eyes sparkled. 'Your husband.'

'You should be a fortune-teller. You would be rich.'

'I am rich already. I have everything I want.'

'That is why you are unique. A man who wants nothing.'

'It is true. You are safe with me.'

Helen could never explain why she felt so comfortable with Sukanashvili. He had made his first fortune after the break-up of the Soviet Union, at a time when a tolerance of corruption was a prerequisite for business success, and a willingness to deploy physical violence counted more than an MBA. There had been a story in the Moscow embassy that at the time first secretary Stephen Million had done Sukanashvili his mysterious favour, the Georgian's second-in-command – a man called Jules Beridze – had met a grisly death in a penthouse flat in London. Yet Helen always felt safe around Sukanashvili. He seemed to derive pleasure from seeing her from time to time, and from helping sort out her life. A man who never let you down. How rare was that?

'It's about Nigel,' she said. 'I might see him tonight.'

'Do you want to see him?'

'Kind of. We always like to have a good argument about children, and careers, and living in the same place.'

'If you want a great thing, you must fight for it.'

'We fight, all right. Actually, it's not funny. He has said some awful, stupid things after a drink or two. Probably I have, too. I don't know if I could live with him again.'

'A routine story. A woman says she does not need a man. The man has to say he does not need the woman. Both are lying.'

'He seems so upset with me all the time. Yet he never gets angry.'

'You hurt him. It is like these protesters. They sense that the world is unjust. Therefore, they want to harm the people who they think are responsible. The problem is, they do not know how.'

'The terrorists seem to know how.'

'The terrorists. Yes. But what is a terrorist? *Danke.*' Sukanashvili nodded at the waiter, who had delivered to the table two plates overflowing with lamb, salad and garlic sauce, together with two small beers. 'Terrorism, it means using violence to obtain something from a country, or a people. Someone who causes such violence is a terrorist. But that person may look like you, or me. Or a member of a government, whether democratic or not.' He picked up his doner and sank his teeth into it.

'But violence in the name of a democratic government has more legitimacy.' Helen waved a sliver of bread.

'It is true that democracy makes governments – and generals

– more careful. That is good. But it also breeds hubris. That is bad. Sometimes it may be harder for an elected president or prime minister to be wise than it is for a dictator. The voters are behind me, the elected leader thinks. My decisions must be the right ones. Those who disagree with me must be wrong. They do not know all that I know.' Sukanashvili was speaking with his mouth full. His kebab had disappeared.

'This is a vicious circle, as we sometimes see with our friends in the West. A president in a democracy is buried with facts, more than any person can absorb. The result is that he pays attention only to those facts which support his decisions, and ignores the rest. Maybe the president's advisers filter out all the wrong facts, the bad facts. The result is that the president finds his decisions have always been right. This makes him think his next decision must be right, also.'

'So how do you make decisions?'

'What do you think, Helen?' The Georgian dabbed his mouth with his handkerchief. 'What is the most important thing in life?'

'People, obviously.'

'It is not obvious to everyone. But you are right. The most important things are people. And ideas. It does not take many people with a strong idea to dominate a country. Look at the communists. Or the Nazis. Beliefs are more dangerous than bombs. Unfortunately, there is no relationship between how strongly someone believes something, and whether it is true. The only defence is humility. A humble man is resistant to being sure that he is right.'

'Which of the G8 leaders is the humble one?'

'You are correct. Humble men do not usually enter politics.'

'Or business. You know Uktam Zholobov is supporting the legal case against me?' Suddenly she had an idea. 'Do you know him? Could you tell him to lay off?'

'I knew him once.' Sukanashvili's face was shrouded in uncharacteristic uncertainty. 'But now, he is very powerful.'

'He seems desperate to sink the Summit.'

'He opposes the Summit. And he hates the Russian government. That is not yet illegal.'

'I sometimes feel like the last person left alive who doesn't have strong opinions on everything,' Helen said. 'Have you looked at the Internet recently?'

Sukanashvili shrugged. 'People who are sure about many things usually understand few of them.'

'How can they believe so passionately? I don't believe in anything.'

'You believe. But you do not know it. Do you not care about your friends?'

'Friends and family.' Helen smiled. 'Sounds like a mobile phone tariff.'

'You see. There is something in which you believe. Friends and family. A good place to start.' Sukanashvili drank the last of his beer. 'Those who champion distant peoples and causes believe they are struggling for justice. But in reality, they are terrified by their own insignificance. By making a noise, they try to convince themselves they matter in the world.'

'What do you care about?'

Sukanashvili looked out of the window. 'Myself. And those close to me. Nothing gives me more pleasure than to help them.'

'OK.' Helen leaned forward. 'Here's a challenge. These embassy bombings. Someone in Berlin must know about them. Could you find out?'

'I do not think these are Russian criminals. Or Chechens, or anyone from the former Soviet Union.'

'Can you try? I need all the help I can get.'

'For you, Helen, I try.' The Georgian picked up a shred of lettuce between two massive fingers. 'Is that your mobile telephone?'

It took Helen a moment to realise that her phone was indeed ringing.

'Helen, it is Ram. Come back now, please.'

'What is it?'

'It is – what can I tell you – a video. Discovered by a friendly power.'

The US must have found something, Helen thought. Probably the National Security Agency. 'What else can you tell me?'

'It is a new claim of responsibility. On the Internet.'

'For the bomb at the US embassy? Or ours?'

'Neither. Our, shall we say, friendly power found it sitting in an anonymous Internet account; it was supposed to be transmitted in two hours' time. We do not know what it is claiming responsibility for. All we know is, it is an atrocity at the Reichstag and it has not happened yet.'

CHAPTER 16

BECAUSE ULI WENGER KEPT UP WITH THE TELEVISION NEWS on the same computer he was using to make his final preparations for the assault, he sometimes felt as though he was already controlling events. It was like playing a computer game where the figures moved on paths he had determined. He watched the British Prime Minister descend the aircraft steps to shake the hand of the German Foreign Ministry Chief of Protocol. Behind the Prime Minister, two armed protection officers scanned the crowd. One was watching each person the politician approached, the other searching for more distant threats. Both looked jumpy. Uli suppressed a smile. The bodyguards could not imagine what they really had to be nervous about.

The Prime Minister disappeared from sight. Once on German soil, the British leader would be under the protection of the most elaborate security regime the authorities could devise. Uli knew every detail.

First, the Prime Minister would climb into one of several identical convoy cars. Then, the armoured limousine would whisk its precious cargo down streets cleared of traffic, parked cars, post-boxes or any other place where a bomb might be concealed, towards the safe haven of the Reichstag. Drain covers had been welded shut. Police officers had visited every apartment block along the route, warning the residents against opening a window or waving a greeting. Schools, kindergartens, car parks and museums had been closed for the duration of the Summit.

Street cleaning and rubbish collection had been suspended; bus and tram services discontinued; roads closed to provide a wealth of route options for the convoys from the airport. Hospitals had suspended non-urgent admissions and put beds on stand-by for the victims of any attack.

Even the air space over Berlin was closed and patrolled by fighter aircraft. Under the German air safety law introduced after the attacks in New York and Washington in September 2001, pilots could be authorised to shoot down civilian aircraft entering the exclusion zone. Uli shook his head. The politician responsible for authorising any strike would be the German Minister of Defence, Irmgard Schneider. She was inside the Reichstag, with the rest of the German cabinet, waiting to greet the Summit participants. One hour from now she would not be in a position to authorise anything.

Even Berliners who did not oppose the Summit found the security regime irksome. Grumbling locals had been on the news all week, complaining that they would have to take the day off work. What else could they do, they asked, except swelter in front of the TV? Uli scowled. Insects. Sitting in front of the television was all they were good for. Well, he would give them something to watch.

It was several minutes later, as the French President came down the steps of the Air Force jet to be greeted warmly by the German Chancellor, that things began to go wrong. Instead of introducing the President to the receiving line, the Chancellor guided the new arrival back towards the runway apron, where a helicopter stood beside two squat armoured personnel carriers manned by GSG 9 personnel. Uli knew the transport plans had made no provision for helicopters. There was an urgency in the action which had nothing to do with protocol.

'You'd better see this.'

Uli looked up to see the Chaos Team member with the phonetic codename Gustav holding out a scrap of paper. Their eyes met. 'It is key,' Gustav said.

Now Uli's heart was pounding. "It is key" was a codeword which members of the Chaos Team were to deploy in the event of a crisis, just as "All is secure" was the code for initiating the attack. But Gustav seemed calm. The paper in his huge hand was steady. Uli felt a surge of confidence. His team was the best. He should know. He had chosen them himself.

'Thank you.' He took the paper. It was an access code for a piece of intelligence. Eight digits. What was this? He punched the numbers into his terminal.

After the usual round of warnings about the need to protect the confidentiality of the information he was about to see, a video image appeared. A figure sat at a table, shrouded in a black and white keffiyeh and wearing dark glasses. Behind him on the wall was a poster with an Arabic slogan. The man looked down at a text on the table and began to speak in heavily-accented English.

'Praise be to Allah, who promised his faithful slaves victory…'

Uli was conscious of Gustav watching the screen over his shoulder. This would be hard for the big man, Uli thought: he loathed all foreigners. But Gustav remained silent as the masked figure began to read out a list of barbaric acts committed against what he called "our people" by the forces of tyranny and oppression. Some of the words were obscure: both sound and image were fuzzy. But the message was clear. Injustice and oppression were everywhere. Now was the time to fight back.

The figure raised his head to gaze at the camera. 'And I say to you, this is why we have done this thing,' he said. 'Some of you will call it an atrocity. An act of terrorism. But is it terrorism to defend our nation, our women, our children? To punish those who hurt us? Should a man be blamed for protecting his home against a brutal enemy?

'You ask yourselves: what can we do now, in the face of what has happened at the Reichstag in Berlin? How can we save our people? How can we prevent more deaths? I tell you this: your salvation is in your hands, and those of the corporations whose fingers are stained with the blood of children. Our demands are simple. No-one who has justice in his heart can be against these things. But hear my words. If you choose the path of aggression, the gates of hell shall be opened before you and all shall perish.' The screen went blank.

Uli stared at the monitor. Should he admit to Gustav that he knew nothing of this video? But it was no time to admit ignorance. It was time to show authority. He stood.

'Thank you,' he said to Gustav. 'This explains the increased security for the French President.'

'I saw the helicopter.' Gustav was choosing his words carefully. 'What do you make of the video?'

There was something in Gustav's eyes, Uli saw. Not fear – that was impossible – but doubt. That must not be allowed.

Leading people was what Uli did best. That, and killing them. Building up and training the Chaos Team, preparing them over months and years for an operation which would start forty-five minutes from now and would last in total just eight hours, had been a masterpiece of motivation. With their help, Uli would become one of the most famous men in Germany. Thanks to Herr Kraft, he would also become wealthy.

None of the Chaos Team would ever know the scale of Uli's achievement. By midnight, they would all be dead. But between now and then, he had to keep them at the highest possible pitch of aggression and determination.

Uli glanced around the room, checking that they were alone. The Chaos Team always worked on the assumption that anything they said might be recorded. Especially here. Operational security was vital. But Gustav needed reassurance.

'Have you seen this?' Uli pointed to a space on his desk which was not overlooked. On it lay a sheet of blank paper. Gustav looked at it. He knew the procedure. 'It could be relevant,' Uli said. Then he picked up a felt-tipped pen – nothing which could mark the surface of the desk – and wrote the words:

VIDEO WILL CAUSE PANIC

GOOD FOR US
ATTACK GOES AHEAD

As soon as Gustav had read the text, Uli folded the sheet in half and dropped it into the cross-cut shredder beside his desk. Then he turned to Gustav.

'Any thoughts?'

'Not really,' Gustav said. The answer was in his eyes. The doubt had been replaced by determination.

'Good,' Uli said. 'Let us get to work.'

CHAPTER 17

'**T**HIS IS THE MOTHER OF ALL RESPONSIBILITY CLAIMS,' RAM Kuresh said to Helen. He froze the image, and pointed to the screen. 'The black and white keffiyeh is the Palestinian head-dress we find sported by revolutionary movements and their sympathisers world-wide. Also, as a fashion statement. On the poster is the Arabic slogan: "The land belongs to those who liberate it." This is straight from the resistance fighter's handbook. The hooded gentleman could be anyone, from a terrorist mastermind to someone's next-door neighbour to an out-of-work actor. Maybe all three. We do not know if the fellow at the table and the man reading the words are the same. Finally, the warnings are the usual bloodcurdling guff.' He spread his hands. 'The gates of hell – it is almost self-parody.'

'What about the reference to the Reichstag?' Helen said. 'He says a terrorist act has taken place. Yet he also talks about us trying to save our people and prevent more deaths. As if he has someone in his power.'

Helen found it easy to think in Ram's office. There were no windows: one of the recruitment criteria for SIS officers seemed to be the ability to work in artificial light. Unlike her office in the embassy, the room was fully air-conditioned, and comfortably cool.

'Most perceptive,' Ram said. 'In among the anti-establishment flimflam are some nuggets of information. What do they mean by warning us not to attack them? SIS are checking with

113

Washington for any current operations against terrorist targets. But this fellow in the head-dress seems to assume we know what he is talking about.'

'Was any of the earlier intelligence on video?'

Ram's phone rang. He picked it up, listened, and replaced it. 'Mr Short wishes to see us in the embassy conference room before I finish this sentence,' he said. 'Whoops. We missed it.'

'Maybe you should use longer sentences.'

Kuresh looked at Helen. 'You are being a particularly naughty girl today. Why are you always doing the opposite of what our esteemed Head of Political Section wants?'

Helen shrugged. 'I tried being a good girl when I was little. I thought it would make the world a nicer place. Then my dad left, my mum got depressed, and my world fell apart. Who needs good behaviour, anyhow?'

'Ah.' Ram blinked. 'Well, I like you naughty. And your point about videos is interesting. As your forceful friend Mr Dieter Kremp knows only too well, we have been lucky enough to intercept a host of communications intelligence which seems to refer to plans for terrorist action in Berlin during the Summit. At the last count, I believe it was twenty-three telephone calls, faxes and e-mails. And nil videos. You do not have to look so shocked. This room is secure.'

'Go on.'

'These intercepts were made in or between seven European and Middle Eastern countries and, in one case, the United States. The phone calls were digitally enciphered, and were made using mobile networks on stolen hand-sets. E-mails were sent using once-only accounts, faxes from public numbers such as grocery stores.'

'So, this is a sophisticated organisation.'

'Yes and no. They used off-the-shelf encryption programmes. These are jolly good, these days. But for the NSA and GCHQ, they are a piece of cake. Same story for the e-mails and so forth.

We could access the messages, but could not identify the people sending and receiving them.'

Helen pressed her lips together and thought back to her time in the assessments staff. Making sense of intelligence was as much an art as a science. 'OK,' she said. 'What are the differences between those intercepts and the video?'

'I am guessing you are in no hurry to go and see Jason.'

'I am never in a hurry to see Jason. Can he find us here?'

'He cannot open the door to our office. Unless he has stolen the password. In that case, I would have to kill him.'

'Could you encourage him to steal it?'

'Good, Helen. You are thinking like a spook already.'

'Two more minutes. I want to know who injured that child.'

'OK. One big difference. The intercepts were enciphered. But their meaning was clear. In fact, by intelligence standards, they were unusually specific. This video, on the other hand, is not enciphered. But we have no idea what it means.'

'Maybe they wanted us to intercept the phone calls.'

Ram shook his head. 'Why would they give us advance warning?'

'I don't know. But if they did, this video could be our first break. Didn't you say it was meant to be transmitted in two hours' time?'

'About one hour, now.'

'That's thirty minutes after the Summit is due to begin. What can they do between now and then?'

'Nothing,' Ram said. 'The participants are arriving at the Reichstag already.'

'We're missing something.'

'We are missing Mr Short. Two minutes are up.'

Ram's computer began playing Ravel's "Bolero". He stared at it.

'That is a first,' he said. 'An encrypted video call from…' he ran his finger down a list of numbers on the wall. 'A number assigned to a well-known military unit based in Hereford. One has to admit, they are quick.'

Ram typed a password on his computer, then plugged in and switched on the web-cam above it. Helen saw a blank screen, with herself and Ram peering out of a window in one corner. 'Any second now,' he said.

A woman's face appeared. She was about Helen's age, with dark, shoulder-length hair and no make-up. She didn't need it, Helen thought: she looked like an athlete, her strong features enhanced by perfect skin and an air of total confidence.

'Thank God for that,' the woman said. 'Is this the British Embassy Berlin? I hope you're Ram Kuresh.'

'Indeed,' Ram said. 'And you are?'

'Could you identify yourself?' The woman was looking at Helen.

'I will if you will,' Helen said. 'I'm Helen Gale. First secretary for – '

'You're the one who's being sued. Post Security Officer. Got it. I'm Captain Elle Morgan, 22 SAS. The squadron is in Hereford now, on standby. I'll be with you in about two hours on a commercial flight. I'm supposed to be part of the FCO advance team, but I can't wait for them.'

'Could you run that past me again?' Ram said.

Elle Morgan nodded. 'Right. You're aware of the premature video.'

'We have been looking at it,' Ram said.

'Along with every counter-terrorist analyst in London. It's set off alarm bells all over the shop. We're in the early stages of preparing for a major overseas terrorist incident involving British interests. COBRA, the Cabinet Office Briefing Room, is being opened: the Deputy Prime Minister is on his way there now.'

'But…' Helen recalled what she knew of counter-terrorist procedures. 'COBRA is only opened for a crisis. Are you proposing to fly out here on the strength of a video?'

'Helen.' Elle Morgan's voice was steady. 'The situation before yesterday was that we had intelligence suggesting a terrorist attack might be in preparation in a city where the Prime Minister was attending a conference. That happens. If the PM never went anywhere there was a risk of terrorist attack, it would rule out half the world's cities.

'After the two bombs, most of us here breathed a sigh of relief. Not too bad, we thought. Then this video shows up. It's not a hoax: no-one intended us to find it. The video suggests a bigger and more sophisticated attack is imminent, possibly on the conference venue itself. It could be a conventional bomb, a chemical or biological weapon, even a nuclear explosion. Or something else completely. Maybe there will be no attack. That's what we're all praying. But if something happens in the next few hours, no-one's going to want hear afterwards how we wasted time in London when we could have been preparing our response, or even preventing the attack itself, on the ground in Berlin.

'My advice to you is, get some rooms ready for an advance party of around ten people with the best comms you can find.' She blinked twice, quickly. 'And there's no need to meet me at the airport.' The face disappeared.

'What's that noise?' Helen said.

'It is our doorbell.' Ram shrugged. 'Perhaps Mr Short is trying to find us.'

But it was not Jason Short whom Helen and Ram found waiting outside. It was his secretary, Elaine Hunter. Her thin face twisted into a smile as Ram opened the door.

'The Head of Political Section asked me to find out,' she said, 'and I quote, where the fuck those two wankers are, and to persuade you to, um, shift your arses down to the conference room. He's in a bit of a tizz.'

Helen and Ram looked at one another. No-one knew whether Elaine's tendency to repeat verbatim Short's obscenities was fuelled by a dedication to accuracy, or an urge to make her boss seem absurd.

'I think we were just in the process of shifting our arses,' Helen said.

The conference room was a large office in the confidential zone of the embassy which was sometimes used to house visiting delegations of officials. For the duration of the Children's Summit, it had been fitted with a row of desks, telephones and computer terminals and a small meeting table.

Short stood in the doorway.

'Ah,' he said. '*Les inspecteurs des travaux finis.*'

'I don't speak French,' Ram said.

Short sighed. 'It means people who turn up when all the work is done.' He sniffed at Helen as she entered the room. 'Have you been drinking?'

'Can we get started?' Helen sat down at the table next to Basil Nutter, who was reading a thick black ring-bound folder. Her doner and beer with Sukanashvili seemed weeks ago. 'We've just had the SAS on Ram's fancy video phone. A Captain Elle Morgan will be here in two hours.'

'What?' Short said.

'And COBRA's open. London seem convinced a major attack is imminent.'

'I told them they should have called the Summit off,' Short said.

'It sounds to me like they might cancel it any minute.' Helen saw another copy of the black folder, labelled UPTAKE, on the table. She pulled it towards her. 'What's this?'

'That, Helen, is the British government's contingency plan for a terrorist crisis overseas,' Short said. 'But its value is moot, since no-one in Berlin or London is answering their fucking phones.'

No-one spoke.

'Answering their phones, I'm sorry,' Short said. 'But everything's falling apart already, and the terrorists haven't even done anything.'

'Are we sure something's going to happen?' Basil Nutter's voice wavered. 'Perhaps it's a false alarm.'

'All I know is, they have activated this so-called UPTAKE plan because the video, pardon my French, is scaring everyone shitless. I know COBRA is open, because every minister and official in London seems to be on their way there. Meanwhile, until it's up and running, and for as long as the Prime Minister's stranded somewhere between the airport and the Reichstag, no-one is making any decisions.'

Helen looked at Short. The imminence of the Summit was making him literally shiver with anxiety. Yet his judgement was spot-on: a collapse of decision-making capacity was a sure sign that a crisis was about to get worse. 'What do the Germans say?' she asked.

'They are in the same fix. The State Secretary at the Interior Ministry wants to stop the Summit now. But he can't do that without asking the Chancellor, who arrived at the Reichstag by helicopter a few minutes ago and is standing in the East Lobby with the Interior Minister greeting guests.'

'Where is the Prime Minister?' Helen said.

'I have located the PM.' Ram Kuresh had a laptop computer open on the table. 'ARD are showing live TV coverage of the opening ceremony. Our leader is shaking the Chancellor's hand… right now.'

Everyone crowded round the screen.

'It doesn't look as if there's been a terrorist attack yet,' Basil Nutter said.

'It's like a game of chicken,' Helen said. 'When the bomb went off at the US embassy, no G8 leader wanted to be the first to pull out. Now we have another threat, literally as people are arriving at the Reichstag. The Germans can't do anything until everyone has arrived.' Helen watched as the Prime Minister exchanged a few words with the Chancellor. 'When they sit down, the first thing they'll do will be to decide whether they should all go home again. Could be the shortest summit in history.'

'Look at the children. That'll be on the front pages,' Basil said.

Helen peered at the screen. The children were lined up on a stepped stand behind the German Chancellor. They looked relaxed and happy: one hundred youngsters from every corner of the globe, beaming at the cameras. Several business and political leaders, having shaken the Chancellor's hand, had wandered over to seize the photo opportunity Basil had identified. Maxim Wild, trailed by a gaggle of photographers, was talking to a Chinese girl at the end of a row: whatever he had said made her laugh out loud, then cover her mouth. There was a burst of camera flashes.

Off to one side, Helen saw Tilo Pollex, the German Interior Minister, talking on his mobile phone. Somewhere in the lobby, out of sight of the cameras, would be several SSU officers and a team of experienced Secret Service agents. You had to pity the terrorist who tried to enter the Reichstag.

'Here comes the US President,' Ram said. 'I think that completes the set.'

Two tall, powerfully built men in dark suits and dark glasses trotted up the stairs. Behind them, the President of the United States was almost hidden from view. Two more Secret Service agents followed, again concealing the President as they passed the camera position.

'Not taking any chances,' Ram said.

'Good,' Helen said.

The scene froze as, behind the shield of Secret Service agents, the Chancellor greeted the President. It was impossible to see the expressions on either of their faces. Then there was a flurry of movement. The Chancellor began shepherding the heads of state and government towards the plenary chamber. At the edge of the picture, Helen spotted some SSU officers moving with them. She wondered where Nigel was. Probably waiting in the plenary room, fiddling with his mobile phone.

'At least they've made it into the Reichstag,' Helen said.

Basil Nutter tittered. 'We're going to look silly if this turns out to be a lot of fuss about nothing.'

'Well,' Jason Short said, 'let's hope that happens. Because if something does go wrong with the Summit, and it turns out that Helen's middle-of-the-night advice played a role in allowing it to go ahead, some of us are going to look even sillier. Particularly Helen.'

CHAPTER 18

U LI WENGER WATCHED WITH ELATION AS THE PRESIDENT OF the United States arrived at the Reichstag. But his face remained impassive. Everything was on track. The G8 leaders, the business tycoons and the German cabinet were all inside the building. Whatever the purpose of the video the Americans had found, it had not affected his plans. On the contrary: he sensed a heightened state of urgency, bordering on panic, around the Reichstag. Maybe that had been Herr Kraft's intention: to stir up confusion. No-one had any idea what the video meant. Not even the deputy head of the Summit Security Unit, Dieter Kremp, who liked to pretend he had everything under control. Well, Dieter would not have to worry about the Summit much longer. In ten minutes, he would be dead.

The politicians, business people and security personnel were moving off now, towards the plenary chamber. Many were still smiling for the cameras. Only the American President was grim-faced, cocooned inside the safety-cell of agents. Much good they would do. What did the President and the rest of them think they were going to talk about at the conference table? Might someone dare to suggest that they scrap the Summit and run for their lives? Would anyone realise that was all that mattered?

Uli took a long, deep breath and felt his heartbeat slow. Of course, it did not make any difference what the world's leaders decided to discuss first. The instant they sat down, the attack would begin.

CHAPTER 19

DIETER KREMP EYED THE STAIRS LEADING UP FROM THE EN-
trance tunnel as the delegates moved into the plenary
chamber. Next to him, Johann Frost was doing the same. Where
would any threat come from? For a moment, Dieter thought a
television camera was pointing straight at him; it made him feel
exposed. But it was focused on the children, gathering to enter
the plenary chamber and sing the song to launch the Summit.

Dieter allowed himself to relax a little as he ticked off the
security measures. To cut down on the number of people cleared
for the Safety Zone, all cameras were controlled by an SSU
technician in the communications centre on the top floor of the
Reichstag. In addition to half a dozen high-definition TV cameras
in the East Lobby and the plenary chamber, every meeting room
and corridor within the complex was covered by closed-circuit
TV monitors. So were the access tunnels. But the cameras had
been positioned to avoid compromising security assets such as the
flak shield or the spots around the building where SSU officers
would be stationed. Red masking tape had been fixed to the
floors of the main meetings rooms and corridors, outlining areas
where security staff could stand without appearing on camera.
To people watching the ceremony on TV at home, security in
the Reichstag would be nearly invisible.

'Herr Frost!'

Dieter turned to see the Minister of the Interior, Tilo Pollex,
striding towards them. Johann Frost stood to attention. Dieter

followed suit, although the gesture seemed out of place in the midst of a potential crisis. As if to confirm this, the minister nodded irritably.

'We are moving the Summit to a new location,' Pollex said. 'Immediately. We can't cancel. It would look like panic.' He paused. 'We don't do panic, right?'

'We don't know the word, sir,' Johann spoke without a smile.

'The Chancellor is about to tell the delegates that the meeting is being moved to the new Bundesnachrichtendienst HQ, up the road.' Pollex grimaced. 'It has conference facilities and it's far enough from here to escape any blast or assault.'

'Yes, sir,' Johann said. Dieter liked the idea at once. The headquarters of Germany's intelligence service, the Bundesnachrichtendienst or BND, was built like a fortress to protect the spies and their secrets.

'Most important, we only decided to relocate to the BND two minutes ago. The terrorists, if they exist, cannot possibly have anticipated it.' Again, the Interior Minister looked at them: beneath the veneer of confidence, his concern was plain. 'Do you think there is a real danger? Herr Frost?'

'I do not know, sir. But even if there is only a five per cent chance of an attack on the Reichstag, I agree we should move the Summit.'

'Good. Start the transfer immediately.' Pollex looked at Johann. 'What is the soonest we can start moving people?'

Dieter watched to see how the head of the SSU would respond to the jettisoning of over two years of detailed security planning. Johann did not even blink.

'We will have to talk to the spooks, sir, and set up transport and security. If you do not mind some rough edges, we could have the first cars waiting in the Dorotheenstrasse in ten minutes.' He turned to Dieter. 'I will supervise the close protection details and liase with the Secret Service. You go back to the Bunker and talk to the BND, the police and the transport co-ordinators.'

'I'm on it.' Dieter took out his mobile, already thinking about convoy orders.

Johann turned to the Interior Minister. 'Ten minutes. I suggest the Chancellor tells the delegates to get ready to move as soon as possible.'

Tilo Pollex nodded and turned back towards the plenary chamber.

Dieter ran towards the stairs. But before he could descend, he heard a shout. He turned.

Johann Frost was standing, his gun slung over his shoulder, in front of the crowd of children. He looked very alone.

'Dieter. If you see any sign of trouble beyond the perimeter I want the heavy security doors in the tunnel closed at once. We cannot take any chances.'

'What about the evacuation?'

'The evacuation goes ahead only if we and the Secret Service are one hundred percent confident the perimeter is secure. Call me as soon as you reach the Bunker.'

'I'll call.' Dieter risked a smile. 'Do you think you can keep the politicians under control for the next ten minutes?'

Uli Wenger smiled back. 'No need to worry,' he said. 'I know what I am doing.'

CHAPTER 20

ULI WENGER WATCHED THE DEPUTY HEAD OF THE SUMMIT Security Unit move away and fought the urge to gun him down. Dieter was dangerous. He knew the SSU team and the security set-up. He would be the first to understand what had happened. But killing him now was impossible. Both of them were visible on the closed-circuit monitors. Leaving the Reichstag had saved Dieter's life.

In the centre of the East Lobby, the children had gathered to enter the plenary chamber. One of the teachers was approaching. She saw an SSU officer, committed to protecting the Children's Summit. The perfect disguise. Uli flipped the D-mark in his pocket.

'How can I help you?' he said in English.

'They don't want us in there!' The teacher was a short, plump woman with curly blonde hair and a silver cross around her neck. She waved a piece of paper. 'We are meant to go into the chamber before the Summit starts, to sing the Song of Peace and Courage. What is happening?'

'There is a change of plan,' Uli said. 'The heads of state and government are discussing an emergency matter. It will not take long.'

'Emergency? What about the children?'

'I would like to suggest you keep the children where they are for a few minutes. There is no need to panic.'

The woman drew herself up to her full height. Beads of sweat had formed along her hairline. 'I am not panicking,' she said. 'But I need to know what is going on.'

The way the teacher squared up to him triggered deep-seated fears in Uli Wenger. But the sweat told him that beneath the bravado, she was scared. That helped him keep calm.

'Please stay with the children.'

To his relief, the woman sighed and turned away.

While he had been speaking, Uli had backed towards the edge of the lobby, where red tape on the floor marked the limits of the area visible to the closed-circuit cameras. He came to a halt at the base of the great steel propeller-blade meant to protect the summit participants from terrorist attack. He checked his watch. Then he switched on his microphone.

Now.

'Participants have assembled,' he said. 'All is secure.'

Uli knew his words would be heard by all twenty-three members of the Summit Security Unit. Twelve of these, including Dieter Kremp, were around the perimeter of the Safety Zone. The other eleven – including Uli – were inside the Reichstag. Of these eleven, seven were members of Uli's Chaos Team.

As Johann Frost, Uli had spent months touring Germany, interviewing hundreds of would-be members of the SSU. Provincial police forces, army and paramilitary units had encouraged their best officers to apply to join the new elite counter-terrorist force. Uli could tell within the first few minutes of an interview that an officer was highly-trained, disciplined, and loyal to his or her sworn duty to uphold the law. All these he rejected outright.

Only one applicant in every hundred had the spark of hate, resentment or gross arrogance which made Uli want to dig deeper. It had been from these precious misfits that he had recruited the eight fighters he needed to take hostage the Children's Summit. Then Petra Bleibtreu had wavered, giving Uli no alternative but to kill her.

Seven people were not enough.

Ranged against them inside the Reichstag were six Secret

Service agents and four members of the SSU who were not part of the Chaos Team. The Secret Service detail was led by David Kowalsky, an American close protection specialist of nine years' experience who never left the President's side. Outside the security bubble, swarming across the Safety Zone perimeter, were over one thousand more Secret Service agents and special forces troops.

That was why it had been vital to make the Reichstag impregnable.

One member of the Chaos Team would now be responding to his coded instruction ("All is secure") to begin the attack. Her assault would take sixty seconds. Until he heard her report back, he would not know whether the seizure of the Reichstag had been launched successfully. Uli stood behind the line of red at the foot of the futile propeller blade and waited.

Also waiting in the lobby were the children. Each had been selected to represent a city, a country or even a continent at the launch of the Summit. Their behaviour was correspondingly untypical: ninety-nine of them were standing still. The exception was a tiny black girl, who had taken advantage of her position at the front of the group to go strutting off around the vast red carpet where the dignitaries had gathered, her face fixed in a vacant grin. A few children were laughing. She looked absurd, yet somehow familiar. Uli watched her approach the Chinese girl, who giggled and covered her mouth. More children laughed. *She's imitating Maxim Wild*, Uli thought. He saw the teacher with the curly hair set off after her.

At that moment, inside his helmet, Uli heard a woman cough twice. He felt adrenalin flood his system. Dieter Kremp and the rest of the Summit Security Unit would hear someone who had inadvertently left her microphone on. Uli and the Chaos Team heard the team member with the phonetic codename Ida reporting that the assault had begun.

One insect was already dead.

Now it was Uli's turn. He had ninety seconds, compared

with Ida's sixty. His task was harder. But there was nothing he could not achieve. He, Uli Wenger, had been fooling the whole world since he was a child. Now would come the final glorious act in a lifetime of deception. He moved towards the stairs down to the main tunnel entrance and activated his own microphone.

'SSU, please ensure all microphones are off,' he said. 'Dieter, I want the first vehicles ready to go in five minutes, maximum.' He waited for his deputy to acknowledge, then continued down the stairs. He needed to keep Dieter busy a little longer. The cars would not be needed.

One minute earlier, in the third-floor comcen, Katia Vonhof, phonetic codename Ida, had not reacted to the words "All is secure". Her first priority was to do nothing which might excite the attention of the Secret Service agent standing next to her. His assignment was to maintain an overview of events in the Reichstag using the comcen monitors. He had no reason to be suspicious of the woman whom the Secret Service advance team had marked up as an SSU operative with particular responsibility for CCTV technology. But she had noticed that he stood well clear of her, away from the console, so that his arms were free at all times. His dark glasses made it impossible to be sure where he was looking.

On the console were six screens. The picture on each was divided into four, making it possible to observe the images from up to twenty-four CCTV cameras at any one time. As there were over one hundred cameras within the Reichstag and around the perimeter of the Safety Zone, the images were set to rotate between different views. The supervising technician could override the system manually to check anything which looked like trouble.

In the CCTV supervisory role which she had played as Katia Vonhof, Ida had set the images to change every fifteen seconds and had slaved the monitors in the comcen to those in the Bunker on the edge of the Safety Zone. Now, she watched until she saw an image of the comcen appear on one of the monitors, showing herself and the Secret Service agent standing at the console. Then she waited fifteen seconds until it disappeared. That gave her forty-five seconds.

She glanced towards the monitor nearest the Secret Service agent, as if she had spotted something.

The agent looked down at the screen.

Ida slid her pistol from a holster which she had oiled every day for the last two months, raised it to the Secret Service agent's head, and fired. The action took less than half a second. The American sensed the motion of her arm and spun towards her, his hand moving to his own firearm.

He died as he drew his weapon, his blood and brains decorating the plain white wall behind him.

Ida had planned their positions so that the agent's blood would not soil the electronic equipment on which their plan depended.

The agent dropped heavily to the ground. Ida fired two more 9mm shots into his face at point-blank range. It was not enough to kill them, Uli had said. They must look dead. Then she seized the body under the arms and dragged it to the door, beyond the field of the CCTV camera. Twenty seconds left. She holstered her weapon, turned back to the monitor, activated her microphone and coughed twice.

From the East Lobby, Uli Wenger ran down the stairs to the main tunnel entrance. He kept behind the red floor-tape at all times. At the base of the stairs, he found himself staring down the barrel of a gun.

'Jesus Christ.' The Secret Service agent guarding the tunnel entrance was a squat African American with a gleaming shaved head. 'I could have shot you.' He shook his head and lowered the weapon. 'Kowalsky's going apeshit about the unnecessary voice traffic. He's closing the tunnel doors.'

'I have dealt with the microphones,' Uli said. 'We cannot abort the evacuation because somebody coughed.'

'Well, he's ordered them closed,' the agent said.

Uli saw he had a problem. The Secret Service man was

spooked: he stood with his back to the wall, gun in hand. His behaviour had unnerved the three SSU men guarding the tunnel entrance. They too had their weapons drawn. All of them were trained combat specialists on high alert; any one of them could obstruct what he had planned. Here at the tunnel entrance, all of them were in full view of the CCTV monitors. Uli checked his watch. Twenty seconds to go.

He activated his microphone and called Christian Gulas, the SSU officer who was manning the console in the Bunker.

'Do not, repeat not, close the tunnel doors. I will talk to Kowalsky.'

'What did you say?' The black Secret Service agent did not understand German.

'I said to hold closing the doors until I talk to Kowalsky. There is no danger here.'

The agent frowned and turned to look down the tunnel. At the far end, the two armed officers from the Bundespolizei, the Federal Police, were crouched down in their concrete booth. Both were looking the other way, towards Jakob-Kaiser House North.

'Video capture board is down.' It was Ida, in the comcen. *'We have lost monitor coverage. We are tackling it.'*

Uli stepped up behind the Secret Service agent and looked past him along the tunnel. 'Maybe we should close the doors,' he said. Then he reached into his pocket and detonated the explosive charge which Chaos Team member Gustav, alias Peter Sturm, had planted that morning under the counter of the security booth at the far end of the corridor.

Dieter Kremp was running up the stairs from the basement of Jakob-Kaiser House South when he heard someone cough. It struck him as odd that any member of the SSU could be so unprofessional as to leave a microphone activated. Perhaps he should issue a reprimand. But surely Johann would do so.

'SSU, please ensure all microphones are off.' That was Johann,

all right. *'Dieter, I want the first vehicles ready in five minutes, maximum.'*

'Roger that,' Dieter said. He ran to the top of the stairs, out onto the Dorotheenstrasse, and surveyed the Safety Zone around the Reichstag. It was reassuringly empty. It had begun to rain, and he could see movement on the towers of the Reichstag as the snipers covered up. The impenetrable steel curve of the Safety Zone perimeter curved off into the distance. A GSG 9 helicopter hovered overhead. Total security. He heard Johann telling Christian Gulas in the Bunker to keep the tunnel doors open. In a few minutes, the Reichstag would be empty.

Dieter had almost reached the Bunker when he heard Katia Vonhof's voice.

'Video capture board is down. We have lost monitor coverage. We are tackling it.'

For a long moment, Dieter did not breathe. It was inconceivable that the main video capture board could fail, blanking out every monitor in the Safety Zone. It could only have been sabotaged. *The Reichstag was under attack.*

Dieter Kremp turned and began to sprint back towards the entrance tunnel.

The Bundespolizei security booth in the main Reichstag tunnel was made of nested slabs of reinforced concrete. Gustav had placed the bomb with care. Most of the blast was channelled upwards or back into Jakob-Kaiser House North, killing instantly the two Bundespolizei officers manning the post. But eighty metres away, where Uli was standing at the Reichstag end of the tunnel, the shock was still immense.

The SSU officers in front of Uli were used to explosions. All three, recognising that some kind of attack was happening, fell to the ground and trained their submachine guns down the tunnel. The Secret Service agent went down on one knee, aiming his pistol at the site of the explosion.

Uli was still standing. One of the SSU men tugged at his leg. 'Main tunnel under attack! Get down!'

'*Close the doors!*' Uli Wenger shouted into his microphone as he drew his pistol. '*Close the –* ' Then, holding his weapon at arm's length, he fired four shots in rapid succession. The first killed the Secret Service agent whose kneeling position and hand-gun posed the most immediate danger to Uli. The three SSU fighters lying on the floor with their submachine guns extended down the tunnel stood no chance: Uli shot all three in the back of the head. Then he fired a further shot into each body, re-loaded his pistol and watched as, activated by Ida in the comcen, the great steel doors sealed the tunnel. The stage was set for the main event in the plenary chamber. Uli turned and climbed the stairs.

The plenary chamber of the Reichstag was a lofty, light-saturated auditorium. Normally it was filled with blue seats and black desks arranged in rising tiers for meetings of the German parliament. For the Children's Summit, the front few rows of seats had been removed and a horseshoe-shaped conference table installed, its two ends curving towards the speaker's podium which formed the focus of the chamber. The table was covered in a sky-blue cloth, custom-made for this event, which hung low on both sides. This was to ensure propriety for those top-table participants who wore skirts. It also concealed from view the mass of wiring which connected the microphones, headphones and other electronic equipment on which the smooth functioning of the Summit depended.

On one side of the table the heads of state and government were gathered. The President of the United States and the Prime Minister of Great Britain shared a joke and engaged in a show of togetherness as they took their seats, which for reasons of alphabetical order and mutual convenience were next to one another. Opposite, arranged in such a way as to imply an adversarial relationship, sat the eight business leaders.

Behind the table, in the first two rows of blue seats, sat three delegation members from each country and seven German cabinet ministers. The latter were due to leave the Summit after the children's song and the opening address. Also in the plenary chamber were four members of the SSU belonging to Uli's Chaos Team; and four US Secret Service agents.

The President's close-protection detail had been Uli Wenger's prime concern ever since the US government had forced their inclusion in his security concept. The agents were armed, highly-trained professionals. The presence of no less than four of them in the plenary chamber posed an immense challenge. That was why Uli had concentrated over half of his team in the same room. Any more would have been impossible to explain. Any less would have had no chance of eliminating the Secret Service agents at the start of the attack.

The Chaos Team contingent in the plenary chamber was led by Peter Sturm, phonetic codename Gustav. With him were Lukas and Phillip Klein, alias Viktor and Wilhelm, the two brothers from the Rhineland who were the best marksmen in the team; and Nicole Braun, alias Dora, a Sudeten German with a quick intellect and a streak of independence. When Ida had coughed twice, each of the four Chaos Team members had begun tracking a separate Secret Service agent. The instant the bomb exploded in the tunnel, all four were to draw their weapons and open fire simultaneously. Success depended on the Secret Service team suspecting nothing until that moment.

But David Kowalsky, the head of the Secret Service detail, was already on his guard. The experienced agent was familiar with every aspect of the security regime for the Reichstag, and hypersensitive to any irregularity. As soon as he heard someone cough, he felt instinctively that something was wrong.

'Not good,' he told the rest of his team on their independent, encoded radio frequency. 'That's not in the script. Could be a signal. Barry, tell the SSU to close the tunnel doors. Plenary team, secure the chamber entrances. Rojas, switch the CCTV cameras to manual and check the perimeter, if the SSU aren't already doing it.'

'Roger that.'

'Roger that.'

'Roger that.'

'Roger that.'

The last-named agent, Antonio Rojas, did not hear Kowalsky's instruction. He had already been shot dead by Ida in the comcen.

Kowalsky noticed the omission at once.

'Rojas? Do you copy? Rojas.'

There was no answer. Kowalsky placed his hand on the butt of the pistol in his shoulder-holster. Two things not in the script. That meant a crisis. Behind him he heard the German Interior Minister, Tilo Pollex, announcing to the conference participants that the entire Children's Summit was to be shifted immediately to a new location. There was a groan of disbelief from the politicians and business leaders, and everyone started talking at once.

Kowalsky felt a flicker of relief. The change of venue was a complication, fraught with challenges and risks. But the great stone mass of the Reichstag suddenly felt more like a tomb than a fortress. *The tunnel doors.* He'd just told the SSU to close them. How long would they take to open? He heard the voice of Johann Frost, on the SSU frequency, say something in German. His own name, Kowalsky. Was the SSU chief ordering the doors to be kept open? If so, that was good.

He scanned the room for danger. Kowalsky himself was standing directly behind the President at the conference table, so that his own Kevlar-clad body would act as a shield in the event of an attack. Several people around the table had stood to leave the room. But the four members of the Summit Security Unit had not reacted to the announcement about the evacuation.

One of them, whom Kowalsky knew as Peter Sturm, was looking straight at him. Or was he looking at the President?

At that moment, in the third floor comcen, Ida hit a switch. Every monitor screen in the Bunker and throughout the Safety Zone went blank. Then she made an announcement, her voice steady.

'Video capture board is down. We have lost monitor coverage. We are tackling it.'

Kowalsky made an instant decision.

'Plenary team, we are extracting the President from the Reichstag immediately,' he said. 'Repeat, we are extracting the President.' But as he spoke, he heard the sound of an explosion. There was no shockwave. A grenade, maybe. From the direction of the tunnel.

'Secure entrances – ' Kowalsky began to shout. But the words took too long to say.

To his right, he was aware of the three Secret Service agents who were guarding the entrances to the plenary chamber turning towards the lobby. In his ear, an SSU man was shouting in German, something about the tunnel. Behind him, conference participants were standing, or shouting instructions. Several junior delegation members were moving towards the table. The German Chancellor and Interior Minister were both trying to make calls on their mobile telephones. Behind Kowalsky, the British Prime Minister and the President remained seated, their heads close together.

Kowalsky's gaze was fixed on Peter Sturm. The moment the bomb exploded he saw the huge SSU man's hand move towards his holster. The Secret Service agent was aware of the other SSU officers moving too, but his focus was on Sturm and the way he seemed to be staring at the President.

Could the SSU man himself be a threat?

David Kowalsky spent a minimum of three hours a week on the firing range. As the SSU man brought his weapon up to fire, the Secret Service agent was a fraction of a second ahead of him. But as he squeezed the trigger, something hit his back. *The President.* The President was standing up. Half the delegates at the table were scrambling to their feet, but Kowalsky didn't care about them. He pulled his left arm behind him and brought it down hard on the President's shoulder, forcing the politician back down into the chair behind the bulk of the Secret Service agent's body. Unbalanced by this action, Kowalsky's shooting arm jerked up and his shot disappeared into the upholstery of a chair in the empty spectator's gallery.

At that moment Chaos Team members Dora, Gustav, Viktor and Wilhelm opened fire with their hand-guns. Each had a separate target. The three Secret Service agents facing the entrances were exposed. But David Kowalsky was already ducking for cover, dragging the President with him. Gustav's first shot grazed his scalp. As Kowalsky pulled the President to the ground, Gustav's second shot caught the Secret Service agent full in the chest, leaving him winded and bruised, but – thanks to his body armour – uninjured. The third shot caught Kowalsky in his right shoulder as he tried to pull the President under the conference table. The shock of the impact sent the agent's handgun spinning away from him. Even under fire, Kowalsky was conscious of a remarkable fact. The assassin was shooting at him, not the President.

Gustav saw the Secret Service agent and the President disappear under the hanging fabric of the table covering and stepped behind a heavy black desk. It would be a difficult shot for Kowalsky from under the table, through the legs of the G8 leaders, assuming he had a second gun. But Gustav did not take chances.

He waved his Heckler & Koch MP7 submachine gun towards the delegates. 'Nobody move,' he shouted in English. 'We will kill you if you move.' He was aware of Dora, Viktor and Wilhelm running down the stairs to finish off their targets. But his own failure to kill Kowalsky had left the situation dangerously unpredictable. Gustav crouched down behind a blue chair and activated his microphone.

'Explosion in Reichstag tunnel,' he said.

Uli Wenger was running through the East Lobby when he heard Gustav's voice.

'Explosion in Reichstag tunnel.'

There was a problem in the plenary chamber. It must be the Secret Service agents. Uli ran on. Several teachers and children were watching him. For them, he was still Johann Frost, SSU chief, rushing to investigate the gunfire.

As Uli entered the plenary chamber, he was sheltered from sight by two security screens. He glanced around to check no-one could see him, then reached for the silk face-mask he had ready, folded, in his pocket. But before he could pull it out, a hand grasped his shoulder. He spun round. It was the blonde teacher who had approached him earlier. She was holding the hand of the black girl who had been imitating Maxim Wild. The child barely reached the teacher's waist.

'That explosion. The shooting.' The teacher was making an effort to sound calm. 'What's going on?'

'I do not know.' Uli looked at the child with interest. 'How are the kids?'

'OK, I guess.' The teacher, noticing they were out of sight of the others, lowered her voice. 'Some of them are scared.'

Uli nodded. 'Of course. How about this one?' He pointed at the black girl. 'Where is she from?'

'Jasmine's from Washington DC.' The teacher turned towards the child. 'She's cool. Aren't you, dear?'

'I'm cool. And I'm pleased to meet you,' Jasmine said to Uli Wenger, and held out her hand. She had the darkest skin Uli had ever seen. Her hair was braided in neat rows, secured with tiny twists of red cotton.

Uli looked at the teacher and child. They had seen his

face. If he took them with him into the plenary chamber, he was sentencing them to death. But so what? Their lives were worthless anyway. And if there was a problem with the Secret Service agents, the child could come in handy.

'I need you for a moment.' He grabbed the girl's hand. 'Come with me, please.'

'Wait. No,' the teacher said.

'It is important.' The teacher's attempt to exert authority brought a fog of anxiety boiling up in Uli.

'I am coming with you.' The teacher was pulling Jasmine away from him.

'You're hurting my hand,' the girl said.

The fear in the child's voice strengthened Uli. He took out his pistol and pointed it at the teacher. 'Come, now, both of you. And make no noise.' He took out his black face-mask and pulled it on.

The teacher stared at Uli, the blood draining from her face. 'Don't hurt her.' She released the girl's hand. 'God will judge you.'

Uli said nothing. He used his access code to open the bullet-proof glass door, then pushed the teacher ahead of him into the plenary chamber, dragging the child after him.

Within, he saw a scene he had imagined many times. Fifteen of the most powerful people on earth were seated around the narrow conference table. All were as still as waxworks, staring at him. Two more rows of chairs held what he knew to be thirty-one other individuals: members of the German cabinet, officials and ambassadors. Johann Frost had pushed hard for the size of each delegation to be slashed to the minimum, then cut some more. For security reasons, he had said. Forty-seven hostages were at the limit of what Uli and the Chaos Team could manage. But the number would fall. The children and teachers must be disposed of.

Gustav, too, had donned his mask. 'Kowalsky has dragged

the President under the table,' he said in German. 'The Secret Service man is wounded. He may be armed.'

The big man and the three other members of the Chaos Team in the plenary chamber had taken up position high in the seating which shelved upwards on each side. It would minimise the risk of being caught by friendly fire, and increase their protection should Kowalsky attempt to shoot at them. Their four Heckler & Koch MP7s were capable of firing the one hundred and sixty rounds in their magazines in under three seconds.

Uli felt an overwhelming sense of power.

'OK.' He unholstered his pistol and sank to his knees next to the little black girl. He spoke clearly, in English, so everyone in the room could hear. Especially Kowalsky and the President. 'Jasmine, you are from Washington DC, is that right?'

'Yes.' Very quietly.

'I will now fire a bullet over your head. The barrel of the gun may spit out some hot gas, which can burn your face. Close your eyes.'

The girl closed her eyes. 'Please don't shoot me, sir.'

'That is up to Mr Kowalsky and the President.' Uli turned towards the conference table. 'You have five seconds to come out.' He waited a second.

'Five.' Jasmine opened her eyes wide, staring at Uli's masked face. Then she screwed them tightly shut.

'Four.' The blonde teacher with the curly hair opened her mouth to scream, then held back, seeing the gun at the little girl's head.

'Three.' Around the table, the heads of state and government stared at Uli. They had just seen three Secret Service agents gunned down by what appeared to be members of the Summit Security Unit. Now a masked man in the same uniform was threatening a child. Would anyone dare stand up to him?

'Two.' Under the table, Kowalsky peered through a gap in the blue tablecloth. He could see neither the newly-arrived terrorist nor the girl he was threatening.

'One.' Next to Kowalsky, the President of the United States glimpsed Jasmine's head above a seat-back, with the barrel of the pistol almost resting on it. The man holding the gun was hidden from view.

'Zero.'

The pistol roared. Jasmine screamed, then screamed again and again until she ran out of breath.

'Stop it, for pity's sake,' a voice said in German. Tilo Pollex, the German Interior Minister, had risen from his seat. 'She is a child. Shoot me, if you want.'

Uli looked at the minister with a curious smile. 'I shall gladly shoot you,' he said. 'If you do not sit down at once.'

'Leave the girl,' Pollex said.

'Sit down.'

'First, leave the girl.'

Uli replied by turning his pistol towards Pollex, taking careful aim, and shooting him in the thigh. The politician gasped and fell back into his seat, his face contorted in agony.

'Good.' Uli turned back to Jasmine, whose face was grey with fear. He took her ear between the finger and thumb of his left hand, and with his right hand placed the mouth of the barrel against the exposed flap of flesh. 'This time,' he announced, 'I will shoot through Jasmine's ear. This will hurt her, and afterwards she will not hear so good. People under the table, you have five seconds to show yourself. Five – '

'David. We have to come out.' The voice of the President of the United States was unmistakeable. 'We cannot let him shoot the girl.'

'Roger that.' There was a stirring of table-coverings. The President and David Kowalsky appeared at the far end of the horseshoe. The Secret Service agent gripped the edge of the table and hauled himself to his feet. His right shoulder was soaked in blood. With his left hand, he helped the President to rise. 'I am sorry.'

'It is not your fault, David.' The President's voice was sombre.

'Stand away from the other hostages,' Uli said to Kowalsky. 'Unless you want them to be killed too.'

Kowalsky squared his shoulders and walked slowly away from the table.

'Do not shoot.' The German Chancellor spoke with dignity from a place at the table opposite a plastic place-marker bearing the Children's Summit logo and the word GERMANY. 'Handcuff him. He is no danger.'

Uli took no notice. 'Pistol,' he said to Gustav.

The big man raised his weapon and, without speaking, fired three times at the helpless form of David Kowalsky. Then he descended the stairs and, at point-blank range, fired two times more. The silence after the shots was absolute. Even Jasmine's sobs were silent, hidden behind her hand.

Uli Wenger addressed his captive audience.

'Now,' he said in English. 'I will tell you what we will do next.'

CHAPTER 21

HELEN WATCHED ON RAM'S LAPTOP AS THE DELEGATES ENTERED the plenary chamber. Then she returned to her office. Thank God the Summit had started. Now she only had her life to sort out, starting with the damages claim. She thought of the trauma counsellor at the hospital, tearing up her card. Dieter, scowling at her in the Reichstag. Jason Short, saying that anything that went wrong at the Summit would be her fault.

She shook her head. Maybe nothing did matter very much. But it would be good to talk to Nigel tonight. What would she say if he suggested getting back together? She pictured herself sipping a glass of wine in the kitchen while he pottered around the hob, chatting about politics and movies. The image was delightful. But were there any children in the picture? And where was Helen working?

She looked around her office. Life was impossible. Nothing could change that. But sometimes talking helped.

At her desk, she kicked off her shoes and started sorting through her e-mails. It was still oppressively hot. Maybe a thunderstorm would clear the air. She quickly deleted dozens of messages, including several old ones from Elaine Hunter urging Helen to come to the meeting with Short, and from Short himself, threatening dire consequences if Helen did not appear forthwith. She smiled. If she worried about what Short might write in her next annual appraisal, she would have no time for anything else.

More disturbing was a message from the Foreign Office

Press Office drawing her attention to a story in the Times online edition, with a couple of hyperlinks. Helen clicked on the first to find a factual account of the cases which the Victims' Legal Support Group had launched in Germany and the UK. There were four actions altogether, two in each country, each for fifty million euro. In Germany, the defendants were the embassy and Helen herself. In the UK, the targets were Helen and the Foreign Office.

Helen called Julia Strang. The young Foreign Office lawyer was not answering. The Germany desk officer was permanently engaged. Helen's contact in Press Office picked up, only to shout 'Can't talk now. Sorry' and slam the phone down. All busy with the Summit, presumably. Helen frowned. Was the Office backing her up? Or not?

She clicked on the second hyperlink. It led to a leader article, also in the Times, entitled "Blood on Her Hands". Helen read it with a sense of growing horror. The piece urged the British government to explore fully allegations that the Post Security Officer at the British embassy in Berlin, Helen Gale, had failed to warn those organising a demonstration in the street outside that a terrorist attack might be imminent. If embassy employees were to blame for deaths and injuries from a bomb blast everyone but the demonstrators had known was on the cards, the FCO should not try to shield them by claiming immunity. "Diplomats are as human as the rest of us", the leader concluded. "Like the rest of us, they should be held to account for their mistakes."

Helen gripped the edge of her desk. Times leader articles were not attributed to individual journalists. But one of the leader-writers at the newspaper was Nigel. Could her husband be so vindictive? He had said he cared about her. He had promised to intercede on her behalf. Now this. There was no point in seeing him tonight. She dialled his mobile. But there was no service.

She checked her phone messages. The last was from a

kindly-sounding woman in the Foreign Office Medical and Welfare Unit.

'I'm calling for Helen Gale in Berlin, in response to a message from her reporting officer, Mr Jason Short. Mr Short has suggested that some time off might help you cope with emotional difficulties you've been having after the break-up of your marriage. He also mentioned pressure at work. If you'd like to talk about it, here's my number.'

Helen gritted her teeth. It was tempting to call the woman back, to give her some home truths about Jason Short. But the priority now was to ensure the Summit was a success. She turned on her television to catch the end of the opening ceremony. At that moment, in the street outside, it began to rain.

'How are you coping with your mental ordeal?' Ram Kuresh had wafted into the room. 'I am so sorry. Is the stress of my presence too much for you?'

'It's no laughing matter,' Helen said. 'Stress can be deadly. In fact, I think I might murder Jason if he doesn't lay off me.'

'Clearly you are deranged already.' Ram sat down on the end of Helen's desk. 'And you are turning to drink, as the future ambassador to Bangkok has already pointed out.'

'Jason might not get Bangkok. Someone with some leadership skills might apply. The ambo won't give him much of a write-up.'

'No worse than the appraisal you are likely to receive from Jason. What is the latest on the damages claim? Would you like me to arrange a whip-round in the embassy?'

'I've only heard what's on the news.' Helen's telephone was ringing. 'Hello?'

'What are you watching?' Ram moved towards the television. 'What on earth is happening in the Reichstag?'

'Helen? Is that you?'

'Mum?'

'Oh, darling. You poor thing. How awful!'

'What is it?'

'I've just had a man here from the Daily Dispatch. Freddy

Acton, his name was. He says you killed someone and they're taking you to court. It's not true is it, darling? Tell me it isn't.' Her mother's voice dwindled into an awful silence.

'Mum. It's OK. I've done nothing wrong.'

'That's not what he said. Fifty million euros, he said they want. That's an awful lot of money. Oh, Helen.'

Helen was conscious of Ram pulling up a chair in front of the screen.

'Don't worry about it,' she told her mother. 'What did he want?'

'He wanted to know about you. What you were like. Said it was wrong, them writing all those bad things about you. He showed me some of the things they wrote. On the Internet. He had a tablet.'

'What did you tell him? Did you keep a note of what you said?'

'A note? What for?'

'In case he lies about what you told him.'

'Why should he lie? I gave him a slice of cake.'

'Well, at least that's something.' Helen saw Ram waving his hand. 'I'm sorry, Mum. I've got to go.'

'Look after yourself, love.'

'Don't worry. You too, and don't talk to any more journalists.'

By the time Helen had concluded the call, Ram was flicking through the channels.

'It seems something has disrupted the TV transmission from the opening ceremony,' he said. 'The Cable News Network is talking about a technical failure.'

'Put on ARD.'

The principal German television channel had been transmitting the opening ceremony. Now Helen saw a commentator in a studio, speaking in the monotone adopted by broadcast journalists obliged to speak live on air with nothing to say.

'That is the situation now. Yes. We are reporting to you live from our studio at the edge of the Safety Zone. Our technicians are

working to restore coverage of the opening ceremony of the Children's Summit in the Reichstag from our cameras inside the summit venue. A few minutes ago, the leaders of the world's major industrial nations were greeted at the Reichstag by the federal Chancellor…'

Pictures appeared of the oversized Secret Service agents climbing the stairs from the tunnel, the US President barely visible behind them.

'We've seen this,' Helen said. She felt the hairs on her forearm standing up. 'Something's happening.'

'Indeed. But what?'

Helen's phone was ringing again.

'Hello? Is that Helen Gale? This is Alexander Graves, foreign editor at the Times. I'm trying to reach our correspondent Nigel Ferguson.'

'He's not here. Good bye.'

'Wait! It's urgent. We've been preparing for months for Nigel to be embedded in this bloody summit. He's meant to be tweeting out a running commentary, you know, a sitrep each time the drinks run out or the PM caves. But since the TV pictures went off, we haven't heard a word.'

'Maybe his computer's crashed.' Helen didn't believe it.

'Nigel's computers don't crash.'

'Did he write today's leader? Blood on my hands?'

There was a pause at the end of the line. 'Don't take it seriously. By tomorrow, everyone will have forgotten.'

'I won't have. Come on. Did he write it?'

'No comment.' Another pause. 'You can ask Nigel, if you want.'

'How can I do that? He's off-air.' Helen felt as if her hand might crush the receiver. 'It matters, because I have to know whether I hate my husband or not.'

'OK.' Alexander Graves sounded nonplussed. 'He didn't write it. But we did run it past him.'

'What did he say?'

'He told us to tone it down.'

'And did you?'

Another pause. 'If you hear anything from Nigel, call me.'

The phone went dead, then rang again immediately. Helen stared at it. A moment ago, she'd been cursing Nigel. Now she felt grateful to him.

'We need more telephones.' Ram was moving towards the door. 'And people. I will start getting calls put through to the conference room.'

'OK. I'll move down there once I've answered this.' Helen picked up the phone.

It was Basil Nutter.

'Thank God,' he said. 'Every journalist in Fleet Street is calling me. Not that there are any journalists in Fleet Street, these days. Did you know you're constantly engaged?'

'What is it, Basil?'

'There's a story about a bomb in the Reichstag. Underground.'

'What?' Helen jumped to her feet. 'They've blown up the Reichstag?'

'No. Not that big. Nothing to see. But loud enough to hear outside, apparently. Everyone in London wants to know where the Prime Minister is.'

'The Prime Minister is in the bloody Reichstag, of course. Or have they been evacuated?'

'That's what I was hoping you'd tell me.'

Helen spun round to look at the television. 'There's a picture of the Reichstag on the telly.' It was a relief to see the familiar outline of the dome and the four towers.

'I'm looking at it. There's no sign of anyone leaving the building.' The press officer's voice was rising.

'If they leave, they'll come through the tunnels. I'll call Dieter.'

'Not much good us being here, really, if all we can do is watch the telly,' Basil said.

'Goodbye, Basil.'

But as soon as she slammed the phone down it rang again. Of

course, Helen realised. There could be dozens of people trying to ring her. Who would be next?

'Helen? Congratulations. No increased danger, you said.'

'Is that Danny McGregor?'

'I'm calling from the Cabinet Office Briefing Room on behalf of the Deputy Prime Minister. Where's your ambassador?'

'In the Reichstag.'

'Still? The Germans told us it was being evacuated.'

'I don't know.'

'Do you know where the Prime Minister is?'

'No. All the heads of state and government arrived five minutes ago at the Reichstag.'

'What about this alleged bomb? Can you confirm it?'

'No.'

Danny McGregor sighed. 'What is the point of having an embassy in Berlin if you don't know any more than we do here in London?'

'If you get off the phone I can try and find out for you.'

'OK. You know what UPTAKE is?'

'Yes. I heard it's been activated.'

'The Foreign Office is putting together the advance team now. People from the Home Office, a Scotland Yard negotiator, some spooks, a couple of SAS people. They'll be with you in a few hours.'

'Is this an open line?'

'We don't have time for that now. The main SAS team, with all the kit, will take a bit longer. We're talking to the Germans about clearance for them and the advance team to fly in.'

'Did you know someone from the SAS is already half-way here?'

'What? Who is it? No, don't tell me, I'll check at this end. How's he getting to Berlin?'

'Easyjet, I think. And it's a she.'

'Christ. Well, tell her not to do anything daft. The Deputy Prime Minister keeps using words like co-ordination and control.'

'Dream on. What are the Americans doing?'

'Getting ready to invade Berlin, I think. The CIA and the Pentagon are talking major logistics. Someone from the London embassy is due into COBRA any minute. But I don't think co-ordinating with other people is their top priority.'

'How about the Russians?'

'God knows.'

'At least they have experience of invading Berlin.' Helen was trying to think. 'Don't forget the whole German government is in the Reichstag too.'

'So what? When was the last terrorist attack on the German government?'

'I still can't see how any terrorists could have entered the building.'

'Well, someone seems to have planted a bomb inside. And now all communications have been broken off.' There was a pause as Danny McGregor spoke to someone in London. Helen heard shouting in the background.

'No-one can have got in,' she said. 'It's physically impossible.'

'No time, Helen. How big is our delegation in the Reichstag?'

'Tiny. Just four people. For security reasons.'

'Worked well, didn't it? Who are they, apart from the PM?'

'Sir Timothy Speed from No.10 – '

'Tim Speed is in there?' For the first time, Danny McGregor sounded shaken. 'I suppose he would be.'

'Plus our ambassador, Leonard Lennox, and – ' Helen stopped. 'Who's the fourth?'

'It's Nigel Ferguson. The embedded journalist.' She could hardly speak.

Danny McGregor seemed not to notice. 'Where's the rest of the delegation? Hello? Helen?'

She fought to focus. 'The note-takers, translators and every-one else are in Jakob-Kaiser House South, two blocks over from the Reichstag. They're – '

'I'm hanging up. The TV's back on.'

Helen rushed to the television. The paralysed news studio had vanished. In its place was a glistening red mass which she could not at first identify.

The camera zoomed out. The red mass was the exploded skull of a tall man in a dark suit, lying on the ground with his feet facing away from the camera. He looked not so much dead as destroyed. Helen felt light-headed. It must be one of the US Secret Service agents. What had happened in the Reichstag? Where was Nigel? The Prime Minister? The President? The camera began moving unsteadily along a row of bodies. Helen counted six in dark suits. All the heads seemed crushed or broken; a grotesque parade of naked flesh.

The seventh body wore the grey uniform of the SSU. So did the eighth, and the ninth. The camera was panning out, now, bodies were piled on top of one another, all in SSU uniforms. Was that Dieter, lying there? The first SSU corpse had a gaping wound where his face should have been. *Count them.* There were twenty-four members of the Summit Security Unit. No, twenty-three. Petra Bleibtreu was already dead. How many had been on duty at the summit venue?

The television company had placed some text at the bottom of the picture: CHILDREN'S SUMMIT: LIVE PICTURES FROM THE REICHSTAG. SOME PEOPLE MAY FIND THESE SCENES UPSETTING.

Helen licked her lips. Where were the children? How many bodies were in that heap at the end? Had they been executed there? No. There was too little blood on the floor. Maybe the bodies had been moved. But why? Six Secret Service agents, plus ten or more SSU officers. That accounted for most, or maybe all, of the security personnel inside the building. The rest were guarding the perimeter, or on the towers of the Reichstag, or on adjacent buildings with the sharp-shooters.

For a moment, Helen felt relief. *They've only shot the security people.* Then shock. *Terrorists have seized the Summit.*

She lowered herself into a chair. There had been a cataclysmic failure. She was partly to blame. What could she do now? She gripped the arms of her seat. She wasn't a soldier. She was an analyst.

So. Analyse this.

There was a flicker and a chubby woman with curly blonde hair appeared, sitting in one of the blue chairs of the plenary chamber. She looked catatonic with shock; the front of her dress was wet, as though something had been spilt down it. A silver crucifix hung round her neck. The woman glanced off-camera, then began to speak.

'My name is Ashley Anderson. I am a teacher at the John F Kennedy School in Berlin. I have the following message from the Action Group for Peace and Justice.'

CHAPTER 22

DIETER KREMP WAS SPRINTING BACK TOWARDS THE SECURITY barrier under the Dorotheenstrasse when he heard the blast. *'Main tunnel under attack! Get down!'* The words inside his helmet were so clear, Dieter flinched. He recognised the voice at once as one of the SSU team guarding the Reichstag end of the main tunnel.

'*Close the doors!*' That was Johann Frost. '*Close the* – '

Shots rang out. Johann's voice fell silent.

Dieter ran up to the barrier and placed his eye to the retina scanner. The door slid open to reveal two of the SSU team assigned to the perimeter of the Safety Zone. Each had a Heckler & Koch trained on him.

'Lower those weapons!' Dieter did not move until he was sure they had recognised him.

'There's been a small explosion in the primary tunnel,' one fighter said. She seemed calm. 'Could be a diversion. All monitors are still off. We are maintaining perimeter security.'

'Good work.' Dieter felt a spike of confidence. He activated his microphone. 'All SSU personnel remain at post. Prevent access to the Safety Zone until further notice. I am investigating the explosion.'

He left the barrier and ran through the basement of the deserted Jakob-Kaiser House North, beneath the suspended rowing boats. A bomb in the Safety Zone? It was impossible. The SSU had swept the summit venue repeatedly with electronic chemical profiling equipment, backed up with old-fashioned sniffer dogs. Peter Sturm had completed a final sweep this morning, after the security tour had been broken off. Could a delegate have smuggled something in? But the alarms at the entrance to the Safety Zone could detect even the tiniest quantity of explosive. *Main tunnel under attack.* What had the American journalist said about a suicide assault? But that was impossible too. Any attackers would have had to penetrate the Safety Zone to reach the tunnel. There was no sign that the perimeter had been breached.

The entrance to the tunnel was ahead of him now, a sharp turn to the left. The floor was littered with debris, including a large pink and black work of art shredded by the blast. His back to the wall, Dieter edged towards the corner where the tunnel opened into the basement, cocked his pistol, and listened.

Nothing.

He could see into the first few metres of the passage. The acoustics seemed wrong. Had something been destroyed in the blast? The explosion had taken out the lights, leaving the tunnel entrance a gloomy cavern with a smear of smoke across the ceiling. The bomb must have gone off around the corner. Where the Bundespolizei guards had been stationed.

In the year leading up to the Children's Summit, Johann Frost had often invited Dieter Kremp to sit down with him and try to enter the minds of the terrorists who opposed them.

'Put yourself inside their heads,' Johann would say. 'Imagine you are trying to murder the G8 leaders. Assume you know everything about our security regime. How would you do it?'

'But terrorists are fanatics,' Dieter had said. They do not think the way we do.'

'Terrorists are people,' Johann had replied. 'Some are brilliant, some are fools. We have to stay one step ahead of the smart ones.'

Now Johann was dead. Somehow, a terrorist had got a step ahead of him.

Standing beside the tunnel entrance, Dieter tried to imagine how he would secure the area if he had seized the Reichstag. A sniper at the far end of the passage? Booby traps? Suddenly it was obvious. He dropped to his knees and stole a quick, waist-level look down the tunnel. Then he stepped into the centre of the passage and cursed.

The wreckage of the Bundespolizei security post he had expected. The terrorists had entered the building down the tunnel, that was clear. There had been a fire-fight, and a grenade blast. The corpses of two guards lay on the tunnel floor, their bodies hurled from the security booth by the force of the explosion. Their deaths were a grim reality. But the sight of the mighty steel security doors which blocked the tunnel was worse.

The Summit Security Unit had trained for the sealing of the tunnel doors a dozen times. But Dieter had always been on the inside, with Johann Frost, preparing to repel an imaginary terrorist assault. Now Johann was gone, Dieter was outside, and terrorists had somehow gained control of the building the doors were meant to protect.

Dieter glared at the wall of steel. Whoever was in the building had no need to mount a guard here. The barriers at each end of the passage were seventy metres apart. The quantity of explosives needed to destroy either set would threaten the fabric of the tunnel itself; to attack both doors simultaneously was impossible. Whoever had seized the Reichstag was occupying a building which Johann, Dieter and the Threat Assessment Committee had done their utmost to render impregnable.

How could Johann's carefully-constructed concept have failed so utterly? Was Johann to blame? Dieter shook his head. Johann Frost had designed a perfect security plan. He had died defending the Reichstag. He could not be at fault.

Dieter Kremp spat on the floor and turned back towards the Bunker. He was in charge now. It was time to reassert control.

CHAPTER 23

HELEN GAZED AT THE WHITE-FACED TEACHER ON HER TV screen. Ashley Anderson was nodding, as if listening to someone. Did she know half the world was watching her? The blonde woman glanced off-camera. There was a flicker, and a glass of water appeared in her hand.

It's not live. The thought deepened Helen's foreboding. How could the terrorists have produced an edited video message within minutes of seizing control of the Reichstag?

'First of all, I want to say that none of the children has been hurt.' Ashley Anderson was staring into the lens of the camera. 'The Action Group for Peace and Justice regrets their suffering and will release them as soon as possible.

'Second, I am to tell you that the Action Group has taken control of the communications centre in the Reichstag. They are using existing CCTV cameras to monitor all approaches to the summit venue at roof, ground level and sub-ground level. They are also observing every corridor and room within the Reichstag complex. From now on, all areas monitored by CCTV cameras are prohibited for anyone except hostages released from this building. If anyone else enters the prohibited area, hostages will be executed.'

Ashley Anderson took a sip of water before continuing. 'The Action Group for Peace and Justice has a list of the VIPs held hostage in this building, including the President of the United States; the President of Russia; the Chancellor of Germany; and the British Prime Minister. That list sets out the order in which the hostages will be killed if our demands are not met. The first hostage on the list is Herr Tilo Pollex, the German Interior Minister. He has been chosen because he has disobeyed the orders of the hostage-takers and is already injured.'

There was another flicker and Pollex appeared. Helen gasped. The minister's authoritative figure was slumped in another of the blue chairs from the plenary chamber. The camera zoomed in on his thigh, where blood had soaked the fabric of his trousers. Then the camera moved to his face, which was slick with sweat. His lips moved, but there was no sound.

Ashley Anderson reappeared. 'The Action Group for Peace and Justice wants to keep misunderstandings to a minimum,' she said. 'To avoid confusion, I will now name the prohibited areas. Reichstag exterior north: Paul Löbe Allee. Reichstag exterior east: Friedrich Ebert Platz. Reichstag exterior west…'

Helen shook her head. To anyone tuning in who had not seen the rows of slain Secret Service agents and SSU fighters, the painstaking listing of areas the security forces were not to enter would give the impression that the hostage takers wanted to avoid casualties. In reality, they were demonstrating their grip on the Reichstag. Ashley Anderson continued to stare into the camera as she read a list of several dozen locations. Had she memorised all this? The teacher drew to a close.

'Finally, at sub-ground level, the basement of Jakob-Kaiser House North, adjacent to the main tunnel doors; and the basement of the Paul-Löbe House adjacent to the north tunnel doors.

'You will ask, what is the Action Group for Peace and Justice? It is an organisation of citizens in favour of peace and social development for the world's poorest people and nations. The Action Group sees the governments of the rich world and the corporations which support them as the enemies of peace and the oppressors of those who seek justice. The Action Group does not seek anarchy. Nor does it oppose the creation of wealth, or deny human nature. Its aim is not to replace governments, but to encourage them to behave in a more humane and equitable fashion. Experience shows that the only way to achieve these goals is through direct action of the kind which has begun today.

'The Action Group has three simple demands. The first is addressed to the eight corporations whose chief executives the Group holds in the Reichstag. This is for those corporations to increase ten-fold the development aid paid by their countries to the eight poorest nations of the world. The sum of money involved amounts to a few tens of billions of dollars. A single year's profit. For each nation offered an aid package in the next eight hours, one business leader will be released.'

Ashley Anderson looked off-camera again before she continued.

'The second demand is directed to the governments of the G8 nations whose leaders are in the Reichstag. For too long, rich-country governments have pursued military adventures in nations too poor or weak to defend themselves. The rich countries use every kind of argument to justify these actions. The simple fact is that these military occupations make rich countries richer, and poor countries poorer. The Action Group for Peace and Justice demands that each of the G8 governments promises to withdraw all military forces from the countries of South and Central America, the Middle East, Central Asia and Africa within one month. For each G8 country making such a pledge at the United Nations in New York before midnight, a G8 leader will be released from the Reichstag. Leave her – '

For a moment, it looked as if Ashley Anderson was about to leap up from her chair; then the teacher was staring at the camera again, her eyes blinking. Her voice had risen a tone.

'Finally, the Action Group calls on the governments of the G8 to withdraw from the World Trade Organisation, the International Monetary Fund and the World Bank, and thus to terminate three destructive neo-liberal bodies whose purpose is to keep poor countries poor. For each G8 nation which fulfils this demand by midnight, the Action Group will release the remaining hostages held in the Reichstag who are not heads of state or government.

'In every case, the deadline is midnight, Berlin time. If any demand is not met, hostages will be executed.

'Use the next few hours wisely. Do not try to rescue the hostages. No rescue is possible. The Action Group will consider demands to have been met when the actions of corporations and governments are reported on all of the BBC, Wild TV, CNN and Al Jazeera TV news channels.

'The Action Group knows that it is normal for governments to try to establish contact with hostage-takers and begin so-called negotiations as a way of exerting pressure. There will be no negotiations with the Action Group, which has all the food, drink and other facilities needed for an indefinite siege. All mobile phone signals have been jammed. The only form of outward communication will be the four-channel TV feed which the Group is making available from the communications centre in the Reichstag via direct transmission, and by web-cast. There will be no form of inward communications to the Reichstag except for the TV news channels which the Action Group will monitor inside the building. If any attempt is made to censor or cut off the feeds from inside the building, hostages will be executed. Thank you.'

The picture changed to a stretch of hallway. A display at the base of the screen identified it as the East Lobby of the Reichstag. Helen found she had stood up, driven perhaps by the urge to do something.

What must Ashley Anderson be going through?

Analyse this.

Helen pressed her lips together. No hostage seemed to have been killed yet. That was good. The hostage-takers valued their lives. Nigel was a hostage. But he was not a politician. Did that make him more, or less at risk? The thought that someone she once had loved might be shot dead at any moment threatened to overwhelm her. The fact there were many others, all with loved ones longing for their release, simply spread the horror.

She must get them out. Not just Nigel. All of them.

The picture on the television changed again, to a deserted street outside the Reichstag. Her phone was ringing, but she ignored it. She changed channels: one, two, three, four, five, six. Everyone was showing terrorist TV. Four feeds, Ashley Anderson had said. The BBC was the first to split its screen into four, to show all the feeds at once: four different stretches of street, or corridor, or conference room, the scenes changing as the Reichstag security system switched from camera to camera.

The images were mesmerising. Eight hours. Then, if any demand was not met, hostages would die. Helen tried to remember the exact words. What if only some demands were met? Everything depended on how the governments and corporations responded. But what if the hostage-takers were being deliberately ambiguous? And who were they? The Action Group for Peace and Justice could come from anywhere. The video retrieved from the Internet had seemed of Arab origin. Yet the demands were global in scale.

Analyse this.

Helen took out a pad of paper and began noting down the demands attached to each set of hostages. Business leaders. Heads of state and government. Other delegation members. She stopped, her pen poised over the paper. In addition to the German Chancellor, there were seven other members of the German government in the Reichstag. The hostage-takers hadn't mentioned them. Why not?

On the television, Helen suddenly saw a man appear. A figure in uniform. Tunnel entrance, Jakob-Kaiser House North, the tag said. Helen recognised the intruder. It was Dieter Kremp. He was alive. He stood, pistol in hand, staring into the tunnel.

'Someone has entered the prohibited area,' the TV commentator was saying. Did she realise she was using the terrorists'

terminology? *'We do not know if this action has been approved by the authorities, but it seems to contravene the instructions of the terrorists.'*

What was Dieter doing? He must leave. Now. Helen reached for the phone on the desk, which was still ringing, slammed it down to get a clear line and used the speed dial to call Dieter's mobile. It was busy. As soon as she tried to call again, her own phone rang. She took if off the hook, fumbled for her mobile, and called again. Dieter's phone was still busy. Yet there he was, standing in front of the camera, as if he had all the time in the world.

'Get out! Get out of there!' She was shouting at the television. As if in response, Dieter spat on the floor, turned, and ran out of the picture. Thank God. She was trembling with desperation to get Dieter out of the terrorists' prohibited area.

Already, she was doing what they wanted.

The picture on the screen changed again. Ashley Anderson had her hand in front of her mouth, and was shaking her head. Then she turned off-screen; nodded; and began to speak.

'The Action Group for Peace and Justice regrets to announce that the armed forces surrounding the summit venue have violated security conditions designed to ensure the safety of the hostages. The Action Group wants to prevent further bloodshed. That is why it has set up a transparent system to allow both sides to monitor the security conditions. You have seen with your own eyes that an armed member of the Summit Security Unit has entered the prohibited area. This leaves the Group with no alternative but…' Ashley Anderson paused, then continued at a faster pace, as if rushing to complete her message. '… to execute the German Interior Minister, Tilo Pollex.

'The execution will take place on this channel in one hundred and twenty seconds.' She was gabbling now, stumbling over words. 'These images will be disturbing, but are necessary to show that the Action Group are true to their word. Channel two, at the same time, will show the release of ninety-nine of the children trapped in the Reichstag, and all but one of their teachers, at the exit of the north tunnel in the basement of the Paul-Löbe House. The Action Group has no argument with these children, and is making this release as a gesture of good will. It is essential that no security forces enter the prohibited area at this time, or hostages will die. Channels three and four will continue to show the prohibited areas. Thank you.'

For a moment, the picture changed to show Tilo Pollex, slumped in his seat. Then a news editor made a decision, and the image switched to show the inner of the two doors in the north tunnel begin to open.

Helen watched the teachers hurry the children through. The inner door closed behind them. Only then did the outer door begin to open. It closed as the last teacher reached the empty prohibited area. Helen checked the time, and wrote on her pad CHILDREN RELEASED. Yet they had said they were going to kill the German Interior Minister, live, on-air. Her fingers moved on the remote control, then stopped. She did not want to see Tilo Pollex shot. Yet she felt impelled to seek out the images. Was it the need to know if the terrorists were serious? Or simply fascination? She found herself changing channels. The first few were all showing the steel doors. At last she turned to Al Jazeera.

She hadn't counted the seconds since the announcement that Tilo Pollex would be killed. That made the brutality of what she saw next even more extreme. One moment she was watching a door in a tunnel; the next, she saw the German Interior Minister sitting in his seat, looking into the camera. He seemed about to speak when his head erupted in a brief red flower, jerked sideways, recoiled almost to a vertical position, then lolled forward as blood continued to spurt from a gaping wound where –

Helen turned away, gasping for breath. How long would they show the picture? But when she looked back, the minister's body was still there. She gazed at the floor. The silence seemed to last forever. At last, she heard the exhausted tones of Ashley Anderson.

'The image of Mr Pollex will remain on channel one for the next fifteen minutes, so that the governments of the G8 countries can assure themselves that he is dead.' The teacher's voice cracked, and she began to sob. 'That's what they told me to say. But I just saw him shot in the head, he's dead for sure. And now they've let out all the kids except Jasmine, and all the teachers except me, so I can go on talking to you. I've only one thing more to say. For the love of God, get us out of this place.'

CHAPTER 24

MARIA VON BOCK AND SABINE WOLF WERE COMPLETING A lunch of sour soup, Chinese mushrooms and snow peas with tofu at the Dong Huong Café in the Hackescher Markt when the Reichstag was seized.

The Dong Huong was a new arrival on the Berlin ethnic food scene. Its owners, a Vietnamese couple from Paris, had set out to attract custom by providing huge portions of vegetarian food at low prices in an ambience of industrial warehouse architecture. This had proved a winning combination with budget-minded Berliners, and several dozen demonstrators from the airport protest had moved on to the Dong Huong for a consolation feast after the failure of their efforts to disrupt the arrival of the G8 leaders. Everyone was tired and hot. Cold beers clinked under the slowly-revolving ceiling fans as the day's events were debated.

In the noisy restaurant, the wave of mobile phone calls and alerts which presaged big news went largely unheard. But when a girl in a red T-shirt stood up and yelled *'There's been an attack on the Reichstag!'* the room fell silent; and everyone either realised that their phones were ringing, or got out their phones to hit the nearest news site.

Maria von Bock pressed her phone to her ear. 'Wow! Unbelievable.'

'What's the attack? Who is it?' Sabine said.

'Quiet. Let me listen! Wait. It's on TV and on the Internet. Live.'

It seemed as if everyone in the room was shouting to everyone else, or into a phone, or trying to call someone to pass on the news. The data networks were overloaded, freezing phones and leading to more shouting, dialling and cursing. In the confusion, it was several minutes before the owners of the Dong Huong could be called on to activate the grimy television jammed into an angle of wall and ceiling. Sabine peered up at it. What was happening?

The first images to appear were of Ashley Anderson describing the Action Group for Peace and Justice. The protesters at the Dong Huong, having missed the earlier images of the dead security guards and the injured Tilo Pollex, received the teacher's account largely in silence, although one demonstrator observed that a group which did not aim to replace governments must be run by wimps. When the teacher announced that the Action Group's first demand was for a tenfold increase in aid to the world's poorest countries, however, the whole café burst into applause.

'Whoo! That's it!'

'A single year's profits!'

'Make it twenty countries!'

Sabine leaned across the table. 'This sounds brilliant. But why do they want it?'

'Because it's right, stupid.' Maria's eyes were shining. 'At last someone's doing something.'

The noise died down briefly as Ashley Anderson demanded the withdrawal of military forces from around the world. This time the reaction was tumultuous.

'*Amis* go home!'

'Stop the killing!'

'These guys rock!'

'Where can I join the Action Group?'

'Let's go show some support.'

Maria von Bock punched the air. 'It's like we've won the war.'

'Nothing has happened yet,' Sabine said. 'They're just making demands.'

'Don't you see? They have the President. They have everyone. The rich countries have to do what they say.'

'But why are they letting us see these pictures? Maybe it's a CIA trick.'

'Get real. You think the CIA would make demands like that?'

'And how can they pull their troops out in eight hours? There's no time.'

Maria rounded on Sabine. 'That's your trouble, scaredy-puss,' she said. 'Your can't-do mentality. Why do you have to be so negative?'

'I'm sorry.' Sabine shrank back. 'But that blonde woman looks terrified.'

'We're watching history here. One day you'll tell your kids where you were the day they seized the Reichstag.'

The Action Group's third demand, for the dissolution of the IMF and other international financial institutions, coincided almost exactly with the aims of the demonstration at the airport. But it seemed small beer after the calls for massive aid packages and military withdrawal; and drew only a modest round of cheering amid the din of discussion.

'They've achieved more in half an hour than I have in my whole life,' Maria said.

'But they did it through violence,' Sabine said.

'Will you shut up?' Maria jabbed a finger at Sabine. 'You of all people should know your Karl Marx. *Philosophers have only interpreted the world. The point, however, is to change it.* These people have taken the bossiest bastards on the planet and rubbed their faces in the dirt. I'd have though that would be just your scene.'

'It is true that my experiences of authority are not good.'

'Right. How many times were you abused in that work-house in Finsterwald? I bet you'd like to see those bastards taught a lesson.'

'Yes. But how do we know if these hostage-takers are any better than the staff at my children's home?'

'And what about your brother?'

Sabine stared at the table. 'They said it was an accident.'

'The place was burned to the ground.'

'My brother is dead. I know this.'

'Poor you.' Maria leaned forward and touched Sabine's arm.

'He was a kind, gentle person,' Sabine said. 'The best.'

'*Quiet! She's back!*'

The diners in the café had been paying little attention to the television, which had been showing a series of empty streets and corridors. The reappearance of Ashley Anderson brought silence. When she announced the imminent execution of Tilo Pollex, reactions were mixed.

'Kill him! Nazi swine.'

'Look! He's wounded.'

'He's not a Nazi.'

'His leg is bleeding.'

'He likes asylum seekers to drown.'

'They're letting the children out.'

'What children?'

'Switch over! I want to see the children.' A woman's voice.

'Let's see them kill Pollex.' A man.

'I can't watch this.' Sabine was standing up to change the channel when Pollex was shot. The cafe fell silent. The politician's head was still being displayed, bleeding, on the television when at last someone spoke.

'Cool.'

'Gross.'

'Who else do they have hostage?'

Sabine Wolf sank back into her seat.

'He was helpless. They shot him.'

'Yeah. But look what they're trying to achieve,' Maria said.

'The carers in my work-house had noble aims, too. They were trying to turn us from bad little children into good little communists.' Sabine took off her glasses. 'Maria. They shot a helpless man.'

'I know. Killing people is disgusting.' The lawyer frowned. 'But thousands of children starve every day. If this makes the world better, it's worth it.'

'How do we know it will make the world better?'

'Well – ' Maria von Bock shook her head. Then she stood up, her eyes blazing. 'Why don't we go and find out, instead of whining that it's all too complicated?' She waved her arms for silence, then addressed the crowd in the café. 'My girlfriend here thinks maybe these so-called terrorists are bad people. I think they're heroes. Who's coming to the Reichstag to see for themselves?'

CHAPTER 25

ULI WENGER LOOKED AT THE CORPSE OF THE GERMAN Interior Minister. One down. So far, everything had gone to plan. Except for the escape of Dieter Kremp. Yet another reason Tilo Pollex had deserved to die.

'Hey! Mr Murderer!'

The President of the United States was trying to attract Uli's attention. It felt good to take no notice. In the world outside, many people thought the President more important than other citizens. A leader. A supreme commander. Now, the President and all the others around the horseshoe-shaped table had joined the community of insects.

What a pity Mouse could not be here to relish this sweet moment of revenge.

'I'm talking to you! Child-beater!'

Still Uli took no notice. These *very important persons* weren't used to being ignored. They hated it. But what could they do? Power lay with Uli and the Chaos Team. Uli had told the hostages they were moving to a new location; and that anyone who stood up before then would be shot. They had seen him kill Tilo Pollex. Their fear was palpable. It was easy to ignore frightened people. More than that. Ignoring them gave Uli pleasure.

He looked around the chamber. The guards, the hostages, the teacher and her brat, all waiting for his orders. None of them knew his plan. Not even the Chaos Team knew how the siege would end. Everyone had a surprise coming.

'Are we moving, then?'

Chaos Team member Nicole Braun, alias Dora, was sitting at the TV camera. She had been editing texts for Ashley Anderson's teleprompter even as the teacher delivered them. Dora sometimes reminded Uli of Mouse. She had the same pale skin and wiry energy, the same brutally short hair. She was smart: she doubled with Ida as the Chaos Team's technical guru, and spoke perfect English. Like Mouse, she sometimes failed to show Uli sufficient respect. And like Mouse, she hated authority.

Dora's grandparents were Sudeten Germans who had lost everything when they and millions of others were driven from their homes in Czechoslovakia in 1945. Many Sudeten Germans had fought to keep alive the cultural traditions of the lost villages of Bohemia. But Dora's parents had immersed themselves in the most extreme forms of anti-Czech hatred and revanchism. They called themselves German patriots; others called them neo-Nazis. In this bitter soil, Dora had been raised.

Uli had found Dora working as a police officer in Passau as he travelled Germany seeking recruits for the SSU. After a first interview, he had marked her down as a possible for the Chaos Team. Two return visits had confirmed his assessment. On the surface, the young Bavarian was a model police officer: diligent and quick-witted. But beneath her patriotic facade lay a baleful demon of hate. At last, in a quiet pub in the Old Town, Uli had recruited her to his inner circle, promising her revenge against the government which had wronged her; and an extraordinary adventure.

'We have a complication,' Uli said.

'Is it the teacher?' Dora jerked her thumb to where the schoolgirl, Jasmine, was helping Ashley Anderson clean vomit off her dress. 'I can kill her.'

'No. The teacher is good for TV. She will say what we want while we have the girl. But we did not plan for them. With Pollex dead, we have forty-nine hostages. We planned for a maximum of forty-eight.'

'You mean it is time for hide-and-seek?'

Uli nodded. 'The North Lobby awaits.'

'Who is playing?'

'I will do it. With Gustav.'

'And the world can watch?'

'Ida will black out the rooms we pass through en route to the third floor. But she will leave on other monitors, including the North Lobby.'

'Is there no risk they could send a message?'

'They will have no sound. And no time. All mobile signals are blocked. They will be running for their lives. A game of hide-and-seek, live on television, with death as the prize.'

'Good for our ratings.'

'Today, in the Reichstag, we are staging the ultimate reality show. The world will want to watch every minute.'

Uli summoned Gustav, Viktor and Wilhelm to brief them on his plan. Then he addressed the hostages.

'We move now,' he said. 'Please leave behind all your papers, your briefcases, and any mobile telephones.'

'They're not working anyway.' It was the British ambassador, Sir Leonard Lennox.

'No. We have activated a jamming device. But we must be sure. Anyone who is found to have kept a telephone after we leave this room will be executed.'

'You're one hell of a tough guy, aren't you?' It was the American journalist, Karen Daniels. Her voice was powerful.

'Our demands are fair.' The blind woman's confident manner made Uli anxious. 'We do not forbid you to talk, or smoke. These things do not matter. But when we give an order, you must obey.'

'What's your problem? Got a tiny prick? Why don't you go jerk off and leave the rest of us in peace?' The journalist was practically shouting. Several hostages laughed. Uli felt a wave of fear and anger. They said blind people could feel more than others. Could she sense his vulnerability?

'We do not wish to kill you,' he said. 'But you must do what we say.'

'If I'm not mistaken, you've already murdered numerous people.' The British ambassador again.

'We will move, now.'

'Are you proposing to leave the bodies lying there?' The ambassador looked disgusted.

'Yeah, Mr Terrorist. You got an obsession with order, you should tidy your room.' Karen Daniels had her hand on the head of her dog. There was more laughter.

'Silence!' Uli felt he was losing control. It was the fault of the American journalist. She was not on the list. But next time she mocked him, he would show her who was boss. 'We have plans for the bodies. Everyone stand!'

He unsheathed his pistol and pointed it towards the hostages. They all rose at once, even Karen Daniels and her dog. Maybe she heard people moving. 'We go upstairs.' He stepped down from the rostrum and made for the West Lobby where Sara Lutz, alias Martha, the seventh member of the Chaos Team, was waiting.

A tall, heavily-built woman with a square jaw and thick forearms, Martha had been stationed at the north tunnel with another member of the SSU when the bomb exploded. Her first task had been to kill him. Her second task was to help move the hostages upstairs. Uli noticed Gustav nod to her: the two shared a primitive political ideology of race hatred and nationalism.

Uli watched them herd the hostages. It was ironic that Gustav and Martha hated America's global power and influence, since most of the websites from which they drew their so-called ideas were run by American white supremacists. But Uli did not care what motivated each member of his team; if anything, the fact that they had different goals made them easier to control. If the prospect of striking a blow against the "Zionist Occupation Governments" which Gustav and Martha believed ran most G8 countries made them ready to risk their lives, that was good enough for Uli.

To leave the plenary chamber, everyone had to pass the bodies of the dead Secret Service agents and SSU guards. The corpses lay on the floor where Dora had filmed them. Herr Kraft wanted the hostage-takers to maximise confusion for the security forces. Before the filming, several of the Chaos Team had smeared themselves with gore and lain in a heap at the far end of the line of slaughtered guards to make it look as though all the SSU defenders had been slain.

'They will soon guess the truth,' Dora had said to Uli as they dragged the bodies into place. 'If not, they are idiots.'

'The world is full of idiots,' Uli had said. 'And conspiracy theorists. The more sand we can throw in their eyes, the better.'

Now it was time to take deception to a new level.

Uli thought of Ivan, Herr Kraft's Russian courier. He wouldn't like what was about to happen. But Ivan could do nothing. The thought made Uli smile.

They moved through the West Lobby towards the stairs. Martha, Gustav and Dora were on the left of the forty-eight hostages; Viktor, Wilhelm and Uli at the rear. No-one guarded the right, where the Russian delegation were bunched, closest to the North Lobby. This was where it would happen.

The Russian President had just begun to climb the staircase when the two young men in his entourage whom Uli had marked down as security agents broke loose. If either of them thought it strange that the doors to the North Lobby should be open, they did not show it; in a moment they were gone, concealed amidst the stonework, sculptures and telephone kiosks of the hallway. A few hostages on the staircase cheered. But their enthusiasm was dampened by the fact that the Chaos Team seemed untroubled by the break-out.

'Gustav,' Uli said. 'Come with me. We shall deal with them. Martha, take the hostages to Room 3N001.' He moved towards the North Lobby. 'What is Ida saying?'

'She is monitoring them from the third floor comcen,' Gustav said.

'Tell me.'

'One is trying to break open the door into the East Lobby. Now he has moved behind a pillar. The other is in the women's toilets, trying to smash a window. It is impossible of course. Both are trapped.'

Uli entered the North Lobby. 'Keep behind the red lines.'

'The man in the toilets has broken a pipe from the wall. A useful weapon. He is behind the door, on the right.'

'That is a partition wall.' Uli moved around the edge of the room. 'We can shoot through it. They are lucky not to have guns. If they did, they would be dead already.'

'At least this way they get on TV.' Gustav was whispering now.

'I will take the one behind the column first. You take the one in the toilets.' Uli set his Heckler & Koch to automatic fire.

'Yours is trying to work his mobile phone.'

The Russian had kept a phone. Behind the metre-thick pillar of stone which shielded him from his prey, Uli Wenger shook his head. This act of disobedience made him almost feel sorry for the Russian. The world needed more people who refused to obey orders. Unfortunately, Uli knew what happened when you broke the rules.

You had to be punished.

CHAPTER 26

ASHLEY ANDERSON'S PLEA FOR RESCUE LEFT HELEN SHAKEN. Who would the terrorists kill next? She stared at the wall of her office. The teacher's tears were as much a part of the terrorists' strategy as the execution of Tilo Pollex. So was their list of demands. And the bombs outside the US and British embassies.

The ingredients didn't belong together.

'Aha! A sane person has penetrated the embassy.' Ram Kuresh poked his head around the door and peered at Helen as if assessing her state of mind. 'A gruesome business. But so far as we can tell, all the Brits are still alive.'

'Do you think so?' Her voice sounded quiet.

'Yes. We must be prepared for the worst. But we can still try to stop the worst from happening. Helen. You are the only person in this building thinking clearly. What should we do?'

'I'll do anything to get Nigel out of there. And Karen, and the ambassador. And everyone else. But it's running out of control.'

'You did not mention the Prime Minister.' Ram grinned.

Helen grimaced. 'Obviously, the Prime Minister is the top priority.'

'So. What is going on? And what do we do next? Analysis, please.'

'We have to work out a motive.' It was a relief to talk.

'Go on.'

'For a start, why did the terrorists kill the German Interior Minister first? Why kill him at all?'

'A good question.' Kuresh nodded. 'But not the focus of attention in London at the present time.'

'And if the terrorists are against globalisation, why are they blowing up anti-globalisation protesters outside our embassy?'

'Another good question. But again, not what most people are asking.'

'What are they asking?'

'Actually, no-one is asking any questions. Mostly, they are shouting and running in circles. But the tenor of the shouting is, how do we get the Prime Minister out of the Reichstag? It is to address this question that the Deputy Prime Minister has summoned Mr Short to a video conference with COBRA.' Ram Kuresh pronounced the acronym of the Cabinet Office Briefing Room with relish. 'I think you should take part also.'

'Why does the DPM want to talk to Jason?'

'I agree it seems improbable that the Deputy Prime Minister wishes to hear the views of anyone but himself. But I assume you are not declining to take part.'

'No. You assume right.'

Helen pulled on her beige jacket with a sinking feeling. London's decision to consult the embassy was welcome. But she hated video conferences even more than ordinary meetings. The format, with two or more sets of interlocutors lined up in front of cameras in different countries or continents, seemed to distil in concentrated form the worst elements of face-to-face encounters: formality, deference to hierarchy, and the crushing of spontaneity.

This meeting was no exception.

When Helen entered the conference room she saw Jason Short and Basil Nutter wearing expressions so grave as to be almost comical. The big television screen on the wall was dominated by the great, squat form of the Deputy Prime Minister, his face set in a mask of solemnity. Next to him sat a thin, anxious-looking man with glasses and grey hair whom Helen recognised as Graham King. King was deputy at No.10 to the Prime Minister's Chief of Staff, Sir Timothy Speed, now captive with the Prime Minister inside the Reichstag. Behind them was a sea of faces she took to be members of the crisis management staff in London. Helen recognised none of them.

My God, she thought. *It's the B-Team.*

The Deputy Prime Minister was in the midst of what seemed to be a lengthy peroration. He showed no sign of having noticed her arrival.

'The policy of not giving in to terror has served us well for years,' he was saying. 'If terrorists know that's our policy, they won't bother taking our people hostage, because they know they'll get nothing for 'em.'

He paused, nodded as if agreeing with himself, and looked around the meeting. Helen wondered if anyone would point out that the Prime Minister had just been taken hostage, but no-one intervened.

'The choice we face is two-fold,' the DPM went on. 'Option one is to call their bluff. Tell them they're wasting their time making demands. Meanwhile, we take forward military options to resolve the situation in Berlin. Option two is to make some show of meeting the terrorists half-way. Would a statement at the United Nations General Assembly pledging to withdraw our troops from some countries have legal consequences?'

The DPM seemed to be addressing Short, who coloured and fiddled with his silk tie. But the question was answered by a disembodied voice from the television. When Helen tried to identify the speaker, she realised that there were even more people in the room at the London end than those she could see on-camera. How could such a huge meeting agree anything?

'There are legal precedents,' the voice said, 'for arguing that a treaty or contract entered into under duress is not binding.'

'But the British government doesn't, um, normally say things at the UN which it doesn't mean,' Graham King said. He took off his glasses and put them back on again. 'Unless the Foreign Office tells me otherwise.'

'You've obviously never worked in New York.' Another unidentifiable voice, followed by a ripple of grim laughter in London.

'So that's the Foreign Office advice, is it?' The Deputy Prime Minister still seemed to be staring at Short. 'Lie through our teeth at the United Nations. What if the terrorists think we're pulling a fast one?'

'We'd have to back it up, um, by press briefings.' Graham King made this sound a perilous procedure. 'And talks with close allies. To show we were serious.'

'What? Lie to the press as well? And our most trusted partners?' The Deputy Prime Minister shook his head. 'You mean, we tell Washington we mean it, and they tell us the same thing, and we both know we're fibbing. How long will the press buy that?'

No-one spoke.

This was going nowhere. Helen cleared her throat, sat up straight, and spoke as confidently and clearly as she could. 'Maybe to get the Prime Minister out, we need to think laterally,' she said. 'Who could the hostage-takers be? Who would gain if their demands were met? Who is gaining from the chaos they've caused? Unless we can answer those questions, we won't know how to respond to their demands.'

There was a moment's silence. Then Jason Short was almost spitting in her ear.

'Didn't you hear the Deputy Prime Minister?' he hissed. 'We're not meeting their demands. It would be giving in to terrorists.'

'Address the microphone,' someone said in London. 'We can't hear you.'

The DPM looked at Short. It was as if Helen had not spoken. 'What's the ETA for the US Delta Force in Berlin?'

'One or two hours.' Short was reading from a sheet of paper covered in handwritten notes. 'There's a unit on R&R

in Germany on their way home from the Middle East. They're diverting them here.'

'The Germans will love that,' the DPM said. 'What's happening on the ground?'

'GSG 9, the German counter-terrorist force, has the Reichstag surrounded. But the Americans are telling them to hold off any attack until their people get there.' Short cleared his throat before continuing. 'A committee of state secretaries, or junior ministers, has been set up to take over the functions of the government with most of the cabinet taken hostage. But the fact is, the Germans are incapable of making any difficult decisions at this stage.'

Unlike us, Helen thought.

'That's, um, three or four hours, minimum, before any rescue is feasible.' Graham King looked unhappy. 'Even the Americans won't want to go storming in the minute they arrive.'

'They will if they have to.' Clipped military tones from London. 'They'll put together an immediate plan even before they get there, for use if the hostage situation deteriorates. Then they'll keep refining the plan until the time comes for them to go in.'

'What do you mean by the hostage situation deteriorating?' the Deputy Prime Minister said.

'If they start killing many hostages, sir.'

'How many is many?'

'That would depend on who they were, sir, and how risky the assault. The Americans would be more likely to go in if US citizens were threatened.'

'Right.' The Deputy Prime Minister looked around. 'Where are the SAS?'

'They and the Foreign Office advance team are still waiting for, um, permission from the Germans to deploy to Berlin,' Graham King said. 'As Mr Short points out, German decision-making is handicapped because their government is inside the Reichstag. The Americans were cleverer. They didn't bother asking.'

'What about this SAS woman who's flying out?' Sweat had

plastered Jason Short's long, thin hair to the nape of his neck. 'Do the Germans know about her?'

'She is acting in an informal capacity,' Graham King said. 'She's not armed.'

'Not armed,' the Deputy Prime Minister said. 'So, for the time being, our military options are zero. What's our assessment of the terrorist reaction if we tell them to bugger off? Will they kill someone?'

'Well…' Graham King scratched his head. 'Based on events to date, further hostage deaths cannot be, um, discounted. The longer we decline to meet the terrorists' demands, the greater the risk that the Prime Minister will be harmed. Particularly as midnight approaches. We would also face criticism from the hostage families, and from the media, if we were seen to do nothing to secure their release. The sister of Miss Ashley Anderson, who is British, has already appeared on the BBC calling on the government to show flexibility.'

'And there's no way of cutting off the TV broadcasts?' The Deputy Prime Minister's expression was sombre. 'The oxygen of publicity, and all that.'

'No,' someone in London said. 'The terrorists are broadcasting live signals from the Reichstag communications centre for anyone to pick up. The whole area is crammed with television vans and people with smartphones and other mobile devices. In theory, the Germans could block the signals if they had the right equipment. But then they wouldn't know what was happening inside. And the terrorists have threatened to kill hostages if the signal is cut.'

'It's, um, worse than that,' Graham King said. 'The only way we have of sending messages to the terrorists is through the TV channels they're monitoring. We have to go on television to talk to them. That means any message won't be very private.'

'Anything else?' the Deputy Prime Minister said.

'Their reach is much greater than traditional TV. Thousands of live Internet channels are carrying images from the Reichstag, including the most graphic scenes,' Graham King said.

'How on earth do they do that?'

Helen listened to the discussion with horror. How did the hostage-takers expect eight governments to make vital decisions within hours when the key decision-makers were held in the Reichstag? Maybe that was the answer. They expected no such thing.

She opened her mouth to speak, then closed it. No-one had listened the first time. The meeting was a charade designed to convey the impression of useful activity. Like every other meeting.

But Nigel – the man who could hold the key to her future life – was a hostage. She had to do something.

'Wait!' Her voice was higher than she had intended. But she had everyone's attention. 'What if the terrorists don't care about their demands? Maybe they will kill the hostages however we respond.'

'What?' The Deputy Prime Minister was shaking his head.

'Think about it. Why did they kill Tilo Pollex? In theory, it was because Dieter Kremp trespassed on their so-called prohibited area. But I called Dieter while he was on camera and his phone was always busy. That's because at the time I was calling him, he was already somewhere else. The terrorists were showing us old camera footage. Dieter Kremp entered the area by the tunnel before the hostage-takers even told us it was prohibited. He didn't do anything wrong. But as soon as the terrorists felt like killing a hostage, they replayed the old pictures, and wham! It's all our fault.'

The Deputy Prime Minister frowned. 'I don't understand,' he said. 'Who is this person in the prohibited area?'

'*It wasn't a prohibited area.*' Why was no-one hearing her?

Short put his hand on Helen's arm. 'Helen is first secretary in the embassy responsible for security at the Reichstag,' he said. 'She's been under a lot of pressure.'

'I am perfectly calm.' Helen pulled her arm away.

'The German police officer who caused the death of the

hostage is a close friend of Helen's.' Short adopted a sympathetic expression. 'It's natural she should want to protect him. You should also know that her husband is Nigel Ferguson, one of the hostages. It may be affecting her judgement on how we should respond to the terrorists' demands.'

'This is not about Nigel.' Helen could hardly speak through her anger.

The Deputy Prime Minister misinterpreted Helen's emotions. 'I understand how hard this is for you,' he said. 'We'll do our best for your husband, I promise.'

'You promise? Like you'll promise at the UN?' Helen stood to leave. 'No thanks.'

'Excuse me.' Short followed her to the door. He spoke in a low voice, his sour breath in her face. 'You can't talk to the DPM like that.'

'We should be working out what's happening, not sitting around hoping something will turn up.' Helen waved at the clock on the wall. 'Two hours have gone already.'

Jason Short's face was red, but his eyes were unwavering. 'That's why we can't have a hysterical woman at the heart of our crisis management machinery,' he said. 'Leave the embassy now. I don't want to see you here again until the siege has been resolved.'

CHAPTER 27

HELEN HEADED FOR THE STREET. SHORT DIDN'T NEED TO banish her from the embassy: the thought of spending another moment there disgusted her. She pushed through the revolving doors, leaving them spinning behind her. The rain had stopped, but the thunderclouds overhead made the grey canyon of the courtyard seem gloomier than ever. In the Reichstag, they would have the lights on. What would Nigel be doing? Probably interviewing a top hostage. Karen would be making life hard for the hostage-takers. Leonard Lennox would be acting as though he were taken prisoner every week.

To imagine anything else was too horrible.

Helen had thought she knew how government worked. But the chaotic response to the crisis astonished her. She took a deep breath of the warm, moist air. She'd tried to help. Short had thrown her out. What more could she do?

In the centre of the courtyard stood an oak, transplanted to the site when the rebuilt embassy was opened in the year 2000. Helen rested her hand against the trunk. The bark was cool against her palm. She closed her eyes, listened to the wind stir the leaves, and imagined the roots spreading out through the earth beneath her.

'Helen Gale, isn't it?'

Helen opened her eyes to see a short, dark-haired woman dressed in jeans and a black bomber-jacket. It was a moment before she recognised the face she'd seen on the computer screen in Ram's office.

'Are you from the SAS? I thought you'd be taller.'

'You try getting a big bloke through a small hole,' Elle Morgan blinked twice. 'And I thought you'd be carrying a pile of secret intelligence with the times and places of terrorist bombs to refuse to give to the public.'

'I have the intelligence on a USB stick in my pocket,' Helen smiled. 'In case I meet a member of the public who might appreciate it. At least the newspapers have gone quiet.'

'They'll be back. Just don't expect anyone to help you.' The SAS officer's eyes were cold. 'Best thing is to give the media something else to work with. A different story. Keep them off your back.'

'You mean it might help if we rescued the hostages.'

'Right. I suppose you know the Germans won't give permission for the boys to fly out of Brize Norton?'

'What about you? Does anyone know you're here?'

'Why should they? I'm sightseeing. But there's only one sight I want to see. Which way is the Reichstag?'

'There's a video-conference going on upstairs with COBRA, if you fancy being bored and patronised.'

Again, Elle Morgan blinked twice, quickly. 'I don't want a meeting. I want operational intelligence, so we can start planning the assault.'

'What's the point, if your guys are stuck in England?'

'The more info we scoop up now, the quicker they can engage when they get here. The big question is what's happening in the Reichstag: number of terrorists, locations, weapons, everything. We'll focus on that.' She looked at Helen. 'What's your excuse for missing this vital video-conference?'

'Can you imagine a meeting with no leadership, no agenda and fifty men in suits panicking?'

'Been there. Done that.'

'Me too. Also, they threw me out. Let's go to the Reichstag.'

'I'm guessing that if anyone around here knows an expert on the summit venue, it's you.'

For the first time in what felt like hours, Helen grinned. 'As a matter of fact, I know just the man. But I'm not sure he'll want to talk to us.'

Dieter Kremp stared at the blue-uniformed Bundespolizei officer blocking the entrance to the Bunker. 'I'm *what?*'

'Excluded. Don't blame me, sir. It's the Interior Ministry.'

'Out of the way.' Dieter considered shoving the man aside. It was hard to hear over the noise of the demonstrators gathered nearby. 'I'm acting head of the Summit Security Unit. It's my command centre.'

'Not any more, sir.' The Bundespolizei man was an immense, simple-looking lad who seemed torn between respect for Dieter's rank and delight that the SSU had been put in its place. 'Everyone is saying it was you got Tilo Pollex killed. Because you went into the prohibited area, sir.'

'But I didn't know it was prohibited.'

The man in blue shrugged. 'Maybe you should have known.'

'Call your superior officer. I can't command the SSU without access to communications.'

'Don't you know, sir? There is no SSU.'

'What?'

'Its job is finished.' The big man was gaining confidence. 'You remember the SSU's job description?'

'To protect – ' Dieter stopped.

'Right, sir. To protect the Summit. Well, the Summit doesn't need protecting any more, does it?'

'Half my people died today.'

'Sir, I'm sorry. But you're not going to get a medal, are you? GSG 9 has taken over the Bunker. All the SSU troops that are left have been suspended.'

'GSG 9? What are they going to do? Storm the Reichstag?'

'Yes, sir. That's what they're trained for.'

'What about the *Amis*?' Dieter could feel the sweat coursing down his back. 'If there's an assault, the Delta Force will want to be there.'

'We don't need the Americans.' The man shrugged again. 'I don't know why we're letting them come.'

'So, I'm relieved of my duties?'

'That is correct, sir.'

'Show me your authorization.'

The big man hesitated. 'It's all a bit crazy now,' he said. 'Pollex is dead. There's that lot to deal with.' He jerked his thumb towards the chanting mass of protesters at the edge of the Safety Zone. 'And no-one knows if we're going to kill the terrorists or give them what they want, sir.' He lowered his voice. 'They say Germany could easily withdraw its soldiers from the places the terrorists talked about. And any one of them big firms could pay the aid for all eight poor countries, if they wanted. So maybe they'll let the German hostages go.'

'Except Tilo Pollex.'

'Well, yeah.'

'You don't have authorization, do you?' Dieter stepped forward.

'Sir. Can I speak honestly?' Suddenly the man in blue patted Dieter on the arm with his huge hand. 'I know this was your patch. But you're finished. No-one's signing anything right now. But when they do, it's a toss-up whether you'll be fired, or arrested. There's even some people asking how you got out of the Reichstag before the shooting started, when you're meant to be inside.'

Dieter retreated. His anger had melted into shock. It was the pat on the arm. A few hours ago, no junior Bundespolizei officer would have dared touch him, Dieter Kremp, deputy head of the Summit Security Unit. He had been part of an elite squad of fighters, charged with a vital mission. Now he was an object of derision. He walked away from the Bunker and stared up at the towers of the Reichstag, a hundred metres across a stretch of bare concrete. A fortress. How had they seized it?

His telephone rang.

'Dieter. It's Helen.'

'Calling to gloat, are you?'

'I need to see you. As close to the Reichstag as possible.'

'Are you still trying to improve security?'

'Stop it. Where can we meet?'

'Nowhere. I've been kicked out.'

'Kicked out of where?'

'The Bunker. The SSU has been disbanded.'

'Oh.' Helen paused. 'I have someone here from the SAS. She wants to meet you.'

'A woman? From the SAS? That I'd like to see.'

'Now's your chance.'

'What does she want, this woman?'

'She wants to see the Reichstag. She wants to talk to the Summit Security Unit. And she wants to free the hostages. But if you don't want to – '

'Bring her over.'

They met in Room 6.556 of Jakob-Kaiser House South, overlooking the Reichstag. When Dieter arrived, he had to clear out a dozen members of the Japanese, Italian and Russian delegations who had gathered at the tall windows. More were clustered around a television in the corner. It was typical of the chaos which had descended on the Summit, Dieter thought, that no-one had yet evacuated this building, which housed hundreds of officials. With the Reichstag full of terrorists with live weapons, any building nearby was dangerous. But at least the SAS woman would get a good view.

Dieter was looking out of the window when the door opened. He held out a hand, registering with surprise that the British diplomat's companion was tiny. But the dark-haired woman radiated purpose.

'You must be from the SAS,' Dieter said in English. 'Welcome.'

'The name's Elle Morgan.' The woman's grip was strong. 'And I'm here unofficially. Thanks for seeing me.' She moved to the window and stared at the Reichstag. 'God, it's big.'

From where they stood the Reichstag was a glistening mountain of stone. At each corner rose a squat tower surmounted by a flagpole and a limp, sodden flag; at the centre was the glass dome. The sides of the building were populated by statues representing the German people: a man in a fishing jacket, a woman in a bonnet. The towers were populated by snipers: four on each summit, Dieter knew. But their weapons were useless against an enemy inside the building.

'Helen tells me you know more about the security of that place than anyone alive,' Elle Morgan said.

'That is correct,' Dieter said. 'The only man who knows more is my boss, Johann Frost. He is dead.'

'How do you know that?' It was the first time Helen had spoken.

'They are all dead.' Dieter scowled. 'We saw the bodies. On television.'

'Since when do you believe everything you see on television?'

'You have a better theory?' Dieter, struggling with his English, could feel his face reddening.

'Dieter.' Elle Morgan sat down. 'Talk me through what has happened. I need your help.'

Dieter glanced at Helen. 'Sometimes, we get more help than we need.'

Elle blinked twice. 'Helen, do you have any contacts with the US team here? Perhaps you could check where their special forces have got to.'

Helen took the hint and opened the door. 'I'll call the US embassy.'

Dieter watched her as she left. Then he turned to Elle Morgan. 'Do you have a computer? I can show you plans of the Reichstag.'

Helen went into the corridor. It felt good to have Elle Morgan here. But she and Dieter could not storm the Reichstag. No-one could. That was exactly what the assembled might of the G8 security agencies – including Helen – had tried to achieve.

Blore Harl answered at once.

'Helen! Where are you?'

'Jakob-Kaiser House South. I need to talk.'

'Me too. I'm in the US delegation rooms on the second floor, downstairs from you. It's insane. Everyone's trying to take control: the Secret Service, the military, the ambassador. No-one can believe the President's been taken. And the Germans told us five minutes ago the Delta Force can land in Berlin, but may not take any military action unless the Committee of State Secretaries authorises it. It's like they want to tell us to get lost, but they feel they might need us.'

'That's how most people feel about America.'

'Thank you, Ms Gale. Succinctly put.'

'What are you doing there?'

'I'm getting in the way, mostly. It's standing room only. The military want to invade the Japanese and Italian delegation rooms to get more space.'

'Invade?'

'They're making it sound like a dry run for storming the Reichstag.'

'Can you come up for a few minutes?'

'Sure. I'm not helping here.'

As soon as Blore hung up Helen's phone rang again.

'Freddy Acton, Daily Dispatch. Ten thousand pounds, max.'

'What?'

'For an exclusive interview. With Helen Gale. You are Helen Gale, aren't you?'

'I'm not giving interviews. We're in the middle of a crisis.'

Some residual sense of good manners, and a sense that Freddy

Acton could be an awkward enemy, stopped Helen terminating the call.

'Middle of a crisis. Very nice.' There was a clatter of computer keys. 'Listen, Helen: you're hot property. You're being sued by the bloody Germans. Your husband's a hostage. You're trying to save British lives. You could be a hero. And your mum makes a lovely cup of tea. The Mirror and the Sun won't offer more than five grand.'

'I don't want to be a hero.'

'It's better than the alternative, darling. Isn't it true that you walked out on Nigel Ferguson, the brave hostage, to take a job in Berlin? That you've screwed up the arrangements for the Summit? And caused the death of an innocent protester? I can make the whole mess your fault, if you want.'

'Leave me alone. I'm trying to save the hostages.'

'How? What are you doing?'

'I can't tell you.'

'Well, it's your funeral.'

'Wait.' Helen stared at the phone. Short had cut her off. London was ignoring her. Could this be a way she could make herself heard? She saw Blore Harl approaching. 'Freddy, can I call you back? I'll make it worth your while.'

'I hope so. Give the story to anyone else, and even your mum won't be talking to you.'

Helen turned to greet Blore. The American's dark eyes seemed more intense than normal. But otherwise the diplomat was his usual phlegmatic self. He shook Helen's hand.

'Helen. Am I glad to see you. Washington's hysterical.'

'So is London. Everything is in melt-down, Blore. Things could get worse.'

The American took a step back. 'Hey. Take it easy.'

'You know Nigel is in there? And Karen? They could already be dead.'

'They're alive. So far, the terrorists have made a big noise each time they killed anyone.'

'I was going to see Nigel tonight,' Helen said. 'He wanted to talk about our future together. If we have one.'

Blore's gaze was steady. 'We'll rescue him.'

'We must.'

They entered the room. Dieter and Elle Morgan were sitting at a laptop. The SAS woman looked up.

'He's a smart one, your man Dieter,' she said. 'I've sent off a first situation report, with plans of the Reichstag. Pity the boys can't be here.'

'Why are you calling them boys?' Dieter said. 'You are not a boy.'

'We couldn't think of anything shorter.' Elle held out a hand to Blore. 'Are you from the US embassy? Where are your special forces?'

'We have a Delta Force assault team arriving in Berlin any second,' Blore said. 'But what they do when they get here, no-one knows.'

'That's why we need to kick some ideas around,' Elle said. 'Have you got any?'

Blore nodded. 'Washington's awash with ideas. There's one debate about how to free the President. Then there's a whole different argument about the terrorists' demands, which everyone agrees we should ignore – '

'Even if they threaten to kill the President?' Helen said.

'I'm coming to that. The deadline is so short, we can't see how they expect us to meet it. The administration is arguing for a clear, quick statement of why US policies are already in line with everything the terrorists want. For example, it's our policy to withdraw US troops from all conflict zones at the earliest opportunity.'

'But the demands make no sense,' Helen said. 'They must know there's no chance of eight governments responding in a few hours.'

'Maybe the deadline is short to prevent a military response,'

Elle Morgan said. 'If they had more time, the US would start flying in whole army divisions.'

'Maybe they don't want a response,' Helen said. 'Just chaos.'

'I think they have achieved this,' Dieter Kremp said.

There was a silence as they listened to the demonstrators chanting outside.

'Do your people know anything about the Action Group for Peace and Justice and their Arabic slogans?' Helen asked Blore.

'No. Except that we never heard of them before. And the Secret Service say it's impossible for any terrorists to have got inside the Reichstag.' He looked at Dieter. 'Right?'

'I thought it was impossible,' Dieter said. 'Until today.'

'Could they have been hidden in there before the conference?' Elle Morgan said. 'Some kind of secret room? It's a big building.'

'The Reichstag has been sealed off for weeks and searched repeatedly,' Dieter said. 'Even if they were hiding, how could the terrorists kill everyone so quickly? The SSU officers and Secret Service agents were spread through the summit venue.'

'It's a sophisticated media operation,' Blore said. 'We think the Ashley Anderson statement was written in advance, edited after the shootings, and delivered using a teleprompter.'

'They're smart,' Elle Morgan said. 'The whole point of terrorism is to influence people. It's no use killing hostages if no-one knows about it.' She looked at her laptop. 'Maybe Ashley Anderson is one of the terrorists.'

'I don't think so.' Helen's mind was racing. 'But what about someone else who had the right to be in the Reichstag? Someone in a delegation, maybe.'

Dieter shook his head. 'They were scanned when they entered the summit venue.'

'Who else was inside? The Secret Service? What about the SSU? They're armed to the teeth.'

'But they're all dead, aren't they?' Elle Morgan said.

'Remember when we saw the bodies in the plenary chamber?' Helen said. 'There wasn't enough blood.'

'*Nein. Nein.*'

Everyone looked at Dieter Kremp. The German was staring at the floor.

'Helen is right,' he said. 'She asked before how I could be sure Johann Frost was dead. I said we saw the bodies of the Secret Service agents and Summit Security Unit officers, on television. Some of them were certainly dead: their heads were destroyed. All the bodies were covered in blood. We expected an attack from outside. Therefore, we saw a pile of dead people.' Dieter shook his head. 'Maybe some of them were alive.'

'So what?' Elle Morgan said.

Dieter continued to stare at the floor. *He can't look us in the eye.* Helen felt a pang of pity.

'What Dieter means is that the hostage-takers could be members of the Summit Security Unit,' she said. 'It makes sense. We have said all along no armed group could penetrate the Reichstag. What if an armed group was already inside?'

'It sure as hell wasn't the Secret Service agents.' Blore's face was dark. 'I never saw anyone so dead.'

'But what about clearance?' Elle said. 'Surely these SSU people were vetted?'

'Of course,' Dieter said. 'Especially Johann. I cannot believe he is involved. He comes from a family of absolutely respectable civil rights activists in East Germany. His parents were both killed on the inner-German border, trying to flee to the West. I have seen his school reports: he was a brilliant pupil, dutiful and loyal. His record is perfect.'

'How about the others?'

'Nearly all of them were recruited by Johann. He was responsible for vetting the whole team. But when you are drawing recruits from the police and the army, you expect them to be loyal.'

'Is there any other potential leader?' Elle's gaze was fixed on Dieter.

'No. Johann is a fantastic boss. He has a way of knowing

how to motivate people. It is as if he can see inside your soul.'
Dieter shook his head. 'I would have died for him myself.'

'Suppose Johann did lead the attack.' Helen frowned. 'He
could have recruited a team of people loyal to him, and made
sure all of them were in the Reichstag at the start of the Summit.
What about Petra Bleibtreu? Did he recruit her?'

'Yes,' Dieter said.

'Maybe she found something out. Or she was a team member
who changed her mind. Johann had to kill her. That would
make the embassy a secondary target, and explain why it was
hardly damaged.'

'It cannot be Johann,' Dieter said.

'But if it is, he and his team have had access to the Reichstag
for months,' Helen said. 'They could have stashed anything in
there.'

Dieter said nothing. There was a moment's silence. Then
Elle Morgan jumped to her feet and stared out at the Reichstag.

'OK. The idea that the SSU are the terrorists is the best
theory we have so far,' she said. 'But even if it's true, and we've
ID'd them, they're still laughing. Why did I fly out here? Because
military success is based on good intelligence. What do we know
so far about what is happening inside the Reichstag? Nothing.
We don't know how many terrorists there are. Or who they are.
I know – ' she held up her hand to Helen. 'We think they may be
members of the SSU. But we don't know for sure. Meanwhile,
they know every move we make. They have surveillance of the
whole perimeter, and guns to the heads of people who matter
to us.' She looked at Dieter. 'Why does the Reichstag have its
own control room?'

Dieter barely raised his head. 'To increase security. All
systems in the summit venue are independent. Power, water,
communications, everything.'

'Remind me,' Elle said, 'why we were so worried about
attacks?'

'There was a whole lot of intelligence,' Blore said. 'Pointing to a threat against the Summit. It's been vindicated now, I guess.'

'No.' Helen had a sensation of falling. 'It hasn't been vindicated. The intelligence was about known terrorist groups. Yet the Reichstag seems to have been taken over by members of the SSU.'

'Where did the intelligence come from?' Elle Morgan said.

'Intercepts.' Everything seemed clear now. 'Designed so we could decipher them. The intelligence was fake. They wanted us to feel threatened, and to make the Reichstag strong. Because they knew they'd be inside, and we'd be outside.'

'What about the bombs at the US and British embassies?' Blore Harl said.

'That was the final act. To make sure we believed the threat was real. Remember this morning? We were still trying to get extra security for the Reichstag.'

'Yes,' Dieter said.

'But we nearly called the whole thing off after the second bomb,' Blore said.

'We didn't, though, did we? It's as if they knew exactly how far they could push us.' What had happened after the second bomb? Helen could not recall.

'OK,' Elle Morgan said. 'Let us assume members of the Summit Security Unit have taken over the Reichstag. Why are they doing it? And what does that tell us about what we should do next?'

'The first thing is, I must inform the authorities of this theory.' Dieter stood up.

Elle Morgan nodded. 'Why don't you and me go to GSG 9 together? And I guess Blore and Helen will want to talk to Washington and London. But first, a reality check.' She gestured through the rain towards the Reichstag. 'That place is a fortress. The people inside are armed and disciplined. We don't know who they are or where they are. It's great that Blore's friends from the Delta Force will be here soon. But with all respect to them, there's no way on earth they GSG 9 or anyone else can seize that building before every hostage inside has been killed several times over.'

CHAPTER 28

SABINE WOLF SAT ALONE WITH A POT OF GREEN TEA IN THE Dong Huong Café. Around her the tables were strewn with empty glasses and half-eaten plates of food.

'Why not come with us, scaredy-puss?' Maria had said as she prepared to leave. 'Everyone else is.'

'I can't. What they are doing in the Reichstag reminds me of Finsterwald.'

'Your children's home? Well then, come and protest about it. Don't just sit there.'

'Why? We can't change anything.'

'That's where you're wrong,' Maria said. 'We can change the world.'

'Let's hope you make it better.'

'It can't get any worse.'

'Can't it?'

'And they've let the children out.'

'Not all of them. One is still inside.'

'OK. Stay here, then.' Maria had stood up and squared her broad shoulders. 'Be miserable.' Then, without a backwards glance, she had joined the crowd streaming towards the Reichstag.

The television in the corner was tuned to Wild TV. Sabine could not bear to watch Al Jazeera, where the killings were being shown constantly. The hunting down of the two Russians in the North Lobby had been like a macabre game show, with the two men being gunned down at close range then executed with shots to the head on live television. And why had the hostage-takers not released the hundredth child? Perhaps it was already dead.

The idea of more violence away from the cameras fuelled Sabine's sense of horror. Should she go to the Reichstag to join the protests in support of the terrorists' demands after all?

She called Maria's number. No connection. Maybe the network was down. Or the government was blocking phone signals round the Reichstag. Or both.

She sat and gazed at the television.

For the past half-hour, the only images coming out of the Reichstag had been shots of the prohibited area. The empty halls and corridors were good to fill a corner of a TV screen. But they were not dramatic enough for the big picture. So, the producers were filling programming with recycled images and reactions to the siege.

Governments around the world had made statements deploring terrorism, and calling for the release of the hostages. But many had endorsed the call for increased development aid, and criticised over-strict IMF or World Bank programmes. Dozens of countries had stated their principled opposition to interference in the affairs of sovereign nations and called on others to withdraw their forces from disputed territories in order to restore peace and stability.

A leading liberal academic in the United States had gone on record condemning the hostage-taking. But for as long as the neo-colonialist western powers continued to attack the economic interests of the poorest nations of the world, she said, there would always be those prepared to "defend the defenceless" against the "pitiless aggression" of the US and its allies. Sabine agreed with every word, but this did not stem her anxiety. Nor did a press statement released by Uktam Zholobov, the Russian energy magnate, listing the occasions on which the oligarch had condemned the use of violence to settle political disputes. Zholobov called on the terrorists in the Reichstag to release the hostages and denounced reports "propagated by media in the pay of the Kremlin" that he supported the hostage-taking "either morally or financially".

Even the chaos on the financial markets caused by the collapse in the share prices of the eight companies whose leaders were in the Reichstag did little to cheer Sabine. It was good that giant corporations were being forced to pay a slice of their obscene profits to the poor. If that made their shareholders sweat, so much the better. But did that justify shooting people live on television?

Now an anchorman in a Berlin studio was talking to a reporter at the scene. A banner at the foot of the picture paired photos of the Reichstag and the US President with the words *BERLIN SIEGE*.

'I am outside the Bunker now.' The reporter was standing by a red-and-white crowd-control barrier. Behind him rose the steel plates of the Safety Zone, surmounted by a Berlin bear lying on its back, balancing a child on each paw. 'The crowd has swelled, and new contingents of riot police continue to pour in. But so far, the atmosphere remains calm.'

'Is there anything new on the children?'

'The police have confirmed that ninety-nine children were released from the Reichstag one hour ago, together with some teachers. We understand they are being debriefed and treated for shock in the Paul-Löbe House. None of them is physically injured.'

'Have they been able to reveal anything about the terrorists?'

'No. I understand that neither teachers nor children saw any terrorists.'

'Are there signs of an attempt to re-take the building?'

'There are reports of soldiers entering the Bunker,' the reporter said. 'But we do not know if these are members of our own GSG 9, or special forces units from the US, Russia or other countries.'

'How about people leaving?' The anchor glanced at his notes. 'Can you confirm that the Summit Security Unit has been disbanded?'

'According to military sources, a new command structure is

now in place. About half the members of the SSU were inside the Reichstag at the time of the assault. They are all believed to be dead. The remaining members have been redeployed.'

The anchor turned to face the camera. 'That was one of our reporters live at the Reichstag, with reports of the tragic loss of life amongst the elite force guarding the Children's Summit. But who are the Summit Security Unit, and what is their role? Retired Police Director Tobias Keller is a former GSG 9 commander.' He turned to a guest in the studio. 'Mr Keller, what can you tell us?'

Keller, a lean, grey-haired man in a blue suit and tie, nodded at the presenter.

'Of course, I cannot say much about the SSU, for reasons of operational security,' he said. 'We cannot broadcast any information which might help the terrorists.'

'Naturally.' The anchor shifted in his seat. 'What can you tell us?'

'The only two members of the Unit whose names are in the public domain are its head, Johann Frost, and his deputy, Dieter Kremp,' Keller said. Pictures of the two appeared behind Keller. 'We do not know if either of these men was inside the Reichstag at the opening of the Summit. But it is normal in cases of this sort...'

Slowly, the retired Police Director got into his stride. The anchor took care not to interrupt. None of the other networks had managed to track down so qualified a commentator. The producer hoped that if Keller kept talking, he might still be on air whenever the next dramatic development took place at the Reichstag.

Sabine Wolf was not listening. She was staring at the television screen, her mouth open.

A few minutes later, the Vietnamese owner of the Dong Huong Café came over to Sabine. He was wondering if he might ask the woman in black to settle up.

'Terrible thing, eh?' he said. 'What's it all for, that's what I'd like to know.'

The woman did not reply. The proprietor, whose command of German was shaky, wondered if he had got his word order wrong.

'Terrible thing.' He peered at the woman, and recoiled.

Her face was white. She stood motionless, staring at the television, clutching her wrists to her bosom as if constrained by invisible bonds. Was she in shock?

'It's not possible,' she said.

'Unfortunately, it is,' the Vietnamese said.

She turned towards him. 'I must tell someone. But who?'

'Tell them what?'

'The killings in the Reichstag. I know something.'

The Vietnamese took a step back. 'You could tell a policeman. I'll find one.'

'No!' The woman was trembling. 'I fear them.'

'Perhaps you could call one of your friends.' The owner was keener than ever now to eject her. 'Do you have a phone?'

'Nothing is working. You are right. I will tell my friends. They are at the Reichstag. They will help me.' She grabbed his hand. 'Thank you.'

And before he could even mention the bill, she had run out into the rain.

CHAPTER 29

ULI WENGER HAD THE HOSTAGES WHERE HE WANTED THEM. Room 3N001 of the Reichstag was a *Fraktionssaal*: a space allocated to the more conservative of Germany's main parliamentary groupings. The irony that the politicians whose room he occupied favoured tough sanctions against terrorists was of no interest to Uli. He had brought his captives here because it suited his purpose.

The hostages sat in one corner of the room at white tables with shiny metal legs, watched over by CCTV monitors suspended from the ceiling. A line of buckets stood along the wall behind them. On the way up to the third floor, the hostages had been allowed to scavenge as much food and drink as they could carry, from the freezers and fridges of the MPs' restaurant. Now, the floor of the *Fraktionssaal* was littered with bottles of mineral water and fragments of food. Uli had placed Ashley Anderson and the little black girl, Jasmine, a few tables apart from the rest. He might need the teacher to perform again on television. He would kill both of them before midnight. But for now, he had allowed Karen Daniels and Otto to join them. The dog seemed to steady the girl, and Uli wanted the hostages calm.

Uli sat next to Dora behind a table which ran along the front of the room. Like the rest of the Chaos Team, both wore their masks. Two wide-screen televisions on movable gantries stood in view of the hostages. One showed Wild TV; the other, feeds from the CCTV cameras controlled by Ida in the comcen. Across the room, Viktor and Wilhelm were sitting by a two-metre high sculpture of what looked like a nail penetrating a piece of wood. The two marksmen were watching the hostages, Heckler & Kochs across their knees, hoping for some activity which might require them to intervene. Gustav and Martha were in another part of the building, preparing a surprise for anyone who dared attack.

Everything was on course. Each member of the Chaos Team was focused and motivated in their different ways. None of them knew all that Uli had planned: not even Ida in the comcen, to whom Uli had confided the core of his strategy. Ida thrived on trust. To be part of a team engaged on a historic mission, informed of details he had revealed to no-one else, had given her life the focus she craved. But even she did not know Herr Kraft's final instruction. How could she? It would destroy her.

Dora glanced at her watch. 'Three hours to midnight,' she said. 'Think they'll try anything?'

'They are trying everything now,' Uli said. 'GSG 9 will have flown in reinforcements from Meckenheim. Maybe the American Delta Force are here. And the British SAS, perhaps the French GIGN, the Russians – who knows? The more the better. Then, confusion will be perfect. The first priority before any attack will be technical surveillance. They will try to find out where we are, and how many. But it will not be easy. They will focus listening devices on the windows. But the Reichstag is full of rooms like this, with no windows. They will drill into walls, to place microphones. But they are too far away to drill into anything useful; and if they try to approach the building, we will shoot a hostage. They will try thermal imaging; but the Reichstag's walls are solid. They are groping in the dark.'

'What about the snipers on the towers?'

'They are dangerous. But the rest of the roof and the rooms beneath the towers are covered by Ida's cameras. If they move off the towers, they are sentencing hostages to death.'

Dora ran her hand over the weapon which lay on the table in front of her. 'How many would we kill?'

Uli shrugged. 'A few seconds of automatic fire would be enough to kill them all. Even if the special forces could somehow identify this room, approach it without our knowledge and detonate stun grenades before we were aware of their presence, we could kill many hostages. Our situation is perfect. We have a kitchen next door; beyond is Ida's communications centre. A fine broadcasting studio. Also, a slaughterhouse.'

'Why not execute them here?'

'When the deadline nears, the hostages will become desperate. We must control the broadcast environment. Also, this room will become unpleasant enough in a few hours without corpses.'

'The captives seem quiet now.'

'They have no choice.'

Constrained to the rear of the room, the remaining hostages seemed infected by lethargy. The British journalist, Ferguson, was writing something in a notebook. The Russian and US Presidents were sitting at a table with their backs to Uli, the British Prime Minister to one side. The German Chancellor and the French President shared another table. But most of the captives were staring at the televisions.

Allowing the hostages to watch live TV posed dangers. But Uli believed the benefits outweighed the risks. Coverage of the crisis would remind the hostages that their situation was hopeless and allow them to witness executions in the studio next door. More important, the hostages might notice developments on the news or CCTV footage which members of the Chaos Team missed. Now Uli saw that his strategy was paying off. There was a stir of excitement in the corner of the room several seconds before a jingle announced a "breaking news" story. Several hostages nudged their neighbours, or turned to face the television.

The TV moderator was torn between alarm and animation.

'Wild Media,' he said, 'has announced it will shortly make an official response to the demands of the hostage-takers in the Reichstag.'

The picture shifted to a hastily-called news conference outside the headquarters of the Wild Media Group. A well-groomed young man with slicked-back hair was approaching a dais thick with microphones, accompanied by an older man in horn-rimmed glasses. Both were sheltered from the rain by assistants holding black umbrellas.

The younger man held up two sheets of paper. There was a storm of camera flashes. He moved to the podium.

'I represent the law firm Krüger, Hahn & Kaiser of Frankfurt and Bad Homburg,' he said. 'We were engaged in a private capacity by Mr Rudolph Wild, Chief Executive of the Wild Media Group, for thirty-four years until his murder by the Red Army Faction in 1982. Since that time, we have been engaged by his son, Mr Maxim Wild.'

Uli noticed that several German-speaking hostages had moved to the front of the group in the corner. Among them was Maxim Wild himself. His trademark smile had been replaced by an expression of dismay.

'I have just delivered to the board of the Wild Media Group a copy of a sworn deposition made by Mr Maxim Wild at the offices of Krüger, Hahn and Kaiser, three weeks after the death of his father,' the younger man said. 'The board has asked me to relay the contents of that deposition to the media. They have authorised this disclosure, first, because that was the express wish of Mr Maxim Wild himself, as set out in his 1982 deposition, and, second, because the contents of the deposition have a bearing on the demands of those now holding Mr Wild hostage in the Reichstag.'

The young lawyer paused before continuing.

'Mr Maxim Wild was deeply distressed by the murder of his father. He was, however, disturbed also by the willingness of the then German government to capitulate to the terrorists' demands. Mr Wild believed this policy would encourage the Red Army Faction and other terrorist groups to engage in further attacks. Mr Wild also disagreed with the decision of the then board of the Wild Media Group, supported by the German government, to meet the financial demands of the RAF. The subsequent payment of a ransom to the terrorists did not prevent the murder of his father. Against this background, Mr Maxim Wild's sworn deposition instructs the board of the Wild Media Group as follows.' The lawyer cleared his throat.

'In the event of Mr Maxim Wild ever being taken hostage by the Red Army Faction or any other terrorist or criminal organisation, and irrespective of threats made against his person, no action should be taken to accede to any demands made as a condition for his release. I repeat: no action should be taken to accede to any demands made as a condition for his release. Thank you.'

Uli watched the hostages in the Reichstag digest the lawyer's statement. Several people had turned to look at Wild. The portly tycoon was staring at the television as if his life depended on it.

The lawyer had been replaced at the podium by the older man, who was sweating heavily. Before he spoke, he wiped his cheeks, forehead and neck with a cotton handkerchief.

'I wish to make a statement on behalf of the Wild Media Group,' he said. He stopped, and wiped his forehead again. 'The board have discussed Mr Maxim Wild's deposition. They have taken account of the many years which have elapsed since the deposition was made, and the changed political circumstances, including the reunification of Germany and the dissolution of the Red Army Faction itself. They have also examined the terrorists' demand that the Wild Media Group pay billions of euro to finance so-called development aid to a country in Africa. And they have taken into account the critical financial situation in which the Wild Media Group finds itself, thanks to adverse trading conditions and the unhelpful policies of the German government. To accede to the terrorists' blackmail would have a profound negative impact on the stability – indeed, the very survival – of Wild Media.' The older man paused.

'The board wishes to draw attention to the Wild Media Group's extensive engagement in charitable initiatives in a number of developing countries, most recently the Wild Zeitung's "Sponsor an AIDS orphan" project of March this year. The Wild Media Group also wishes to point out that taxes paid by the Group, and by the workers it employs, help pay for development assistance in the poorest countries of the world by the German government, by the European Union, and by the governments of many other countries in which subsidiaries of the Wild Media Group operate.

'Mr Maxim Wild at present holds some thirty-five per cent of the shares of the Wild Media Group. As such, the instructions contained in his deposition from the year 1982 carry great weight. The existence of Mr Wild's deposition was not known to the board until earlier today. But the firm Krüger, Hahn & Kaiser has drawn the board's attention to a resolution ratified by the board of Wild Media, under Mr Maxim Wild's chairmanship, shortly after his father's death in 1982. That resolution commits the Group to reject out of hand all future extortion attempts against Wild Media by terrorist or criminal organisations and to place the matter at once in the hands of the police.'

The man in the horn-rimmed glasses paused and mopped his face and neck again. He stared down at his prepared text. Then he gripped the edge of the podium with both hands and took a deep breath. 'Taking all these factors into account, the board of the Wild Media Group wishes to make clear that it will not under any circumstances submit to the blackmail attempts of the self-styled Action Group for Peace and Justice in connection with the illegal detention of the Chief Executive of the Group, Mr Maxim Wild. In particular, the board will not accede to the demand that the Wild Media Group should provide aid to a developing country. The board appeals to those holding Mr Wild to release him at once. Thank you.'

The two men turned, ignoring a tumult of questions, and re-entered the headquarters of the Wild Media Group.

In Room 3N001 of the Reichstag, Maxim Wild stood in the front row of hostages. He seemed to be trying to compose himself as he sought to catch the attention of Uli and Dora at the front table.

'Take no notice,' he said. 'That deposition is ancient history. I can send a message now, to the board. They'll do the aid thing.'

'Yes.' Uli stood up. 'You can send a message.' He took out his pistol, and pointed it at Wild. 'That message will show what happens when people refuse to meet our demands.'

'*No!*' Maxim Wild screamed; and with an agility which belied his girth, ducked behind the other hostages and began worming his way towards the back of the group.

Uli did not move, but observed the behaviour of the other hostages. Most of them shrank away from Wild, pressing themselves against walls or under desks so that he could not take cover behind them. But a minority, including the German Chancellor, several German cabinet ministers and the British ambassador, did the opposite, pressing themselves together to form a human shield to shelter the portly tycoon. To Uli's right, by the nail sculpture, Viktor and Wilhelm had also drawn their pistols.

'I see him,' said Viktor. 'Can I take him out?'

'No.' Uli kept his voice level. 'Leave it to me.' He ranged his pistol along the hostages sheltering Wild. 'You are making a mistake,' he said. 'If Wild does not come forward, I shall shoot a hostage at random – not necessarily one of those protecting him. If the shot does not kill the hostage, the person I shoot will be executed next.'

There was a scramble away from the cluster sheltering Wild. But the clump of people around him did not move.

'Very well.' Uli picked out a hostage standing close to the wall and shot her in the arm. It was the type of difficult shot Viktor and Wilhelm were desperate to try out on a human target. Uli smiled. That sense of power, and the pleasure it brought, was like a drug. It was his privilege, as leader. Just how powerful he was, the rest of the Chaos Team did not yet understand.

The woman Uli had hit was the German Minister of Defence, Irmgard Schneider. She had dyed red hair and red-framed glasses and was unpopular both in her own party and in the country at large more for her lack of charisma and poor public speaking skills than for any deficiency in the formulation or execution of policy. She had not been amongst those shielding Wild, but had taken off her jacket, leaving her arms bare. When the bullet struck her she looked down in astonishment at the wound, which began to ooze blood, and issued a low moan.

'Frau Schneider. Come to the front,' Uli said. 'How many more people must I shoot? Wild! This is your fault.'

Such was the hostages' fear of drawing attention to themselves that it seemed no-one would protest, or even speak, as the white-faced Defence Minister stumbled forward, clutching her arm. Blood was streaming down to her elbow and dripping on the floor. Uli shook his head. Insects. Then he saw that the American journalist, Karen Daniels, had risen to her feet and was feeling her way along the edge of a desk away from Jasmine.

'Sit down,' Uli said. 'Or I shall shoot you, too.'

'Listen, big boy.' The American turned her sightless eyes towards Uli. 'I don't know what the hell you want, but whatever it is, you're not getting it. Your demands are crazy. You can't escape. Release us now, and you'll spend the rest of your life in a German prison while the US tries to extradite you. It's not so bad, they say.'

'Shut up.'

'You shut up. Tell your buddies to let us go. Now.'

The journalist's voice carried so much force that Uli felt himself longing to obey. To resist meant punishment.

'Uli?' Dora was nudging him. Uli nodded and bit his lip. He must assert himself.

'You! American journalist! Come to the front!'

'What? You going to shoot a blind woman, now? You're pitiful.'

'Come to the front!'

'I'm leaving Otto with Jasmine.' If Karen Daniels heard the edge of unreason in Uli's voice, she gave no sign of it. She inched forward between the white tables. Irmgard Schneider moved towards her and held out her uninjured arm.

Uli shouted again. 'Wild! Come out now. Or I shoot someone else. Do not think this is hard for me. I shall be happy to kill everyone.'

There was movement at the back of the human shield, as if some of those protecting Wild felt it was time for him to reveal himself. But the media boss remained hidden.

'Very well, then.' Uli pulled the trigger. It was another tricky, beautiful shot. This time he hit Irmgard Schneider in her other arm, the one which Karen Daniel had been holding. The way the blind, bossy journalist leapt away in shock as the bullet struck the woman she had been trying to comfort filled Uli with intense joy. The Defence Minister crumpled to her knees, her face contorted in agony. Panic broke out as hostages scattered. 'Silence!' Uli felt an almost supernatural strength. 'Stay still!'

The hostages froze. Incredibly, the Chancellor and one or two others were still shielding Wild, their bodies rigid with tension.

'Who is next? Perhaps the Chancellor.' Uli raised his pistol. 'No! Wait!'

The bowed form of Maxim Wild emerged from behind his diminished band of protectors. He sidled to the front of the room in a submissive, sideways motion and gently took the arm of Karen Daniels.

Uli addressed the remaining hostages.

'I hope nobody else has left instructions telling their companies, or their governments, not to give in to the demands of kidnappers,' he said. 'The portion of the money due from the Wild Media Group will now have to be raised by the remaining enterprises.'

Several business leaders groaned.

'Mr Wild will deliver his final message on television in a few moments. You may watch, if you wish. Before that, Frau Schneider will deliver her own message. For a few moments, she will be more famous, and perhaps popular, than she ever thought possible. Who can say such a life was not worth living? The last message will be from Miss Daniels.'

'It's Ms Daniels,' Karen said.

'Silence!' Uli clenched his fist, then realised he was losing control. 'Now, we shall all go to the TV studio. You!' He addressed Irmgard Schneider. 'On your feet. The story is finished for the three of you.'

With that, he led Maxim Wild, Karen Daniels and the weeping, broken figure of the German Defence Minister from the room.

CHAPTER 30

HELEN AND BLORE HARL WATCHED THE WILD MEDIA PRESS conference in the room overlooking the Reichstag.

'My God,' Helen said. 'I never thought I would feel sorry for Maxim Wild.'

'It's high risk,' Blore said. 'The logic is, by refusing to pay ransoms, you make hostages worthless. If they're worthless, the terrorists have no reason to keep them. But do terrorists think logically?'

'Maybe we can't see their logic.' Helen thought of Nigel. 'I can't see why no-one is trying to understand the motives of the hostage-takers.'

'Tell that to the Delta Force.' Blore Harl turned and stared out at the Reichstag. Night had fallen, and floodlights picked out every detail of the wet stonework. 'They have a simpler theory: to free the hostages, they have to kill the terrorists. Somewhere out there is a squadron of US special forces getting ready to go into harm's way.'

'A frontal assault is impossible.'

'I don't think "impossible" is a concept they major on at Fort Bragg.'

Helen crossed her arms. 'You know the problem with crisis managers? When the heat is on, they can't resist the pressure to do something. So, they look around for something to do – like launching a useless attack on the Reichstag – and say "this is something. Let's do it."'

'That's Trollope,' Blore seemed untroubled by Helen's sharp tone. 'Phineas Finn. *It has been the great fault of our politicians that they have all wanted to do something.* Still true.'

'No-one has learned anything in a hundred and fifty years.'

'Nope. I guess you can blame the voters. It's a while since a politician was elected on a platform of doing nothing.' Blore turned back to Helen. 'If you don't want the Delta Force to rescue the hostages, how will you get them out?'

'Look at what has happened so far.' Helen saw the problem laid out before her. 'Two whole years before the Summit, the terrorists launch a recruitment drive into the heart of the SSU. They also start laying a false trail of intelligence half-way round the world so that we will beef up security at the Reichstag. This is a global organisation we're dealing with. Then, before the assault begins, a video pops out of the internet implying the hostage-takers are religious fundamentalists. Yet, if we're right, in fact they're all German, recruited by Johann Frost. They are consistently trying to blind us to what is really happening.'

Blore nodded. 'The British press will froth at the mouth when they find a bunch of Germans have taken your Prime Minister hostage.'

'This could happen anywhere,' Helen said. 'Johann Frost can't have toured police and special forces units in Germany looking for religious nuts. He must have recruited people who would buy into something else he had to offer.'

'Like what?'

'I don't know.' Helen shook her head. 'Some terrorists have a political cause – especially the guys at the top. But the foot-soldiers can be driven by anything. Some are like high-school killers: they want an adventure, or to strike back at someone who they think has humiliated them. Others want to be famous. Like Herostratus. Or they find being in a close-knit group gives them the sense of belonging they crave. Like football fans.'

'Who's Herostratus?' Blore said.

'He was a Greek pyromaniac who destroyed the temple of

Artemis at Ephesus in 356 B.C. When they asked why he did it, he said the name of the architect who designed the temple would be forgotten, but the name of Herostratus would live on forever.'

'Who was the architect?'

'No-one knows.'

Blore sighed. 'If everyone who felt like destroying something did it, there'd be nothing left standing. I can think of a few places I'd like to blow up myself.'

'Me too.' Helen looked out at the rain. 'Suppose we assume Johann Frost has an agenda and the rest of his team has a mix of motivations. Why should they demand world peace?'

'You said it before. Confusion. Their whole strategy has been based on misinformation. Why should their demands be any different?'

'But if the demands can't be met, they're condemning the hostages to death.'

'Maybe it's money. Hold it.' Blore took out his phone and touched the screen. 'The share prices of the eight corporations crashed as soon as the terrorists demanded they pay billions of dollars in aid, or lose their CEO. Anyone who knew that was going to happen would have made a fortune.'

'What about Wild Media?'

Blore tapped his screen. 'A crazy day. They've been on the brink of a financial meltdown all year, with the government hammering them on media regulation and the banks talking about calling in their loans. Their shares fell further than anyone else's when the terrorists seized control. But since the announcement that Wild Media will not pay anything to get Maxim Wild out, the shares have soared. I guess shareholders care more about billions of dollars on the bottom line than they do about Wild himself.'

'Think they'll really kill him?'

'Looks like we're about to find out.'

In the corner, the television showed a picture of a woman with red hair and glasses, sitting in a chair facing the camera.

'That's Irmgard Schneider.' Helen's heart raced as she recognised the woman. But the shock of seeing someone who might be murdered in front of her already seemed less since the death of Tilo Pollex. A threshold had been crossed, and diminished. At least it wasn't Nigel.

'She's injured,' Blore said.

'Two Germans,' Helen said. 'Two cabinet ministers.'

Irmgard Schneider disappeared, to be replaced by a panel of counter-terrorism experts. Two were staring open-mouthed at a TV screen with its back to the camera. The third was looking away. A banner at the foot of the picture named a channel to which anyone wishing to watch the feed showing Irmgard Schneider could now turn.

'Do we switch?' Blore picked up the remote control.

'We have to know.'

Irmgard Schneider reappeared. The Defence Minister was slumped in a swivel chair. Both her arms seemed to be slick with blood. Her mouth was slowly moving, but her voice was indistinct.

'My god,' Dieter Kremp said. 'What have they done to her?'

'Where is the teacher?' Helen said. 'Why aren't they telling us what's happening?'

'Maybe they think this is all we need to know.' Blore leaned forward in his chair.

'Why should they shoot her?' Helen said. 'No-one's approached the building.'

'No reason,' Blore said. 'Maybe – '

Both of them gasped as Irmgard Schneider's head burst open.

'Holy shit.' Blore turned away, coughing.

For a few moments, the corpse of the Defence Minister lay slowly rotating on the swivel chair. Then the screen turned blue.

Helen's hand was over her mouth. Dieter was staring at the screen. At last he spoke.

'I cannot believe they would kill a woman like that,' he said.

'What's the difference?' Helen felt an illogical rage. 'Why should a woman's death be better or worse than a man's?'

'They must be animals.' Blore licked his lips.

'Murdering people to force countries out of the World Trade Organisation,' Helen said. 'What the hell is that about?'

'Do you think the WTO doesn't matter?' Blore said. 'That the Children's Summit was a waste of time?'

Helen looked up. 'Say that again.'

'What? That the Summit was a waste of time?'

'With all the talk about the terrorists' demands, I never thought of it. One thing they achieved with the first shot was to stop the Summit. Who's always opposed it?'

'Apart from a million anti-globalisation protesters? Uktam Zholobov, the Russian energy oligarch.'

'But also Maxim Wild. Wild Media was always against everything the Summit was meant to achieve. Action against monopolies. It was going to cripple Wild.'

'So what?'

'But then he changed his mind. He started pushing for the Summit to take place.' Helen looked up. 'What's happened to the share price now?'

Blore looked at his phone. 'Still soaring. In theory, Wild is now rich. But he may also be dead.'

'Look.'

Maxim Wild sat in the swivel chair. He looked terrified. As they watched, he shook his head and his eyes widened. Then he began to speak.

'Friends.' Wild tried to smile. His voice wavered. 'They are going to kill me. Because the board of Wild Media refused to bend to the will of these terrorists. At first I was angry. But now I know that decision showed strength and courage. It is right to live according to principles. These people will kill us whatever we do. We should never reward them for it.'

'He's showing strength and courage himself,' Blore said. 'I'd be begging for my life.'

Helen was watching the screen through half-shut eyes. It felt ghoulish, waiting to see a man killed.

'Why are they letting him say this?' she said.

'I want to say goodbye,' Wild went on, 'to my dear wife, Heike. My sons, Paul and Sven; and my granddaughter, Lily. I love you all. Do not forget me.'

Again, Wild shook his head.

'No! Wait!' He began rising from his chair as a shot burst out.

'His face!' Blore Harl murmured. 'They shot his face.'

At first it seemed as if Maxim Wild would continue to rise, even though part of his jaw was disconnected, a fleshy bundle hanging loose. Then he began to sink back into his chair. There was a second detonation. A fountain of blood erupted from the top of Wild's head. This time, the unseen executioner had hit his mark.

Helen stared at the body until the screen turned blue. Then the picture flickered. Karen Daniels sat in the chair, her sightless eyes facing the camera.

'Karen!' Helen scrambled to her feet. 'Oh no. Not Karen. If they touch her – ' Helen turned away. 'Blore, I can't look.'

'I don't know if I can.' Blore, too, was shrinking from the screen.

'Wait,' Helen said. 'Why is there no sound?' She glanced back at the television and saw Karen's lips moving in silence. Then the sound came on.

'…don't watch because it'll be messy. If anyone in Russia knows where my eyes are, tell them I'll be joining them soon – '

Helen felt rather than heard the explosion of the gun as she turned away. Then a second shot. She counted to five. The room was silent.

'Are you looking?' she said.

'I'm looking.' Blore's voice

'Is she dead?'

'Yes.' The American placed his hand on Helen's shoulder. 'Karen Daniels is dead.'

CHAPTER 31

DIETER KREMP HAD KNOWN MANY WOMEN SOLDIERS. THERE seemed to be more every year. Most had a tough time of it: always a minority, always struggling on the assault course, always with something to prove. Sometimes he'd made their lives a bit harder. That had been fun.

All this made his feelings about Elle Morgan hard to explain. The young SAS Captain didn't seem to care what anyone thought of her, least of all Dieter. That should have fuelled his efforts to bring her down a peg or two. Yet she seemed oblivious to his attempts to assert his authority. It was like trying to browbeat a glacier. What was happening to him? The disasters of the past few hours must have sapped his confidence. That, and Helen Gale spotting before he did that it could only be the SSU itself which had taken over the Reichstag. The blonde diplomat had shown him up in front of Elle Morgan. Now he had another chance to prove himself.

Dieter was with the SAS Captain at the back of the main briefing room in the Bunker. The room was crammed with German and US special forces. Yet he, Dieter, would not even have got in without the help of Elle Morgan.

When the dolt on the door said Dieter was barred, Elle had insisted on talking to the major in charge of the GSG 9 unit. He in turn had been in the middle of an argument with the US Army colonel commanding the Delta Force troops, a sniper detachment of whom had already deployed to positions on the perimeter of the Safety Zone *without German authorization* – a direct contravention of German sovereignty – and sixteen of whose specialists were now inside the bunker.

To make things worse, Elle Morgan knew the Delta Force colonel from a tour in North Carolina two years previously. Outnumbered, outranked and incandescent with rage, the GSG 9 commander had agreed to Dieter entering the Bunker simply, it seemed, to reduce by one the number of problems confronting him.

Now, the GSG 9 major stood at the front of the room, attempting to brief his audience of German and US special forces on the situation in the Reichstag. The US colonel leaned against the wall nearby, watching the German with an expression of studied indifference.

'We start from the assumption,' the major said in English, 'that it is members of the former SSU who are the hostage-takers.'

'You don't know that,' the US colonel said.

'We are not sure, no. But it is the best guess we have. Analysis of the pictures from the Reichstag suggests that all the Secret Service agents inside were killed by the terrorists in the first assault. Of the eleven members of the SSU who were stationed in the Reichstag, eight are accounted for by the bodies in SSU uniform visible in the TV pictures. But of those bodies, only two showed clear evidence of fatal injuries. Six did not. So, we estimate the number of terrorists in the Reichstag at between three and nine.'

The US colonel nodded.

'Our surveillance of the building,' the major continued, 'suggests activity on the third floor, the so-called *Fraktionsebene*. This level contains several large rooms to which the hostage-takers may have moved.'

'How do you know they've moved?' the colonel said.

'We have studied the pattern of feeds from the closed-circuit television cameras controlled by the terrorists, together with the murder of the two Russians in the North Lobby. These are consistent with an attempt to conceal the movement of the terrorists from the plenary chamber to another location.'

'Could be a bluff,' the colonel said.

'Yes. Finally, thermal images of the south and east sides of the building in the past few minutes show intense heat in a meeting room belonging to the Green Party on the third floor. We do not know the origin of this heat. It is consistent with a fire. But there is no sign of burning in the rest of the building. It is possible that the terrorists are close to the fire.'

'You mean, we don't know where they are,' the colonel said.

'We are not certain, no.'

There was movement at the door. Half the participants craned round to see the new arrival.

'What is it?' the GSG 9 major said.

'Video analysis, sir. We've found something.' A young woman stood in the door in a black assault uniform. 'You'll want to see it.'

'Now?'

'Yes, sir. We've set up the video feed.'

The GSG 9 major's eyes narrowed. 'Go ahead.'

'This had better be good.' The Delta Force colonel glanced at his watch.

The major said nothing. The lights dimmed. A beam of light shone onto the screen behind the podium.

'This is a CCTV image from the communications centre in the Reichstag,' the GSG 9 woman said. 'We have studied the tapes from every CCTV camera in the building from the hour before the first explosion to the time the terrorists took control of the feeds. We started by viewing the seventy-five percent of images taken while cameras were out of rotation.'

'These are the pictures the cameras took while other images were displayed on the monitors,' the Delta Force colonel said.

'That is correct, yes, sir.'

The screen showed an image of the comcen, taken from above the console. A woman in the grey uniform of the Summit Security Unit was standing watching the monitors. Next to her, at an angle, stood a man in a black suit and dark glasses. There was no sound.

'The woman on the left is SSU officer Katia Vonhof,' the GSG 9 woman said. 'Next to her is Secret Service Agent Antonio Rojas. Watch closely now. At this moment, the image from this camera disappeared from the consoles in the Bunker and the comcen.'

What happened next was a movement so small as to be almost invisible. Katia Vonhof's head moved slightly to the right.

'We think she said something to distract him,' the GSG 9 woman said.

The Secret Service agent looked down at the monitor. In the same moment, the SSU officer pulled out a pistol and shot him in the head at point blank range. The agent, who had begun to move as she drew the weapon, sank to the floor. Katia Vonhof fired two more shots into his face.

Inside the Bunker there was silence. Then the Delta Force colonel spoke.

'Thank you,' he said. 'That confirms our enemy. I guess our Secret Service friends will want a word with Miss Vonhof, in the unlikely event that we capture her alive.' He unfolded himself from the wall, ignoring the GSG 9 major, and addressed the Delta Force soldiers.

'The Reichstag is a hard target: large, heavily fortified and well defended. We do not want to assault this building unless all other options have been exhausted. If we do have to attack, we shall maximise our chances of success by doing so in the company of two further assault teams which are en route from North Carolina.'

The colonel looked around the room. 'But if the situation degrades, we are ready to go in at once using the immediate attack plan. Are you all familiar with that plan?'

'Yes, sir!' The sound of the US soldiers confirming their familiarity with the immediate attack plan was deafening.

'Good.' The colonel turned to Dieter. 'Our task now is to use what time we have to improve that plan. I would like Mr

Dieter Kremp, an expert on the terrorist stronghold, to share with us his thoughts on how we can defeat the surveillance cameras. Any ideas on ingress also welcome.' The colonel paused. 'Any assault in the next few hours will be high-risk. Statements to the effect that such an operation is too dangerous to contemplate will, however, result in the speaker being used for target practice.'

No-one spoke.

Dieter moved to the front, conscious of the baleful gaze of the GSG 9 major. He had given hundreds of briefings in this room over the past two years. This was the most important. His audience was divided down the middle: sixteen Delta Force soldiers on the left, sixteen GSG 9 on the right. All were watching him. Treating him with respect. He drew himself up to his full height.

'The first things which are important,' he began in English, 'are the red lines on the floor of the Reichstag corridors and main rooms. These mark areas not covered by the CCTV monitors…'

Dieter was completing an account of the weaknesses of the third-floor windows when a hand-held radio on the desk next to the Delta Force commander squawked. At the same moment, a young GSG 9 man burst in.

'They have started to kill more hostages,' he said. 'A minister.'

The Delta Force colonel took a step forward. 'Who?'

'Irmgard Schneider. The Minister of Defence.'

The colonel turned to the GSG 9 major. 'Are you launching an assault?'

'No.' The German frowned. 'The crisis staff of state secretaries has not authorised military action.' He paused. 'Either by GSG 9, or by the US Delta Force, which is at present on German territory.'

'That's too bad,' the colonel said. 'If we go in, we'd like your men with us.'

'US forces cannot deploy military force inside Germany without the agreement of the German government,' the major said. 'Unless you are at war with Germany. I hope you are not.'

'I understand you have to say that.' The colonel said. 'But if you think the US military can stand by and see the President threatened while we wait for authority from a foreign government, you're living on another planet.'

'You need to hear this, sir.' It was a US Delta Force soldier staring at a smartphone. 'They've just killed Maxim Wild. They're preparing to execute the hostage, Karen Daniels, who is a US citizen. Washington want us to go in now, and go in hard.'

At once, in a clatter of boots and equipment, every American in the room was standing, eyes fixed on the colonel.

'OK, boys,' the colonel said. 'Let's rock and roll.'

CHAPTER 32

U LI WENGER STARED AT THE WALL OF THE *FRAKTIONSSAAL*.
Every vertical surface was clad in sheets of brilliant white
laminate, scored at the base with rows of black parallel lines. The
pattern of white and black was so dazzling that the members of
parliament who usually occupied the room joked it would render
the calmest person aggressive in less than fifteen minutes. Uli
smiled. He'd felt aggressive all his life.

The door to the lobby flew open. The big man, Gustav, was
covered in blood: his arms up to his elbows, his torso, his legs.
Even his face was spattered. He strode across to Uli.

'It is done. We watched them burn for ten minutes.'

Uli looked at the blood. 'You should have been a butcher.'

'Have you ever tried chopping up a body? It's not easy.'

'Where is Martha?'

'I left her smashing jawbones with the blunt end of a fire axe.
Never saw her so happy.'

'She should get out of there. How is the fire?'

'Hotter than hell. Fireproof sheet on the floor, supported on
each side with metal furniture. Body parts in the centre, doused
in petrol. We piled them around a couple of chairs to help the
air reach the flames.'

'Did the windows smash OK?'

'Sure.' Gustav grinned. 'They're not armoured up here.'

'The extra blood?'

'Done. We put a litre of your blood on the edges of the

fireproof sheet, then poured the rest on the floor. So, it looks like we cut up your body there. Once all the body parts were ready to burn, we dumped the torso of one of the Secret Service guys in your blood, dragged it towards the fireproof sheet, and threw it in. As if your body was on the top of the heap. Where it burns hottest.'

'Did you leave plenty of blood on the floor?'

'We cut up two Russians, and two Secret Service men. There is blood on the floor.'

Uli nodded at the big man. 'Good work. Fetch Martha, quickly.'

'Sure,' Gustav said. 'What was the point of the extra blood, anyhow?'

'It will confuse the hell out of the police later when we have all disappeared. Go.' Uli watched Gustav move away.

There was a gasp from the hostages. Uli whirled towards the televisions. The floodlights illuminating the outside of the Reichstag had been extinguished. Since the lamps were on the Reichstag's own anti-tamper circuit, that could mean only one thing. The lights had been shot out.

They were under attack.

Uli had planned for this moment. All members of the Chaos Team knew what they had to do. There was only one way seven fighters could repel an assault by an elite special forces squad.

'Attack in progress. Viktor, Wilhelm – take the hostages to the studio. I will bring the teacher. Gustav, Dora – automatic fire. If anyone enters this room or a stun grenade goes off, kill everybody.'

'What about Martha?' Gustav said.

'She should not have stayed so long smashing bodies. She will have to take cover in the lobby.' Uli cursed silently. If Martha opened fire at the wrong moment, the situation could spiral out of control.

He grabbed Ashley Anderson. Viktor and Wilhelm pushed their way through the hostages and emerged with the Chancellor of Germany and the President of the United States. Both held their heads high. The other captives shrank away. Uli saw the British hostage, Nigel Ferguson, still bent over his notebook.

There was a round of distant blasts.

'They are in the Green committee room,' Uli said. 'Attracted by the heat. Like moths. They are using stun grenades.'

'To subdue defenders.' Gustav bared his teeth. 'Everyone in that room is subdued already.'

'They must be using helicopters to enter the upper windows.' Uli pushed Ashley Anderson ahead of him towards the studio. 'That will take time. And they are on the wrong side of the building.'

'What if they put out the fire?' Dora said.

'They are soldiers, not fire-fighters.' The thought worried Uli. What if the bodies were not fully burned?

With three hostages and four members of the Chaos Team, the studio seemed crowded. Ashley Anderson sat down in the killing chair before she realised the seat was drenched in blood. She made to stand up, but Uli pushed her back. Viktor restrained the German Chancellor. Wilhelm had the muzzle of his pistol pressed under the President's chin. Ida watched the console.

'Ten seconds,' Uli said to the teacher. 'Ida. Run the tele-prompter.' He pointed to the hostages. 'Cuff them both. Guns to heads.'

'They are coming into the lobby.' Ida was staring at the banks of screens. 'Three. Four. Five. Six.'

'Can you see Martha?'

'No. But I can see them as clear as day.' Ida smiled. 'Kremp must have told them about the red floor-tape. They are staying behind it.'

'Good thing we moved the tape.' Uli turned to Ashley Anderson. 'Get this wrong, and the President dies.'

The teacher sat up straight and looked at the camera. At this moment, Uli knew, she would be going out to a worldwide audience of millions, swarming in front of their televisions. Nothing hooked the insects like violence and celebrities.

'You have attacked the building.' Ashley Anderson addressed the teleprompter on the front of the monitor. 'We will now show pictures of your special forces. Unless they leave at once, the German Chancellor will die.'

Ida worked the console. Uli pulled the teacher out of the chair and Viktor shoved the Chancellor into it. The TV feeds from the Reichstag now showed a line of special forces troops moving along the wall of the third-floor lobby. Because a line of red tape ran parallel to the wall, the soldiers believed themselves invisible. Instead, in their black helmets, goggles and body armour, they looked absurdly vulnerable in the brightly-lit space. Uli guessed they were American Delta Force, but it was hard to be sure. Instantly the transmission went on-air, the soldiers stopped. Some looked down at the tape on the floor, others scanned the ceiling for cameras.

'Going live,' Ida said.

Now the main feed out of the Reichstag showed the German Chancellor, sitting in the chair in which viewers had already seen three hostages murdered. Uli imagined the sense of shock across Germany. Would it be enough?

'Special forces have stopped,' Ida said.

'They must retreat.' Uli stared at the screen.

More and more of the black-clad soldiers had appeared in the white-tiled lobby. Uli counted sixteen. 'They are conferring,' Ida said. 'Taking orders. Or deciding what to do next.'

'The Germans will be screaming at them to get out of the Reichstag before we shoot the Chancellor,' Uli said. 'They cannot attack us if they know for sure we will kill hostages.'

'They are pulling back.' Ida scrolled through her screens. 'Wait. They have seen something. It must be Martha. They're turning.'

'No!' Uli said.

But it was too late. An extended burst of firing rang out

beyond the door, two or three seconds, Uli judged, maybe a whole forty-round magazine from Martha's Heckler & Koch MP7. In the same instant, the CCTV screens in the comcen showed five or six black-suited figures fall writhing to the floor. She'd gone for their hips, to avoid the body armour. Immediately the lobby outside exploded with noise as the special forces soldiers returned fire. Uli tried to count the bodies on the ground. Martha would be dead. But only ten or eleven Delta Force were still fit to fight. Less: some would care for their injured comrades.

There was no time for Ashley Anderson. Uli leaned towards the microphone. He spoke English in the thickest German accent he could muster. 'Tell your forces they are stopping their shooting right now and pulling out,' he shouted. 'I am counting from five. Five. Four. Three...'

The noise outside was dying down.

'Two...' Uli aimed his pistol at the Chancellor's head and glanced at the CCTV screens. Were they pulling back? Did the US Delta Force care if the German Chancellor died?

'One...'

Outside, the firing had come to a stop. No-one seemed to be moving. Uli thought of the pictures Ivan had shown him in the woods, and pulled the trigger.

The Chancellor of Germany died instantly. The President, who was standing behind Uli, flinched. Even Viktor and Wilhelm blinked at the familiar figure, lying dead in the chair. As if one corpse was worth more than another, Uli thought. Only Ida, faithful Ida, was still watching her console.

'Put the soldiers on camera!' Uli yelled. He and Viktor pulled the Chancellor's body onto the floor. Then Wilhelm manoeuvred the President of the United States into the killing chair.

'They are moving forward,' Ida said. 'They must have new orders. Clearing rooms round the lobby. We have less than a minute.'

'If they find us, the President will die.' Uli turned to Viktor and Wilhelm. 'On the floor,' he said. 'Train your weapons on the door. If it opens, automatic fire outside.' He looked at Ida. 'Go live on the President. And give me sound.'

'Sound is on.'

Uli addressed the microphone again. He felt calmer now, in control. The attackers had no chance. 'Stop the attack.' Again, he tried to disguise his voice. 'If you do not, we are killing the President.'

But as he spoke, the President jumped up from the chair. Uli felt the President's head smash into his chin and fell to the floor, his mouth filling with blood. He felt the President attempt to kick him, but the blow was feeble. Uli scrambled to his feet.

'Viktor. Help me.'

Between them, they grabbed the President by both arms and wrested the struggling politician back into the killing chair. But the President fought and kicked. Only when both Uli and Viktor crouched down on the floor and held one arm each could they hold their captive still.

'The special forces are right outside,' Ida said.

'Pull back your soldiers now,' Uli yelled into the microphone, 'or I am shooting.' He looked at Ida. 'Why are they still moving? Is the chair not on-camera?'

Ida was on her feet, scrambling to raise a tripod from the floor. 'The President kicked it over,' she said.

'They must see.' Uli was shouting. 'The President's head, and a gun. It is our only defence.'

'Camera is up.' Ida was back at her console. 'On-air now.'

But at that moment a heavy boot kicked open the door and something clattered into the room. Stun grenades. Two. Four. Viktor and Wilhelm, on the ground, opened fire with their Heckler & Kochs. There were shots outside. Someone shouted in English.

'The President! Hold your fire!'

There was a series of terrific explosions and blinding flashes. The room was full of smoke. Wilhelm was still firing. He must have reloaded. Ida would be shooting, too. The grenades were meant to disorientate defenders for a few vital seconds. But that depended on surprise. The Chaos Team had tracked their attackers right across the lobby. The Delta Force could not risk shooting a man who had a gun to the President's head. They could not win.

Uli again thought of the pictures in the woods and did not hesitate. He placed his hand against the wall behind him; held the pistol at arm's length; felt his finger tighten on the trigger, and fired: once, twice, three times.

CHAPTER 33

HELEN SAW KAREN DANIELS LYING IN THE KILLING CHAIR AND screamed. The roar of grief poured out as if some reservoir of fury had been building ever since Nigel and Karen had first been taken hostage. Ever since Jason Short had thrown her out of the embassy, taking away what little power she had to shape events.

Karen's picture blinked out. A blue screen. Helen was back in the room overlooking the Reichstag, staring at the television. Blore had his hand on her shoulder. Helen brushed it away and leapt up.

'Sorry, Blore, I can't – '

'It's OK.' The American backed off. 'It's OK.'

They stood opposite each other. Helen gulped air. Blore jerked round towards the window.

'There's something happening at the Reichstag,' he said. 'Helicopters. A fire.'

'No!' Helen moved to the window. 'It won't work.'

'They have to do something,' Blore said. 'What's the alternative?'

'I don't know.' Helen said.

The television came back on. They saw chaos. The Chancellor of Germany in a chair. Threats. A countdown. Pictures of special forces soldiers, somewhere in the Reichstag, moving forward then halting. Then the Chancellor was shot.

'Jesus,' Blore said.

Helen tried to calm her breathing. The death of Karen

Daniels had filled her with emotion. The death of the German Chancellor, like the killings of the other politicians, seemed more abstract. Yet she felt a dizzying sense of loss and anguish. The terrorists were winning.

'Who's the man making the threats?' she said. 'He can hardly speak English. And why did he shoot? The soldiers had stopped.'

Then she saw the President shoved into the killing chair.

'Oh, no.' Blore's face was pale. 'I must go.' He rushed from the room.

Helen was alone. She watched the struggle between the President and the two terrorists wearing SSU uniforms. Suddenly the picture showed a close-up of the carpet. The camera must have been knocked over.

She stared at the grey square and a thought sprang into focus. Why were the terrorists wearing masks? Did they hope to escape? Why else would they care who knew their identities?

There was no time to pursue the idea. The TV picture spun as someone picked up the camera. She saw the President, held down. A gun at point-blank range. Smoke. Again, the image jerked and disappeared. She heard explosions and automatic gunfire, then three staccato shots, then – nothing. No pictures. No sound. It was as if a curtain had fallen. Could the attack have been successful? Or had something happened to the feed?

She ran to the window. Helicopters were still visible, hovering over the Reichstag. A fire raged in one of the top-floor rooms.

She grabbed a phone. Engaged. She tried again, and again. At last someone answered.

'Helen. Where are you?' Ram Kuresh sounded subdued.

'Looking at the Reichstag. Did the assault succeed?'

'No.' There was a silence.

'What happened?'

'Did you see the President? On TV?'

'Yes.'

'As soon as Washington saw a gun to the President's head,

they pulled the plug. To go on would have been like murdering the Commander-in-Chief. The special forces have withdrawn.'

'Is the President alive?' Helen found it hard to say the words.

'No-one knows. The theory here is that the assault damaged a cable, or a camera.'

'I can't see why they shot the Chancellor. If the hostage-takers had threatened the President first, they would have stopped the assault quicker.'

'Your fertile brain is still in fine fettle, Helen. But I do not know the answer.'

'What has happened on the demands?'

'Ah.' Ram paused. 'It seems the appearance on television of the President of the United States restrained by two bloodstained terrorists has helped to oil the wheels of diplomacy. What was impossible may now, after all, be possible.'

'Tell me you are kidding.'

'I am quite serious, Helen. You will recall your theory about members of the Summit Security Unit taking over the Reichstag. Since then, we have seen that the chaps in balaclavas holding onto the President are indeed wearing SSU uniforms. That, and the rather disciplined response of the terrorists to the special forces assault, and their readiness to shoot important hostages, has already led one or two governments to conclude that if they wish to get their people out, they will have to do something.'

'Surprise me. What have they done?'

'The French, Russian and Italian governments have announced their withdrawal from the World Trade Organisation and other International Financial Organisations.'

'What about us?'

'The British are holding firm, because we, of course, do not give in to terrorists. The Germans are also hesitating; in their case, because their Chancellor seems to be dead, and because their provisional government has launched a full-scale diplomatic row with the Americans for the unauthorised attack on the Reichstag which caused the fatal shooting. The Americans are refusing to meet any demands until the terrorists confirm that the President is alive.'

'But what if the hostage-takers don't care about the demands?'

'Actually, that adds to the confusion. There is uncertainty about whether meeting some of the terrorists' demands will lead to some hostages being released; or whether all the demands must be fulfilled. We cannot ask the terrorists to clarify, because the only way we can talk to them is by television broadcast. Neither we nor the Americans want to do that, because it would show the world that we do not know what is happening.'

'But we don't.'

'No. Meanwhile, our own Deputy Prime Minister has asked the Attorney General for legal advice on two issues. First, the DPM wants to know whether the unilateral withdrawal of two or more key members from the World Trade Organisation amounts to a de facto suspension of the WTO itself. If the WTO is, in effect, moribund, the British government would be able to announce the suspension of its own membership on operational grounds, unconnected with events in Berlin.'

'So, we cave too.'

'But in our own unique and highly-principled manner.'

'What about the Americans?'

'The Vice-President has been too busy to share his thoughts with anyone for the last few minutes. But the present US administration has never been a friend of the WTO.'

'Surely the US can't meet the demand to pull out its military forces?'

'There you have a good example of the muddle we are all in.' Ram lowered his voice. 'The terrorists must know we cannot start abandoning countries around the world in the space of a few hours. But ministers in COBRA want to know what their options are. Hence the Deputy Prime Minister's second question to the Attorney General. He wants to know whether a decision by the United Kingdom to withdraw our troops from the areas named by the terrorists could leave us open to damages claims from people we are now protecting. It seems we would not want the victims of future massacres complaining to us later that we should have stayed put.' Kuresh put his hand over the phone for a moment, then continued. 'Most of the British units involved are UN peace-keepers.'

'Where are the SAS?'

'Still on the runway at Brize Norton. They could be here in an hour if the Germans agreed. But our lawyers are clear we would be opening a ghastly can of worms if we gave ourselves the right to move combat troops into a friendly country in direct opposition to that country's wishes.'

'But that's what the Americans have done.'

'Come now, Helen. Everyone knows the flexibility with which countries approach international law is in direct proportion to their military might. Also, strictly speaking, the US special forces troops engaged so far were already in Germany.'

'How about the development aid?'

'The developing countries have all said that they do not want money extracted by terrorism. But it seems several corporations whose CEOs are inside the Reichstag have begun to assemble the necessary finance. Except Wild Media, of course.'

Helen thought of the executions of Tilo Pollex, the German Interior Minister, Irmgard Schneider, the German Defence Minister; and now the German Chancellor. The deaths of Karen Daniels and Maxim Wild. The US President, held down in the killing chair.

'They are wasting their time,' she said. 'Think about it – '

'Please do not tell me. Tell the excellent Mr Jason Short. Tell the wise men of the Cabinet Office Briefing Room.'

'Jason is refusing to talk to me.'

'We need you here in the embassy, Helen. Jason cannot cope. Outwardly, he has the appearance of a fully-functioning diplomat. He writes things down, attends meetings, promises to take action. But underneath, the mechanism is broken. He is not talking to the Germans. He is not running the embassy. In fact, thanks to the efforts of Mr Short, this embassy's contribution to the engine of British policy formation is to throw a handful of spanners from time to time into the gearbox. Please come back, Helen.'

Helen looked at the Reichstag. She had to do what she could.

'Of course I'll come,' she said.

'Thank you,' Ram said. 'Please be quick.' He rang off.

Helen looked up to find Dieter Kremp standing in the doorway.

She saw at once something had changed. An hour ago, the deputy head of the SSU had been in shock. Now he radiated power. It was as if contact with Elle Morgan and the Delta Force had recharged his self-esteem. Staring at him, Helen felt a glimmer of attraction, then revulsion as she realised this was the first time they had been alone together since the previous night.

'The attack has failed,' Dieter said.

'They killed Karen.'

'I told them it could not work.'

'Did you hear me? They killed Karen. A blind woman. My friend.' Helen wanted to slap Dieter. 'Where is Elle?'

'Elle is with the Americans. They are blaming me for their failure. Because the terrorists decoyed them to the wrong side of the Reichstag. And because the floor-tape was moved.' Dieter slammed his hand against the wall.

'Are you angry? Good. Me too.'

Dieter moved into the room. 'They are not listening to me.'

Helen held Dieter's gaze. When he was fired up, Dieter was more himself. Arrogant. Self-obsessed. Desirable.

'Me neither.' She stepped towards him. 'Here's a challenge, Dieter. Can you listen to me? For once?'

'Why?' Dieter scowled. 'What are you saying?'

'I'm asking questions. Like why the terrorists have killed three German cabinet ministers.'

'It means nothing. They also killed Wild. And the American journalist.'

'We'll come back to Wild. Karen probably attacked them with her bare hands.'

'And the US President?'

'We don't know if the President is dead or alive. Or did the assault team see something?'

Dieter sat down. 'The Delta Force team are raging,' he said. 'They never wanted to attack such a hard target so early, with too little information and too few people. But Washington sent them in. A suicide attacker took six of them down. The rest could have made it. Then Washington pulled them out. The soldiers want to finish the job.'

'Did they see the President?'

'Yes. For a moment, in the middle of a firefight, before they came out.'

'A firefight?' Helen stared at Dieter. 'They were shooting into a room where the President was being held?'

'They were attacking a room full of terrorists.'

'You mean the Delta Force could have shot the President.'

Dieter shook his head. 'These people do not shoot wildly,' he said. 'But it is possible in theory, yes.'

'My God. What else did they see?'

Dieter frowned. 'A strange thing. The room where the fire was burning was swimming in blood. In the centre of the room was an incinerator with a fireproof sheet and some petrol, and burning body parts.'

'Who?' Helen thought of Karen.

'The Delta Force saw nothing to identify.'

'Did they bring anything out?'

'Their orders were to leave at once. The fire was still burning.' Dieter was watching her. 'You said something about Wild.'

'Yes. Didn't it strike you? His execution was different. They allowed him practically to make a speech. When they shot the Defence Minister, her chair spun round. When they shot Wild, it stayed put. Then when Karen started talking, the sound was off to begin with.'

Dieter frowned. 'Maybe the speech was his reward. Because the Wild Zeitung campaigned to make the Reichstag stronger.'

'That's right. All the Wild media did. And remember, I asked why we didn't cancel the Summit after the second bomb? Something happened, I couldn't think what. It was Maxim Wild. He came out of the US embassy right after the explosion and made a speech about why the Summit should go ahead. He said we shouldn't give in to terrorists.'

'Wild makes mistakes too.'

'It was almost like he was trying to make it harder for any G8 leader to pull out of the Summit.' Helen's mobile was ringing. She was on the verge of understanding something. But what? She snatched up the phone.

'Helen. It is Oleg.'

'Oleg. It is good to hear from you. All this is horrible.'

'Yes,' the Georgian said. 'Maybe I can help.'

'You are kind. But we know who the terrorists are.'

'Maybe you do.' Oleg Sukanashvili paused. 'But I have someone here who says he knows who paid for the attack on the Reichstag.'

CHAPTER 34

Sabine Wolf pounded down Unter den Linden in the rain. She must tell someone what she had seen on the television at the Dong Huong. But who? Her clothes and shoes were drenched. Her legs and feet ached. She would never get to the Reichstag in time. Everyone would be dead.

At the Bebelplatz, where the Nazis had burned books, she stopped to catch her breath. Her throat was burning. There were people all around, but no-one she could trust. She saw a policeman and turned her face away.

Across the street towered the bronze statue of Frederick the Great on his horse, the floodlights forming bright cones in the rain. What was the Pushkin poem they had learned in the Kinderheim? The Russian words resurfaced in her mind. A bronze horseman chasing a crazy guy through St Petersburg. Maybe she was going mad. She was not even sure what she had seen on the television. Could she, Sabine Wolf, really save lives? She rubbed her wrists: it was years since they had ached like this. The pain reassured her. That, at least, was real.

The Reichstag was near. Maria would be there. Maria would do something.

She set off running again. People with umbrellas looked at her, shook their heads. A dishevelled, hysterical woman. The Russian embassy loomed ahead, massive and imperious. It had been built in the days when the Soviet Union still held sway over East Germany. When Sabine Wolf had been locked in a children's home for a crime her parents had died committing. Now, the Russian President was locked in the Reichstag. Maybe she could tell someone in the embassy. They would know what to do. But the great metal doors filled her with dread. She ran on.

Not far to the Reichstag now. When she neared the Brandenburg Gate, her heart sank. The streets were jammed with protesters. She fumbled for her mobile. No service. She could never find Maria in such a crowd.

What if you had a secret and no-one to tell?

At the corner of the Wilhelmstrasse she saw it. A modern building, with brightly-coloured angles sticking out over the street. The British embassy. This was where the demonstrators had been blown up. Where Helen Gale worked. The security expert from the embassy. Sabine pictured the diplomat in her cotton print dress at the hospital. A woman, who acted at least as if she cared, who was connected somehow to authority. *Who better to tell?*

Sabine's phone was in her hand. She could do this. Yes.

She pulled the fragments of the torn, damp card from her pocket and dialled the number. No service. She checked her watch. Ten o'clock. Would Helen Gale be working this late? She took a few steps nearer. In the narrow street, the downpour seemed heavier than ever. Then, she saw that the entrance was bristling with police and Bundespolizei officers with guns. Any moment now they would see her. She stepped back. What was she thinking? This was as much a place of power as the Russian embassy. She did not belong here. Last time Sabine had seen Helen Gale, she had threatened the diplomat with ruin.

'Hello, there. Can I help you?' An English voice, speaking German.

Sabine saw an elderly man in a shabby suit standing in the entrance to the embassy, holding an umbrella above his head. He was looking at her quizzically.

'I do not know if you can help me,' she said.

'Well, is there something you want?' The man's face was friendly.

'I am looking for Helen Gale.' Sabine held out the card. 'She gave me this.'

'I'm afraid she's not here at the moment.' The man eyed the ripped-up card. 'I would normally call her for you, since you have her card, but the networks are overloaded.'

'Will she be back soon? I have information.'

'What information is that, love? Is it important?'

Sabine looked at the man. Although his tone was kindly, he still stood between her and the embassy. Was he a security guard? Why did he not wear a uniform? But his shabby suit reassured her. She needed someone to confide in.

'It is important information,' she said. 'It could save the life of the President of the United States.'

The man's eyebrows went up. 'Is that so? Would you like to tell me about it?'

'No. I must talk to Helen Gale.'

'I see. Well, if you have some ID, you can come inside and wait.' Eric Taylor, the duty security officer at the embassy, stood aside to allow the soaked, black-clad woman to pass through the security arch. 'But I'm afraid I have some bad news for you. The President died half an hour ago.'

CHAPTER 35

'K ILLED?' HELEN RETREATED A STEP FROM OLEG SUKANASHVILI and glanced back towards the door of his office. 'How?'

'The President died when Delta Force soldiers entered the studio,' the Georgian said. 'No-one knows whose bullets were responsible. The terrorists say this shows more heads of state will die if anyone tries to attack again.' He watched her. 'Are you afraid?'

'Yes.' Helen could not help looking again at Dieter being frisked as he sought to enter the room. She had not seen the Georgian's two bodyguards since Moscow. One had a narrow face with swept-back hair and over-large, protruding eyes. The other had wide shoulders and a massive bull-neck. What were they doing here?

'Do not mind Iveri and Merab.' Sukanashvili's voice was grave. 'Usually they stay out of sight. But today we have a visitor who is dangerous. I am not talking about your German friend, by the way.' He did not look at Dieter. 'Who is he?'

'Why would they kill their most important hostage?'

'When guns are fired, people get hurt.'

Helen shook her head. 'So far, no-one has died by accident.'

'I ask again. Who is your friend? He looks like a policeman.'

'Yes. He's OK.'

'You mean well, Helen. But you are young. I do not like Germans in uniform.'

242

'He is helping me.' For once, it felt good to have Dieter nearby.

'Are you lovers? Of course.' The Georgian nodded. 'Do you trust him? Then he is welcome.'

'I don't know.'

'You are lovers, and you do not trust him?'

'Did you trust all of your lovers?'

'A good answer. But none of my lovers were German policemen.'

'Dieter can help us end the siege. He is the deputy head of the Summit Security Unit.'

'The deputy head of the SSU? A man without a job. A failure. Both.'

'Let him in. I will ask him to keep quiet.'

'Do that. I would like to watch his face.'

Moments later, Sukanashvili led the way into an inner office. Four dark-brown armchairs were arranged around a smoked-glass table bearing a pot of tea, four cups and a plate of biscuits. Dieter followed Helen. He and the Georgian had contrived to shake hands in such a way that their fingers barely made contact. Now he watched Sukanashvili as if expecting him to attack Helen at any moment. Behind Dieter stood the two minders.

'Why are there four cups?' Helen said.

'You will meet the man now.' Sukanashvili sank into an armchair. 'I must warn you, Helen. He is a professional killer. I know this. He has left his previous employment. Now he works for me. I believe I can trust him: I have paid him money, and he knows that colleagues of mine have called on his mother and his sister in Vladivostok. But I cannot be sure I have judged him correctly.'

'I thought you knew about people.'

'I have some understanding, yes. But this one is difficult. Ex-navy. Pacific Fleet. Then Russian Interior Ministry, Organised Crime Squad. I met him once before in Moscow, many years ago. Now he is a businessman.' Sukanashvili used the English word transliterated into Russian, with its connotations of dirty dealing. 'It means he will do your business, whatever it is. Yet he also acts as if he is the king of morality.'

'He sounds awful.'

'Wait until you see him.'

'Quickly. We have less than ninety minutes before midnight. I must get Nigel out.'

'Your husband. You were going to see him tonight.'

'Yes.'

'I think, perhaps, Kolya can help you.'

Helen sat forward in her seat. 'If he can, I want to meet him.'

'He may enter,' the Georgian said to the bodyguards. The one with the protruding eyes opened the door. The most beautiful man Helen had ever seen walked in.

He was a Russian, with high cheekbones, blue eyes and straight, blond hair. Sukanashvili's bodyguards drew back as he entered the room.

'Kolya,' Sukanashvili's tone was gruff. 'I want you to tell Miss Gale the story you told me earlier. Speak in German, so the cop understands.'

'With pleasure.' The Russian looked at Helen. A smile played around his lips, as if he knew what she was thinking.

'My name is Kolya Baklanov,' he said. 'I am from the Far East region of Russia, but I have lived for many years in Berlin. First, I must say that Mr Sukanashvili did not find me. I knew he was seeking information. I came to him of my free will.'

'Why did you do that?' Helen said.

'One reason is that Mr Sukanashvili is a generous man. But the main reason is that Johann Frost has killed two unarmed Russians live on television. I warned him not to kill Russians. He has done the opposite. Now, he will die.'

'Johann Frost?' Dieter said. 'You know Johann Frost?'

The Russian ignored him. 'Three years ago, there appeared in a Russian-language newspaper in Berlin an advertisement for a confidential courier. I applied for the job, and was successful.

The duties were simple: to carry messages, or money, from one place to another in the city.'

'Who were you working for?' Dieter said.

'I worked out of a small office close to the Kurfurstendamm, with several other couriers. As the months passed, we became fewer. The jobs grew more challenging, with complex messages, covert entry into buildings, or evading surveillance. The sums of money became larger: sometimes I carried sums of more than one million euro in cash.'

'They were testing you,' Dieter said, 'to see if you were reliable.'

The Russian kept his gaze fixed on Helen. 'In the end, I was the only courier left. It was then, two years ago, that I was first told to deliver a message to a man named Johann Frost.'

'Who was the message from?' Helen said.

'The messages were never signed. They were delivered to the Ku-damm office each Monday. Always the same courier. Always hand-delivery. Good security.'

'Good security? But would they trust you?" The question felt fake to Helen. When she looked at the man's blue eyes, she wanted to trust him herself.

'Because they saw I was reliable. And because I did not know who the messages came from,' the Russian said. 'If something went wrong, if the plot was discovered, I could tell the police nothing. Nor could Frost.'

'But why involve an extra person?'

Kolya smiled. 'To communicate securely between two people, you cannot use a telephone, or the Internet, or the postal service. All of these can be intercepted by the enemy, without your knowledge. Most of them have been intercepted before you even pick up the telephone, or turn on your computer. The safest way is to pass a message by hand, using people you can trust. They gave me many tests before they trusted me.'

Helen watched Kolya. 'What were the messages?'

'The first messages were sealed. I think they contained money.

Later, we established dead letter drops to transfer important papers, and the messages set out the tasks Frost was to perform.'

'There was more than one task?'

'The first was, I think, a test. He was to kill two men and one woman, living in Kreuzberg. I was to confirm that they were dead.'

'Johann Frost killed three people in Berlin two years ago?' Helen felt as if she was understanding less, not more.

'Yes,' Kolya said. 'When I saw this, I knew my own life was at risk. I decided to discover the name of my employer.'

'Why didn't you quit?'

'I was earning too much money. Also, a contract killing is always associated with other important crimes. It is not my business to solve crimes in Germany. But to know who has committed one can be rewarding. So, I decided to try and find out who wanted Johann Frost to kill the eight leading members of the German government, starting with the Chancellor, the Minister of the Interior, and the Defence Minister.'

'You knew what he had planned? And you did nothing?' Before Dieter Kremp had risen to his feet, Sukanashvili's two minders had seized his arms.

'Sit down,' Sukanashvili said.

Dieter stood staring at the Russian.

'Please sit down, Dieter,' Helen said. 'Or he won't talk. Eight German ministers – are you listening?'

Dieter Kremp settled back into his chair, his jaw working.

'I gave Frost his orders,' the Russian continued. 'In return, he briefed me on security for the Summit. This information was taken away by courier each Monday.

'It was not easy for me to identify my employer. I began by searching the office. Rental deeds, tax records, the usual nonsense. I found nothing. All bills were paid through an account in Switzerland. I decided to track the courier who delivered our messages.

'This was a Swiss man, correct, always silent. I did not know how much he knew. But he was the only link I had. He went to the airport. When he flew to Geneva, I bought a ticket and followed. But on arrival, he was picked up by a driver, and I lost him.

'I could not be away from Berlin for long without arousing suspicion. Nor could I involve the police authorities in Germany or Switzerland. So, I stayed in Geneva only long enough to make some simple arrangements, and returned to Berlin.

'When the courier came the following Monday, I was ready. I had already booked a flight on his aircraft, and was able to keep close to him through the airport. When he left the terminal, the taxi I had booked the week before was waiting. I followed the man's car as far as the centre of Geneva, where he entered the office of a legal firm. A few minutes later, he left; by this stage I was sure he was no more than a courier. If I was the first cut-out between Johann Frost and the man who was employing him, the courier was the second; and the lawyer was the third.'

'Three cut-outs,' Dieter muttered.

'Here, my employer made a mistake. If he had chosen a large practice, with hundreds of lawyers, it would have been hard for me to follow the trail. But his representative was a young lawyer with his own practice. This made it possible for me to return to Geneva the next week, after completing my duties in Berlin, and watch his office. On the Friday, three days before the courier's next visit to Germany, the lawyer walked four hundred metres to a building by the Central Station on the Rue de Lausanne. I travelled with him to the ninth floor and watched him enter a door. Twenty minutes later, he returned to his own office. I had reached the next link in the chain.'

The Russian sat back in his chair and rubbed the palms of his hands on his jeans. 'Here I ran into difficulty. The office the lawyer had visited was not a place for doing business. It was a representative office, for companies wishing to have a legal or tax base in Switzerland. On a brass plate outside the door were listed forty-five firms. I made a note of all them. But I felt I had achieved nothing. The fourth cut-out had defeated me.'

'What were the companies?' Dieter Kremp said.

Kolya continued to ignore him. 'I returned to Berlin and my work with Johann Frost. I took care with my personal security. And I decided to approach the problem by another route.'

'The three murders,' Helen said.

'Yes.' When Kolya Baklanov smiled, Helen saw he had perfect teeth. 'These were not people killed at random. I tried to see what they had in common. I found that they were all in the film business. All of them had worked regularly for one company. When I saw the name of that company, I knew I had found my employer.'

Helen nodded. 'Maxim Wild,' she said.

Oleg Sukanashvili roared with laughter: a fat belly-laugh too huge for the office. 'I told you she was smart,' he said to the Russian. 'You work for months, and spend all your salary on air-fares. She puts her finger in the air, and sees the answer. Maxim Wild. Yes!'

'Maxim Wild is correct.' The Russian did not seem put out by Helen's guess. 'Wild Media was one of the companies on the office door in Geneva. And the three dead film technicians worked regularly for Wild TV. The loop was closed.'

'Is that all you have?' Dieter Kremp spoke with such venom that even Kolya turned to look at him. 'Names on a door, and a company which employed dead people? This is useless. It would not convince a court. It would not even convince a newspaper. And Maxim Wild is dead.'

'At last you say something intelligent.' The Russian looked at the former deputy head of the SSU. 'The evidence linking Maxim Wild to Johann Frost is convincing, but not conclusive. Why the terrorists killed Wild, I do not know.'

'Wait,' Helen said to Kolya. 'Suppose Wild did organise this. He tasked you with approaching Johann Frost to do a job for him. But how did Wild know Johann was a potential terrorist?'

'The first time I visited Frost,' Kolya said, 'I was given his address in Friedrichshain, with a photo. Someone else had identified him.'

'Could Wild have approached a lot of people?' Helen turned to Dieter. 'How about you? Anyone ever offer you an envelope full of cash?'

'No. I would have reported any approach.'

'Did anyone ever try to find out about you and Johann? Do an interview?'

Dieter Kremp slowly nodded. 'We did many interviews at the start, when the government was telling the world how safe the Summit would be. The SSU was a new concept: a hybrid of police and armed forces, recruiting only the best. But one TV channel took a special interest.'

'Let me guess. Wild News.'

'They have always been obsessed by terrorism. As soon as the SSU was set up, they came to interview Johann and me. They asked a lot of questions. They wanted to make a documentary. But we told them nothing. The project was abandoned.'

'Or maybe not, if they found out something about Johann,' Helen said. 'Could the dead film people have been the documentary-makers?'

'No,' Kolya said. 'They were working on feature films. The two men were a producer and a make-up artist. The woman was a special effects expert.'

Helen sat still. Her heart was pounding. She stood. 'Oleg,' she said in Russian, 'thank you for finding Kolya. He is perfect.'

'He knows this,' Sukanashvili said.

'I must go. Call me if Kolya remembers anything else.'

'I can do better,' Sukanashvili said. 'I will send him with you. You need help.'

Helen looked at the blond Russian. A professional killer, Sukanashvili had called him. 'Thank you, Oleg. But I have Dieter.'

'That is why you need help.' The big Georgian smiled. 'But tell me, Helen. Where are you going?'

Helen stopped at the door.

'I am going to the embassy. We can stop this. Because I know what is happening inside the Reichstag.'

CHAPTER 36

DIETER COULD BARELY KEEP PACE AS HELEN MARCHED UP THE Wilhelmstrasse. The rain had soaked her hair. Her face gleamed under the streetlights. She looked as if she might do something magnificent, or disastrous. He longed to help her. Yet she seemed as indifferent to him as she was to Kolya Baklanov, who trailed a few paces behind.

The Russian seemed impossible to shake off. Twice, Dieter had told him he was not welcome. Baklanov had kept walking.

They reached the embassy. An elderly man in a suit came out.

'Hello, Helen. Someone's here to see you.'

'Eric. Thanks.' Helen gripped the man's arm and swayed. 'Who is it?'

'A young lady. Name of Sabine Wolf.'

'Sabine Wolf?' Dieter saw Helen glance inside the gate. 'Well, tell her to go die quietly somewhere. She's one of the lot suing me.'

'Is she? That's odd. Maybe she has changed her mind.'

'I need to see Jason.' Helen looked at her watch. 'We have new information about the siege.'

She strode through the gates. The man called Eric seemed about to say something, then stood aside. Almost at once, Helen re-emerged. She held a piece of plastic like a credit card.

'Why isn't my pass working?'

'I'm sorry, love,' the security officer said. ' Mr Short has suspended your entry privileges.'

'He can't lock me out of the embassy.'

'I know. It's shite. But so long as the ambo's stuck in the Reichstag, Short's in charge.'

'I know something which could end all this.'

'That's what your friend says, too.' Eric pointed inside.

As if in response, a woman emerged. Dieter had never seen her in his life. She wore heavy glasses and dark, damp clothing. She grabbed Helen. 'I must talk to you.'

'Let me go,' Helen said.

'Please.'

Helen turned to Dieter. 'I can't cope with this now. Can you make this woman take her hands off me?'

'My pleasure.' Dieter stepped forward. He knew the type. A self-styled anarchist or do-gooder who thought the world owed them a living. He would have to watch she did not throw herself to the ground, then sue him for her injuries. But when he touched her she shrank away.

'Help me,' she said.

'Push off.' He projected her across the street with a fine-ly-calibrated shove.

Helen addressed the security officer. 'What the hell is Short's problem?'

'He's afraid you'll show him up, mainly,' Eric said. 'But I reckon he really does believe you are making things worse.'

Helen's eyes widened. 'Do you believe that? I'm trying to get Nigel and all the rest of them released.'

'I don't know, love.' The security man glanced at the Russian standing across the street. 'I know you're trying to help. But you could land in real trouble.'

'OK. Thanks, Eric. Sorry it has to be like this.' Helen turned away.

Dieter watched Helen walk out into the rain. She looked angry, not defeated. For a moment, she stood silently in the darkness. Then she pulled out her mobile.

'Is that Freddy Acton at the Dispatch? This is Helen Gale.

If you can promise me a TV team outside the British embassy in Berlin in ten minutes, I will give you an exclusive that will make you famous. Sound good? OK then, listen. Here is the story.'

Helen spoke for several minutes. Then she slumped against the facade of the embassy. Her legs felt like blocks of lead.

'What now?' Dieter said.

'Someone is coming.' Helen wondered if it was true.

'Are you sure?'

'No.' Helen checked her watch. There was no sign of any TV cameras. What if no-one came? Why should they? The ground was damp. The minutes ticked by. She felt exhaustion embrace her. Her head fell forward. Her eyes closed. She saw Karen, curled up in an armchair, laughing.

'Helen. Listen.'

There was a rumble overhead. Helen blinked. Had she been asleep? A helicopter was descending towards the junction at the end of the Wilhelmstrasse. A door slid open and a slim, red-haired woman jumped out, an umbrella over her head against the pounding rain, followed by a man with a TV camera.

Helen dragged herself to her feet, breathing deeply. At last: her chance to tell the world what she believed was happening.

But what if she was wrong?

The red-headed woman ran towards her. Helen recognised Michelle York, the BBC's roving crisis correspondent. She looked edgy and intense.

'Are you the wife?'

'I am Helen Gale.'

'Michelle York, BBC.'

'Hello.' Helen licked her lips. 'Do you always travel by helicopter?'

'I wish. The chopper was chartered to shoot footage of the Reichstag. But the Germans wouldn't let us fly near the place. So here we are.' The woman took out a small mirror and inspected her face in the shade of the umbrella. 'Shall we start?'

'I guess so.' Helen's mouth felt dry.

'Freddy Acton has taken a risk, putting out that story with you as the only source.'

Helen said nothing.

'He says you think Wild is still alive. But he left it open whether you're bonkers.'

'You mean the story could be "Junior diplomat goes gaga"?'

'That's it.' Michelle York hardly smiled. 'But people will want to hear you. Freddy's piece makes you sound quite a character. I mean, going on TV because your boss won't listen to you. Not very diplomatic, is it?'

'My boss is about as diplomatic as Oliver Hardy,' Helen said. 'Ready when you are.'

'Right.' Michelle York glanced at the camera and a light came on.

'Helen Gale,' she said, enunciating the words clearly. 'You are a British diplomat locked out of your own embassy here in Berlin because your boss thinks your theories about the Reichstag siege are crazy. You are being sued by victims of a bomb here yesterday. And your husband, Nigel Ferguson, is a hostage. You must be under awful pressure.'

'Yes.' ABC, Helen thought, recalling her media training. Answer the question. Bridge. Core message. But what was the question?

'How do you feel?'

'I feel angry.' That was the question answered. Now she needed a bridge. 'I want to get all the hostages out. Especially Nigel.' Finally, the core message. 'To do that, we must figure out what drives the hostage-takers. The truth.'

'What makes you think you understand them better than anyone else?'

'We know the hostage-takers are all members of the Summit Security Unit. The question is, what is their motive?'

'And you have a theory, is that right?'

'I want to know why there is no link between the hostage-takers – a bunch of Germans with security backgrounds – and their demands, which are idealistic and high-concept. I also want to know why those demands can't be achieved within the deadline.'

'You think the terrorists are stupid?'

'No. I think they want something else.'

'Like what?' The smile on Michelle York's face had been replaced by a quizzical frown. A second TV team was setting up a camera. More crews were lumbering into view.

'I don't know,' Helen said. 'But I have talked to a witness who says he carried messages between the man who planned this atrocity and the hostage-takers.'

Now she was preparing to name Wild, Helen felt panic rising. What if Sukanashvili was working for the Russian oligarch, Uktam Zholobov, and Zholobov had an ulterior motive to attack Wild? What if Kolya Baklanov's story was invented? If Wild was innocent, Helen's life would be destroyed. She thought of Sukanashvili in the Cafe Motiv. A man who never let you down. She pictured Kolya, with his blue eyes. She thought of Nigel, in the Reichstag. Then she took a deep breath and addressed Michelle York.

'The witness identified a man whose news networks have been campaigning to turn the Reichstag into a fortress. Who had the resources to lay a trail of false intelligence about attacks on the Summit. Whose business has doubled its value in the last few hours.' Helen paused. 'That man ordered the murder of the entire German government. His name is Maxim Wild, Chief Executive of the Wild Media Group.'

She had expected shock. Instead, at the back of the press pack, someone chuckled.

'Complicated way to commit suicide.'

Several people laughed. There were four cameras on Helen now. The drumming of rain on umbrellas seemed deafening. *Someone ask a question.*

A man from Wild TV obliged.

'Why should Mr Wild do this? Are you accusing him of manipulating share prices by killing people?'

Helen thought of Karen. 'It's not just about share prices. There must be something else that we do not know about. Maybe Wild hates the government.'

'But...' the man spoke slowly, as if addressing a simpleton. 'Mr Wild is dead. Why should a dead man do all this?'

More people laughed. But Helen felt a surge of confidence. 'Two years ago,' she said, 'Wild made a film faking his own execution. He had the film-makers – a special effects team – murdered. A triple killing in Kreuzberg. Check it out. Today we saw the film they made, alongside real hostage deaths. I believe Wild is still alive.'

'Do you think the President is alive, too?' Michelle York said.

'Yes.' Helen looked at the ring of cameras and stood up straighter. Everything was going right. 'In fact, let us challenge the hostage-takers. If Maxim Wild is dead, show us his body. They say the President is dead. Show me the head of the President, now, live on TV. They won't do it. Because they cannot.'

She knew at once that she had said something wrong. Everyone began asking questions.

'Is there not a risk that by challenging the terrorists to produce bodies, you will make things worse?' the Wild TV man said.

'Is it true you have accepted money from a British newspaper?' someone shouted. 'Doesn't that undermine your credibility?'

'Do you think the terrorists don't care about the demands?' It was Michelle York.

'That is correct,' Helen said. 'The demands are a smokescreen.'

'Then what do you think will they do with the hostages when the deadline expires?'

Helen stared at the journalist. What was the answer? The hostage-takers seemed to think nothing of murdering people. Might they massacre everyone at midnight?

'I don't know,' she said. 'We must rescue them before then.'

No-one was listening. Lights were going out.

Helen turned away. She had shared her big theory with the world. They had laughed in her face. Nearby, she saw Dieter struggling with Sabine Wolf. The little trauma counsellor was stronger than she looked.

'What is it?' Helen said.

'Some stupid story,' Dieter said.

'Please!' Sabine Wolf sounded crazed. 'Listen to me!'

'Shut up.' Dieter swung the woman away. Her glasses fell to the ground.

Helen felt a rush of anger. Sabine Wolf had tried to ruin Helen's life. But to see Dieter mistreating her was unbearable.

'Dieter! Leave her alone,' Helen said.

'She is a waste of time,' Dieter said.

'I want to listen to her.'

'Don't be stupid. She is a protester. She hates you.'

'Don't you dare call me stupid. *Let her go!*'

Dieter released the woman. 'Don't say I didn't warn you,' he said.

Sabine Wolf ran to Helen and embraced her. 'Thank you.' She smelt of cigarettes and wet clothes. Her voice was husky in Helen's ear. 'I knew you were different. You won't regret it. You see, Johann Frost was my brother.'

CHAPTER 37

'**T**HEY WILL NOT ATTACK AGAIN,' ULI WENGER SAID. 'WE ARE safe.'

'Except for Martha and Viktor.' Gustav's broad face was blank, but his eyes shone. 'Two white patriots, dead. For what?'

'The fire you and she started decoyed the Delta Force,' Uli said. 'Without that, we would all be dead.'

'Cutting up the bodies took too long.' The big man stared at his blood-stained arms. 'Why did we do that?'

'Everything is under control.' Uli spoke slowly. Say a message often enough, and people would believe it.

Yet he knew it was not true. Disaster had been just a ricochet away. It was the fault of Karen Daniels. If the US hostage had not provoked Uli into killing her, the Delta Force might have held off their attack. Now, images of the President held down by masked SSU men would have confirmed suspicions that members of the Security Strategy Unit were the hostage-takers. But the outcome Herr Kraft wanted was still possible. No-one outside the Reichstag could know who among the SSU were the victims and who the perpetrators of this crime. When it came to the final act, confusion would be crucial.

Five of them still lived. Martha, Gustav's fellow Aryan supremacist, lay dead in the lobby, riddled with bullets. Viktor had been unlucky: a stray shot had punctured his throat when the Delta Force kicked in the door to the comcen. Uli felt Viktor's loss keenly: he and Wilhelm had been the best marksmen in the Chaos Team, and the easiest to control. Now Wilhelm sat slouched watching the hostages, his finger on the trigger of his MP7. Ida, in the comcen, would stay loyal as long as she felt she was part of the team. Dora, at the front of the room, hated the German government so much she was delighted with events. But Gustav was becoming a problem.

'When will we kill more foreigners?' the big man said. 'How about these Japanese bastards? Or more Russians?'

'The deadline runs out soon,' Uli said. 'Then we will kill.'

'Why wait?' Gustav said.

'Look.' It was Dora, near the televisions. 'An interview.'

Uli and Gustav joined her. Even Wilhelm looked up. The channel they were watching had joined the transmission part-way through.

'Who is she?' Gustav said.

'An English diplomat from the Threat Assessment Committee,' Uli said. 'She is called Helen Gale.'

'That man ordered the murder of the entire German government,' Helen Gale was saying. *'His name is Maxim Wild, Chief Executive of the Wild Media Group.'*

'That's shit,' Gustav said. 'Wild is dead.'

'Yes.' Dora was watching the television, her eyes narrowed.

Gustav looked at Uli. 'It is not true, is it? That we are supposed to kill the whole government?'

'Good thing if we are,' Dora said. 'They're all bastards.'

'She says Wild is alive.' Gustav's voice was rising. 'And the President. How does she know the President is alive?'

'And why does she think Wild is not dead?' Dora said. 'Maybe we should kill the President. Then we can show her a head.'

'She does not know anything.' Uli looked to where the President of the United States was sitting at a table with an adviser. Helen Gale was stirring up trouble. He would punish her. 'The woman is English. So, we shoot an English hostage. Which one is her husband?'

'The Finance Minister is next,' Dora said. 'We should kill him first.'

She pointed to a monitor. The minister sat upright in the killing chair, his spectacles gleaming, as if about to give an interview. The image was grainy: after the main camera had been damaged in the Delta Force assault, Ida had commandeered a CCTV camera to transmit from the comcen. Uli liked the pictures: they made it look as if events in the Reichstag had become cruder. Less predictable.

'Good,' he said. 'Kill the minister. Then the husband.' He turned to the hostages. 'Which of you is married to Helen Gale?'

The journalist, Nigel Ferguson, stepped forward. Uli thought he looked too old to be married to the Englishwoman.

'I am married to her.' He attempted to smile. 'I never thought it would kill me.'

'One moment.' The British ambassador was addressing Uli. 'You said you wanted an English hostage.'

'Yes. They say we only kill Germans. They are wrong in this, as in everything.'

'Then you cannot shoot Nigel. He is Scottish. So am I. But I am willing to volunteer myself, if you insist on a Brit.'

'It's me they want,' the journalist said. 'Because of bloody Helen.'

'Scottish, English, it is all the same,' Uli said. 'We will kill Ferguson.'

'It is not the same.' The ambassador's face was red. 'It is – '

When Uli sent a shot a few centimetres over the ambassador's head he felt filled with power. It was easy to deal with men. The ambassador froze. Uli stepped forward and addressed the hostages.

'First the minister, then the journalist,' he said. 'If anyone else wants to die, you need not worry.' He looked at the clock on the wall. 'It is twenty minutes to midnight.'

CHAPTER 38

HELEN STOOD IN THE RAIN. THE STORY SABINE WOLF HAD told her changed everything.

But no-one would listen to anything Helen – or Sabine – had to say.

Two women with no voice.

Analyse this.

She scanned the street. The embassy gates, closed in her face. The pack of journalists, slowly dispersing. The helicopter, ringed by sightseers.

That was it.

'Dieter.'

'What?'

'She knows something important.' Helen nodded at Sabine. 'About Johann Frost.'

'About Johann?' Kremp frowned. 'She didn't tell me.'

'You weren't listening.'

'What did she say?'

'The real Johann Frost is dead. Sabine was his sister. The man in the Reichstag is called Ulrich Wenger. She knows where he is weak.'

'Johann never had a sister.'

'You are not listening!'

'We do not have enough time,' Dieter said.

Helen's fists were clenched. 'We have time. But we must enter the Reichstag. Now.'

'Impossible.'

'We can end the siege,' Helen said. 'If we can get Sabine inside – '

'Me?' Sabine's face was pale. 'No.'

Helen stared at her. 'But please – you must.'

'I cannot. I fear him.'

Dieter grimaced. 'I told you she was a waste of time.'

Helen reached out and gently touched Sabine's face. 'You can do this. You came here, didn't you? That took immense courage.'

'You do not know him.' Sabine's voice was a whisper.

'You are strong. At the hospital, you were strong. When Dieter tried to hold you back, you were strong.'

'I am nothing.' Suddenly the trauma counsellor turned and walked away. Helen reached out for her, but could not move. What arguments were left? *You do not know him,* Sabine had said. Trudging into the rain she looked defeated and alone.

Alone.

That was it.

Helen was running.

'Sabine. Wait.'

The trauma counsellor turned, but said nothing.

'They are still holding a child captive. Inside the Reichstag.'

Sabine's eyes flickered. The muscles of her neck tautened.

'Uli kept one when the others were released. One child. We do not know why.' Helen said.

'The hundredth child.' Sabine spoke slowly.

'Uli knows you. You must face him. Without you, the hostages will die.'

Sabine took a step forward. 'Uli will kill that child. I know him. Otherwise, he would have let all of them go.'

'You can stop him.'

Sabine gripped Helen's arm. 'Maybe I can.'

'Will you try?'

There was a pause. 'Yes. I will try.'

The intense pressure of Sabine's fingers seemed to infuse Helen with a surge of strength. 'Dieter. She will do it.'

Kremp was leaning against the wall of the embassy. 'Do what?'

'Enter the Reichstag.'

Dieter snorted. 'I told you. It is impossible.'

'Stop treating me like an idiot. How did the Delta Force get in?'

'By helicopter. They blew out the third-floor windows and abseiled in. Can you abseil?'

'There's a helicopter at the end of the road.'

'The Reichstag is a no-fly zone.'

'But how could they stop us flying in?'

'They would shoot us down. There are anti-aircraft batteries for this purpose.'

'They would never shoot down a helicopter full of security people and diplomats. Why should they?'

Dieter hesitated. 'If we land on the roof, the terrorists will kill us.'

'Dieter Kremp. Chicken. I don't believe it.' Helen moved towards the journalists. 'Is Michelle York still here?'

Several faces turned their way. The BBC journalist appeared.

'Helen. Hi. The jury is still out on whether you're nuts. But I've told the editor I think you're sane.'

'I need a ride in your helicopter,' Helen said. 'Now.'

The journalist blinked. 'Where to?'

'To the Reichstag. We are going to end the siege.'

Michelle York shook her head. 'I'll have to call the editor back.'

'No time.' Helen stepped close to the journalist. 'They may kill everyone in the Reichstag in eighteen minutes. We are trying to stop them. Do you want the story? Exclusive?'

'Not if I'm dead afterwards.' Michelle York eyed Dieter in his SSU uniform. 'How dangerous is this?'

'It is dangerous,' Dieter said. 'And stupid.'

'That's quite a recommendation,' the journalist said.

'Wait,' Helen said. 'Why not talk to your pilot?'

Michelle York looked from Dieter to Helen. 'OK. But what he says, goes.'

They approached the helicopter. Helen was aware of the Russian, Kolya Baklanov, moving along the opposite side of the street.

The pilot was a desiccated, silver-haired American wearing dark blue overalls with a military flavour. He listened to Helen. Then he shook his head.

'I'd like to help you, ma'am,' he said. 'Flying in a war zone's what I do best. I was in the Navy fifteen years. But now I obey the rules. Air traffic control say I can't do it, I can't. End of story.'

'You could save the President,' Helen said.

'Sorry. No can do.'

Helen felt despair well up. A cameraman, already strapped into a seat inside the fuselage, said nothing. Michelle York began talking to another journalist.

Was this where it ended?

Dieter glanced towards the embassy. Helen turned and saw Jason Short approaching with four German policemen, rain drumming on their flat hats.

Short stopped in front of Helen. 'That's her,' he said.

The senior police officer stepped forward. 'Are you Helen Gale?'

'I am.'

'You are under provisional arrest for incitement to murder. Anything you say may be used against you. You have a right to a lawyer. You have the right to remain silent.'

'Arrest me? But I'm trying to save the hostages. The Prime Minister. The President. If we do nothing before midnight they will all be dead.' Helen looked from the police officer to Jason. 'I'm a diplomat.'

'That won't wash, Helen.' Short looked grim. 'The embassy has waived your immunity.'

'You have, you mean.'

'Do not try to make this personal. I waived your immunity at the request of No.10. Do you think the Deputy Prime Minister enjoys watching members of the Diplomatic Service on television urging terrorists to decapitate the President of the United States?'

'I – '

'Do you realise that if they do put the President's head on a plate, it will be thanks to you? The Vice-President has spoken to No.10 personally to express his anger in the strongest terms.'

'But why arrest me?'

'Maybe they want to shut you up before you say anything even more stupid.'

The German policeman was pulling a pair of handcuffs from his belt.

'Jason.' Helen fought to keep her voice level. 'Don't you care about rescuing the hostages?'

'You should stop fantasising about things you don't understand.' Short lowered his voice. 'Within the next hour, London will issue a joint statement with Washington on military policy. And we will quit the WTO. It's crippled anyway, with so many others leaving.'

'We're caving? Because they have the Prime Minister?'

'It's not a concession if we leave an organisation which doesn't exist.' Short spoke as if it were obvious. As if repeating something often enough made it true.

'An hour is too long. We only have twenty minutes to midnight. Anyway, the terrorists don't care about their bloody demands.'

'We don't know that. And if concessions don't work, there's another assault planned, this time with the Germans.'

'What if they kill the hostages at midnight?'

'Helen. It is you who is putting lives at risk. More than you think.'

'What?' Helen took a step forward. 'Don't you think I want to help Nigel?'

Short hesitated. Why was he not meeting her gaze? When he spoke, his tone was brusque.

'The fact is, Helen, you are not helping anyone. Did you know they've just shot the Finance Minister?'

'Another German politician?' Helen grabbed Short by the lapels. 'Can't you see? That shows I'm right.'

'What about your friend, Karen Daniels?' Still Jason would not meet her eye. Helen felt a chill.

'All the others were German,' she said.

'The two Russians?'

'They tried to escape.' Helen slackened her grip on Short's jacket. 'Jason. What is it?'

'I – ' Short paused. 'I wasn't going to tell you. The terrorists say they are shooting your husband next. Because of your interview.'

'Oh, no.' Helen staggered, dragging Short sideways. She saw only Karen, and Nigel, and a cloud of blackness.

'Helen? Are you all right?' Short's face was a mask of fake concern.

Her vision began to clear. She tightened her grip on Short's lapels. 'You bastard! You shabby little git! What have *you* done to save the hostages? Nothing! Nothing! Nothing!'

Short did not resist, but let her shake him, a bedraggled marionette. Then, as her fury ebbed, he withdrew a handkerchief and wiped his face. 'I know you need someone to blame, Helen. But if they shoot Nigel Ferguson, it will be your fault.' He turned to the policemen. 'Take her.'

'Leave me alone!' Helen darted away, and scrambled up into the helicopter. 'Dieter! Sabine! Come with me.' She glared at Short. 'They are threatening Nigel, and you tell me to do nothing? What kind of man are you?'

Sabine was gazing up at Helen, her mouth slightly open. Without a word, she climbed on board. But Dieter shook his head. 'No. It is too dangerous. The pilot is right.'

'What else can we do?' Helen tugged at Dieter's shoulder. 'Come on.'

Dieter did not move.

Across the road, Helen saw Kolya Baklanov. He was watching her, arms folded across his chest, his beautiful face gleaming in the rain. Whose side was he on?

There was nothing else. She yelled, in Russian.

'Kolya! Help me!'

Short and the German policeman turned. The Russian was already running. He threw himself into the helicopter behind Helen. Suddenly his arm was around her neck, choking her. She gasped. Something was pressing against her head. The barrel of a grey pistol.

'Take off immediately,' the Russian said to the pilot in English. 'Tell the air traffic people I force you.'

The pilot did not move. 'How do I know you're serious?'

'I am serious.' The Russian fired a shot above the crowd. Helen flinched. People screamed. Jason Short threw himself to the ground.

'Thank you kindly.' The pilot's face remained expressionless. 'Now I can get airborne.'

Kolya's arm was tight round Helen's throat. She stared at Dieter. Their eyes met. The helicopter was beginning to lift. Dieter's nostrils flared; he shook his head; then he climbed aboard. 'I will come,' he said to Helen. 'You need me.'

'Prepare for lift-off,' the pilot said. At the last moment, Michelle York darted forward and threw herself inside.

The helicopter rose into the storm.

CHAPTER 39

HELEN CLOSED HER EYES AS THE HELICOPTER LIFTED OFF. SHE had to shut out all she could. The scream of the engine. Kolya's arm around her throat. The pistol at her head. But as they rose, the Russian released her.

'I am sorry,' he said. 'It was all I could think of.'

Helen felt a moment of relief. Then she thought of what lay ahead. Sabine's plan was all they had. Yet even if the trauma counsellor was right about Johann Frost, they were about to place themselves in mortal danger.

Someone was shouting. The pilot.

'Air traffic say we must land,' he said. 'What is my answer?'

'Tell them if you try to land anywhere but the roof of the Reichstag I will kill you.' Kolya put the pistol to the pilot's temple. 'Your choice.'

'They say if we approach any nearer, they'll shoot us down.'

'Let me talk to them.' Dieter scrambled into the seat by the pilot and pulled on a headset. Helen peered out into the rain. They were hovering over the Holocaust Memorial, a few hundred metres from the Reichstag.

Dieter yelled into the microphone. 'We have on board one member of the Summit Security Unit, one news team, one trauma counsellor, one diplomat, and – ' he looked at Kolya ' – a businessman. None of these people threatens the hostages.'

Helen could not hear the reply.

'To fire on us would not be legal under the rules of engagement

268

for the missile batteries.' Dieter indicated to the pilot that he should fly forward. 'The batteries are to protect the summit participants. That is our goal also.'

The helicopter passed over the Brandenburg Gate. Ahead, the Reichstag loomed. A fire still burned on the upper floor.

'Missile battery below,' the pilot said. 'Wait.' He put his hand to his ear.

Helen could hear it, too: a dull roar, rising in pitch.

A black helicopter appeared in front of them. It was far bigger than their own craft, and bristled with military hardware. It came to a halt, hovering so close Helen could see the other pilot. Next to him sat a black-visored figure.

'That is a GSG 9 Puma,' Dieter said. 'Now we know they will not use missiles.'

'They want to talk to you.' The pilot turned to Helen. 'Assuming you are Helen Gale.' He passed her a headset. 'The other lady wants a word.'

Helen looked at the black helicopter. The second figure had removed her helmet. It was the SAS officer, Elle Morgan.

Helen pulled on the headset.

'Get out of here!' Elle Morgan was shouting. 'Don't you know they have Nigel Ferguson in the killing chair?'

Helen stared across the void. The din of the helicopter had faded away. All she could hear was the SAS Captain's voice. 'Are you sure?'

'They are showing him live on TV, Helen.'

Helen pictured Nigel. Waiting to die. *Yet there would always be someone in the killing chair.* If she turned back now, she might be condemning all the hostages to death. Should she abandon everything because they were threatening Nigel?

Maybe they would shoot him anyway.

'You don't have to go in,' Elle Morgan was shouting. 'The Germans and Americans are launching a joint assault.'

'When?' Helen said.

'What?'

'When is the assault? And why should it work better than the last one?'

'More time to prepare,' Elle said. 'Overwhelming force. And we know now where they are in the building. It will work.'

'But when is it?'

'Any time now.'

'Before midnight?'

Elle said nothing.

'It is twelve minutes to midnight now. If the assault goes in after midnight, it will be too late,' Helen said.

'But if you blunder in, there will be a bloodbath,' Elle said. 'We will have to stop you.'

Helen shook her head. 'No.' She looked across the space between the helicopters and shook her head at the SAS Captain. 'We have to do this.' She tore off the headset and put her hand on the pilot's shoulder. 'Can you get past?' she said.

'That depends,' the pilot said. 'Think they want a mid-air collision?'

Helen looked at him.

'That is a transport machine,' the pilot went on. 'I guess it flew the special forces up from Meckenheim. But it ain't that nimble.'

There was a lurch, and they hurtled upwards. Helen caught her breath. She had the sensation they were passing over the other helicopter. Then they were plunging through the air.

'Easy does it,' the pilot said. 'We are above the Reichstag. He is following, but there is no space for him to get below us. Do I put down?'

'What about snipers?' Kolya was peering from the window.

'They are still in position on the corner towers,' Dieter said.

Helen turned to Dieter. 'Would you give the order to shoot? If you were in charge?'

'I would not, no,' Dieter said. 'But I am not in charge.'

'Put us down,' Helen said. 'We have eight minutes.'

The other helicopter was in the air nearby. Its door was open. Helen saw special forces troops throwing out ropes.

'They are going to abseil onto the roof,' Dieter said. 'To stop us. Why don't they land?'

'Only space for one chopper,' the pilot said. 'Hardly even that.' He shifted the controls and their own machine drifted towards the hanging ropes. 'No fun, jumping into rotor blades.'

The other helicopter moved away.

'He is going the other side of the dome,' Dieter said. 'How quickly can we land?'

'Ten seconds,' The pilot said.

'They will take sixty.' Dieter pulled open the hatch. 'Everyone out.'

The roar of the rotors dipped as the helicopter touched down. Dieter jumped out, followed by Helen, Kolya and Sabine. Michelle York and the cameraman stayed on board. Helen was aware of the lens pointing towards them, and the journalist yelling into her microphone, but all she could hear was the engine and the thunder of the rain.

'Run!' Dieter shouted. 'The emergency stairs are blocked by a security door. But I have the access codes.'

Helen saw the other helicopter sinking towards the roof beyond the glass dome. Dieter reached a steel door, flipped open a box by the lock, and moved his fingers across a panel.

Nothing happened.

'They have changed the codes,' Dieter said.

'I can see GSG 9 soldiers on the ground,' Kolya said.

'They are coming!' Sabine yelled.

'What about the retina scanner?' Helen said. 'Aren't you registered?'

'I am.' Dieter placed his eye to the scanner. She could see beads of rain on his eyelashes. Then he was pounding on the metal. 'My access is cancelled.'

'Wait.' Helen pushed Dieter aside. 'Let me try.' She placed her eye to the scanner. Nothing. She blinked and tried again.

The door clicked open.

'They are too close.' Kolya's hand went for his gun.

'No!' Dieter seized the Russian's arm. 'They will not shoot unless they are in danger.'

He tugged open the door, and they threw themselves inside. A concrete staircase descended into gloom. The GSG 9 troops were running towards them. At their head was Elle Morgan.

'Helen!' she shouted. 'Don't do it.'

Helen turned. 'It is too late,' she said. 'This is our only chance.'

She slammed the heavy door behind her. They were plunged into darkness.

CHAPTER 40

SABINE WOLF HEARD THE BLACK-SUITED FIGURES HAMMERING on the door at the top of the stairs and covered her mouth. Men in uniform were trying to kill her. They must not sense her fear.

A light came on. Dieter Kremp held a battery-powered torch. He shone it upwards. 'Can you hit that camera?'

The Russian, Kolya, drew his pistol and took careful aim at the CCTV camera on the ceiling. He hit it with his first shot.

'They know we are here,' Helen Gale said.

'Yes,' Dieter said. 'But now they cannot see us.'

'Are you ready?'

Sabine realised Helen Gale was talking to her. 'Yes.' She looked into Helen's eyes. 'I am ready.'

'For what?' Dieter loomed over the two women.

'I must talk to Uli Wenger,' Sabine said. 'The man who calls himself Johann Frost. Face to face.'

Dieter shook his head. 'If we enter the lobby, they will shoot us.'

'Uli will not shoot me,' Sabine said.

'Will he recognise you?' Helen said.

'He will know me,' Sabine said. 'I will make sure of it.' She pulled her soaking black top over her head. Underneath she wore only a black bra. Her pale skin glistened in the torchlight.

'What are you doing?' Dieter was staring at her.

'I need a blade,' Sabine said.

Both Dieter and Kolya held out knives. Sabine noticed Dieter glance at Helen Gale as he did so.

'What happened to you?' Helen said.

Torchlight played on Sabine's arms. Long, parallel scars ran from her wrists to her elbows. Seeing them gave her confidence. He had done this. She had survived. Now, he must be stopped. 'I was cut,' she said. 'Now, I am cut again.'

She ran Kolya's blade over her skin. The knife was mercifully sharp. The cut burned, but the skin parted easily. The gash looked trivial beside the old, deep scars.

'There is not enough blood,' Sabine said.

'You want blood?' Kolya inspected the wound. 'Give me the knife.'

'Don't hurt her,' Helen said.

'I need blood,' Sabine said.

'This may hurt.' The Russian was gripping her arm tightly. 'Are you sure?'

'Do it.'

Kolya picked a spot along the wound and inserted the point of the knife. Sabine cried out. At once, blood came bubbling to the surface.

'What did you do?' Helen said. 'She will bleed to death.'

'No,' Kolya said. 'The bleeding will stop.'

Sabine watched the blood drip onto the floor. 'Now my hair. As short as you can.'

'Quickly!' Helen said.

Kolya took hold of Sabine's thick, dark hair and hacked at it with his knife. She felt an unaccustomed coolness around her scalp.

'Do not cut it neatly,' she said.

'It is not neat,' the Russian said. 'There. I am done.'

Sabine put her hand to her head. Kolya had butchered her hair, all right. But she was still wearing her glasses. She took them off and put them on a concrete step.

'When we get inside, all the men must remain absolutely

silent,' she said. 'And you must keep behind me. Our lives depend on it.'

'If Johann is still alive, I will tell him what I think,' Dieter said.

'Dieter, listen,' Helen Gale said. 'Keep your mouth shut.'

Dieter looked at her. 'Helen. You cannot give me orders.'

Helen turned to Sabine. 'What about me?'

'Maybe you can speak. But you must sound powerful. In control.'

'That won't be easy.'

'No.' Sabine smeared blood from her wrist onto her other arm, and on her face. 'Nothing is easy.' She felt faint already, as if the blood she had lost were weakening her. Quickly she sat on the stair and took off her shoes and socks. Then, without looking at Helen or the men, she removed all the rest of her clothes and threw them to the side of the stairwell. She felt calm, as if her nakedness somehow made her invulnerable. Finally, she wiped blood across her chest and legs. 'I am ready,' she said.

'For what?' Dieter Kremp said.

'I am ready to meet Uli Wenger.'

CHAPTER 41

IN ROOM 3N001, ULI'S RADIO CRACKLED.
'Perimeter breach in sector 7.' It was Ida, in the comcen.
'Roof door opened with a retina scanner by Helen Gale, British embassy.'

'The wife of the hostage,' Gustav said. 'Maybe she has come to rescue him. She will join him.'

'Why did we not cancel her access?' Dora said.

Uli looked at the Sudeten German. Since Helen Gale's interview, Dora had begun to challenge his authority. It unsettled him. 'We blocked access for all security personnel,' he said. 'No-one expected a diplomat to break in.'

'We should have expected everything.'

'We shall kill them in the lobby,' Uli said. 'Wilhelm, Dora, Gustav, get in position outside.' He called the killing room. 'Ida. Shoot Nigel Ferguson as soon as we open fire outside.'

'What about the other hostages?' Dora said.

'Ida will watch them on camera.' Uli addressed the hostages huddled at the rear of the room. 'Stay where you are. Anyone approaching the doors will die.'

One or two hostages looked at the clock on the wall. It was four minutes to midnight. The child, Jasmine, was asleep on a bed of clothes. The journalist's dog lay next to her, eyes open, ears flat.

'You will kill us anyway,' someone shouted.

'Perhaps.' Uli looked at the sleeping child. When she and

the teacher had seen his face, they had condemned themselves to death.

He followed Gustav into the third-floor lobby. The white tiles were smeared with blood and littered with cartridge shells after the passage of the Delta Force soldiers. Blackness filled the circular shaft in the centre of the room which opened into the plenary chamber below, the night sky reflected downwards by hundreds of mirrors in the cupola above. Martha's shattered body lay at the angle of two benches, surrounded by congealed gore.

'I have the stairs covered.' Gustav took up position on the floor, his rifle stretched out in front of him. 'They will be dead before they see us.'

'I am ready.' The remaining marksman, Wilhelm, lay next to Gustav. He seemed almost in a trance as he gazed down the barrel of his gun.

Dora stood, next to Uli. 'We have more firepower than we need,' she said. 'Unless there are a hundred of them.'

'Quiet,' Uli said. 'Shoot only on my order.'

They waited in silence. No-one appeared. Where were they? Uli checked his watch. Helen Gale's intervention would complicate everything. Why could she not have waited a few minutes longer?

'They have lost their nerve,' Gustav said.

'Wait.' Uli pointed.

Across the lobby, a door swung open. Uli's finger tightened on the trigger. But instead of an armed fighter, a naked, blood-stained, close-cropped girl stumbled forth.

'Is that Helen Gale?' Even Dora sounded shocked.

'No.' Uli's mouth had fallen open. How could this be? 'No.'

'I'm taking her down,' Gustav said.

'Do not shoot!' Uli took a step forward.

'It could be a trap,' Gustav said.

'Of course it is a trap,' Dora said. 'Uli. We must kill her.' She paused. 'Uli!'

Uli stared at the girl and shook his head. Her arms were

streaming blood where he had cut them. What had he done with the knife? His hands were sticky with the blood of Johann Frost. Would Johann be the next ghost to appear?

'There is someone behind her.' Gustav looked up at Uli. 'You are in camera shot. Have you gone crazy?'

'It is Mouse.' Uli took another step forward. He could hear the roar of the flames. Someone was screaming.

'What?' Gustav was staring up at him.

'Mouse. She is alive.'

'She dies.' Gustav steadied his weapon and took aim.

Uli's Heckler & Koch was set to automatic fire. When he pulled the trigger, a stream of bullets sliced open Gustav's waist where his body armour ended. Gustav's hand clenched reflexively and his own weapon jerked upwards in a spasm of firing, but the shots flew wide. There was a clatter of breaking glass.

On the floor beyond Gustav, Wilhelm groaned. Blood was pooling round him.

'I am hit.' The young Rhinelander's voice was weak. 'Why?'

'Gustav was disobeying orders,' Uli said.

'But I did not shoot.' The boy was coughing blood. 'I was waiting for your order.' His weapon slipped from his hands. 'I always did what you said. But you never gave me a difficult shot.'

This was the plan, Uli remembered. Of course, he had to kill Wilhelm. And Gustav. And Dora. Once they had served their purpose. But Mouse should not be here.

'You must have caught a ricochet,' he said to Wilhelm.

'Or five,' Dora said. 'This floor is marble, laid on solid concrete.' She stared at Uli. 'You just shot two of our people. What is wrong with you?'

'It is time.' Uli blinked. Mouse was halfway across the lobby. Naked. Wet. She had risen from the dead.

Dora slowly turned towards Uli. 'What do you mean, it is time?'

'Time to end this.'

Dora's weapon was trained on the naked girl. 'What are

you saying?' Her voice was low and strong. 'Why are we not shooting? Is she one of ours?'

'Yes.' Uli's mouth hung open. 'She is mine.'

'There is a woman behind her. Helen Gale. And two men. One is Kremp. Shall we shoot them?'

'No!' Uli's breathing was ragged. 'They are too close to Mouse. But Mouse is dead. I saved her.' He took another step forward, and pulled off his face-mask. 'Mouse! It is me, Uli.'

'You are not making sense,' Dora said. 'They are too close. I have a clear shot at Kremp.'

'Do not fire!' Uli realised he was shouting.

'We cannot wait.'

'OK.' Uli closed his eyes and felt an instant of calm. 'Leave it to me.'

He raised his weapon. Then he swung the barrel towards Dora. '*It is midnight.*' As he spoke, he fired a burst of shots at her head and neck. The impact slammed her against the wall, her gun tumbling to the ground. She seemed to sigh as she slumped to the white marble. Uli felt the weapon in his hands. Who was left to kill? The teacher. The child. And Ida, in the comcen. But he was not wearing his mask. That was wrong. Mouse was close. She was bleeding. She was staring at him. She was dead.

'Uli.' Mouse's voice. An order. 'Uli. You must stop this.'

'It is already over.'

Mouse frowned. 'Already over?'

Her uncertainty broke the spell. Uli saw a naked woman, Johann's sister from the *Kinderheim*, older, heavier, standing in front of him. Behind her were Helen Gale, Dieter Kremp and – Ivan, the Russian. How could he be here? Was this a double-cross by Herr Kraft? Uli gripped the Heckler & Koch. He could kill them all in half a second.

'*Put the gun down!*' Mouse screamed at him, a huge voice, filled with anger. At once her power returned. Uli saw her waste away. A slender, pale-skinned, dark-haired girl, her arms slashed from wrist to elbow. A knife in his hand. The water turning red.

'On your knees, Uli.'

'You cannot be here.' He fell to the floor. 'They killed you.'

'You tried to kill me!'

'I tried to save you.'

'You came to my bed that night. You promised to protect me.'

'I loved you,' Uli said.

'I hated you!' Mouse shouted. 'You beat me, and dragged me to the basement. You filled the tub. You made me strip. Then you cut my wrists. Four times.' She thrust out her arms.

'No.' Uli's voice was a whisper. 'I saved you.'

'You are living a lie.' Her voice pierced him. 'You made me get in the water. The house was burning. The smoke was choking. But you waited for me to bleed to death.'

'The director was hurting you.'

'You hurt me more.' Mouse was so close he could feel her breath on his head. Her voice was relentless. 'You are finished, Uli Wenger. You are evil. A monster. You should die of shame.'

Uli knew it was true. He raised his hands to his ears. In the distance, he heard his weapon crash to the tiles. His head was filled with noise. He was worthless. Nothing. Zero. He lowered his face to the floor.

Behind Sabine, Helen watched the man she had known as Johann Frost crumple, his face twisted in horror. Her body ached from the effort of driving herself forward towards the guns.

Sabine had been right. This man was Uli Wenger. He was a manipulative killer. And yet *he feared the power of women.*

That didn't explain why he had shot the other terrorists.

It didn't explain where Nigel and the other hostages were.

Helen had not planned beyond entering the lobby. If Sabine was right, and Uli Wenger stopped the other terrorists from opening fire, Helen had hoped she might order him to disarm his companions.

Instead, he had murdered them in cold blood.

Why?

She stepped forward past Sabine. She had to find Nigel.

'*Where is he?*' She loaded the words with all the power she could. The man on the floor answered at once.

'In the comcen. Behind a panel in the wall.'

Behind a panel? Helen hesitated. 'Is he alive?'

'I am.'

The man standing in the doorway was not Nigel. It was Maxim Wild. He wore a GSG 9 combat uniform.

Helen could not speak. She knew now. Nigel was dead.

'Congratulations to our new media star, Miss Helen Gale,' Wild said. 'In other circumstances, I might offer you a job. You have been right about many things. But on the most important thing, you are utterly wrong.' Wild showed his teeth. 'Much good it will do me.'

'What do you mean?' Helen said.

'You were right, of course, that I hated the German government. Their persecution of my businesses was bankrupting me. The agreement they planned to sign at the Children's Summit would have exterminated Wild Media. The bungling of their predecessors encouraged terrorists to execute my father in 1982. The government murdered him. I wanted to kill as many of them as I could.'

'You loved your father.' Helen's voice was soft.

Wild's eyes narrowed. Then he cackled with laughter. 'My father? I hated him! All my life he humiliated me. He was repulsed by the thought of leaving to his son the media empire he had built from the scorched earth of 1945. He said I would wreck everything. He would rather have destroyed Wild Media than have me inherit. But before he could cut me out, the terrorists murdered him. It was the happiest night of my life.' Wild scowled. 'That was before I realised how death would glorify him.'

Helen said nothing. Wild was trembling with emotion.

'My father was a cruel man,' Wild said. 'He poisoned

everything he touched. How could I have guessed that by inciting terrorists to kill him, the government would make him a hero? When I took over as Chief Executive, I was always the son of Rudolph Wild. When Wild Media ran into financial difficulties, the comparisons were harder still. I was a second-rater.'

'But why all this?' Helen spread her arms. 'The G8 Summit? The Reichstag?'

Wild's mouth twisted into a grin. 'I wanted something to eclipse my father forever. Something which would turn his pathetic death into a footnote to my own, sensational story. I would become one of the most famous men on earth. And one of the richest. Because at the same time I was murdered live in front of a global audience, the strength and courage I displayed so conspicuously in refusing to allow a ransom to be paid would bring me wealth beyond my father's wildest dreams.'

'You made that deposition in 1982.' Helen's mind was beginning to work again. 'You can't have planned this then.'

'The negotiations between the government and the Baader-Meinhof terrorists over the life of their hostage made my father look impotent,' Wild said. 'So, I told my lawyers to draw up a statement refusing any ransom. To show, if I should ever be kidnapped, that I was stronger than my father. But from that time on, I studied terror groups, and tasked my media companies to focus on the pathetic efforts of the German government to combat them. Then, several years ago, Wild TV began a documentary about the Children's Summit and I came across Johann Frost. I saw he could provide the stage for me to mount the greatest show on earth.'

The tycoon looked down at the man kneeling on the floor.

'Of course, he needed help. If I had not spoken out after the American embassy bombing, the Summit might have been called off. That bomb was a risk. But it was vital to reinforce the false intelligence which had turned the Reichstag into a fortress for Johann to defend. Luckily, the herd instinct is strong in politics.

Once I had said I would attend, and accused anyone who stayed away of cowardice, the story was over.'

'And the share prices?'

'That should have been the crowning glory.' Wild's eyes narrowed. 'It was too late to save Wild Media. But the impact on the markets of threatening eight vast enterprises with crippling costs, and then removing that threat for one of them, was predictable. Without you, I should have become several billion euro richer. I was ready to live out my days as the wealthiest murder victim in history.'

Helen shook her head. 'But you could never have got out of here.'

'I planned to leave the Reichstag by doing what I do best,' Wild said. 'Controlling information. But for you, no-one would have been looking for me. The tape of my untimely death was made with the highest production values by a team of special-effects experts: it was their last job, of course. Combined with DNA from a litre of my own blood, spilt in a room where several corpses had been butchered and burned, it should have convinced a coroner who had seen me shot dead. Johann had one final instruction, once he had ended the siege. This was to close down the remote sensing equipment in a sector of the Safety Zone perimeter so I could escape. Once people rely on one source of knowledge, it is easy to deceive them.'

Helen swayed on her feet. 'Ended the siege? What do you mean?'

'I said you were wrong about *the most important thing*.' Maxim Wild's face flushed red. 'I never planned to harm any non-German hostages. No! On the contrary, Johann had specific instructions to protect my friend, the President of the United States. Johann's orders were to kill as many members of the German government as possible. Then, at midnight, he was to eliminate whichever hostage-takers remained and present himself – minus his mask, of course – as a surviving SSU member who had saved the day.'

'But they killed Karen. And the Russians.' Helen's voice died away. 'And Nigel.'

'Casualties of war. The point is, you should never have accused me on television. If you had done nothing, my plan would have been a total success. The remaining hostages would have been released unharmed at midnight. Every country, except a mourning Germany, would have breathed a sigh of relief. I would have slipped away. And Johann Frost would have become an anonymous special forces hero.'

Helen fought for breath. 'But you both would have got away with murder.'

'So what?' Wild said. 'I have not killed anyone myself. Who can say their actions have never caused anyone to die?' He looked at Helen. 'Can you?'

Helen thought of Nigel. Then she shook her head. No. She hadn't killed him. Uli Wenger had killed him. Maxim Wild had killed him. Maxim Wild, who was trying to accuse her of murder. She looked up at the ceiling.

'You cannot escape. You are live on TV.'

'I knew it was over when I saw your interview. You planted a seed of doubt about whether I was dead. From that moment on, my plan was finished. I could no longer leave the Reichstag. People would have ransacked the building and found me hiding in a cupboard. That was not how I wished to be remembered.' The corner of Wild's mouth curled up. 'But you see, I always knew I might have to rise from the dead one day. The absence of a body would have been certain to fuel debate among conspiracy theorists. Others might have spotted anomalies about my execution. The authorities might even have tracked me down. Had it become necessary, I planned to emerge from hiding in Germany: a country with safe prisons and no death penalty.'

Wild smiled faintly. 'Yes, thanks to you, I shall now go straight into captivity. But that is not so bad. When I confess my crime, I shall become the most celebrated prisoner in the world. People

will be queuing up to interview me. My father will be forgotten.'
Wild raised his arms. 'I surrender.'

Helen stared at the tycoon. Was this really a victory for Wild?
He knew the media. He would have the best lawyers. She heard
a woman's voice.

'Is it true? You planned to betray us? To kill all of your
Chaos Team?'

A hostage-taker had appeared behind Wild. She held a
Heckler & Koch. A black mask lay on the floor by her feet.

Helen recognised the SSU surveillance expert, Katia Vonhof.
Vonhof had always sounded confident to the point of arrogance.
Now her authority was overlain with rage. She had addressed
Uli Wenger.

'Yes.' It was the first word Uli Wenger had spoken since
falling to the floor.

'Even Ida? Me, who you trusted more than all the others?'

'Ida. Yes. I am sorry.' Uli seemed to shrink further.

'I believed, when I joined you, that I was part of something.
I thought you cared for me. Now, I see my life had no more
meaning for you than any other insect.' The woman's voice fell.
'But maybe I can do one thing with my life.'

There was a burst of fire and Wild fell forward. His face still
wore a smile, overlain with a slight look of disappointment.
Behind him, Katia Vonhof lifted the barrel of the submachine
gun to her mouth.

'There,' she said. 'I made the world a better place. Now, I
will do it again. Goodbye, Uli.' She pulled the trigger.

Helen turned her head away. Were any other terrorists left?
Where were the hostages? Where was Nigel's body?

By the time she became aware of Dieter stepping from behind
her, it was too late. He stood over Uli Wenger.

'Johann,' he said. 'Uli. Whoever you are. You are going to
die for this.'

'*Quiet!*' Sabine cried.

At the sound of Dieter's voice, Uli's head jerked up. The look of fear had been replaced by a resolute calm.

'I think, Dieter, that you of all people have nothing to say.'

In a single motion, he threw himself up at Dieter Kremp. A knife was in his hand. For a long moment, they seemed to embrace. Then Helen heard a shot, and the two men slumped to the ground. Kolya Baklanov lowered his pistol.

'I told him not to kill any Russians,' Kolya said.

The man who had been Uli Wenger sprawled face-down on the floor, the back of his head matted with blood. Next to him, Dieter Kremp lay on his back, mouth working. The front of his grey uniform was punctured by a single, gaping knife-wound.

Helen knelt down. But he seemed not to see her.

'Shit,' he said. His hand felt clammy in hers.

'Dieter?'

'Shit.'

His body shuddered. He was still staring at the ceiling. But Helen knew he could see nothing.

There was the sound of a door opening. Sir Leonard Lennox stood in the entrance to a large, brightly-lit room. Behind him, Helen saw other hostages.

'I volunteered to come out first because I have died several times today already,' he said. 'Helen. Well done. We saw everything on television.'

'Ambassador!' Helen's voice cracked. 'Is Nigel in there? Is he – ?'

'No. They took him away. He can't be far.' Leonard Lennox looked around. 'Maybe in here.'

The ambassador stepped over the bodies of Wild and Katia Vonhof towards the comcen. Silence. Then Helen heard him shout. 'Quickly! Come.'

She could not move.

'In here!'

Slowly, as if pushing against a powerful current, she entered the room.

She saw Leonard Lennox hunched over the body of a man tied to a chair.

She saw the man's face, the mouth taped shut. It was Nigel. She saw his eyes move.

'Here we go. Sorry if this hurts.' Leonard Lennox managed to seize one end of the tape. 'Off it comes.' He stepped back.

Nigel Ferguson looked up at Helen. His eyes blazed. His lips moved.

'You didn't care whether I lived or died, did you?' he said.

EPILOGUE

'**A**sk away all you want. I might just decide not to answer.'

'I understand.' Sir Leonard Lennox sank back into his armchair. 'But there are questions I must ask. As chairman of the Commission of Inquiry.'

Helen said nothing.

'This is a bit formal,' the ambassador said. 'But I wanted somewhere private.'

'Thank God for that.'

'Press still bothering you, are they?' He glanced at a news magazine on the table. The cover showed Helen in the rain outside the embassy, giving her press conference in the glare of the TV lights. *GALE FORCE*, the headline read.

'You know I have had to move my mother down here to stay in my flat? To stop Freddy Acton and his mates ringing her doorbell every ten minutes?' A smile lit up Helen's face for a moment. 'She is enjoying it, actually. She thinks she is looking after me.'

They sat in one corner of a large, formally-furnished room in the Foreign Office in London, overlooking Horse Guards Parade. The window was open; she could hear the sounds of the city. A clock ticked on the mantelpiece above a sealed-up fireplace. Leonard Lennox watched her, eyes warm under his bushy white eyebrows. Suddenly, she couldn't stand it.

'I was useless,' she said. 'I made everything worse.'

'Not so.' He didn't offer her a tissue. She was grateful for

288

that. 'If you hadn't gone in, additional hostages would have been killed. Nigel for certain. More German ministers. Maxim Wild would have got away. And Uli Wenger – or Johann Frost – would have got a medal.'

'If I hadn't done my interview, Nigel would never have been singled out.'

'You should ignore what he said when we ripped off the tape,' Leonard Lennox said. 'He had been staring down the barrel of a gun. He had no idea what you had achieved. The early sections of that blog he wrote in captivity are practically a love poem, he was so sure you would get him out.'

'But I signed his death sentence, did I? I came into the Reichstag, even though I knew he was in the killing chair. He knows it. I know it.'

'He is alive. That is what matters.' Leonard Lennox leaned forward, but he did not touch her. That was good. 'All the hostages heard Uli Wenger tell Ida – the terrorist in the comcen – to kill Nigel as soon as they opened fire in the lobby. But she must have seen on CCTV that Uli had lost control. So, she killed Maxim Wild instead. And then herself.'

Helen shook her head. 'Nigel will never forgive me.'

'You don't know that.'

'You don't know bloody Nigel.'

Leonard Lennox shuffled his papers. He cleared his throat. 'I have here a question from SIS. Who was the Russian?' He smiled. 'And do you have his telephone number?'

'His name was Kolya. That is all I know.' Sukanashvili had spirited the beautiful blond Russian back to Vladivostok at the first opportunity. The media had feted Kolya as a hero after his intervention had helped resolve the siege. But he was not staying to answer questions. Helen wondered if she would ever see him again.

'Very well.' The ambassador turned a page. 'Now. Wild told you the remaining hostages – minus the remaining German cabinet ministers – were to be released at midnight. Do you think that is credible?'

'That was what he said.'

'Yes. But the man was a pathological liar. He will go down in the record books as the biggest con-artist of all time.'

'So he will end up being famous for something.' Helen paused. 'Just what he wanted. Sometimes I feel like a fraud myself.'

Leonard Lennox looked at her. 'Let me be clear, Helen. I don't want to hear about anything you think you did wrong. The CCTV pictures showed your intervention resolving the siege with no further hostages killed. A tremendous achievement.'

'I suppose that's what the British government wants.'

'The Germans are grateful also. As they should be: you saved the lives of four members of the cabinet. Do you know they have expelled ten US diplomats? They say the Chancellor might still be alive if the Americans hadn't sent in the Delta Force without authorization.'

'Blore told me. But Wenger would have shot the Chancellor anyway.'

Leonard Lennox looked up. 'What do you know about Ulrich Wenger?'

'Only what Sabine told me at the embassy. Can I start with her?'

'Do.'

'Her real name was Sabine Frost. She had a brother, Johann. Their parents were civil rights activists, killed trying to cross the border from East to West Germany. Sabine and Johann were sent to a *Spezialkinderheim,* a home for under-aged delinquents, at a place called Finsterwald, in Saxony.'

'Why the new surname? Wolf, wasn't it?'

'The idea was to turn enemies of society into model communists. The children were given a new name, Wolf, like the so-called wolf orphans from East Prussia after the war. The wardens encouraged other children, many imprisoned for acts of violence, to pick on the political prisoners. That was where Uli Wenger came in.'

'How old were they at this point?'

'Sabine was twelve, Johann thirteen. Uli was fourteen: one of those misfits communism threw up who hated authority, yet was a genius at adapting to it. He had come to Finsterwald after he killed a boy with a knife.'

Helen paused. Leonard Lennox said nothing.

'Uli made Johann's life hell, bullying and torturing him. Then he started demanding sexual favours of Sabine. She agreed, to protect her brother. She pretended to admire Uli, even to love him. Uli wasn't used to any kind of affection. He became obsessed, telling Sabine everything he did, seeking her approval. He called her his Mouse. Until, one day, she refused to praise him for beating up some kid. That night, Uli nailed Johann's hands to the frame of his bunk-bed as he slept. The wardens did nothing.

'Sabine was desperate. She went to the director of the Kinderheim and said she would do anything to protect Johann. The director locked the door, and told her to show him what she was prepared to do. Excuse me.'

Helen walked to the window and breathed deeply. Then she continued.

'A few weeks later, an eighteen-year-old girl arrived from a women's prison in Leipzig. On her first day, she picked a fight with Uli and broke his jaw with a claw-hammer. He was chained in a punishment cell, where she visited him every night for a month. When he came out, he feared women. They had only to speak with authority, and he would obey. Some of the women who he had bullied took their revenge and harassed him mercilessly.'

'What about Sabine's brother?' Leonard Lennox said. 'Johann?'

'When the Wall came down, everything fell apart. No-one knew what would happen to the Kinderheim. The uncertainty reawakened something in Uli Wenger.

'One night Sabine woke to find him with a knife to her throat. Uli said he had come to stop the director hurting her. He had already rescued Johann, he said. Sabine was so terrified, she could not speak. Uli dragged her downstairs to the cellar. Then he set the Kinderheim on fire.'

'In the middle of the night?'

'Everyone was asleep. Uli showed Sabine the body of her brother, Johann. Then he filled a tub in the basement with warm water. He slashed Sabine's arms, and forced her to lie in it. He said she would soon be free – like Johann.'

'Good God.'

'The fire spread quickly. Sabine blacked out. She came around in hospital. The bleeding had stopped as the water cooled. When the Kinderheim burned to the ground, the water protected her. She was the only survivor. But in the chaos of reunification, no-one cared about the deaths of a few juvenile criminals. Sabine never knew what had happened to Uli. Until, on the day of the siege, she saw a picture on television of the head of the Summit Security Unit, Johann Frost. She recognised him as Uli Wenger. He had stolen the identity of her brother: a loyal, dutiful boy. Uli's first victim.'

There was silence.

'Where is Sabine Wolf now?' Leonard Lennox said.

'On holiday with her girlfriend. I think she wanted to put the relationship on a new footing.'

'This has been an ordeal for you. I am sorry.'

Helen looked down. 'It must be some kind of a record, having your husband and your lover murdered the same day. Even if the husband survived. Poor Dieter. He didn't deserve that.'

'I meant the way the Office treated you,' Leonard Lennox said. 'Jason's lack of support was inexcusable.'

'Julia Strang told me the legal case collapsed when Uktam Zholobov withdrew his backing.' Helen wondered whether Sukanashvili had played a role in that. 'And once they knew the intelligence was faked.'

'A dangerous precedent. If we can only take action on the basis of reliable intelligence, we shan't be able to do a damned thing.'

For the first time, Helen smiled. 'At least Bangkok has been spared a horrible fate.'

'I do not think Mr Short impressed the No. 1 Board,' Leonard Lennox said. 'Whereas I know Press Office were keen to have you. How is it?'

'I could never have stayed in Berlin.'

'Of course not. I suppose I and the embassy will manage without you, somehow.' The ambassador rose to his feet. 'That about wraps it up. Unless there is anything else you want to say.'

'If you have any way to pass a message to Captain Elle Morgan, 22 SAS, tell her she rocks.'

'I will.' Lennox made a note. 'Anything more?'

'Any idea how I invoke my right to be forgotten on the Internet? Anyone who craves fame needs their head examining.'

'I'm afraid those CCTV videos from the Reichstag will be played for years,' the ambassador said. 'Grainy, silent and spell-binding. A soupçon of cinéma-vérité, Ram Kuresh said. Hollywood will probably make the movie before too long.'

'I always wondered why Ram told Jason he didn't speak French.'

'I believe he was needling Mr Short for being pretentious.' The ambassador held open the door. 'Have you anything planned for this evening?'

Helen pressed her lips together. Should she reveal that she was meeting Nigel for a drink? He had said he wanted to talk. To try and come to terms with the Children's Summit. He had not mentioned getting back together. Neither had she.

She said nothing.

Leonard Lennox paused in the doorway. 'Good luck, Helen. Thanks for everything.'

'No.' She turned. 'Thank you.' Quickly, she leaned forward and kissed him on the cheek. Then she turned and walked away down the tall, bright corridor.

AUTHOR'S NOTE

This is a work of fiction. None of the politicians, officials, security operatives or terrorists who people its pages are based on anyone I've met, or even seen on TV. Nor does this book contain any information which I think might endanger the security of real individuals.

The G8 as a political entity has been in abeyance since Russia's suspension in 2014. I am aware of no plans at the time of writing to hold a Summit in the Reichstag, or to turn that building into more of a fortress than it already is. The crisis in US-German relations which forms the background to the Children's Summit is, of course, invented.

There is no town in Saxony called Finsterwald. But *Spezialkinderheime*, or special children's homes, did exist in the German Democratic Republic to house both minors convicted of serious crimes and the children of enemies of the state.

If you enjoyed my book, I would welcome it if you would write a short review on Amazon. Reviews are gold-dust for writers.

If you would like to learn more about my writing, see my website at http://robertpimm.com/.

Thanks again for reading.

Robert Pimm
Vienna, November 2017

Printed in Great Britain
by Amazon